I0590138

Philadelphia Legend: The Story of Jade
by
Derrick J. Truesdale

© 2002, 2026 Derrick Truesdale. All rights reserved.

No part of this book may be reproduced or transmitted in any form or by any means, electronic or mechanical, including photocopying, recording, or by any information storage and retrieval system, without permission in writing from the publisher, except for brief quotations in reviews.

To Mother,
your boys love you very much.

To Guorong,
look dude—the first book!

To Monique,
thank you for putting up with my working late nights

To Christina,
Thank you for always believing in me

Energy cannot be created or destroyed; it can only be transformed from one form to another.

— First Law of Thermodynamics

PROLOGUE

THE NIGHT AIR was brisk and frigid. As the light from the moon beamed down onto the hospital doors, revealing their gloomy and dull exteriors, the building sat there next to the almost empty parking lot in its melancholy clothing, looking as if it felt lonely, empty and lifeless.

Empty and lifeless, the interior of the hospital rarely saw activity around this time either. The smell of the pine cleaners the custodians used just a few short hours ago still ran the halls along with the bleach and ammonia.

In an effort to keep the hospital clean, the custodians cleaned the building in a meticulous manner, making sure they never left a stain. However, in making sure they had never left a stain, they left an acrid smell of the cleaners throughout the halls. They knew the odor was strong but were sure the halls would see little to no activity until around six o'clock in the morning. The smells, by then, would be gone.

And even though there was little to no activity, squeaking wheels could be heard getting louder and closer, if anyone were around to hear them.

It was October 3, 1973, at three a.m. when Lee Anne Thompkins was being pushed on a gurney in what appeared to be a dimly lit corridor of the empty hospital. This woman, with light brown skin and disheveled auburn hair, was sweating profusely while holding her baronial belly.

Lee Anne looked down from the white square ceiling tiles above her and peered ahead to see where she was being pushed. As she was being carted down the hall, Lee Anne felt as if every breath would be her last. She could feel her body dragging the chemical filled air deep into her lungs and then releasing it as if she were a small child trying to blow a makeshift sailboat across a lake. The astringent smell of the pine cleaners, along with the forceful knot constantly moving around inside of her, proliferated her feeling of nausea.

"I don't wanna lose my baby, I don't want to lose my baby," Lee Anne cried frantically as the tears and sweat, with little effort, blurred her vision.

Alex Fordham, the young orderly who was pushing her, empathically looked down at her with eyes of pity, wishing he could ease her pain.

Fordham was a massive giant, whose relative size was reminiscent of Lou Ferrigno as *'The Incredible Hulk'* in the television show of the same name. He had the incredible charming looks of a young Dean Caine, but with a head full of blond hair instead of brown, and with baby blue eyes which accented his hair very well. His charming, good looks told the true tale of his gentle side as well. Fordham had won the affection of many people, patients and staff alike, just because of his gentle and empathic nature.

Alex lowered his head and in a low voice said, "remember what I said Lee Anne, if they hear you talking about aliens while you're in there, no matter what you say in court, you'll be committed, and the only time you'll get to see your kid is when your sister brings him here to visit you."

As Lee Anne looked up at Alex, her teary and sweaty face worried the young orderly. Just two days before he saw Lee Anne glowing radiantly when she was talking with her sister, Pauline, who had come to visit with her often. As a matter of fact, he thought to himself, he has known Lee Anne for at least seven months now, since the time she was first committed. This was the first time he had ever seen her look this bad. He took into consideration she was about to give birth, but Alex had seen several women right before they gave birth, none of whom looked the way Lee Anne did now.

"Alex, I don't wanna lose my baby," she cried again while looking up at him. She then screamed as the pain returned.

With the help of the barren hallways, Lee Anne's words echoed in Alex's mind like the sound of a forty-five on wax with multiple scratches.

With a doleful facial expression, Alex looked away from Lee Anne and looked back up at the plain blue doorways lining the halls. He continued to walk past the doors until he came to a set of double doors with a large, dimly lit sign which seemed to be tarnished yellow with dark letters spelling out the word, 'surgery'.

Right before they entered the room, a young nurse, whose neatly pressed uniform was comparable to the sharpness of a teenager in dress, spruced up for a date, had walked out, looked down at Lee Anne as she was being pushed in, and started down the long hallway. She was headed in the same direction Lee Anne and Alex had just come from.

As the young nurse quickly moved down the hallway, her trimmed red hair flowed back as if blown by a light gust of wind. Upon reaching the end of the hallway, the nurse turned left and walked a few feet until she was at a pay phone.

Katherine O'Mally, or Kat as her friends and colleagues referred to her, was ambitious at twenty-four years of age. She became a registered nurse two years ago and worked part time in the Jefferson Hospital Operating Room and has very recently gained more drive to achieve her goals of future wealth. A friend of hers, a young lawyer, was going to help her with that goal once she acquired a substantial amount of capital.

Picking up the receiver as she retrieved a folded piece of notebook paper from out of the pocket in her uniform, the young nurse placed a dime in the phone and then dialed a phone number she had scribbled on the piece of paper earlier in the week. As she listened to the phone ringing, the nurse then folded the tiny piece of paper back up and returned it to the pocket of her uniform while looking around the barren halls.

Someone answered the phone.

"Hello? May I speak with Tanya James?" she asked. She brushed her hair behind her left ear as she waited until she heard the familiar voice on the phone.

"Tanya it's Kat, they just brought the woman into the delivery room, is the agreement still the same?"

She paused as she listened to the response of the woman on the phone. "No, no need to worry, no one will ever find..."

Hearing the loud and steady gait of someone's footsteps walking down the once empty hall, the nurse quickly paused, cupping her hand over the phone as someone had turned the corner and walked past her.

She then watched Alex Fordham, the young orderly, walk down the hall until he turned another corner and was no longer in sight.

3

"I'll worry about that you don't have to worry," she continued in a low voice. "We don't have the staffing census needed here for anyone to state otherwise; besides, no one is looking closely at this hospital."

She paused.

"The mother? She's not a problem; she doesn't even want the child."

Another pause.

"Just have the money ready, I'm leaving work early and making my way straight there. I'll call you when I'm in the area...be ready!"

Kat then hung up the phone and ran back in the direction from where she had just come.

When she walked back into the surgical room, Kat noticed the doctor, who was alone with Lee Anne, was visibly upset from the present situation.

"Kat, where have you been? You know we're severely understaffed! I told them we should've sent this woman out to a medical facility earlier, never mind, just please scrub in and try to stabilize her."

"Me?" she asked.

"Unfortunately, yes," Harding started, "in leu of an anesthesiologist, I need to depend on you, please give her no more than fifteen ccs of that epidural." He pointed to a tray with the medicine on it. "I'm gonna grab Doctor Barnett," said the young Doctor Michael Harding as he rushed quickly out of the operating room.

Kat immediately started washing her hands and scrubbing in.

The surgical room was of mediocre decor. There were plain gray walls with nothing decorating the room, which would suggest imagination. Two old porcelain sinks surrounded with pushcarts of very shiny and very metallic tools, which reflected the light from above as they lay on the top surfaces of the carts.

The floor and the ceiling were twins, devoid of any warm primary colors, devoid also of secondary or even tertiary colors.

The bed was the gurney upon which Lee Anne had arrived on.

Kat slipped on a pair of latex rubber gloves and grabbed the needle. She looked back at the door the doctor had just left out of and then filled the syringe with an additional fifteen ccs of the

4

medication. She then picked up another needle with Ketamine and slowly walked over to Lee Anne who, with knees in the air and both hands resting on her belly, was still sweating as she looked back at Kat with her blood shot eyes, which were caused from the pain and heavy crying.

"Please...help me!" cried Lee Anne as the nettlesome pain found its way from her stomach to her pelvic cavity.

"Don't worry Lee Anne," started Kat as she slowly injected the ketamine into the hysterical woman's thigh, "I'm giving you ketamine so the epidural will not be so uncomfortable to administer, but I'mma need you to try and sit up a bit so I can give you this epidural."

Lee Anne steadily complied, feeling somewhat better with help from the ketamine.

Kat then raised the back of her patients' gown and administered the epidural as Lee Anne winced a little and cried out a bit from the discomfort.

When Kat finished, she assisted Lee Anne with laying back down on the gurney.

After a few minutes passed, Lee Anne slowly stopped crying as she felt the numbing sensation of the medications working. She soon stopped sweating so hard as she felt as though she was floating above the gurney upon which she was resting.

Kat leaned into Lee Anne and whispered in her ear, "It's okay to let life go!"

As Lee Anne turned her head to the side, a glowing figure materialized out of thin air, standing before her.

Kat couldn't see him.

The figure, who shined as if his body were made of yellow sunlight, walked over towards Lee Anne and reached out for her face, but his hand passed right through her.

He knew something was wrong.

This brightly lit being was in love with Lee Anne. Currently, he was unable to visit with her in the physical world, so he often visited with her when he sensed she was dreaming, what Lee Anne referred to as his tunnel vision, since they were only able to see each other through this method when she slept. The visitor knew though at the current moment, Lee Anne was very much awake, and this troubled him.

An individual drop of light then fell from the right eye of the glowing figure and hit the floor, dispersing, like a single raindrop in the beginning of a violent rainstorm which had been first in finding its way to the ground.

Lee Anne started feeling weird and realized something was wrong. "I love you too," she said as her marble white teeth and soft dimples imposed a beautiful smile upon her sweat soaked face, touching his brightly lit heart.

Kat quickly turned around and looked at the doorway, thinking the young orderly who had befriended Lee Anne may have walked into the room. When she saw no one was there, she turned back around and drew a nefarious grin across her face, realizing the overdose of pain killers she administered to Lee Anne was kicking in.

As a tear came slowly out of her left eye and rolled down the side of her face, Lee Anne slowly stopped breathing.

In the distance, the tapping of running feet could be heard getting louder and closer.

Kat immediately walked over to the body and started pouring out the fake tears.

Doctor Harding soon ran back into the room with an older looking doctor and saw the nurse crying.

Lee Anne was lying still with her eyes open. Nothing on her was moving. she was lifeless.

"What happened?" asked Harding as he rushed in and looked over his patient.

"I, I think her heart stopped," said Kat as she continued to cry while hovering over Lee Anne 's large belly. "I was trying to resuscitate her but couldn't."

The young doctor discourteously moved the nurse aside and placed two fingers under Lee Anne's chin, checking her pulse.

Nothing.

Doctor Harding immediately placed his hands over her sternum while locking them and brought his shoulders directly over his hands as he began cardiopulmonary resuscitation on Lee Anne.

Harding gave her fifteen-chest compression's, followed by two breaths and then rechecked her pulse. "Kat, prep me 5 mg of epinephrine for an I M injection."

Doctor Barnett looked at Kat as he was applying his cranial flashlight and signaled the young nurse to wait; he then looked over Doctor Harding's shoulder as he went back to doing the chest compressions. "We can't do that Michael."

Doctor Harding turned and looked back at Doctor Barnett as he continued to do the chest compressions. "Whatta you mean we can't..."

"A shot of adrenaline to her heart could compromise the child and cause it to experience a severe excitatory dysrhythmia."

Doctor Harding signaled Kat to continue prepping the medication and pulled the gown tie over her head and pulled it down exposing her breast. "Let's save the mother first, then we'll worry about the babies."

Doctor Barnett then grabbed a hold of Doctor Harding's wrist, stopping him from doing any more compressions. "If we put the infants and mother at risk by improperly trying to revive the mother," Barnett started solemnly, "we will be sanctioned and I for one am not going to let that happen to me."

Doctor Harding stared blankly at Doctor Barnett with a glossy look in his eyes. He then looked back at Lee Anne.

Lee Anne's face continued to stare blankly towards the ceiling as Doctor Harding's hand closed her eyelids.

Harding then looked at the other doctor and then at the young nurse in frustration and feeling deficient as a physician. He had failed this young woman, Lee Anne Thompkins, who was already dealing with a multitude of problems. Then with a plaintive facial expression, Harding looked at his wristwatch. "Time of death for the record is three thirty-five a. m."

Harding then looked up from his watch and over towards the other physician as Kat jotted in the time on the log. "We should move forward with a c-section and make an attempt to save the babies, " he said.

Using her arms to wipe the spurious tears from her eyes, Kat then walked over to the counter from where she had gotten the rubber gloves and retrieved two surgical masks. She tied a mask around each of the necks of the two physicians, covering their mouths and then looked at Doctor Harding with a puzzled expression on her face as she passed him the scalpel.

"What do you mean babies?" she asked.

Harding looked briefly at her and then at the sizable belly as he created his incision from the top of her belly down to the pubic bone. He then used the forceps to expose the belly more, as Doctor Barnett applied the clamps on order to keep the belly exposed as Harding worked to expose the babies.

Dr. Michael Harding was considered a hunk by European standards. His ice blue eyes nicely accented his well-groomed jet-black hair. He stood at six-foot two inches and weighed a modest one hundred and ninety pounds. Although he was what every woman wanted in a man, he was married. Happily married. With one very small child and one on the way. And Harding planned on staying happily married.

"When checking her most recent ultrasounds," started Harding as he continued his precision like surgical cutting around the babies, "I discovered that the umbilical cord looked as if it were longer than it should be, and after continuous review, I consequently learned there was another child hiding behind the first. In other words."

Harding paused as he pulled back the folds of skin, subcutaneous tissue, and adipose tissue, revealing more of the interior of Lee Anne's stomach.

Harding said, "I discovered she was having twins."

The young nurse looked down into the stomach and saw the two infants were intertwined within each other's umbilical cord.

The older doctor, Doctor Barnett, quickly grabbed first child as it was positioned closest to the vaginal opening, untangled the other child's cord from around it, and clipped the umbilical cord as the child started crying.

"This one's okay," exclaimed Barnett gleefully as he started wiping the watery blood off of the child.

Kat thought to herself that if she had someone waiting in the parking lot for her, she could have easily doubled her profit.

Doctor Harding grabbed the second baby and clipped its umbilical cord. After seeing no movement from the infant, he then tried to get the child to respond to bottom tapping.

There was still no movement from the child.

Harding then grabbed a suction bulb and attempted to clear the infant's oral and nasal cavities before again bottom tapping, but there was still no response from the infant.

The young doctor again raised his arm and looked at his watch, while cautiously holding the lifeless infant.

"Time of death is three forty-one a.m.," he said solemnly. Being a parent himself, he took the lives of children seriously and always felt badly when it came to the death of a child. Harding then grabbed a towel and gently wrapped it around the dead infant. "Kat, please take care of this child properly," said Harding as he handed her the dead infant.

Kat took the baby from the young physician.

"After you take care of the child, I want you to take the rest of the morning off, I'll explain everything to the hospital administrator later today."

Kat looked in confusion at the young doctor, and then looked from him to the older doctor, Doctor Barnett, who was holding the neatly wrapped crying infant in his arms.

Doctor Barnett was a stout older man with silver white hair and a soft white full beard to match. He was not quite as plump, or as tall, or as jovial as the mythical representation of Santa Clause. Because of his lifelong career as a physician, seemingly seeing more death than life, Barnett rarely wore a smile.

Barnett nodded in agreement. "We understand how observing a death can be a traumatic experience for a young woman such as yourself," he said.

Kat looked between the two physicians. "You don't want me to check..."

"No it's' okay," interrupted an angry Harding, "we'll take care of this child."

Upset by the sudden interruption of her plans, the young nurse then stormed out of the surgical room, forcing the doors open as if she were running with a football and trying to make a touchdown by pushing her way through the defense.

The nurse then marched down the hall with the dead infant in her arms. "Damn male chauvinist," said Kat out loud and to herself. " I'll just wait 'til the two of you go back to your quarters and then I'm gettin' that baby! "

The young nurse soon turned the same corner she had turned earlier and passed the phone she was on earlier confirming her sale with her buyer.

She soon turned into a room and switched on a light switch.

The interior of the room shined with the brilliance of silver, housing sterilization products of all types. The nurse then placed the dead infant on the metal table over by the door and then turned and faced the sink. She ran the water in the sink as she reached for a couple of cloth towels. As she unwrapped the baby and started wiping him down, Kat failed to notice the baby's eyes open and twinkle in reception to the light in the room.

The baby then started to cough, scaring the shit out of Kat as she jumped back.

The child then started to cry as if he had just come out of the birthing canal as she just stared at it in shock.

Kat then looked around while still in shock and then used her backside to close the door. "What the?" she started. She then continued to wipe the baby until he was clean. She reached for a thick and soft burgundy blanket from off a nearby shelf, wrapped the child up in it, and left out of the room.

The nurse then continued down the hall the same way she had been walking before she had entered the room.

Kat moved quickly in order to avoid any unwanted spectators such as Harding, Barnett, Fordham, or any other employee of the almost barren hospital. *Thank God for under staffing*, she thought.

She soon reached the North Hall nurses' station as the cries from the baby echoed chaotically throughout the halls, almost as if he were attempting to alert someone to his whereabouts.

Kat soon reached an unoccupied office in which sat a wooden coat rack in the corner, a large wooden desk with a matching wooden chair and a telephone. Kat closed the door as she removed her latex gloves while still holding the baby.

She picked up the receiver of the black phone sitting on the desk, placed the pointing finger of her free hand into the rotary dial of the base, and quickly dialed the telephone number of a taxicab company she had committed to memory.

"I would like to get a cab at the northeast corner of Southampton Road and Roosevelt Boulevard," said Kat as she paused and waited for the response of the operator. "Fifteen minutes? Okay, thank you."

She quickly hung up the phone and left out of the office as the baby stopped crying. "Thank God you finally shut up," she exhorted.

She then reached the South Hall nurse's station, where no one was at, grabbed a pocketbook from under the desk and then retrieved a jacket from off the back of a chair.

In a hurry to leave, Kat made her way to the stairwell at the end of the hall, ran up to the first floor, and left out of the building and into the cold air with the ten-minute-old infant.

Thankful for the fresh air she just walked into, Kat walked swiftly towards the street whose sign named it Southampton

Road as the spiritless night welcomed her with open arms. While walking down Southampton Road, Kat kept looking back at the well-lit sign of *Byberry State Hospital*, wondering if she would be lucky enough to get away with her crime.

As soon as she reached the boulevard, her cab pulled up.

The driver got out of the cab, walked around the car, and opened up the back door for her.

Kat got into the cab with the baby.

After closing the door, the cab driver walked back around to the driver's side and got in. "Where to lady?" he asked in order to ascertain as to whether or not he had picked up the right fare.

"Grant Avenue and Krewstown Road," she replied.

The driver then took the car out of park and sped off, confident that he had indeed picked up the right fare.

Not one person was around to question her about the baby as she made her way out of the hospital.

The doctors with whom she worked both believed the baby she had to be deceased. They would not mention the stillborn child to Lee Anne's family, the ramifications of the intricacies of two deaths in this one night would be more than the family should have to deal with; besides, they would have a baby, and no one would ever know about the twin.

* * *

Later that same morning, the autumn wind blew, signaling that it was aware of the approaching winter season. The sun generously shared its light with the tops of the cars in the hospital parking lot, which gave the view from above the impression of a rainbow.

A metallic blue, nineteen sixty-nine Chevy Nova, soon sped into the parking lot of the state hospital and circled a row of cars until the driver of the car found an empty parking spot.

Pauline Thompkins' heart raced as she pulled into the hospital parking lot. She could feel her mother's concern radiating from the passenger seat, and it only added to her own anxiety.

The humming engine was immediately silenced as she turned the key and shut off the car.

She knew her mother needed her, but Pauline also needed to brace herself. After scrambling to get out of the car, she slammed the huge door shut and headed to the entranceway of the hospital.

The sun was beating down on her, but she barely noticed. Her thoughts were consumed with what was waiting for her inside.

Her sisters' death had come as a shock, and now they were facing a long road ahead, having to care for a baby without its' mother or father. Pauline was determined to be there for the baby though, no matter what.

Pauline's mother sat on the passenger's side, her tears staining the fabric of the seat.

Pauline had never seen her mother so vulnerable before. It had been a stark reminder of just how serious the situation was. She knew her mother was initially putting on a brave face for her, but Pauline could always see the pain in her eyes and then eventually, the tears poured out.

Pauline took a deep breath and steeled herself for what was to come. She would be her mother's rock, just as her mother had always been for her.

Pauline hurried into the building she had just left two days before, rushed up the steps and walked quickly over to the nurse's station where a single nurse rested, seemingly engrossed in her work or whatever lay in front of her on the desk.

"Excuse me," said Pauline after clearing her throat.

The lone heavyset nurse, with the head full of gray hair, looked up from her desk with the look of surprise on her face someone had snuck up on her.

"My name is Pauline Thompkins; I was notified earlier this morning that my sis..."

"Come with me sweetie," interrupted the nurse as she got up from behind the station. She knew why Pauline had come and she was well aware of who her sister was. Everyone in Byberry State Hospital knew who Lee Anne Thompkins was.

Nurse Barnett was a pleasantly plump woman whose appearance would remind anyone of the strict female penis identifying physical fitness instructor from the 1980's movie 'Porky's', a woman whose demeanor was anything but pleasant. Nurse Barnett, however, had a very soft and comforting personality.

Despite being admitted for a supposed mental breakdown and experiencing delusions, Lee Anne's amiable demeanor and kind heart quickly won over most of the hospital staff, leading them to question if there was truly anything wrong with her. In the eyes of the staff, who's to say she hadn't been taken by extraterrestrial beings? After all, tales of alien abductions were not uncommon, and many who have made the claim still roamed the streets freely. However, for Lee Anne, the issue was such claims were unheard of in Philadelphia.

Nurse Barnett led Pauline around the building, passing a number of people who were walking around in a zombie-like state, obviously side effects from the overdoses of the medication they were receiving. They then went down several flights of steps until they reached a set of double doors devoid of any tell-tale signs as to their current location.

They arrived at the morgue.

The nurse and Pauline silently entered the dim and chilly chamber, where Stanley, the undertaker, was so preoccupied with preparing a cadaver for pick up, he never even acknowledged their presence. As he worked, Stanley emitted a low, eerie croon.

As Stanley turned around, he jumped at the surprise he had living guest in his secluded domain.

"Sorry to bother you Stanley," started Nurse Barnett as she held her hand towards Pauline. "This is Lee Anne's sister, Pauline."

Thin and frail, Pauline noticed Stanley looked as if he himself should have had a bed down in the morgue. Dark circles sat comfortably around Stanley's eyes, and he seemed to be without words, as if he was waiting to share his knowledge with someone worthy of it. If he were to change into an animal, Pauline thought, it would be an owl.

Stanley's cold, black, beady eyes rested on Pauline as he, without saying a word, directed the two women over to a wall of metal drawers. Stanley then looked over the numbers until he reached drawer number one – nine – nine – six B – the drawer with which he was sure would contain the body of this woman's sister.

Stanley pulled the metal drawer out and as Pauline observed the sheet covered body, a knot of anticipation mixed with a dab of anxiety formed in her gut and tears started to flood her eyes.

Pauline's mind raced as she desperately tried to convince herself the body on the hospital bed couldn't be her sister Lee Anne. *Surely, there must have been a mix-up and they had mistaken her for someone else.* But as the gaunt coroner pulled back the sheet to reveal the face of the deceased, Pauline's worst fears were confirmed. It was indeed her sister, and she was gone.

Trembling, Pauline approached the lifeless body and gently touched her sister's pale face. Unable to contain her anguish, she covered her mouth and let out a sob. Lee Anne lay there, unmoving and unresponsive. The realization of her sister's death hit Pauline hard, leaving her devastated and in shock.

* * *

Nurse Barnett escorted Pauline to the administration office where she was introduced to the social worker. Together, they completed the necessary paperwork to transfer her sister's remains to the funeral home of her choice and gathered all the essential documents for her to begin caring for her sister's infant child.

Afterwards, Nurse Barnett and Pauline walked together down the dispiriting and monotonous halls of the building.

Barnett took Pauline's hand in hers and warmly said, "I'm sorry about your sister."

Pauline wiped a tear from her eye. "I never thought I would have to bury my baby sister," she said sobbingly.

"Well, it's never easy to bury someone you love, whether they're older or younger than you." Nurse Barnett lost a mother the month before and so sympathized with Pauline.

Pauline, still wiping her eyes, nodded in agreement as they walked up to a door where another nurse, a younger nurse, was sitting outside of the room reading a book.

The young nurse appeared to have a disposition towards Nurse Barnett, obviously a result of a dislike of authority, which, being the charge nurse, Barnett had.

"Why are you outside the room?" Barnett asked of the younger nurse.

"I had a cough and didn't want to wake him," she replied.

Nurse Barnett shook her head in the negative as she opened the door and led Pauline into the dreary room which only had four plain yellow walls, no windows, and a crib.

Byberry State Hospital was not initially designed to accommodate infants or toddlers; it was mainly a behavioral correction facility for adults. However, when the hospital started getting patients who were either expecting a child or somehow ended up pregnant while at the institution, the hospital administrator had to make several adjustments.

Usually, the children birthed in the hospital remained in the hospital for up to three months, the amount of time it usually took a social worker to find temporary placement for each child. Things moved much faster when family was involved.

"Here's the wittle fellow now," said Nurse Barnett as she picked up the infant.

The baby's facial expressions seemed to have made him smile. The child, upon first glance, appeared to be healthy. He was indeed very healthy. His skin tone was a light brown and his eyes, were still kind of squinted, because he was less than twenty-four hours old.

Pauline looked at the child and smiled as a tear found its way out of her eye. She was then startled briefly when she thought she saw a sparkle of light in the infant's eye. Pauline brushed the thought off; *just a tear from my eye, which glimmered in the light,* she thought.

Nurse Barnett handed the child and a slip a paper to Pauline. "If you go to Children's Hospital and ask for Doctor Emily Barnett, she'll help you out with all of the initial medical care you'll need. Just give her this note, she's my daughter." She said proudly as she also handed Pauline a bag with some formula, diapers, onesies, and barrier cream.

"Thank you," replied Pauline as the two left out of the room. "As I told the social worker, my sister's body will be picked up soon."

Nurse Barnett looked at her sorrowfully. In her opinion, Pauline looked almost exactly like her sister Lee Anne, with the exception that she was slightly thinner and that Pauline's skin tone was slightly darker than her caramel complexioned sister.

Nurse Barnett also thought of the other baby, who was still born, and didn't have the heart to tell Pauline about what her husband, Doctor Barnett, had told her about the child. After all, she figured Pauline had enough to deal with and she didn't need to be upset any more by any additional revelations.

"My prayers are with the two of you sweetie," said Nurse Barnett.

***

Three weeks later, Pauline walked into a medical clinic located on the corner of Fifth Street and Girard Avenue in

Philadelphia. Pauline chose this small clinic, because she herself had been treated here for over five years, and she appreciated the treatment she had always received. She also heard that the pediatrician here was good.

As the door closed, it hit a little bell situated near the top, which jingled with the same sound made by a jingle bell at Christmas time.

With difficulty because of holding the infant in her arms, Pauline signed in at the front desk, which was exactly six feet in front of the entrance door of the clinic. Afterwards, she then sat down in the reception area next to an older woman who was smiling at her, revealing her own pride and joy, a couple of missing teeth.

With the uniform look of a nanny who might have worked for Scarlett O'Hara in 'Gone With The Wind', the old woman smiled annoyingly at Pauline and the baby, unknowingly making Pauline slightly uncomfortable.

"You not here to see Docta Jacoby are you?" asked the woman.

"As a matter of fact I am," started Pauline. "Why?"

"Well he aint here no more," replied the woman. "He done went to Wisconsin or someplace like that. They got this young, new ingine docta in though, and I heard he's pretty nice."

Pauline, upset by the update, looked around the small reception area of the clinic as the baby continued sleeping.

There were a couple of magazines on an old wooden coffee table and in the corner to her far right; there was a radio, which was at this moment, soundless.

Pauline then looked down at the baby as he started cooing and waking up.

The baby looked up at her, appearing to comfort her by smiling.

"Poline Tombkins!" called a voice from up front.

Pauline looked up after hearing her name called by someone with a heavy Indian accent. She saw a young Indian doctor who was signaling with a hand wave for her to come with him.

As the old woman watched her and smiled, again revealing her missing teeth, Pauline got up and followed the young doctor into the office.

The doctor closed the door behind them and then offered her a seat as he himself sat down. Doctor Benjamin Nassir did appear to be incredibly young with his light brown, clean shaven complexioned skin, hazel eyes and jet-black hair. He had a medium build and appeared to be well in shape. Although he appeared to be an eligible bachelor, the wedding band all but told the tale of his real life, which was that of a newlywed.

Pauline, with slight disappointment, noticed the ring immediately.

"You have such a pretty baby," said the young Doctor as he looked from Pauline to the baby. "Whut can I help you wit today?"

Pauline started feeling a little uneasy but decided to open up anyway. "I was kind of hopin' that Doctor Jacoby, would be here. I wanted him to be my nephew's primary."

"Nephew? Where are the child's mutter and fadder?" asked the young doctor with apparent surprise in his voice.

"His mother was my sister; she died three weeks ago while giving birth to him. I never found out who the father was...I have his birth certificate and his immunization record right here."

Nassir accepted the paperwork, took a quick glance at it, and then set it to the side. "I am, very truly sorry to hear about your sister," interrupted the young doctor as he dolefully looked at the baby. He placed his finger in the hand of the baby and allowed the child to grab hold of it. "Nice little grip there son. What is your name?"

Pauline, looking at the doctor as he was looking at the infant, smiled and said, "Johnny."

Nassir looked at Pauline with a grim facial expression on his face, which made her feel a little uneasy. "Well Doctor Jacoby is no longer here; he moved to Wisconsin to be wit a sick relative." Nassir then smiled warmly at Pauline. "But I am here, and the good news is I specialize in both pediatrics and family medicine. We'll just have to see what we can do to make this little one's life just a little bit easier."

He then looked excitedly at the baby. "Hello there Johnny, my name is Doctor Nassir, but you can call me Doc, I hope you'll allow me to be your new doctor."

The baby appeared to have smiled in response to the doctor.

Pauline continued smiling as she thought to herself, *he's kind of nice.* She knew at that moment she had found Johnny's new pediatrician.

***

"What can I say? He is so beautiful," started Tanya as Kat took a seat and watched the woman as she held her new baby and smiled joyfully at him. "At first he cried for almost two days straight, but then he just started warming up to us more and more."

Tanya wore a pullover hat to cover the bald head, which was a result from months of chemotherapy. She couldn't have children of her own, and she and her husband had a difficult time with adoption so, she decided she would take an illegal route. She would never tell this child he was adopted. Tanya figured by the time this child was old enough to notice her head, her hair would have grown back. She also thought she could tell her new son she had gotten ovarian cancer sometime after he was born. The child would never know the truth.

Thinly built, Tanya used to be a dancer. She met her husband Michael when she auditioned for a musical he was producing at the time. Now ill, she had to stop dancing. Her soft brown skin hid her ailment well. She turned to Kat, whom she had met on a bus from New York at one time and made a joke about hoping to find someone who would be willing to sell her a baby for the sum of twenty-five thousand dollars.

Kat gave Tanya her home phone number and asked her to call her, claiming she knew a woman who was about to give birth and who didn't want her baby.

The rest is her story.

"It was nice of you to do a follow up visit with us," said Tanya.

"Well," started Kat who was sitting there looking at the two of them interact, "Since the birth mother took a turn for the worse during the delivery, I just wanted to make sure everything was okay with medical care and..."

"Oh you don't have to worry about a thing we have really good doctors," interrupted Tanya. "But I didn't have a lot of medical history to give the doctors, you said that his mother died while giving birth to him?" asked Tanya as she rocked him.

"Yeah, she had heart failure," Kat lied. "I felt sorry for her, she was only there because she said she was abducted by aliens." She smirked. "I guess I know what not to say in public."

"What a shame," replied Tanya as she became disgusted with the callousness with which Kat spoke of regarding the infant's birth mother.

As they both sat there, Kat thought about how Doctor Harding had pronounced the baby dead, and how moments later he remarkably came back to life.

Kat really came to the house out of curiosity. She was glad things had worked out for herself the way they had but still couldn't help but to wonder how this baby managed to come back from the dead without any type of resuscitative measures.

"So will you and Michael junior be okay until big Mike gets back?" asked Kat.

"We'll be fine," said Tanya as her and Kat stood up simultaneously, "we're going back to Pittsburgh in about a month." She then walked Kat over to the door.

"Well don't hesitate to call if you have any problems, any problems at all," said Kat.

"I won't," replied Tanya as Kat left out of the door.

After Tanya closed the door, the baby started crying again.

The presence of Kat made him uneasy, but as an infant, he was unable to say so.

Tanya looked down at the infant and slowly moved her arms in a swinging motion, calming him down.

Michael soon stopped crying.

Tanya looked down into Michael's warm brown eyes, forcing a smile out of him. She smiled. "Don't worry Michael, everything will be just fine.

CHAPTER 1

THE DAY WAS sunny and eerily quiet as if it were a Sunday morning. Quiet as if there would be no witnesses for anything going on because of it being a weekend, but it was in fact, a weekday. In fact, it was Monday.

Just after the group of four masked men entered the bank, they immediately spread out into different directions, immediately catching the attention of a guard who started to grab at one of the masked figures as the masked figure quickly twisted the guard's arm behind his back and threw him down to the floor.

Mikey fired his gun in the air, "EVERYONE DOWN, NOW!"

The small group of three never addressed each other by their real names while they were doing business; it was part of the rules. If any of them were to ever be caught, they were to never mention their boss, by name, any of his affiliations, or otherwise.

That was his rule. He always gave them information on where there would be the least police activity, and they would go where he sent them in order to rob a bank or any other local business, whichever he said to hit.

Hands now in a locked position behind their heads, while they themselves were lying outstretched and face down on the floor, the hostages were nervous and scared.

"STY DOWN! Sty - DOWN! Don't nobuddy move!" yelled Mikey with his phony British accent as he kicked the man lying on the floor beside his feet. He then gave the man a swift and hard finishing kick in the left side of his abdomen. Mikey then smiled and waved the gun around the bank. "The next purson who tries to play hero will get their bloody head shot off!"

John Marshall, father of three, husband, and security guard at First Federal Bank, tried to play hero but was apparently unsuccessful, and the attempt almost cost him his life. Lucky for him this time it only cost him a rib.

Mikey looked over at Tom, who was already behind the teller's station collecting money with a large felt laundry bag. He then walked away from the would-be hero, who was crouched on the floor in a fetal position and in pain. "YO ICE!" yelled Mikey. "WE GOT ONE MINUTE!" He was really saying Ace but intentionally said ice to play into the accent.

Tom turned around and looked back at Mikey. "That's cool," he said smugly, "I'm already finished." He then hopped over the counter as Mikey tuned his head around and looked at Chris.

The ski hats they were wearing were rolled down all the way over their heads, covering their eyes, nose, and mouth, yet these guys could see everything clearly.

"How's it lookin' Mack?" asked Mikey, really talking to Chris who was just exiting a room sized vault.

"Like Christmas in September man," started Chris laughingly while looking at the large felt bag he was holding, "like Christmas in freakin' September."

"LET'S GO!" yelled Mikey.

The four bandits all left out the front door of the bank after fifteen minutes, as planned.

As the morning sun hit their masks, Mikey pressed a button and the masks the quartet were wearing immediately dissolved, appearing to have never been covering their' faces. The four of them laughed as they jumped into the unmarked black SUV which pulled up just before their exit.

They quickly hopped in and the vehicle sped off, tires screeching in the street.

It was nine thirty a.m. on September sixteenth, nineteen ninety-six, near 11th and Chestnut Streets in Center City

Philadelphia. The streets were surprisingly quiet, and there wasn't a cop in sight.

CHAPTER 2

SPRING GARDEN STREET hummed with the frantic energy of college students hurrying in different paths, eager to make it to either their initial or second lectures.

The orange, red, and sometimes yellow leaves from the trees, some of which were either already on the ground or about to fall to the ground, marked the beginning of the fall season.

The sun shined brightly just as noticeably as the cool wind blew as some students stopped to talk with each other, ordered breakfast from food trucks, or just sat around reading as they waited out the time to go to a class.

Inside the West Building of the Community College of Philadelphia, as Johnny Thompkins ran through the halls with his backpack situated over his right shoulder, his sneakers squeaked on the recently buffed floors. Johnny dodged the few people who were in his way. He then looked at his watch and thought, shit, late for class today, again.

It was only his second week of classes and Johnny had already been late for two out of three of them. He wasn't the kind of student who was tardy because of apathy or because of his reluctance to attend; there was no reason as deep as him trying to contemplate the wonders of the construction of the universe after waking in the morning. He just had difficulty with being on time.

As Johnny rushed into his class, he noticed most of the seats in the room were full, especially in the back where he normally liked to sit so he went to the front of the room where he quickly found an empty desk and sat in the chair, which screeched as he pulled it up to the desk.

Johnny then reached into his backpack for his psychology text as he heard the professor starting to call the roll. *Maybe,* he thought, *I'm not late after all?*

As he listened to the list of names being called out, Johnny looked back and waved at Mark Chang, someone whom he had completed a lab project with once before during the previous semester in his anatomy and physiology class.

"Thompkins?" called the professor as Johnny turned back around and looked up front at the attractive middle-aged brunette who was standing to the front of the class holding open a roll book.

The instructor of his psychology class was dressed in a dark blue suit dress and wore a soft white blouse underneath it. Her shoes, which had quarter-inch heels, were also dark blue.

Doctor Margaret Comer was a psychiatrist by degree, but in the last year has opted to also teach psychology. Her facial affect was often flat, she never wore a smile, and her eyebrows arched slightly inward. Her hand, which was devoid of any rings or ring marks, told the world she had never married. Her usual affect also told the same tale.

"You're up front today? What a surprise," said, Doctor Comer as she looked at Johnny.

Johnny turned around slightly, and with his head, gestured towards the back of the room. "All the seats back there were full," he said.

As the class spewed out slight chuckles in response to his comment, Comer gazed at him as if to suggest she didn't approve of it.

Johnny smiled and looked down at his textbook with slight embarrassment.

Doctor Comer finished calling the rest of the names on her list, as Johnny opened up his notebook. She then closed the roll book. "Okay class," she started as she centered herself towards the front of the room. "Today I have a little group assignment for you to do." She then cleared her throat. "First, I want all of you to get into groups of four, everyone in the first seat of each row will be group A, the second seat, group B, and so on. Once you have gotten into your respective groups, I will pass a number to each group."

Doctor Comer turned and pointed towards the chalkboard. "Whatever your group's number is, the scenario on the board that corresponds to the number assigned to your group, must be completed by your group. Any questions so far?" she asked as she glanced round the beige bricked and windowless room.

One young lady who was sitting at her desk which was near the brown wooden door leading to the hallway, and who was wearing a sun hat which allowed her blond hair to flow freely from under it, raised her hand.

"Your question?" asked Doctor Comer.

"How are we supposed to answer the questions with the scenarios?" she asked.

"I was just getting to that," Comer replied. After scanning the room in order to see if there were any more questions, she continued, "within each scenario listed up here," she again pointed to the board. "I want you to determine which is your dependent variable and which is your independent variable. I then want you to set up an experiment using a control group and an experimental group, indicating which group is which."

Doctor Comer then paused briefly. "After you have all of your information," she started again, "I want to know how you conducted the experiment and I want you to hypothesize the results as if you've actually conducted said experiment." She then looked down at her watch as she passed out little slips of paper with numbers on them to the students in the first row against the right-side wall, one paper for each group. "You have thirty-five minutes to complete the assignment, so get started and I'll be around the room to assist you if you have any problems."

As the class started getting with their groups, Comer walked over to Johnny as he looked at her while standing in order to join his group. "Don't be late for my class again," she said.

***

After his psychology class, Johnny leisurely walked through the bustling hallways of the junior college. He observed the other students frantically rushing to their next class, while he had two hours to spare until his next one. To make use of his free time, he decided to work on an assignment in a study booth. As he slowly made his way towards the window in the lounge area of the West Building, not looking for anything in particular, he gazed outside at the clear blue sky.

Johnny couldn't help but appreciate the beauty of the autumn scenery. He took a moment to visually absorb the scene, and it dawned on him that it was the same view he had observed in the hallways earlier; students hurrying to their next destination. As he watched the two lanes of students, resembling cars following traffic rules, Johnny couldn't help but ponder on the constant rush in life. It seemed like from the moment one starts grade school until retirement, everyone is always in a hurry, spending the prime years of their life trying to fit into the societal norms.

"There must be a better way," Johnny said out loud and to himself.

Johnny wanted to enjoy his life and so decided if he worked extra hard now, then he would be able to enjoy at least part of his life later, instead of conforming to the social norms.

As the crowd in the hall started to dissipate, Johnny then gripped his backpack to make sure it didn't fall and as he started continuing down the hallway. He then heard his name called by a pleasant female voice from behind.

Johnny then turned around and saw a young woman who stood at about five nine, with short black hair and light brown even toned skin. She was wearing a pink khaki jumper with a white turtleneck shirt.

He looked at her as if he were surprised, she had even called his name. "Aren't you in my botany class?" he asked with uncertainty in his voice.

The young lady walked closer towards him, extended her hand for him to shake it and said, "April Jenkins."

He slowly took her hand and shook it, while looking into her soft and warm brown eyes. As he shook her hand, he couldn't help but to focus on how attractive this April Jenkins was.

April, catching the stare, started to feel slightly embarrassed and lowered her head a bit just before she started talking.

An African American male who is chestnut brown complexioned with his hair in a high-top fade, Johnny stood at six feet two inches and weighed a modest two hundred pounds. He was wearing a casual dress consisting of blue jeans, and a button-down blue shirt. Under the shirt there laid a white tee shirt which displayed his brawny chest, chiseled arms, and well-defined pectorals. His pair of white high-top Adidas complemented the tee shirt.

Johnny was the picture of perfect health. He worked out three days a week at the school's gym and went jogging early in the morning before he went to school as a part of his daily regimen as well as a few times a week in the evening.

April then continued, "A few of us from the class are planning on getting together a study group for the first exam and I was wondering if you would be interested in join..."

Johnny dropping his backpack and quickly pulling April closer in addition to kissing her passionately, interrupted her words. After a few moments, he then pulled back from her smiling. "I'm not much of a fan of botany study groups, or any study groups for that matter. Gonna call me at work tonight?" he asked as he picked his backpack back up.

"I might," she responded smilingly, slightly embarrassed that he had cut her off the way he had. She then looked him up and down, "yeah, I think I'll do that!" she said, right before she turned around and started walking away. "I'll let you know when the group is getting together," she added as she continued walking away.

"I did say I wasn't much of a botany study group fan, didn't I?" asked Johnny as he watched her walking away.

"You'll be fine!" she insisted as she continued walking without turning around.

Johnny couldn't help but to stare at the five foot nine, hourglass shaped woman walking away from him. After all, his girlfriend of six years was very attractive.

***

After his last class, Johnny usually went straight to work. Today was no different. He was undeclared with his major but, as he was certain he wanted to work in healthcare, he started where he could.

Johnny had been working in the direct health care field with adults with intellectual disabilities for over five years now, and at the age of twenty-three, he seemed to be more passionate about helping others than when he started at eighteen.

Johnny knew the residents of ninety-two fifteen Alton Street very well. He knew all the resident's medications by heart and was astute with reviewing medical documentation in order to be aware if changes took place with anyone since his last scheduled shift. He knew how to implement resident tasks and goals, which helped the residents work towards the goal of independent living. He implemented the care plans in such a way as to not make things seem repetitive or boring to the residents.

Johnny was extremely passionate about his job and the residents he worked with. He had a natural ability to connect with them and understand their needs. He was always willing to go the extra mile to ensure they were comfortable and happy. His positive attitude and patience made him a role model for the other staff members.

Johnny was also skilled in dealing with aggressive behaviors without physical intervention, making him a valuable employee. He loved his job and decided that since he had quite a bit of experience working with people who had developmental disabilities, he would get a second job working in the same field as his current occupation in human services.

Johnny spent the next week putting in applications at every direct care agency that he could find in Philadelphia. If he wasn't putting in employment applications, he was working, studying or spending time with April. Johnny quickly received a telephone call from one of the companies with which he applied, requesting him to come in for an interview.

He smiled to himself as his plan was working.

CHAPTER 3

THE 1996 TURQUOISE BMW 325i sat within the darkened garage at Eleventh and Market Streets with the head lights off but the soft quiet engine humming as the vehicle's occupant sat inside listening to classical music, while inhaling and exhaling the fumes from his tetrahydrocannabinol.

The exterior of the car was clean, not a noticeable speck of dust. The windows tastefully tinted green. The beige leather interior was just as immaculate as the outside.

Martin Cole, a young man of twenty-six enjoyed early success in life as the right hand to one of Philadelphia's most prominent businessmen. He not only played the part well during business hours, but he looked the part. Jet black hair cut short, soft blue eyes, and he wore a a blue Armani dress shirt and tie with the sleeves rolled up now because he was technically finished with work. He also wore gray Armani dress slacks. He tapped his hands on the steering wheel in order to match the beat playing over the radio.

Cole soon looked over to his immediate left as he noticed a silver Nissan Maxima pull up next to his car. He turned off the car and soon got out.

The driver's side door to the Nissan soon opened and his friend Mikey soon stepped out and greeted his childhood friend their customary handshake.

"How'd it go?" asked Cole.

Mikey laughed. "We carried out your plans at First Federal just the way you told us to...and those masks Stern gave us, worked just as he said they would."

"No casualties?" asked Cole.

"One security guard got a bruised ego and likely a fractured rib, but no, no casualties!" Mikey then went around to the back door and pulled out a briefcase. After closing the door, he turned back around to Cole. "Here's the take, minus our fee."

Cole smiled. "As always, "I know I can count on you," he said.

Mikey and Cole had been friends a long time, since junior high, so when Cole needed cronies he could trust to help him with the tasks his boss gave him, Mikey was his obvious first choice. They grew up together and ran the streets together, the only difference was Cole's family could afford to send him to college where he majored in business law whereas Mikey was unable to go to college.

Mikey and Cole stood at the same height, six feet, two inches, but that was where the similarities in their appearance stopped. Mikey dressed in baggy denims and a hoodie. He had stringy blond hair which was shoulder length. The pair looked as if they were from different worlds, but they really weren't. "So can I tell you about this dude Snake from the hood?"

Cole scoffed. "Not this again?"

"I'm telling you, the dude got some sorta strange mind abilities going on...he might be of some use to..."

"How many times I gotta tell you Mikey?" interrupted Cole. "My boss ain't interested in anyone like that at the moment. We don't need it! Besides, if we had someone strange like that on our payroll, we wouldn't need you, now would we?"

Mikey stopped and thought about it for a second. "I couldn't get like a promotion or something?"

"What you do for us...it ain't no legit job," started Cole. "Your promotion would have to be an actual gig, with a serious pay cut...like a door man or sumthin'."

"Doorman? I couldn't get a bodyguard gig or something?"

"Still a pay cut!" Cole then started fake boxing Mikey. "Besides you're too small and too slow to be a bodyguard."

Mikey started fake boxing him back. "Forget that!"

They each got a couple of slaps on the other and then Cole hugged Mikey, "just a few more jobs and you'll be good. I'll help you invest your money."

Mikey sighed, feeling grateful for his friend's support. It wasn't easy having no career path, especially with today's job market. He couldn't help but second guess his decision as he thought about all the bills he had to pay. "Thanks for having my back brotha," replied Mikey. He felt a sense of relief knowing that Cole was there for him. They had been through thick and thin together, and he knew he could count on him no matter what.

"Always," replied Cole.

Mikey couldn't shake off the feeling of uncertainty regarding his financial future, especially with taking care of his 8-year-old daughter, Ava. He had always dreamt of becoming a successful businessman like his friend Martin, but now it seemed like a far-fetched dream. He reminded himself, though, *just a few more jobs, and I'll be set.*

CHAPTER 4

AS THE WEEKEND approached, the cold, dreary weather of the week slowly dissipated. The sun had yet to make an appearance, but the wind had calmed down, bringing a sense of tranquility to the crisp autumn air.

The trees, some adorned with vibrant hues of orange and red, sat quietly in the open air making for a picturesque scene. Despite the lack of sunny skies and chirping birds, it was a perfect day to enjoy the beauty of the season.

Saturday had finally arrived, and with it came a much-needed break from the hustle and bustle of the work week. The weather was on everyone's minds, as it had been quite unpredictable lately. But to everyone's delight, the day turned out to be a pleasant surprise.

The cool breeze had a soothing effect, and the leaves rustled gently, creating a peaceful ambiance. It was a great day to take a walk, go for a bike ride, or simply relax and take in the sights and sounds of nature. Saturday was indeed a much-needed respite from the gloomy days which preceded it. As the week came to an end, the weather seemed to mirror the changing of the seasons. The cool, crisp air and the gentle wind were a reminder that autumn was in full swing. The absence of sunshine and birdsong did not dampen the spirit of the day but rather added to its charm. The weekend had arrived, and with it came a reprieve from the hectic weekday routine. It was a chance to slow down, appreciate the beauty around, and enjoy the simple things in life. Indeed, Saturday was a perfect day, true to the season.

The track was quiet today, but Johnny didn't mind. He enjoyed the peacefulness of the track during the fall and winter months. It was a serene escape from the chaos of campus life.

As he made his way around the track, Johnny took in the sights and sounds of the season. The vibrant leaves, the crisp air, and the distant sound of cheering fans at the nearby football stadium all added to the charm of his Saturday morning run. Johnny wasn't a professional runner, but he took his workouts seriously. He knew the importance of physical fitness for both his physical and mental well-being. Plus, it was a great way to clear his mind and start the weekend on the right foot.

As he ran, Johnny focused on his breathing and the steady rhythm of his footsteps. He was in his own world, without a care in the world. After completing his usual number of laps, Johnny slowed to a walk and made his way to a nearby bench. He took a few moments to catch his breath and stretch his muscles before heading off to start his day.

Johnny couldn't help but feel grateful for the reprieve Saturdays provided. It was a chance to slow down, appreciate the beauty around him, and enjoy the simple things in life.

***

The weekend flew by just as quickly as it had appeared.

After finishing his classes, Johnny made his way from Seventeenth and Spring Garden streets to Girard Avenue to catch the SEPTA route fifteen trolley. He needed to complete a physical for his new second job, so he headed to his doctor's office on the corner of Fifth Street and Girard Avenue. This was the same office his aunt had taken him to over twenty-two years ago. The waiting room was now equipped with a magazine stand and a color television, replacing the old radio that was there when he was an infant.

After checking in at the front desk, Johnny settled in to watch 'The Young and The Restless' which was playing on the television. The arched doorway in front of him now had a buzzer, requiring permission to enter the clinical area.

As Johnny watched the show, a Hispanic woman sitting nearby tried to calm her restless child. "Hector, please sit down and be quiet. Mommy's trying to watch her show," she pleaded.

Johnny couldn't help but smile as he continued to watch the television.

Suddenly, the receptionist called out, "John Thompkins!"

Johnny stood up and looked in her direction.

"Yes?" he asked.

"You can go back now," replied the receptionist as the sound of the buzzer signaled Johnny the door was now unlocked.

Johnny walked through the door as the buzzing sound stopped and let go of the door which closed on its' own accord. He then walked into the third doorway on his right-hand side.

Doctor Benjamin Nassir was sitting at his desk inside the tiny exam room, smiling warmly as he continued writing on a paper tablet.

"Mornin' Doc," said Johnny, announcing his arrival as he walked into the exam room.

"Good afternoon, Johnny," corrected the now middle-aged doctor who spoke with no hint of any type of an accent. The last twenty-two years had been extremely kind to Doctor Benjamin Nassir. Still at a medium build, Nassir's hazel eyes continued to compliment his still jet-black with gray just above both ears, hair, very well. One could not look at him and tell he was married with three grown children, two daughters, and a son. Also, to his credit, Nassir had never been known for having a disposition. If he did, he hid it well.

Doctor Nassir loved Johnny like a son, and Johnny felt the same closeness with him; they have after all known each other for Johnny's whole life. There was very little they didn't know about each other.

Nassir asked, "How are you feeling today?"

"I actually feel great," said Johnny as he looked at his physician with a smiling, glowing expression. His eyes were wide with anxiousness, as if he had just consumed a pot of coffee.

Unbeknownst to him, his body was adjusting.

Johnny said, "I constantly feel as if I'm full of energy, and the best part about it is … I haven't changed my eating habits or my sleeping pattern."

Nassir looked at him with a puzzled expression, seeing how overly alert his young patient was. "You're not experimenting with drugs, are you?"

"What?! Doc, no that ain't me!"

"Even caffeinated products, though legal, can have negative consequences when taken for prolonged periods…"

"Doc, I said no!"

"I have to ask," Nassir said as he pushed the note pad to the side. "I know how the kids like to experiment with the reefer."

"The reefer?" asked Johnny as he laughed, "that doesn't even sound right comin' out your mouth."

Nassir laughed. "Why are you here, you weren't due to see me for at least another 4 months?"

"I can't come and see my favorite physician?" Johnny asked still smiling.

Nassir laughed. "I'm your only physician? You're here because…"

Johnny chuckled and retrieved a medical form from his backpack and handed it to Nassir, who shook his head as if to say I see. "I just need to have this filled out so that I can start a new job."

Nassir looked at the form, put on his glasses and then started reading the form. "You don't work at your utter job anymore?"

"Yeah, I still work there," started Johnny, "but I want another job in order to make something a little extra."

"Don't you think that you'll be spreading yourself a little too thin with school and your current job?" asked Nassir. "What about April, how do you think she'll feel when you'll have to cut down on your time with her because of another job?"

"I'm sure she won't have a problem with it!"

"Ah ha!" proclaimed Nassir smilingly.

"Ah ha what?"

"You didn't discuss this wit April."

"I will," Johnny replied smiling. "If I wasn't on this natural high, I probably would've thought I was spreadin' myself thin too, but for the last few months, not days, months, I've had so much energy, it would be a shame to just waste it. Besides, April will think I'm crazy until she actually sees me in action."

Nassir looked into Johnny's eyes and saw the radiant glow of a healthy person. He knew Johnny took care of himself; his perfect form was evidence of that. Nassir also knew if Johnny didn't feel like doing something, he wouldn't. Johnny had often made good decisions throughout his young life and the man he called Doc knew that. He just couldn't help but wonder why Johnny was on such an energetic high, this was after all, a young man who has been known to oversleep and miss an eleven-a.m. appointment.

Nassir pulled out his stethoscope and sphygmomanometer and rolled up Johnnys sleeve as he held out his arm. "Okay Johnny," Nassir started hesitantly, "after I take your vital signs, we will do the TB and they want you to take a drug test, but along with the tine test you'll be getting, I want to draw some labs. I just want to make sure your levels are all within range."

"Sure Doc," replied Johnny. "But I want you to know I can't afford to miss work or school by being in the hospital or anything like that if my labs come back problematic."

"Then maybe you should forget about the second job," Nassir added in a low monotone voice.

***

That night Johnny lay in bed in the confines of his dark bedroom. He thought about his approaching birthday and wondered what he was going to do.

He would be twenty-three.

Johnny looked up at the ceiling, and as he did every year, started wondering what his life would have been like had his mother been alive to share his approaching birthday with him. He wondered what his life would have been like had he at least

37

knew his mother or father. Even though he never knew his mother personally, Johnny thought about all the stories his Aunt Pauline had shared with him about the childhood her and her two siblings had shared.

With the help of those stories, as well as the photos, Johnny felt he had known his mother, and the feeling of knowing her is what made him miss her. The strange thought occurred to Johnny though, was aside from all the stuff his aunt had told him, he felt he knew more about his mother then what his aunt had shared with him. This, to him, was a strange thought because she had died while giving birth to him, there wasn't any time for bonding.

Johnny also felt as if a large part of him was missing, half of his whole being, but this was a feeling for which he had no explanation. He then brushed off the thought, turned to his side, and attempted to go to sleep.

He laid in bed for two hours and was still wide awake.

His body was still adjusting.

Johnny then got up and switched on the lamp sitting on top of his dresser.

His bedroom was of a simple design. His bed was a twin with no noticeable headboards. Behind his bed, or at the head of it, there was a closet which had a curtain hanging in front of it, different from the standard closets which all had a door of some type. Opposite his bed, which rested lengthwise against the wall, was his dresser, which had a mirror running the same length of the bed. The ceilings were low, like all the other homes in the Cambridge Mall projects.

The living room floors were hard wood and there was linoleum in the kitchen.

Living in the Cambridge Mall housing projects his whole life; Johnny was quite comfortable where most would find discomfort.

When the light came on, the glow revealed to him a brighter reflection of himself through the mirror. He smiled. He was amused even though he had been awake for almost twenty hours, he was not sleepy as of yet. He turned the light back off and walked through the hallway past the two partially closed bedroom doors and turned left, in order to walk down the steps and into the living room.

Once in the living room, he then slid the wooden coffee table sitting in front of the couch over to his left and started doing pushups.

As he thrusted himself up from the floor multiple time, he felt little resistance and attributed his ease with his getting used to doing them.

He did a set of fifty push-ups, which would be his first set of six tonight.

Johnny then turned over and cupped his feet under the couch so he would not slide, and he did one hundred sit-ups, which would be his first set of three tonight. As his adrenal glands continued to work their very rare overnight shift, Johnny initiated a night of what should have been total body exertion.

As the morning hour drew closer, he gave up on the idea of trying to get some sleep. It never dawned on him his ability to work out as much as he had without feeling any soreness or fatigue, should've been impossible.

CHAPTER 5

AT TWO IN the morning there should have been no one outside, but such was almost never the case in Philly, especially on South Street. People of all types could be found gallivanting around doing everything or doing nothing it just depended on whom you were.

In the distance, the song *'Gonna Make You Sweat,'* by C&C Music factory could be heard playing from one of the local establishments.

The night air was crisp and cool. The dark blue night sky was tastefully accented by the presence of bright stars and the night-lights which usually made South Street such a wonderful place to hang out.

Michael Jones, or Snake, as his friends like to call him, had been strolling down South Street trying to clear his head as various people scurried past him. He was a six-foot two and solid two hundred and thirty pounds black male. He wore blue denims, a black sweater with designer gray patches throughout, a beige leather jacket and matching Lugz Boots.

Snake had been drinking a lot tonight, and when he got drunk, he had a temper. Because of the temper he gets when he drinks, Snake never made it a habit to drink. However, tonight was different. He just had to have something. His birthday was fast approaching, and it would be almost ten years since he had last seen his grandmother, the one remaining person in this world whom he loved very much.

Snake would do anything for his grandmother but felt too unstable to be around her, especially of late with the headaches and all. He then had a flashback.

He wasn't sure of why he ran away, but at fourteen years old he should have been in Pittsburgh. But he had a new family now. Michael was in a gang in which he felt he belonged. His best friend Toothpick had a brother who just died, and he had to go to the funeral out of respect.

Hurt from dealing with the grief of another death, Michael quickly decided he would go back to Pittsburgh with some of the money he had earned while with his gang. He needed his grandmother and was sure she needed him.

As a teen, Michael now realized no matter how hard he tried he couldn't escape the presence of death. If he would have gone to Disney World, it was conceivable to Michael the darkly cloaked individual would have taken Mickey Mouse from the world of the living while he watched.

While at the funeral, he decided it was time to go home now, and all would be okay.

Michael was getting off the SEPTA train at the Market – Frankford Thirtieth Street Train sub-station when six youths from a rival gang got off the same train and started to follow him. He hadn't even noticed them.

Upon hearing the train from the opposite direction coming his way, Michael happened to have turned back just before he approached the steps when he finally noticed the group following him.

The fear materialized on his face and then raced down to his heart as he quickly turned around and started to run up the steps, but two of the other youths were quicker as they caught up to him and grabbed him forcefully off the steps.

"Wuz up Snake?" asked the eldest of the small group. "I don't hear you talkin' shit now!"

Although Michael was a bright kid, his mouth usually opened before he thought and he failed to realize his comment, "that's 'cause you ain't let me get a word in yet," would do more harm than good.

The two youths threw Snake on the tracks as the remaining four youths attempted to conceal from passers-by what was happening, about ten seconds before the train arrived.

A woman screamed.

He closed his eyes in fear, and the last thing Michael heard was someone screaming just before the sound of crackling electricity followed by a spiral of red light swarmed around him and caused him to vanish, a fraction of a second before the train would have struck him.

When Michael opened his eyes, he was in his grandmother's house in Pittsburgh. He was shocked yet happy to be there. Then the first headache came, causing him to double over in pain, accompanied by the psychotic thoughts of killing his grandmother.

"No, I gotta get outta here," said Michael as the sound of crackling electricity along with the spiral of red light again circled around him and he vanished from out of the house, before anyone even saw him.

***

The flashback ended.

For the past nine years, Snake has wanted to return home, but knew he couldn't, because of the headaches, which came on a regular basis as well as the random moments of psychosis, for which he had no clue as to where they came from.

Snake didn't just have simple headaches, nothing as pleasant as a migraine. Snake's headaches were the kind which would make any normal person commit suicide. But again, Snake wasn't normal.

For the past decade, Snakes' body had undergone a major genetic alteration. If it were not for the fact of someone trying to kill him, he would've never known about the changes, at least not for a while anyway. Snake had special talents, talents which would allow him to do anything he wanted.

Unfortunately for Snake though, with the blessing of a gift there came the price of a curse, and this was where the headaches came in. Every time he attempted to use his gifts, which he did often, he would have the headaches. It was almost as if something in his system were preventing him from enjoying what he had been blessed with.

The gift, which he and only one other, whom he knew nothing about, had been blessed with.

As he walked down South Street, slightly inebriated but still in full control of his faculties, Snake enjoyed the night air as he attempted to figure out how he could go home, without the headaches.

Snake started looking around but never noticed the large youth who was walking in his direction, when he accidentally bumped into the youth, knocking a little of his drink on himself and the youth.

Snake started brushing himself off. "My fault man, I ain't even see..."

Before he could finish his words, the large youth sucker punched Snake in the jaw and sent him falling back as people quickly moved out of the way, while continuing to become witnesses to the altercation.

The six-five, three-hundred-and-thirty-pound youth laughed. "Maybe next time nigger, you'll watch where you're goin'."

Snake rubbed his chin as he looked up angrily at the youth. He then slowly got up until he was standing in front of the youth and looking up in his face. The three inches in height noticeable to those watching.

The youth looked back at his friend and laughed. "Oh, you must want some more!" He then swung forcefully as the sound of cracking electricity along with a spiral of red light helped Snake to vanish from in front of the youth.

The small crowd who noticed the incident all moved farther away from the youth as he looked around with a puzzled expression on his face.

"Where'd the fuck, he go?" the youth asked as he felt someone grab the front of his neck from behind, slightly cutting off his air.

From behind him Snake said, "If I want to, I can break your neck right now, and no one would ever catch me." And he was right. But now he was starting to have the headaches, and he didn't want them to get any worse.

Snake then threw the large youth to the ground, hard, causing him to bleed from the right side of his head as the youth's friend decided to punch Snake in the back of his head, getting no reaction.

Snake then slowly turned around to face him. "You just saw what I did to your homie here, and still you wanna try me?"

Snakes' eyes then started to glow a bright red as he looked at the second youth who started to float upward involuntarily. Spiraling red light started to crackle around the man's right hand. "Let this be a warning for you and the rest of you who want to try your luck. DON'T FUCK WITH ME!"

A loud cracking sound could be heard as the man's hand appeared to be getting crushed, causing him to scream as his large friend got up and backed away nervously.

Snake then dropped the man who started screaming from the pain of the bones in his hands breaking. "Boy, do I have a fuckin' headache now!"

The sound of crackling electricity along with the spiral of red light helped him to vanish from South Street for the rest of night.

CHAPTER 6

JOHNNY NEVER DID get any sleep last night. He also wasn't as tired as he had been the night before. He spent most of the night exercising and then studied for his botany test.

Morning arrived before he knew it.

Towards the early morning, Johnny remembered he also had to take a test in his psychology class, so he grabbed some index cards and quickly started making up some flash cards. He spent the rest of the morning going over the flash cards after he arrived at school.

On time for a change, Johnny entered his psychology class and sat up near the front of his class behind Tamara Smith.

Tamara had the build of a dancer, which she was, and the face of a beauty queen, which by opinion of Johnny, she was. Her caramel complexion glows with warmth, a smooth honeyed tone which seems to catch light effortlessly, giving her soft skin a luminous sheen. The blend of her African American and Asian heritage shows itself in subtle, beautiful ways-features which feel both striking and harmonious.

Her eyes were almond shaped and expressive, dark and reflective, framed by long lashes which soften their intensity. There's a depth to them as if they carry curiosity, gentleness, and confidence all at once. Her Cheekbones are delicately sculpted, high enough to add elegance, yet rounded with youth. When she smiles, it's unguarded and genuine, revealing full lips with a natural curve which feels warm and inviting.

Tamara, Johnny and April were at one time classmates in biology 101.

April was initially convinced Johnny was trying to put the moves on Tamara, but when she and Tamara became lab partners, and then friends, she quickly realized there was nothing more than a friendship between her boyfriend and this pleasant young woman.

"What's up?" he asked as he tapped Tamara on the shoulder.

Tamara turned around and smiled a soft smile. "Tellin' April you goin' around touchin' other women," she said jokingly.

"Don't play me like that!" Johnny said as he chuckled.

"You ready for the test today?" she asked.

"As ready as I'll ever be," he started as he held up his botany text. "I've been so into my botany class; I forgot to study for this one. As a matter of fact," he again paused as he leaned over closer to her and lowered his voice to a whisper. "Last night was the first time I even looked at the chapters."

Tamara shook her head in the negative while thinking this fool doesn't have a chance at passing this test. She then smiled. "Good luck!"

Simultaneously, Johnny pulled some index cards from out of the zipper pouch located on the front of his backpack. "I outlined all of the important terms from the chapters and put them on these index cards, but I ain't really get a chance to look at them until this morning. I'll be lucky if I get a fifty."

"Why even bother coming in?" she asked him as the professor walked in.

Tamara then turned around as Doctor Comer started giving out verbal instructions for filling out the answer sheet.

"Let's see how many of you pay attention today," started Doctor Comer. "This is your answer sheet," she said as she held up a Scantron Bubble Answer Sheet and displayed it around the classroom. "First, fill in your last name, and shade in the letters of each letter in your name, if your name exceeds the amount of spaces provided, don't worry about filling in the rest of the letters, then fill in your first name, the same way you filled in your last, and fill in your middle initial. After you have done that, write in the month of your birth, the day of your birth and the year of your birth, if any of the numbers is a single digit, please put a zero in front of it."

The class laughed at her comment.

"You're laughing now," started Doctor Comer, "but you'd be surprised at how many students will still fill the sheet out incorrectly. Then where it says student identification number, fill in your social security number. When I give you your test booklet, at the top of the page there will be a number sitting inside of a circle. Write that number at the top of your answer sheet and circle it. If not, I won't know which version of the test you took and will be obligated to fail you if the answers seem wrong." Comer then handed the answer sheets out around the room. "Your papers will serve as my attendance record."

After she handed out the actual test booklets, Johnny opened the test booklet and surveyed the questions, which were all in multiple-choice form.

He didn't understand any of them.

Johnny then closed the booklet back up and sighed. As he looked up at Dr. Comer, he noticed she was looking at him, smiling.

"Good luck!" she mouthed to him.

He smiled at her and then slowly dropped his head back down.

Comer shook her head in the negative. *He obviously didn't study,* she thought.

Johnny then slowly reopened the test booklet and read the first question.

Which answer best describes operant conditioning?

This time Johnny understood the question.

A learning process where voluntary behaviors are modified by association with the addition of reward or aversive stimuli, he thought.

He looked at his paper and saw his mental response was one of the choices. He then smiled as he filled in the bubble sheet and started answering the questions, one by one, marveling at his familiarity of the terms and the definitions.

He ended up completing the test before anyone else in the room did. On his way out of the class, Johnny dropped the test booklet and the answer sheet off in front of Dr. Comer as she looked up at him, wondering how he could have finished the test so fast.

"How was it?" Comer asked.

Johnny smiled at her and in a low voice said, "piece of cake!"

"Piece of cake huh?" Comer said as she examined the paper. She sighed. "You didn't even follow directions."

Johnny looked at her with a look of surprise on his face.

"I told you to put the number of your test booklet at the top of the answer sheet."

Johnny looked at his paper as she wrote the number in for him. He gave her a faint smile as he mouthed the words, "sorry." He then left quickly out of the classroom."

***

After his classes, Johnny went by the doctor's office before going to work, in order to get the results of his tine test read. He stopped by the receptionist's desk and smiled at the attractive Hispanic woman reading a magazine stationed behind the desk. She must be new, he thought.

The receptionist's hair fell in long, corkscrew spirals that framed her face, its dark, swarthy tone giving it a heavy, almost glossy presence under the lights. Each curl seemed deliberately styled yet effortlessly untamed, resting against her shoulders in tight, confident coils. Her lips were painted a deep, wine-red shade, the color rich and deliberate, drawing attention to the slight pucker that gave her expression a perpetually unimpressed air. Without lifting her head, she remained absorbed in the magazine before her, eyes scanning the pages as though the rest of the room—and anyone waiting within it— barely registered as more than background noise.

Johnny said, "excuse me, my name is John Thompkins, I'm here to have my arm read from a TB test I had done three days ago."

"Thompkins?" she asked after she looked up.

Johnny nodded in the affirmative.

The receptionist pushed the roller chair she was on back and went through the alphabetically listed slots, which sat just against the wall behind her. She pulled a file from one of the slots and then retrieved a form from out of the file and handed it to Johnny.

Doctor Nassir did say you would be here, but he had to step out. Nurse Clark will be the one reading your arm."

"Thank you," replied Johnny as he took the form. He then sat in the reception area and waited for his name to be called. He was the only person in the reception area. The television played the cartoon *'Scooby-Doo'*.

***

Two days later, as Johnny rushed through the hallway in order to get to his psychology class, he realized the group of students walking towards him were from the class. He looked at his watch for the first time since getting up this morning and the time confirmed class was indeed over. He stopped running. Johnny then noticed Tamara was walking in his direction.

"Tamara, what'd I miss?" he asked.

"Class!" she started while walking as he followed, "Doctor Comer gave back the test and went over the answers. She's still in there if you wanna get your test back, but I'm telling you in advance, only one person got a ninety-six, everyone else got less than a seventy-five."

Johnny shuddered. *If everyone else got less than a seventy-five, what did I get?* "Thanks," he said stopping as she continued walking.

"Sure," replied Tamara.

Doctor Comer soon exited the classroom and spotted Johnny as he approached her. "Not only late today but missed the class entirely."

"Sorry about that Doctor Comer, but I was wondering if I could still get my test back?"

She stopped, gazed at him and then started digging through the small stack of test she had in her arm over the roll book.

50

"Thompkins," she started. "I just spent the whole class going over the exam," she stopped talking as she looked at his paper. "Oh, you did well," she said as she passed the test to him and continued her way, leaving him standing there. "Only one, I'll excuse your absence today, but don't miss my lecture again!"

"I promise!" Johnny slowly read the results of his test paper and saw at the bottom *'a possible 24 correct out of 25*. He was stunned. *One question wrong?* And according to Tamara, confirmed by Doctor Comer, no one else in his class had done as well.

As he scrutinized the test paper to be sure he was seeing correctly, excitement rushed through his blood. The school year was, after all, getting off to a good start.

***

As April Jenkins looked at her boyfriend and laughed, Johnny continued to sing verses from Michael Jackson's song, *'I'm Bad'*. She sat across from him in the booth seat in the school cafeteria and smiled. She has always loved his sense of humor. Ever since the two of them got together, he has been the romantic comedian. Making her laugh while showering her with love. To her he was the paradigm of what a man should be. Not so much of him being good-looking or well built, but the fact he had a humbling personality. Which was what had attracted her to him. When they first met, as she would look at him, he would always shy away. For April it was a turn on. She took another bite of her cheeseburger as he continued to sing.

"Eat your food," April said.

He stopped. "Not til the whole world knows I got a NINETY-SIX ON MY PSYCH TEST WITHOUT STUDYING! Who's bad?"

She smacked him on the arm as a couple of other students passed by them and looked at them.

Johnny waved to them and mouthed, "ninety-six on psych test!"

The other students laughed.

April said, "Not a big deal block head...get a four-point-o without studying the whole semester and then I'll be impressed?"

"You don't understand," said Johnny. "I should have failed that test. I didn't really get a chance to study while everyone else in my class studied their buts off. Instead of me getting the low score and them getting the high scores, it was the other way around, don't get me wrong, I am in no way getting off on their failures, I'm just getting off on my success."

She gazed at him and smiled as she leaned in towards him. "Maybe you just test well and speakin' of getting off," April said, as she stroked him softly on his face and puckered her lips to emphasize them. "I was thinkin' maybe this weekend we could take a drive, spend a couple of days in the Poconos?"

Johnny smiled. It turned him on whenever April acted in an audacious manner. "Well, I am off this weekend, that can definitely work. You ready to put some miles on that new Escort of yours?"

"It'll be all gassed up and ready to go!" April then started laughing. "I knew I could get your mind off of that stupid test."

Johnny frowned. "Wait, we still get to go to The Poconos, right?"

"Eat your food," April said smiling.

***

On his way to work that afternoon, Johnny sat on the Market-Frankford elevated train as the doors closed.

The SEPTA train wasn't super clean, nor was it spectacular to look at, but it wasn't what Johnny was focused on.

As the train started pulling off, Johnny looked outside the windows and wondered what it would be like to run across the rooftops and jump across the spaces separating the buildings from each other.

He then imagined himself doing just that. *The wind in his face, his heart racing every time he leapt upward and his legs feeling the impact when he would land on the next roof top. Then he leaped again. The next thing he knew flying.*

52

"Next stop, Margaret Orthodox," started the female computerized voice of the train, which then stopped at Margaret and Orthodox station, "Doors are opening."

Johnny opened his eyes and caught himself as he looked up at the sign posted at the station. He only had one stop left to go.

"Next stop, Market Frankford Terminal," again the female sounding computer voice of the train, "with connections to routes, three, five, fourteen, twenty, fifty-eight, and R, thank you for riding SEPTA. Doors are closing." The swishing sound of the doors closing accompanied a hissing sound and then, the train started moving again.

Johnny again looked out the window as the train moved swiftly towards its next destination. The wheels soon screeched while rounding a curve and made its way towards the station.

Johnny got up and made his way to the door so he could make his exit off the train quickly in order to catch his bus. He looked down at his watch and noted he had another forty-five minutes to be at work. *I'm making good time*, he thought to himself.

CHAPTER 7

DOCTOR ROBERT BROOKS had always been irresistibly drawn to the hidden worlds that existed beyond the reach of the naked eye. His fascination with cell biology began early, sparked the moment he received his first microscope at the age of seven. What began as a simple gift quickly became an obsession; hours disappeared as he peered into glass slides, mesmerized by the intricate structures and silent motion of living cells. From that point on, science was no longer just a subject to him—it was a calling that shaped his curiosity, his habits, and his imagination.

By the time he reached thirteen, Brooks's intellect had far outpaced that of his peers. Teachers and researchers alike took notice as he demonstrated an extraordinary grasp of molecular biology, effortlessly navigating concepts that challenged even advanced students. His interests expanded naturally into physics, where he explored the fundamental laws governing matter and energy, and into robotic technology, where theory met invention. Already, he was designing complex systems and asking questions that hinted at a future well beyond conventional scientific boundaries, earning him recognition as a genuine child prodigy with a mind fixed firmly on discovery.While in college, on his way up to medical school, Brooks also decided to focus most of his research on matters dealing with histology and cell physiology. To date, he had never seen anything in a cell he has not been able to identify. This is why this latest discovery has excited him.

Brooks had never seen animal cells with this type of physiology.

Whomever this blood belongs to is one lucky person, he thought. Brooks had just finished observing the blood samples and gave rise to the thought the average working adult would kill to have this type of advantage in his or her physiology over their peers.

The labels on the tubes were coded, as to protect the identity of the person whose blood was being tested, but as Brooks was not affiliated with any lab, he knew his friend Ben would have no problem with divulging this information to him.

Robert Brooks and Benjamin Nassir have been friends for well over two decades. They once met at a medical convention in Valley Forge, Pennsylvania and have been friends ever since.

The lab Brooks did a lot of his research in was a home lab, and looked like any standard laboratory, but the side office within the lab was tastefully decorated with beige walls which had brown paneling running around the baseboards. The large oak desk, which he rarely sat behind when studying his specimens under the microscope, sat in front of the window with the green balloon valence and its' cream-colored mini blinds.

As Doctor Brooks sat at his desk, his blue eyes locked on the open folder in front of him, he seemed to have a look of disbelief on his face as the phone rang.

"Hello," he said dryly after he pressed the button on the speakerphone while running his fingers through his gray-streaked brown hair. His full beard was perfectly matched with the color of his hair.

"Doctor Benjamin Nassir here to see you," responded the voice at the other end of the phone.

"Please send him in Rachel." He then pressed the button again as he stood up.

After a minute, Nassir soon came in and upon seeing his friend, extended his hand. "Robert, you said it was urgent you see me?"

"Yes, Ben," replied Brooks as he nodded in the affirmative and shook Nassir's hand. "I don't mean to startle you with jumping to the point but, who did you get the blood sample from you sent me?"

"I apologize," started Nassir, "but with the tests I wanted you to run, I didn't trust the samples with a regular laboratory so I..."

"No...no," interrupted Brooks, "That's okay but, who did you get it from?"

"It's from one of my patients of course, Johnny Thompkins. He's a twenty-two-year-old male, black, usually the picture of perfect health. He's been my patient since he was an infant. Why do you ask? Is he okay?"

"Johnny Thompkins," repeated Brooks, pondering the name for a moment. "You ever send me his blood before?"

"Never had the need to," Nassir replied, "I only asked you to check it just in case something was in it that could cause him trouble, I want him to avoid problems. Will you tell me what this is about? If he were sick, you would've told me without me having to come all the way down here."

Brooks picked up a Manila folder from off his desk and passed it to Nassir. "Take a look at this," he said.

Nassir opened the folder and read it slowly, while looking at the analysis of the blood tissue. "Where'd this come from?" he asked.

"It's D-N-A from the blood sample you provided," said Brooks as he studied Nassir's facial expression.

"How is this possible?"

Brooks pointed and walked over to a nearby chart which had hand drawn diagrams. "It shouldn't be but somehow, his D-N-A received new information and responded to it, causing a mutation if you will. And because all the information carried in the D-N-A is eventually converted into specific proteins, any change in the base sequence of the molecule can result in a change in the molecular composition of the resulting protein. In general, such changes are caused by a substitution, insertion or a deletion of one or more base pairs within the DNA molecule..."

"Wait, wait a sec Rob," interrupted Nassir, "You're saying all of his extra energy is due to a mutation?"

"So he is experiencing an increase in energy," replied Brooks. "Good, good."

"I don't understand, how can this be possible? I was worried about a metabolic disorder..."

"This is the furthest thing from a metabolic disorder," interrupted Brooks. "Ben, this is the first time, in all my years of studying animal cells, I've ever seen anything like this." He then grabbed Nassir's shoulders and looked directly into his hazel eyes, hoping to appeal to Nassir's love of science.

"I would like to study some of his skin cells, they could probably tell us more about what is going on with his body. What was the catalyst? Where did this start? I believe him to be going through a very unique type of mutation, and I want to see if my hypothesis is right."

Nassir looked back at Brooks, as he seemed to plead with him with the soft blue look in his eyes. "I don't know, you're talking about turning someone who I think of as a son, into a Guinea pig..."

"Ben, whatever is happening with him. I think it be best if we were there to guide him there before he falls down the wrong path, or worse, something bad happens to him."

Nassir looked at Brooks with concern but knew his friend wouldn't mislead him and he cared for Johnny too much to let anything happen to him. "I'll call him into my office as soon as I can..."

"Great!" interrupted Brooks smilingly.

"But I've known Johnny for a long time he's gonna be concerned about your wanting skin cells," replied Nassir.

Brooks said, "Just give him a brief explanation of what's happening to him and let him know everything is going to be fine. Be there for him if he has any questions." As the two physicians started to bid adieu to each other, Brooks added, "I know how remarkable this information is to us, but until we learn more, take care and don't let this get out, not right now anyway."

"I understand," replied Nassir and as he left out of the office, Brooks just shook his head in disbelief.

CHAPTER 8

JOHHNY ARRIVED AT work in a more than jovial mood. He started preparing dinner as he waited for his residents to get home from their day program. While he was in the kitchen, he heard the door open and close.

"Sup Pete?" asked Johnny without looking from the kitchen.

Pete walked into the kitchen and looked at Johnny curiously. "How'd you know it was me?"

"Who else do I work with on pay Fridays?"

Pete shrugged the comment off as he peered into the pot to see what Johnny was making while taking his coat off. "Smells good!" Pete exclaimed as the aroma of seared chicken breast, broccoli, and fettuccini alfredo hovered in the air throughout the apartment.

Peter Bellows was one of Johnny's favorite coworkers. Pete was a five foot seven, pleasantly plump man with brown hair which was cut short, and which was accented well with the presence of baby blue eyes. Pete made it his business to get along with everyone, one of the reasons why Johnny liked him.

While still stirring and without looking from the pot, Johnny said, "just a little somethin' April taught me how to make."

"How long you two been together now?" asked Pete.

"Me an' April?"

"Nah you and Chuck," Pete responded jokingly, "of course you and April!"

"It'll be seven years on December twelfth," said Johnny as he looked around, grabbed the seasoning salt and dashed it into the pot. "Remember...we met at a Thanksgiving dinner? At least I thought I told you."

"You did, I remember now!" Pete asked. "That's like, not even three months away. You gotta do something before someone else steps in!"

"I know, I know and I'm gonna pop the question soon. I'm paying on the ring now, almost done."

"Congratulations," said Pete as he grabbed Johnny's hand, forcefully shaking it.

"Pete, I've had, thee best day." He put the stirring spoon on a towel on the countertop in front of him and turned the stove off as he continued. "I got an 'A' on my first psych test, a test I ain't even study for, I just got another job which I'll be starting soon, which translates into me moving out my aunt's house soon, and April and I are at the top of our relationship ladder."

"Sounds like you are having a pretty good day," replied Pete as the phone started ringing.

"Yeah, things are lookin' pretty good," said Johnny as he walked over to the telephone and answered it. "Ninety-two fifteen ... "

Johnny then paused as he listened and a look of recognition came across his face. "I thought that was you Doc, thanks for hav..." he stopped abruptly and just listened. "Tomorrow, around eleven? Sure, okay, I'll see you then." He hung up the phone and walked into the living room where Pete now was.

"What's wrong?" asked Pete as he observed the disappointed look which willingly laid itself across Johnny's face.

"That was my doctor on the phone," Johnny said. "He drew some labs the other day when he completed my physical and now, he wants to see me in his office tomorrow."

Pete sat on the couch while opening a can of Sprite. "I hope it's nothing serious," he said right before taking a drink.

"Guess I'll find out when I get there," said Johnny.

"I'm sure if it were an emergency, he would've had you go to the hospital or something," replied Pete.

Just then a car horn honked from outside.

Johnny looked over in the direction of the window. "The guys are home."

"I'll get them," started Pete as he got back up. "You just sit there and relax for a minute. I'm sure everything'll be fine." Pete left out of the apartment.

With nothing but his own thoughts to keep him company over the next sixty seconds, Johnny sat down but couldn't help feeling a sense of dread. He replayed the brief conversation with his doctor over and over in his mind, trying to find any clues or hints as to what could be wrong. He couldn't believe that just a few minutes ago, he was sharing his exciting plans with Pete. Now, with one phone call, everything felt uncertain.

"Damn," said Johnny aloud and to himself, his disappointment and worry evident in his tone. He could only hope that his doctor would have good news for him tomorrow, but deep down, he feared the worst.

CHAPTER 9

THE TELEVISION HUMMED softly, casting flickering lights on the walls of the row home nestled within the confines of Cambridge Mall. Even though Johnny's aunt did well financially and could afford to move out of the projects, she decided to stay there because her parents lived in the house most of her life.

Johnny had no objections because he grew up there.

The house was sturdy in construction; it would last longer than the new houses which were built just across the street. Throughout the house, there were pictures telling the tale of a past he knew very little of. He knew his grandparents when he was little, but they both died when he was young. The pictures of the three children on the wall were also familiar to him. One of the girls was his mother and the other was his aunt, Pauline. The young man was his Uncle Eric.

Eric was in the military, so he traveled most of the time.

Johnny admired the highly decorated soldier. Every time he saw his Uncle Eric, the soldier would have a tale to tell him. His most recent tale had to do with him meeting The Reverend Jesse Jackson while he was over in the Persian Gulf. Johnny knew the great reverend wasn't over there at the time his uncle was, but he never told Uncle Eric because his stories were so entertaining.

Then there was another set of pictures of two children, a boy and a girl.

There were several pictures of the boy, aged through the years. Those were pictures of him.

The pictures of the young girl were his cousin Tanya, his Aunt Pauline's daughter.

Tanya was born only twelve years ago, and the picture hanging on the wall next to his was only taken six years ago. Tanya was the little sister he always wanted, but since he didn't have parents, he knew having any type of siblings was out of the question. Tanya was better than anything he could ever had hoped for.

"What's wrong hun?" asked Johnny's aunt as she descended the steps wearing a solid blue nightgown while watching him stare blankly at the television screen.

Pauline Thompkins was aging gracefully. Now in her late forties, she had aged little in the last twenty-three years. She never married, but she did give birth to a girl, Tanya, who seemed to be the mirror image of her mother when she was a young woman.

Tanya's father was by no definition a deadbeat dad. He and Pauline were good friends who became intimate with each other on more than a few occasions. When Pauline announced she was pregnant, they mutually decided to share the responsibilities of raising their little girl.

"Nothing," replied Johnny as a girl, who appeared to be around twelve years of age, walked in from the kitchen and into the room where her mother and older cousin were talking.

"He probably had a fight with April," said Tanya.

"Tanya!" started Pauline with slight anger in her voice. "Why are you in an adult conversation?" She then looked down at her watch. "As a matter of fact, what are you even doin' downstairs?"

"Mom I..."

"Am gonna march right back up them stairs, better be the next sentence out your mouth," interrupted Pauline. "I want that little but back in bed, and we'll talk tomorrow about what time at night a twelve-year-old should be walking around the house."

Tanya angrily marched up the steps.

"Sorry 'bout that, I told her she could get some juice," Johnny said as he watched Tanya's shadow ascend the steps. He then went back to staring at the television.

Pauline looked at the television and saw Johnny was watching, 'Star Trek: The Next Generation.' "She know better, it's a school night," she started. "You watch this garbage?"

"Garbage? The devil is a liar!" laughed Johnny.

"What would you call it then?" she asked.

"Preferred programming which stimulates neural activity."

Pauline grabbed the remote from off the coffee table and turned the television off. Ever since her sister's tragic death, she hadn't been able to watch anything having to do with space, aliens, or planets other than the one she lived on.

Johnny looked at his aunt and huffed. "I told you I was cool."

"Are you an' April okay?" she asked.

"We're better than okay, we're actually great," started Johnny as he stood up and walked over to the television and then turned around. "Whatever's on my mind, it has nothing to do with April, nothing to do with school, I'm just," he sighed as he sat back down, "never mind."

Pauline moved closer and took Johnny's hand. "I get you're and adult now, but I don't want you to feel like you can't talk to me. I love you very much and there isn't anything I wouldn't do for you."

Johnny looked at his aunt's wrinkle free brown skin and her shoulder length black hair. He knew she loved him. She had taken care of him his whole life. Working hard, day in and day out, to support this child who wasn't even hers.

"I know Aunt Paula," he replied. He leaned over and kissed her on the cheek. "Now you go back upstairs and get some rest, I'll be fine."

"You sure sweetie?"

"Nothing but sure."

She smiled at him as she got up and made her way to the stairs. "You have anything planned this weekend for your birthday?" she asked.

"April and I are going to the Poconos."

"Poconos huh?" she asked. "Better make her an honest woman!"

"You know I'm workin' on it."

"Work harder! And faster!" She smiled as she headed back towards the steps. "Don't forget to straighten up your mess before you go to bed," she added.

"I won't," he replied as he headed to the sofa and swiped the remote off the table and turned the television back on.

"Turn the lights and tv off before you come up," she added as she continued up the steps. "Tanya, you better be in there sleeping!"

"If she was you just woke her," Johnny said aloud and to himself.

Johnny then smiled to himself. He had been so focused on job searching and his questions about his health that he didn't realize until just a few moments ago that April had planned their weekend getaway for his birthday.

***

As it got later into the night, early into the next morning, the television programming bored him and there wasn't anything on of interest to Johnny. They didn't have cable, so the choices were limited to channels 3, 6, 10, 17, 29, and 48.

Johnny fell asleep on the couch while still trying to watch the television, trying to make sure tomorrow took its time arriving, so he could delay the delivery of any bad news from Doctor Nassir.

His body had finally adjusted.

As he was drifting off to sleep, his eyes started getting heavy and he tried to continue staring at the light from the television, his sleepy eyes forbidding him to make sense of what was on the screen.

In a sleepy, dazed voice, Johnny repeated what his aunt said earlier, "and don't forget to turn the TV and the lights off." Trying to remind himself of his aunt's request prior to his coming upstairs. His eyes briefly opened and then closed, and the television instantly cut off.

As a light sound of crackling electricity started to play around his body, Johnny's clothing changed into a tee shirt and a pir of basketball shorts and then he disappeared from off the couch.

***

A light sounding snap assisted Johnny as he reappeared upstairs in his bed.

Everyone else in the house was asleep.

Only the dark silence of the house witnessed what had happened to Johnny as he teleported himself for the first time.

He would never know this happened.

CHAPTER 10

LOOKING AROUND AT the walls in order to ease his anxiousness and trepidation while his left knee jittered up and down, Johnny sat in Nassir's office, believing he was awaiting bad news when Nassir walked in smiling.

The nerve of this guy, he thought. *Here I am, dreading bad news so I can go find out my treatment options, and my so-called friend walks in here wearing a grin he borrowed from a purple dinosaur named Barney.*

"Good morning, Johnny," said Nassir smilingly.

"Is it Doc?" asked Johnny with nervousness in his voice. "Won't know 'til you tell me what's wrong with me?"

"Huh?" asked Nassir in a confused tone as he looked over at Johnny. Then he started to laugh. "No, no Johnny, sorry if I worried you. I don't have any bad news for you," he said as he sat down and as Johnny touched his leg which then stopped shaking. "I just wanted you to come in so I could try to explain to you where we think all your extra energy is coming from. More precisely, to try and explain why you are getting this extra surge of energy."

Johnny sighed with embarrassment; because of the way he was just thinking and how he presented himself to Nassir. "I thought you were going to tell me I was sick or something," said Johnny as he then developed a look of relief on his face. "Okay...so wuz up?"

Nassir closed his office door shut. "Johnny something strange and wonderful has happened to you," started Nassir. "Your body, for some strange reason, has developed a strange mutation which is causing the base pairs in your genetic code to change up." Nassir laughed. "The result of this change up is increasing the rate at which your body is mutating and adding a new type of amino acid into your blood stream. This is causing an increase in adenosine triphosphate production, which is requiring you to eat less but helping you to maintain your energy levels along with slight increases of ener..."

"Wait a minute Doc," interrupted Johnny as he rubbed his neck and look downward. "As you know, I took some time off after high school and started college a little late...so you lost me around base pairs and mutation. I have no clue what you're saying."

Nassir took off his glasses. "The bottom line of your increase in energy is the result of your body's rapid production of adenosine triphosphate or A-T-P, A-T-P is the energy usually supplied by glucose and oxygen in humans and animals. The only thing we don't know, is why this is happening to you."

Johnny was now looking at his doctor with a more confused look than he already had. He wasn't sure if this was good news or bad news. "Isn't this dangerous, shouldn't I be getting help or something?" he asked.

"Johnny, your body is adapting extremely well with this modification, however, I would like to take some cell samples in order to find out what could be going on."

"Why does this sound like it's going to hurt?"

"No, no, it won't hurt a bit," assured Nassir.

***

The following week, after his weekend getaway with April, Johnny was back at work.

Ninety-two fifteen was quiet except for the television which blared the laughs which Martin Lawrence usually received during his television show.

All the residents had been given their showers and were now in bed.

Johnny had another two hours to go before his three to eleven shift ended. While waiting for the end of his shift, he poured a bag of microwave popcorn into a large bowl as he spoke on the phone with April.

He soon walked out of the kitchen, he passed a bowl of popcorn to Jay Smothering, the young guy working with him tonight.

Jay was normally a quiet gut, except for the times when he and Johnny worked together. They usually liked to laugh at everything and because Johnny didn't have many friends outside of work, he liked his job because of the interesting people he worked with.

"Everything's cool now, though," started Johnny followed by a pause. "I didn't want to ruin our weekend with potential health issues that weren't really even concerns," he started. "You know he's been my doctor ever since I can remember, and I trust him."

Again he paused. "I promise!"

Quiet again, then, with his teeth clenched he said, "girl...I said I promise." He switched the cordless phone from his left ear to his right ear and then grabbed a handful of popcorn. He started munching as he listened.

"I'm only going to work two jobs for a little while, just long enough so we have what we need to start our life together."

Johnny grew quiet as he listened to her and started thinking he hadn't even considered the possibility she could financially supplement what he brought in in order to get their lives together started. His Uncle Eric had always told him, "the man is supposed to be the provider."

He stood back up and walked back into the kitchen and said, "I cherish our time together too, but I was just trying to do this for us because I love you."

"And I love the two of you," yelled Jay as he leaned into the direction of the kitchen.

Johnny peeked out of the kitchen and smirked and then into the phone, "Oh that aint no body but Blondie," said Johnny. Johnny usually called Jay Blondie because of his thick blond hair and boyish looks. Johnny paused as he cupped the phone and said, "Jay, April said hello."

Jay simply smiled and nodded back his response as he continued watching the television.

***

Later that night, as he walked up from the steps of the subway at Broad Street and Girard Avenue, Johnny took notice the air was extra frigid, and the night was still and quiet. Usually, the streets were still busy at this time, and it was only twelve-thirty a.m.

The cold air must have kept everyone inside, but Johnny liked this type of weather. He looked over across the street at the closed businesses as he walked down Girard Avenue along the fence which led into the courtyard of William Penn High School. When he got to Thirteenth Street, five young black men who were around his age, turned the corner just as he had gotten there.

Initially startled, Johnny jumped back.

The five men were varied in sizes and shapes, but were all dressed in semi baggy clothing. One of them had on dingy sky-blue jeans and what appeared to be a new goose down. The four remaining youths had on dark colored jeans and new coats as well. The group stopped him as he attempted to walk past.

Johnny became irritated and slightly nervous about the confrontation.

The first thug jumped in Johnny's face. "Zup holmes?" He asked as he looked Johnny up and down. "You think you can help me out wit some cash?"

"Nope," replied Johnny as he nonchalantly attempted to continue walking past, but then one of the other thugs pushed him back.

"He looks like he gots sum ends on em," said a second thug angrily. "I'm sure he at least got some tokens or a trizzy on him, I say we take what we want." He then swung at Johnny, but Johnny blocked him and gave him a hard uppercut before tossing him seven feet above his head.

The thug involuntarily flew up and back and then landed hard on the ground. "Aw shit, damn," he said. The impact to the ground was painful.

Before Johnny had time to be surprised about how he so effortlessly tossed the thug behind him, the other four thugs rushed towards him.

Right before they reached him, Johnny instinctively jumped eight feet into the air and over the heads of his would-be attackers before landing behind them.

While everyone, including Johnny, stood around looking surprised about what just happened, one of the thugs pulled a gun out from under his coat and aimed it at Johnny.

"I dunno wuz up wit this shit," he said. "But game times' over."

"NO Wait!" yelled Johnny, but it was too late.

The thug had already fired three shots into Johnny's chest.

The bullets seemed to have moved slowly, and a yellow light formed around them as they moved closer towards him and as the hot metal pierced its way through his chest, Johnny fell back hard and slow as the radiating pain from the wounds shot quickly all over his body, alerting every sensory nerve he had into defense mode.

"Let's get outta here!" ordered one of the other thugs as his friend tucked the gun back inside of his jacket.

The five thugs then quickly ran away.

Johnny's eyes lit up bright yellow and then quickly dimmed out as his head rolled down to the left and as his eyes closed.

In the distance, a police siren could be heard shrieking through the night, responding to the 9-1-1 call put out by a witness who was peeking out a window from an apartment across the street.

Johnny's right hand twitched slightly with a small amount of blood covering it.

CHAPTER 11

AWESTRUCK, THE SITE they were looking at made their mouths hang open. To think someone could have a cell with which...never mind, read on.

Ben Nassir and Robert Brooks were in Brook's home lab studying the cell samples they were able to obtain from Johnny Thompkins. They had a set up of three microscopes on a table which was positioned against the wall, opposite from the office where the desk Brooks rarely sat at was located.

Each of the microscopes had their own individual magnification setting.

"Remarkable Ben," started Brooks, "I've never seen anything like this in any animal cell I've ever looked at."

Nassir couldn't respond, for he too was astonished at the sight he was able to see.

Brooks continued looking into the microscope. "There seems to be an organelle in the cytoplasm of his skin cells which is remarkably similar to the chloroplast of plant cells, minus the green pigment, otherwise many of the other constituents are there."

Nassir looked up from his microscope and over at Brooks, whose eyes were still locked into his. "You mean, his body is producing the extra A-T-P because his cells are absorbing light?"

Brooks then looked up from the microscope. "That's what it seems like, yes," he said. "This allows for an increase in energy along with a lesser need for oxygen, an increased rate at which the body heals itself and he could potentially have augmented strength and speed." He walked over to Nassir and passed him a folder he had picked up off a nearby table. "The other thing I discovered while observing the samples of blood is, whatever is happening to your friend, it's happening at a faster rate as time goes by. As we speak, his strength is growing and without the proper training on how to handle such strength he could accidentally become very dangerous to himself or anyone else."

"Are you certain that he is pulling in light?" asked Nassir. "I mean it looks as if there were little sparks in the cell.

"That has to be residual," started Brooks. "There's no way he could produce the light himself!"

Nassir shook his head in the negative. "I don't know how Johnny's going to handle this," he said as he walked over towards a window and looked outside.

"All of his special qualities will be at their strongest in the presence of light," added Brooks. "Take another look into the microscope." He directed Nassir over to the microscope he himself had just been looking into. As Nassir studied the microscope, Brooks continued. "If you noticed earlier when looking at the cell membrane, it keeps trying to form some type of cell wall every time the light on the scope is adjus..."

Nassir's pager started going off, interrupting Brooks.

Nassir looked up from the scope as he reached for his pager. He then looked at the phone number displayed into the screen. "Robert, may I use your phone?"

"Sure!" said Brooks. He then headed back over to the scope and turned the switch off.

Nassir picked up the telephone and dialed the number from his pager. He then held the receiver of the telephone up to his face. "Yes, this is Doctor Benjamin Nassir, I believe I was just paged."

He paused as he listened.

"Okay, I'll be there shortly." Nassir hung up the phone walked over to the coat rack and removed his coat.

"You're not on-call are you? One of your patients in dire need of your attention?" inquired Brooks.

"I'm not technically on call," started Nassir, "but one of my patient's is in dire need of my attention, not just one of my patients, but the one we've been talking about for the last few days." Nassir slipped on his coat and located his car keys in one of the outer pockets. "Come wit me, I'll explain everything to you on the way."

***

The incessant ringing of the telephone intruded on the silence of the night as Pauline hesitantly rolled over and pressed the speaker button on the telephone.

"Hello?" she said dryly.

"Hi Ms. Paula," started April. "I'm sorry to be calling you this late but, Johnny was supposed to call me as soon as he got in from work tonight and I just wanted to make sure he made it in okay."

Pauline glanced at the clock radio on her dresser and saw that it was one o'clock in the morning. "Baby I don't think he even came in tonight, hold on let me check." She then got out of the bed and looked in his room.

Johnny's bed was still made.

She then went back into the room and looked down at the speaker phone. "April he never came home, call his job, he might've gotten stuck and had to work overtime."

"Thank-you Ms. Paula," said April. She then hung up the phone.

Pauline then depressed the button on the speaker phone and laid back down.

CHAPTER 12

AT SAINT JOSEPHS' Medical Center, on the third floor, several of the hospital personnel were discussing the strange physiology of their latest patient. He was picked up off the street with three apparent gunshot wounds in the chest. In the emergency room, they also said he was found lying in what was believed to have been his own blood. But almost as soon as he was put into the ambulance, his body started to heal itself.

The emergency medical technicians couldn't figure out what to do with him. And even though he was unconscious on the way over, he still made them nervous.

The physicians at the hospital were also stumped when it came to how this man should be treated. They knew there were bullets in this man's chest, but every time they attempted to cut into his skin, he would heal. All they could do was hope his primary care doctor, would be able to somehow help them with getting the bullets out of him.

Johnny was awake now, but other than providing them with the pager number to his physician, the only questions he was willing to answer, were the ones his lifelong physician were to ask. As he lay in bed, just looking out into the hallway, Nassir and Brooks entered the room and walked over to him.

"What's up Doc?" asked Johnny in a tired and raspy voice.

"Don't say a word Johnny," replied Nassir. He then held his hand towards the man standing behind him. "This is my good friend, Doctor Robert Brooks."

Brooks waved to Johnny who then looked at Nassir as if to ask, who is he?

"He's the gentleman who revealed your unique tissue pattern to me," Nassir replied.

Brooks smiled.

Nassir said, "We were studying the cell samples you had given us when alerted of your condition. Luckily, we believe we have a solution as to how take care of all of this and I will explain everything we know so far to you." He looked at Brooks and then back at Johnny. "But after your surgery, I am having them release you under my care."

Johnny continued to look at the two physicians with a look of curiosity on his face.

***

Johnny spent a few days at the home of Doctor Robert Brooks and had been communicating with his aunt and April about most of what had happened, omitting some of the information because everything still seemed unreal to even himself and he was living through it.

As the days passed, Johnny soon went home and told his aunt of the shooting incident. He told her of how he was on his way home from work when the incident took place, and of how he had to have emergency surgery in order to have the bullets removed from his body. He lied about the surgery.

Johnny decided not to tell his aunt how he was winning the fight with his attackers. He also neglected to tell her of how his body healed itself. He was unsure why, but he didn't want her to question him about those strange facts.

Pauline, who was tearing up at the news from Johnny, was upset about the entire situation. "What do you mean, you didn't feel the need to worry me?" she asked with teary eyes. "What'd you think April calling here at one in the mornin' was gonna to do? Johnny, I have raised you better than that and you can't even have me notified when something like this happens?"

Johnny continued looking down at the floor. "I told you that Doc had everything under…"

"That's another thing," she interrupted. "Ben, also didn't feel the need to tell me anything. Do the two of yall think I'm so fragile, I can't handle stuff like this? I have a right to know what happens to you, God forbid if you get shot again? Or hit by a car? Your coworkers may not be able or know to call me to see if you're okay." She moved over closer to Johnny and lifted his chin up. "Johnny, I love you very much, and I want you to be careful out there but considerate in here."

Johnny gave his aunt a hug. "I'm sorry Aunt Paula; I really don't know what I was thinkin'."

The two fell silent for a moment as Johnny looked away from his aunt who stared directly at him with an angry yet teary eyed expression on her face.

Ringing loudly, the telephone then intruded on their brief silence.

Johnny walked over to it and picked up the receiver. "Hello," he said dryly, as his throat was scratchy from the conversation he just had with his aunt.

Johnny paused as he listened to the voice on the other end of the phone.

"It's me Lisa," said Johnny.

Lisa Sims was Johnny's immediate supervisor at Helpers of All People, or HAP, as the agency was known. Lisa has always felt that Johnny was one of her best employees.

He has had an occasion where he has missed a meeting but has never been late to a shift, all in all he was a good employee and a diligent worker.

The Human Resources department at the company however was pretty strict on how they dealt with attendance problems and since Johnny had a recent no call / no show under his belt, the company wanted Lisa to find a solution to dealing with the problem. If she couldn't, then they would.

"Before my shift starts?" he asked.

Again, he paused as he looked at his aunt and mouthed the words, *it's my supervisor.*

Pauline nodded she understood.

"Well, is two o'clock on Monday okay, 'cause I don't get out of class until twelve, and it'll take me a minute to get there by bus."

He paused.

"I'll be fine, I have a great doctor. Thanks Lisa, see you on Monday." He then hung up the phone. Johnny looked at his aunt and said, "I have to report to the office before I go to work on Monday." He then grabbed his backpack from off the floor and headed upstairs to his room.

Pauline said, "Remember Johnny, please be considerate in here."

Johnny nodded his head in the affirmative and went all the way upstairs. He thought he was being considerate by not alarming his aunt of his condition.

***

The next morning, Johnny awoke suddenly feeling damp and clammy as the sweat continued to pour down his face. He sat up on the side of his bed looking confused, as if he had just lost track of time. He then sat his face inside of his hands as he recalled the uncanny dream, which awakened him about the man who was made of light or at least the man who looked as if he were made of light.

In the dream, the man had vanished several times and he could fly. He also appeared to be broken up into pieces and then coming back together again, as if he were healing himself. Then as the being tried to approach Johnny, the dream ended.

As Johnny re-visualized the strange dream, he yawned and stretched. He then placed his right hand inside of his pajama top in order to scratch an itchy sensation he had on his chest. Out of concern, feeling only the hair follicles of his chest, he hurried and unbuttoned his pajama top, looking at his chest as he did so.

The three bullet wounds from a few nights ago were gone.

***

Later that morning, as the wind blew lightly, Johnny left the house and then crossed over Girard Avenue at Twelfth Street and then walked up the block over to the rear of the courtyard of

William Penn High School and stood next to the part of the fence where he had been shot.

Johnny stood there looking around, and as clear as watching a picture-perfect movie, he observed the whole incident which took place at the time of his shooting as the incident took place.

When he got to Thirteenth Street, five men who were around the same age as him, turned the corner just as he had gotten there.

Johnny jumped back.

The group stopped him as he attempted to walk past.

The first thug jumped in Johnny's face. "Zup holmes." He asked as he looked Johnny up and down. "You think you can help me out wit some cash?"

"Nope," replied Johnny as he attempted to continue walking past, but was then pushed back by one of the thugs.

"He looks like he gots sum ends on em," said a second thug angrily. "I'm sure he at least got some tokens or a trizzy on him, I say we take what we want." He then swung at Johnny, but Johnny blocked him and gave him a hard uppercut before tossing the second thug seven feet above his head.

The thug involuntarily flew up and back and then landed hard on the ground. "Aw shit, damn," he said.

The other four thugs rushed towards him.

Right before they reached him, Johnny jumped eight feet into the air and over the heads of his would-be attackers before landing behind them.

One of the thugs pulled a gun out from under his coat and aimed it at Johnny. "I dunno wuz up wit this shit," he said. "But game times' over."

"NO Wait!" yelled Johnny, but it was too late.

The thug had already fired three shots into Johnny's chest. Johnny fell back hard and slow.

"Let's get outta here!" ordered one of the other thugs as his accomplice tucked the gun back inside of his jacket.

The five thugs then quickly ran away.

In the distance, a police siren could be heard shrieking through the night.

Gasping from the impact into the ground, Johnny's eyes closed slowly as his right hand twitched slightly in the small pool of blood.

The vision ended and he then looked down and saw he was standing on some of his dried-up blood.

"Something wonderful is happening to your body," said Nassir's voice from inside of Johnny's head.

"What the fuck?" he asked out loud and to himself as he glanced down to his chest. He continued to look around the crime scene, looking up at the tall fence which surrounded the courtyard of the school. After looking down at his watch, he then headed back home.

***

The aroma of Italian cuisine danced in the air at the Spaghetti Warehouse on Tenth and Spring Garden Streets, a rich mingling of garlic, simmering tomatoes, and fresh bread that drifted out onto the sidewalk. Inside, the warmth wrapped around patrons like a familiar embrace—steam rising from heaping plates of pasta, the low clatter of forks against porcelain, and the steady hum of conversation blending with soft music in the background. Red-checkered tablecloths bore the marks of many meals before, stained faintly with sauce and wine, while the scent of oregano and basil lingered long after servers passed by. It was the kind of place where time seemed to slow, where hunger sharpened not just the appetite, but the senses, drawing everyone a little deeper into the comfort and promise of a good meal.

"Johnny!" April called as he popped his head up in surprise.

"I'm sorry babe," started Johnny. "Just got a lot of stuff on my mind."

"You wanna talk about it?" she asked.

Johnny looked from her to the other people in the restaurant, who were either eating, talking, or doing both, as he shook his head slowly in the affirmative.

"April there's a lot of weird stuff happening to me, causing me to feel like I'm losing my mind."

She put her fork down without taking her eyes off him, showing him, she was paying attention. "What do you mean?"

"I keep having these strange dreams, it's almost as if someone's trying to tell me something." He started drinking some water as April just watched. "The dreams never make any sense. All I keep seeing is someone flying, people vanishing or changing into beings made of light, this morning, I walked over to William Penn High School, and I swore I watched something that happened to me the other day as it was going on, like a vivid dream."

"You mean like a vivid memory?"

Johnny shook his head no. "Naw, it was more like watching a movie and I was observing myself from the outside, but everything I saw was yellow..." Johnny then suddenly stopped talking. "What?" he asked.

"Whadda you mean what? I'm listening to you."

"Yeah, but the way you're looking at me."

"How am I supposed to look at you?" she asked. "I'm trying to be a consoling ear, and you won't let me. Never mind," she sighed. She then got up from the table, gathered her belongings, and stormed out of the restaurant, leaving all of the attention on Johnny.

With the sign of annoyance hanging on his face, Johnny reached into his wallet and pulled out some money. "I don't believe this girl." After dropping the money on the table, he followed her out of the restaurant.

"April, what's wrong with you?" he asked loudly as he watched her storming away. "We were in the middle of ..."

April stopped and turned to face Johnny as he caught up to her. "What's wrong with ME? Let me tell you what's wrong with me. First of all, for the past month, you have not been yourself; you've been distant and secretive, and I don't know what's going on with you. Secondly, when were you planning on telling me you lost your job? I felt like an idiot calling ninety-two fifteen asking for you. And lastly, if I were ever in the hospital, EVER! I would make sure you and my family are the first ones notified. Why didn't you tell me you were in the hospital? I am the last person you should be keeping something like that from. Let me say this again to make sure you understand."

Johnny looked away and then down.

"See you're lookin' away 'cause you know you're wrong. If something were to happen to me, I would make sure that you and my family were the first ones notified."

Johnny continued to look down with the *'dam I'm caught'* look on his face. He then thought, *I hope she doesn't know I've been shot.*

As they paused and stood there, the thirty seconds stretched out to feel more like ten minutes.

The wind blew heavily and dusk started to announce its appearance, spectators walked by and glanced at the young couple as they stood there.

"Go ahead and keep lookin' away 'cause you know you're wrong," said April. "Why would you keep anything from me?"

Johnny moved closer to April. "Like I started to say April, a lot of weird shit is happening to me and I'm not even sure if I'm clear on what's exactly happening."

"What? Some weird dreams about flying people. A moment of Déjà vu you had at your old school?" April looked at him angrily as her eyes glossed and burned from the tears which were about to come out. "From what I understand, you almost DIED, and you don't think I should know? What kind of life are we gonna have together if one half of us decides it's okay to keep secrets from the other?" April then angrily stormed off in the direction she was initially headed in.

Johnny stood there for a moment and sighed. He then ran after her. "April wait!" he called as he continued after her.

CHAPTER 13

NESTLED IN THE quiet suburbs of Horsham, lay a million-dollar estate belonging to Doctor Robert Brooks. The home was not built just because he had the money to build it. He had it built in order to accommodate himself and his younger brother, Sam.

Reconstructed over twenty years ago, the house was lavishly furnished with Victorian furniture in the living room and in the dining room.

The den, more recently decorated, housed a black plush leather sofa with matching love seat and chaise. The oak washed coffee table, which also resided in the den, was the sister to the mammoth entertainment system, which started at the floor and almost reached the ceiling.

The entertainment system was home to the forty-eight-inch color television and the rest of the home theater system.

Downstairs in the basement, was another laboratory sitting adjacent to a small gym which Robert had built for Sam, who back then, was aspiring to be one of the world's best martial artists.

If Sam had gotten into the film industry, he would have ranked well with the likes of Chuck Norris, Steven Segal or Jackie Chan.

Two weeks had passed since the time of Johnny's attack just outside of the courtyard of William Penn High School. He went with Nassir and Brooks to the estate, which was located just on the out skirts of Philadelphia.

"Damn this jawn is tight," exclaimed Johnny as he eyed over the huge estate.

Brooks smiled at Johnny's approval. He was lucky enough to have been born with a silver spoon in his mouth but if you ran into him in public, one could never tell as he kept his dress simple, a pair of denim pants and a Polo shirt under a sweater when casual. He guided them around the mini-mansion. "My brother and I both were fortunate, our parents however, died in a plane crash while I was in medical school and while my brother Sam was still in high school."

"Sorry to hear that," replied Johnny.

Brooks nodded in appreciation and then changed the subject and they entered the lab. "I have no doubt the personnel at Saint Joseph's Medical Center, will discuss what they know of you to anyone who will listen." He sat down in a lounge chair which sat near his desk in the lab and gestured Johnny and Nassir to each have a seat. "It'll be in your best interest if you keep your gifts hidden for a while and, here is as good a place as any to practice using your abilities or practicing any skills you may have."

"Here? I'm pretty sure I'll be alright," started Johnny as he shook his head in the negative, "I don't make it a habit hangin' around hospitals," said Johnny as Nassir smiled at the comment.

Brooks nodded in the affirmative. He then looked at Nassir and gave him a signal with his head.

"Johnny," started Nassir, "as you know, your D - N - A has mutated in such a way that, you will never run out of energy, but what you don't know is why this is happening." He paused. "Your body seems to have somehow acquired an organelle in the cytoplasm of every cell on the outer part of your body, which mimics the chloroplast found in plant cells. The more your body's D - N -A changes, the stronger and more energetic you seem to get."

"That is why on the night you were shot," said Brooks as he stood up. "All the bullets could do was get inside your body. They couldn't do any major damage because your body started changing on the inside possibly because of the threat of harm. When the E-M-Ts put you into the ambulance, the addition of light healed your body at a faster rate than it would have in darkness."

"Then how come the two of you were able to cut in to me and get the bullets out?" asked Johnny.

"We didn't," started Nassir, "The bullets are still inside of you. We had to sedate you and pretend we were able to perform the surgery and Robert here paid off the circ team for keeping that info close to the cuff. We then had you transported here."

Brooks held up a pair of night vision glasses. "And thanks to these things, we were afforded the chance to fake the game."

As Johnny smirked at the pair and looked at the glasses, Nassir said, "We want you to spend some time here because we wish to conduct a few tests on the changes your body's going through. You know, learn all about your strengths and weaknesses, and about what you can and cannot do. We know, for example, in the dark, your body still has vast amounts of energy which can decrease at any time without foreknowledge, but we still have a lot to learn."

Johnny shook his head no. "You two are starting to scare me," he said. "I don't know what it is yawl expect from me, I've already lost one job and may have forfeited the other, still have to get my thoughts organized enough to focus on my classes, and what am I expected to do about April, just push her off to the side?"

"No Johnny, anything you decide to do is okay with us. We only want any part of your free time you may be able to give us, and I will compensate you generously for doing so. It's totally your decision," Brooks said reassuringly.

"I don't care what," Johnny stopped as he looked between the two docs, "did you say compensate? As in pay me?"

Brooks shook his head yes. "Ben already explained what happened with your job and the work we want to do is extensive. I can legally pay you under my company as a security consultant and the salary would be very generous, enough to allow you to continue living your life."

Johnny shook his head no. "I'm sorry, but I got my own problems to deal wit, so what I can heal fast and have extra energy? Who's to say I won't really get hurt?"

Nassir shook his head in the affirmative. "Johnny, we understand any apprehension you may have."

"Thanks Doc," started Johnny as he grabbed his backpack. "Do you think I can get a ride to the closest bus stop?"

"Sure Johnny," replied Nassir.

"Just be careful out there Johnny and if you change your mind," started Brooks, "my offer still stands."

"Thanks Doctor Brooks," replied Johnny.

***

Impatiently waiting for a bus at Bustleton Avenue and Red Lion Road in Northeast Philadelphia, where Nassir had dropped him off, Johnny glanced over at the McDonalds and decided to grab a quick bite to eat.

"Damn, I hate Sunday schedules," he said as he waited for his food.

The server then gave him his food and soda. "Here you go!"

"Thank you," said Johnny and after getting his food, he left out of the restaurant and headed for the bus stop when the SEPTA bus passed by him.

The bus soon stopped at a red light about two blocks away from where he was standing.

"Damn that, I aint waitin' no hour for another bus," he said as he looked at his watch. He then started running in an attempt to catch the bus. He then looked down at his bag and drink to make sure he had a good grip.

Assisted by the sound of a giant zipper unzipping, a large circle of black space opened directly in front of Johnny as he was running and, not paying attention, he ran straight through.

***

The sound of the giant zipper welcomed the portal as it reopened at Twelfth Street and Girard Avenue and as soon as Johnny ran out, he fell to the ground with his torso landing on his sixteen-ounce soda.

Confused and frightened, he stood up and let go of the McDonald's bag in his hand, dropping it onto the ground. as the large black abyss zipped closed behind him. He then started wiping the spilled soda off the front of his jacket.

A few small children, who witnessed what just happened from the other side of the street, quickly ran across the street and over to Johnny.

"Decent," started one of the kids as they all gathered around him.

One of the smaller kids looked him up and down and asked, "Can you do that again mista?"

"Do what?" Johnny asked nervously, trying to play dumb as he looked at the children and picked up the bag of food.

"Come out of the air like that," asked another child. "How'd you do that?"

Johnny looked around at the children and took notice they were all quite young and thought to himself *they shouldn't be out here at this time of night.* "Shouldn't yawl be in bed right now?" asked Johnny as he looked at the small children. "As a matter of fact, I wish I were in bed right..."

The sound of cracking electricity interrupted him as it started to play around him accompanied by a spiral of yellowish light, causing him to vanish before he could finish his sentence.

"Where'd he go?" asked one of the children as they all looked around with puzzled expressions on their faces.

***

With a light snapping sound, Johnny materialized in his bedroom. To be more specific, he appeared standing at the foot of his bed. "What the F...?"

Interrupting him as he sat down, Johnny suddenly heard his aunt and little cousin walking up the steps. He quickly reached over and pushed the door lightly and as it closed, it made a creaking sound.

"Damn," he whispered aloud.

Thinking no one was home when she got in, Pauline heard the sound, pushed Tanya slightly behind her, and walked towards his door. "Johnny?" called Pauline as she pushed his door open. "Oh, you did get in before us, it looked like...no one...was home."

Johnny sat up as if he had just awakened and groggily said, "I must've fell asleep with my clothes on."

"Oh, sorry to wake you," she said as she noticed the bag of food and wet jacket. She then brushed it off and left out of the room, pushing Tanya back with her on her way out."

"Aunt Paula!" called Johnny.

"Yes?" she replied as she turned back around and looked at him.

"I'm going to be staying over a friend's house for the next couple of weeks, so I can cram for finals. I just wanted to let you know."

She smiled at him and replied, "You're a grown man ...you don't need to tell me all your business, just the stuff I would be concerned about...but thanks just the same." She walked out of the room and directed her attention back to Tanya, closing Johnny's door as her mouth started issuing verbal commands such as get ready for bed young lady.

"You would be concerned about this," he said under his breath. Johnny sighed in relief his aunt had obviously not been home when he teleported in.

CHAPTER 14

SWIMMING IN THE deep sea of his thoughts, Johnny tried to reach his destination, which was the shore of understanding. The *'Quantum Leap'* type experience he had last night unnerved his train of thought, being only certain each time he reappeared he was himself and he, was definitely no Doctor Samuel Beckett.

Johnny wasn't surprised he decided to stay with Doctor Brooks and go through whatever the two physicians had in mind, after all, he did like the peacefulness and beauty which enveloped Brooks' home.

It definitely helped with Brooks being willing to pay him double the amount of his salary from his former job, which he lost due to absence from work when he had gotten shot, an ordeal not believed by his employers as he had no proof of his injuries or any hospital discharge paperwork.

He also lost his chance at the new job for similar reasons.

Johnny then thought about how grateful he was to his Aunt Paula for not telling April he had been shot. April was on a need-to-know basis, and what happened to him wasn't something she needed to know. Without the scars to prove it, he would become less and less credible with those he loved.

Johnny felt telling April he was in the hospital because of food poisoning, was a lot more believable. The true events of what happened would have been hard for him to believe had he not gone through it himself. To try telling the story to April could end his relationship quickly.

For the next few weeks, the plan would be for Nassir and Brooks to study the changes in Johnny's body. His body, his speed, his strength, and his stamina in both light and dark environments in an attempt to understand the full range of his biology.

***

At one o'clock a.m., the canvas of dark blue skies perfectly accented the bright light being emitted from the full moon. A light sprinkle of stars was scattered across the sky reflecting the white light from the hidden sun, reminiscent of Vincent Van Goghs' 'Starry Night'.

On the football field of Bensalem High School, chosen because of its darkened environment, Doctor Robert Brooks held up a stopwatch while Johnny stretched the stretch of a novice athlete preparing to run a marathon.

The suburban nights' companion, the cool air, embraced the two as they prepared to start their test on Johnny's abilities.

"It's a shame Docs' gonna miss this," Johnny said.

"He didn't want to," started Brooks, "but seeing how he has to work early tomorrow, he really didn't have a choice. He'll get a chance to see you the next time." He then looked down at his stopwatch. "Ready?"

Johnny looked around and as the white smoke flew from his mouth, he said, "it's a bit nippy out here." He then looked down the length of the football field. "Yeah, I'm good?"

Brooks, pointing at the goal post at the opposite end of the field from where they were, said, "remember, just run down to that goal post, tag the pole, and then run back, as fast as you can."

"That's it?"

"That's all."

"Sounds easy enough," Johnny said.

"Go!" shouted Brooks, looking down at the watch.

Startled from the quick shout, Johnny hesitated for about two seconds and then started running.

The frigid air opened up around him as he dashed down the football field in swift strides. Johnny was surprised at how fast he was running because he was never much of a runner.

After reaching the goal post, Johnny quickly turned around and started running back towards Brooks.

As Johnny reached him, Brooks stopped the watch.

Gasping for breath, Johnny asked, "how'd I do?"

"I guess it's okay," Brooks said. "My niece only runs point five seconds faster than you, but in all fairness, she does run track for her high school."

Bent over and breathing heavily, Johnny looked up at Brooks.

"She doesn't breathe as hard either," said Brooks. He then smiled.

Johnny stood up all the way up while taking a deep breath. "Well, your niece doesn't have my talents."

"Talents?" asked Brooks, again attempting to antagonize Johnny. "You can heal fast and have an abundant supply of energy. What other talents do you have?"

Johnny smiled. "Start that watch again."

Brooks looked down at the watch as Johnny lowered himself back into a starting position. "GO!"

Johnny then darted back in the direction of the goal post as an aura of yellow light started to form around him grabbing Brooks' attention. At a speed comparable to that of a cheetah, Johnny zipped down the football field and quickly reached the goal post. He then quickly darted back towards Doctor Brooks.

"Johnny that was gr..."

Interrupting Brooks by not stopping, Johnny quickly turned around and darted again in the direction from where he had just come. This time a loud zipper sound opened a portal in front of him and he ran through.

Shocked from what he just witnessed Brooks dropped the stopwatch and put his hand up to his chest as the smoke from the cold air exited his mouth. His eyes searched for Johnny.

A second later, the zipper-like sound reopened the portal directly in front of the goal post as Johnny ran out of the opening, and then another zipper sound opened a portal and

Johnny again ran through, as Brooks looked around trying to figure out where he would materialize next.

Brooks then got a tap on the shoulder startling him, causing him to turn around and see Johnny smiling. "Good Lord!" he exclaimed.

"Whatta you think now?" Johnny asked.

Brooks just smiled as he tried to recover from the shock of what his young friend had just done. "That doesn't count as running!"

"Man get on wit that," Johnny replied laughing as he lightly slapped Brooks on the back. "It counts with regards to timing."

Brooks laughed as he bent over and picked up the watch. "Well I, dropped the watch."

CHAPTER 15

INSIDE THE SEMI-empty cafeteria in the lower level of the Community College of Philadelphia's West Building, Tamara sat across from April, watching her idly stare out the tall window which looked out towards the street. The day light filtered in weakly, casting dull reflections across the scratched tabletops and linoleum floor, while the echoes of distant footsteps and muffled voices reminded them the building was far from alive.

Between them lay the remnants of lunch—half-eaten burgers slumped in their wrappers, fries scattered without order, some cold and forgotten, others crushed beneath napkins. Lidless cups of soda sat abandoned near the edge of the table, each revealing barely half a cup left, the ice long since melted and watered down. The food told a quiet story of distraction rather than hunger, as if the conversation had weighed heavier than their appetites.

"You think he's doing drugs?" Tamara asked.

April turned from the window and faced her, laughed lightly and said, "Oh please, he doesn't even like taking Tylenol." She picked up the cup, which was halfway filled with soda, and took a long sip from it. She then sat the cup back down on the table as Tamara continued looking at her. "I just think he's a little weird lately, and I feel like he's keeping something from me."

Tamara nodded her head, signaling she understood what April was saying.

April then lowered her voice. "He got a ninety-six on his first psych exam last month and I swore he was gonna have a mental break right here in the cafeteria."

"Last month? He got the ninety-six?" asked Tamara with a surprised expression on her face.

April shook her head yes. "I thought you knew," said April. "Yawl are in the same class."

Tamara took a sip from her cup. "Punk never said a word."

"I'm shocked, he usually runs off at the mouth about everything else."

"He didn't even study for that test?" Tamara protested.

"That's what he told me!" exclaimed April. "Another thing that's been bothering me is, ever since his little food poisoning incident, he's been actin' like he's keeping more secrets."

"Your boyfriend!" said Tamara.

"I know and I do love him! but I don't like how he's been acting lately."

"Just so I don't go to the same restaurant he went to, where'd he get the food poisoning?"

April looked at her and they both laughed. "He ate something at work."

"And he still works there?" asked Tamara. "Brave fool."

"Not anymore," April replied shaking her head.

"Keeping secrets and unemployed?" asked Tamara, "maybe you better start investigating your options!"

April put a couple of fries in her mouth and started chewing with her hand covering her mouth. "He got a job working private security for some doctor, making more money too!"

"Lucky fool," said Tamara. She then took a bite out of her burger.

April looked out of the window and sighed.

"Okay, forget about J.T.," started Tamara, "what's going on with your little sister? You sounded weirded out the other day."

"Sorrie?" April laughed. "I thought about it and it's actually kind of cute. I woke up the other night, and it looked like she was praying over me."

"That shit would creep me out," said Tamara. "Ain't she like fourteen?"

April laughed. "She said she was putting a protection spell over me?"

"Yeah, that's not creepy at all!" Tamara picked up her drink and took a sip and made slurping sounds as she finished her soda. She then chuckled. "Protection from what? Never mind, it doesn't matter, talk to your mom, your little sister needs help."

April slapped Tamara's arm. "No she doesn't...she just different. Things have been strange for her since her father passed."

"I remember. Well, I'll keep her, both of you, in my prayers."

"Thanks," started April, "so you now understand why my life's been so stressful or crazy, or whatever you want to label it." She finished her soda and then started eating another fry. "So what's going on with you?"

"Nothing really," started Tamara, "men are dogs, I need a job, hey are they hiring where you work?"

"At Biotech?" asked April as she shook her head no, "I work in finance, not H – R." She then looked at her watch. "Speakin' of which, I better get ready to go!" She started cleaning her trash up as Tamara did the same.

"Well if you see somethin', hook a Sistah up!"

April laughed.

CHAPTER 16

ONCE AGAIN, ALMOST complete darkness became Johnny's co-star, clinging to him like a familiar presence as he stood on the football field of Bensalem High School. The stadium lights were long since shut off, leaving only the faint glow of distant streetlamps and the pale wash of the moon to outline the bleachers and goalposts. The grass beneath his feet felt damp and cool, carrying the quiet scent of earth and cut turf.

Beside him, Nassir stood in silence, his shape more suggestion than certainty in the shadows. The field, usually alive with cheers and whistles, lay empty and still, amplifying every small sound—the rustle of a breeze through the stands, the soft scuff of shoes against the turf, the steady rhythm of their breathing. It was two o'clock in the morning, a suspended hour where the world seemed paused, and the darkness felt less like an absence of light and more like a witness to whatever was about to unfold.

Nassir looked down at his pager as it started beeping unceasingly. "Okay, he's there!"

"Watch this Doc," said Johnny. "This is tight." The cracking sound of electricity as well as a sparkle of yellow light started to circle in the air around Johnny.

Johnny then vanished.

Nassir pulled out his digital mobile telephone and dialed Brooks' number via the speaker function. "Robert?" he inquired.

"He got here just fine," replied Brooks from over the phone. "I'm about to send him back."

With the sound of a quick light snap, Johnny reappeared standing next to Doctor Nassir.

"He's here," said Nassir into the phone.

"Tell him to come back using the portal," said Brooks.

Johnny signaled he heard Brooks. He then turned from Nassir and looked in the opposite direction.

The sound of a loud zipper opened a portal right in front of Johnny and Nassir.

He never heard the sound Johnny heard, but Nassir stood there and stared in awe at the unearthly darkness in front of him, stirring calmly within the boundaries of the seventeen-foot-tall oval perimeter.

The interior was pitch black in appearance and it had a bright yellow light which surrounded the rim. The blackness of the abyss moved around with the appearance of black water being held neatly in place by some magnetic force. It was a magnificent yet eerie sight to behold.

"Can you control how wide that opens?" asked Nassir.

"Not sure," started Johnny. "It's never quite the same size. "Johnny then jumped forward and into the portal which then immediately closed up by shrinking, appearing to have never been there.

"Amazing," said Nassir as he raised the phone up to his face.

"The portal does look amazing," replied Brooks from over the phone.

"His abilities are growing more and more impressive by the day," replied Nassir.

"Didn't I tell you?" asked Brooks. "I'm already questioning my theories."

***

Doctor Robert Brooks, Doctor Benjamin Nassir and Johnny Thompkins were all inside of Brooks' home-gym with numerous objects laid out around them, in a diamond formation on the floor. Dirty old rubber baseball bases sat correctly positioned on the floor of the gym.

There was a hula-hoop on first base, a basketball on second base, a skateboard on third base, a bat and softball on the home plate, a catcher's mitt which also sat on home plate and a battery-operated radio which sat behind home plate.

Brooks asked, "Do you have any questions as to what it is we want you to do?"

"Naw," replied Johnny, "I think I got it!"

Nassir pointed to the right-hand corner of the gym, which was directly opposite to the home lab. "We'll be right over there," he said.

Both Nassir and Brooks moved swiftly over to the corner of the gym as Johnny eyed over the various objects laying around him on the floor.

Auras of light formed around the objects as each of them were picked up by his visual field. Each of them then raised a few inches off the ground, with the exception of the ball and catcher's mitt, which rose up about four feet, and they then glided back fifteen feet to the pitcher's mound.

The radio stayed situated on the ground.

The softball glided quickly through the air towards the bat, which swung at the ball, hitting it past the glove and to the other side of the gym where it hit the wall.

The glove floated to the back of the gym, where it met the ball as it bounced off of the floor, catching it.

Simultaneously, the skateboard darted from off third base and headed home.

Simultaneously, the basketball rolled from off second base to third base and then from third base to home.

Simultaneously, the hula-hoop glided from first base to second base and then from second base to third base, and from there to home base.

As the catcher's mitt was heading towards the imaginary diamond, the bat was rounding second base, heading for third.

The bat passed through third and was headed for home as the catcher's mitt caught up to it.

Suddenly, the radio started glowing and awakened with music as the dials started gliding through the various radio stations.

Nassir and Brooks both smiled with amusement as they observed the phenomenon.

The bat dove and started to slide towards the home plate.

The softball welding catcher's mitt hit the bat as it came to a complete stop.

At the same time, the radio briefly hit an active station, and the word "you're" could be heard. It then quickly hit another station and said, "out!"

As Johnny looked over and smiled at the two physicians, the toys all fell over as the yellow light vanished from around them.

Nassir smiled. "I think the bat was safe," he said.

***

It was three in the morning, and Johnny looked around carefully in order to see if any of the other dedicated athletes had decided to come out and get their jogging on but was relieved to see no one else was around.

The track at Saint Joseph's University was clear, and if he could manage a straight run around the track several laps, he would be happy. Johnny forewent the normal stretching procedures because of his anxiousness to see if he could improve his use of teleportation with his movements.

Johnny walked up to his mark and stood there, shaking his arms out in order to release any tension he may have had. He then crouched down and slowly eased his backside up. He then imagined the firing of a gun and took off in response.

To not much surprise, Johnny was again running remarkably fast, but no faster than he was running when Doctor Brooks had timed him the other night and he already had a feeling that would be the case. As he was running, Johnny opened a zipper-sounding portal about five feet in front of himself and ran in.

The zipping sound then closed the portal and as Johnny ran through, he could see his exit point as clear as day until he reached it.

The portal then reopened with the zipping sound and Johnny darted out, continuing in the same direction he had been going in.

The zipping sound then closed the portal as Johnny kept running. Johnny marveled at himself as he realized he had good control over his portals.

For the next hour Johnny continued to use his portals around the track and then around the whole exterior of the campus. When he finally stopped running and traveling through the portals, Johnny bent over and started laughing to himself. He was happy he didn't have to breathe hard when he ran. He was also getting used to his ability to travel through the portals. Johnny decided that tomorrow night; he would give himself a little more of a challenge.

***

The next night, Johnny knew It was almost time for the train as he waited patiently. As the crisp wind blew lightly, Johnny stood on the ledge of a Motorworks engine shop on Frankford Avenue near Church Street, as he looked westward down the length of the Market – Frankford Elevated train tracks. In the distance, he could see the beaming headlights of the train, as well as hear it's constant chugging sound.

Yes! He thought, *the train is finally here.*

His eyes began to light up and appeared to be pupil less, not that he could tell for everything he looked at still looked the same to him. He soon noticed his reflection in a nearby window, and he was almost half spooked by it.

He then looked back at the approaching train and smiled, mostly because he had been wanting to do something like what he was about to do, ever since seeing it in one of his favorite superhero movies as a child.

The train stopped near his current location, Church Street and Johnny then crouched down towards the ground as if he was about to sprint with the train.

The hood of his sweat jacket began to sway in the wind.

He pulled the hood up over his head and secured it by tying the draw strings together.

"Doors are closing," started the female sounding computerized voice of the SEPTA train as Johnny stood partially up. "Next Stop...Margaret Orthodox...with connections to routes J ... K ... fifty-nine...seventy-five and wheelchair accessible routes three and five."

The doors swooshed closed, and the train started moving again.

Johnny just watched as the train started pulling off, and he started beaming. "Five, four, three, two, one!" Johnny then darted off the first roof and jumped onto the next, moving in the same direction of the train.

An aura of yellow light then started to form around him as he reached the end of the second building and jumped off the ledge.

His jump was upwards, assisting him with landing on the slant of a purple church. Johnny then quickly darted up the slant of the roof and started swearing to himself as he saw the train was speeding off in the distance.

Johnny then did a swan dive off the very top of the church as a zipper sound opened the portal, allowing him to dive in before the zipper sound closed it back up.

The zipper-sounding portal then quickly re-opened up on a rooftop which was adjacent to the trains' current location and Johnny flew out, headfirst and caught himself on the floor of the roof and he quickly hid behind a chimney as the train slowed to a stop.

The zipper-sounding portal quickly closed up.

"Margaret Orthodox station," started the computerized voice as the doors of the train started to open. "Doors are opening...Market Frankford Terminal...making all stops."

A few people got off the train and started heading in their desired directions, oblivious to the fact Johnny was watching them from the rooftop.

"Doors are closing," spouted the female computerized voice of the train as the doors swooshed close. The train started again. "Next and last stop...Market Frankford Terminal...for connections with routes; three, five, eight, fourteen, eighteen, nineteen, twenty, twenty-six, fifty-eight, eighty-four and route R...Thank you for riding SEPTA."

Again, Johnny took off.

***

Inside one of the train cars, there weren't many passengers left. The space felt hollow and tired, filled with the low hum of the tracks and the rhythmic sway of the car as it sped through the night. Fluorescent lights flickered faintly overhead, casting a dull sheen over empty seats and forgotten newspapers. In the middle of the car sat an old man, slouched and unsteady, a bottle of whisky dangling loosely from his hand. His eyes were half closed, his head nodding as though sleep and wakefulness were locked in a quiet struggle.

"You were my one *twue fwiend*," the old man slurred, lifting the bottle with a crooked sense of ceremony. He stared at it with mock seriousness, squinting as if expecting it to answer back. "Now, you don' seem to got any effect on me— not like yer used to. I think it's time we bid each other adieu." He raised the bottle toward the window in a slow, exaggerated toast, his arm wavering as the train rocked.

That was when his expression froze. Reflected faintly in the glass—and then clearly beyond it—was something which did not belong to the ordinary night. Outside, racing alongside the train, a strange young man leapt effortlessly from building to building, wrapped in a glowing yellow light which streaked through the darkness like lightning. The old man's jaw dropped, his breath catching as he pressed closer to the window, blinking hard to be sure his eyes weren't betraying him.

Slowly, he lowered the bottle and looked at it again, his face tight with suspicion and concern. For a moment, the train car seemed to hold its breath. Then, just as suddenly, the man's worry melted away, replaced by a wide, delighted grin.

"Welcome back, pal!" he exclaimed. Without hesitation, he twisted the cap, raised the bottle, and took a long, satisfying drink, the hum of the train carrying him onward through the night.

***

As the train approached the final stop, Johnny made touchdown on the roof of a supermarket, stopped and smiled. He then looked on the platform and saw a small child pointing in his direction when the child slipped down to the tracks as the trains' whistle blew.

"NO!" yelled Johnny as he dove off the roof and as a zipper-sounding portal opened right below him, allowing him to dive in.

The zipper-sound then closed the portal up.

***

"MY BABY!" yelled a woman as the zipper-sounding portal opened up in-between the train and the child.

Fully glowing bright yellow, Johnny flew out of the portal as the zipper-sound quickly closed it back up, and he grabbed the child and flew down the length of the platform before rising and safely landing with the child onto the platform.

As gawkers gasped, the mother started running towards them and Johnny stooped down as the glowing light dissipated and as he looked in the child's five-year-old eyes. "You okay?"

The kid nervously shook his head yes as the mother approached Johnny from behind.

"Thank you very...very much whoever you are!"

"No problem," replied Johnny without turning around as the kid ran past him and hugged his mother. Johnny then produced the sound of cracking electricity along with the bright spiral of yellow light which danced around his body and he vanished.

The woman quickly hugged her son tightly. "Markie!"

"Mommy you saw that?" asked Markie with excitement in his voice. "I was saved by the flame on guy!"

***

On Girard Avenue, outside of the back end of William Penn High School, two young guys had just exited the subway station and had gotten into their neighborhood and were walking down Girard Avenue having a jovial conversation.

From on top of the roof of the swimming pool of the high school, Johnny reappeared with a light snap and looked around as he smiled at the accomplishment of what would be his first good deed. "Yeah, I could be a superhero!" he exclaimed. He then turned around as the zipper sound opened a portal which he started to walk through.

"Wuz up holmes?" said a familiar voice from down on the street.

Johnny slowly turned back around in anger, remembering when he had been shot in this very area. When he looked down towards Girard Avenue, he saw the same thugs who attacked him the night he had been shot, and now it looked as if the same group were accosting the two young men who were walking down Girard. He looked to the right at the fast-food parking lots and down the length of Girard Avenue and saw not one police cruiser.

"Damn, where are the cops when you need em?"

The zipper sound soon closed the portal.

He then produced the sound of crackling electricity along with the spiral of yellow light which helped him to vanish.

***

"You think you can help me out wit some cash?" asked one of the thugs.

"We aint got time for this buster," started the one youth. "We can scrap if you want, you want some of this?" The youth dropped his backpack and threw his fist up as his buddy did the same.

"Let's take these clowns," started another one of the thugs as they all moved towards the two youths.

"Wait a minute...CUT!" interrupted Johnny as everyone turned to look in his direction. Johnny was leaning with his back against the fence, and his hood was propped down over his head, covering his eyes. Without turning in their direction he

106

said, "The line is...he looks like he gots sum ends on em, I say we take what we want! Can we try this again people?"

One of the thugs pulled a gun from under his coat and aimed it at Johnny as the two young men grabbed their back packs and ran down Girard Avenue. "You fuckin' with the wrong people bro."

Johnnys' hood flew back from his head as he turned and faced them, revealing his glowing eyes and angry facial expression. "Wrong answer bruh!" he said angrily.

In response to seeing the glowing eyes, one of the thugs started screaming with a high pitch scream while backing away. He then turned and started to run but fell forward.

The thug with the gun angrily started shooting at Johnny, but the bullets developed a yellow light around them and went around him.

"My turn," said Johnny and he pointed two fingers at the thugs as if they were guns. "Bang, bang, bang, bang, bang." Little balls of light went towards each of the thugs as they all started running.

A ball of light then hit each of the thugs causing each to scream as they fell over, shocked by the sensation of something feeling like electricity, which stunned them just the same.

After the last thug fell over, Johnny blew on his fingers. "I hope that wasn't to...shocking for you fellas." He started to chuckle but then shook his head in the negative. "Too corny!"

A cop car soon appeared turning right from Broad Street and onto Girard Avenue.

Johnny smiled, "oh now they wanna show up?" He then produced the sound of cracking electricity along with the spiral of yellow light which encircled him, and he vanished.

***

It was true the strengths of Johnny's abilities were increasing with time. He learned he could utilize his mind for strength via some telepathy, when his own strength was no longer sufficient. Johnny was also able to lift himself as if he were in flight, but when his body was fully engulfed in light, he could fly effortlessly. It seemed as if every time Johnny practiced, he would learn how to do something new with his abilities or he would discover a way to merge his gifts.

Both Nassir and Brooks felt there was more to Johnny than a simple mutation, but they only had the evidence at hand and Johnny seemed to have been just as ignorant as they were as to why this was happening to him.

Outside of Brooks' home, Johnny went on with his life just as he always had. He was still doing well in school, his aunt had no idea anything had ever changed about him, and his relationship with April was continuing to blossom.

As his sessions with Brooks and Nassir continued, Johnny's powers became somewhat well defined.

Johnny soon moved out of his aunt's house and into a cozy one-bedroom apartment, which he was able to afford with the salary Brooks was paying him. Johnny felt things were going the way he wanted them to go.

One day after his classes, Johnny went to Brooks' home as usual, excited to continue with his training, especially since his rescue incident a few nights before.

"What's on the agenda today?" asked Johnny with anxious eyes.

Brooks and Nassir both looked at each other and then at Johnny.

"Johnny, you have a remarkable gift," said Nassir. "Even though, we're not sure where it came from or how it all really came about, it is one I'm sure you were meant to have." Nassir then looked at Brooks and then back at Johnny. "The only question now is, what are you going to do wit it?"

"Whatta you mean?" asked Johnny, "I'mma keep working security for Doctor Brooks, right?"

Brooks nodded in the affirmative. "Sort of."

"How far are you willing to go with your gifts?" asked Nassir as Johnny shrugged, not knowing how to answer the question. "Before you answer, I want you to take a look at this." Nassir pulled a large box out from behind the desk.

"A gift?" asked Johnny with surprise in his voice. "Christmas is still a few weeks away, and I didn't get yawl anything yet…"

"Not a gift," interrupted Brooks. "Not really. Just open it!"

Johnny retrieved the large box from Nassir and opened it.

His mouth hung open in shock as he peered into the large box. "Whoa, hold up," started Johnny as he shook his head no. "I'm not…wearing this, I can do the hero shit, but I'm not wearing this."

"Well," started Brooks. "My brother Sam is a martial arts instructor, and since this would be a noble cause, he will be glad to teach you the basics in hand-to-hand combat… I mean with your powers, that'll be all you need."

"Did you hear me say, I'm not wearing this?" asked Johnny.

Nassir touched Johnny's arm and said, "You can't tell me saving the life of that child the other night didn't do anything for you."

"Okay, but why do I need this?" asked Johnny as he held up the green and gold costume which was hidden in the box. "Couldn't I just wear a simple mask or something? This isn't even my favorite color."

Nassir started to chortle. "Sure, you could wear a simple mask, but it wouldn't be good for concealing your identity.

And the color thing, I'm sure in time we could make some modifications."

Johnny looked at Nassir and slowly shook his head in the affirmative. "Why would I care if my identity is known? As far as I can tell, I can't be hurt."

"Technically you can," replied Brooks. "If your body is kept from light for a prolonged period of time, then I believe that it, as well as your abilities will weaken significantly, making you vulnerable to harm. Also, there are those who are out there, who will try to hurt you by getting to your loved ones and hurting them, because of your good deeds. If they don't know who you are, then they can't get to you."

Brooks retrieved the costume from Johnny's hands. "This is one of several prototypes we made. It is made entirely of Teflon embedded with solar cells. The part which will be facing your body will be constantly feeding light to it, therefore keeping you as strong at night as you will be in the day. The only thing is, at night, because of the function of the solar cells, you will appear to be illuminated, more so than usual."

Johnny retrieved the costume from Brooks and replied, "I guess that eliminates any possibility of stealth?"

Nassir looked at Brooks.

"Yeah...no, didn't even think there'd ever be a need for stealth," replied Brooks as he picked up a pencil and wrote on a note pad, *stealth version of suit.*

CHAPTER 17

SLAPPED IN THE face, Johnny touched the left side of his face and realized he didn't feel any pain. He felt the hand hit him, but all he received was a little forced movement. However, he was upset.

He didn't really like the idea of someone aiming for his face and hitting it. Johnny then decided it wouldn't happen again and blocked the next throw.

Sam Brooks started training Johnny in the basics of tai kwon do. Because of his willingness to learn, and his ability to retain information, Johnny learned the basic skills well and in little time. Because of his increasing strength, Johnny was taught how to pull his punches and how to hold back on his kicking.

Both Nassir and Brooks became increasingly impressed with Johnny's progression.

One day after one of his routine practices with Sam, Johnny was pulled aside by Doctor Brooks. "So far," started Brooks. "Everything looks excellent. We just don't have any special way for you to put on your costume, so..." he led Johnny over to a tall metal footlocker. "You can teleport here, open the locker, take the suit out and put it on, and then just teleport where you need to be."

"Sounds like a lot of time can pass," replied Johnny. "You mean I don't get to slide down no pole or run out of a phone booth or anything like that?"

"Well if you can think of anything better," started Brooks. "Then by all means..."

Johnny took the costume out of the locker. "I'll think of somethin'," he said as he went into a nearby bathroom.

A few minutes later, he emerged from the bathroom wearing the costume. He looked more muscular, taller, than his 180 pound and six-foot frame would suggest.

The suit, which accented his brown skin beautifully, was made of a sturdy Teflon-like material in black, green, and gold.

The boots were black, encircled by a one-inch gold band, the final band stopping at the top of each boot. From there up to just above his torso, the costume remained black, while dark green panels ran along the outer sides of his legs, beginning above the knees and rising to his hips. A gold band, initially an inch wide, separated the black and green sections, tapering to about three-quarters of an inch as it curved from the hips to the waist.

The torso was predominantly dark green, except across his pectorals where the suit turned black and continued up to the neck. Cutting through the center of his chest was a bold, V-shaped gold band that extended outward to each shoulder. From just below those shoulders, matching one-inch gold bands ran over his biceps, traced the front of each arm, and connected seamlessly to black gloves. The gold wrapped once around each forearm before ending fully at the wrists, while the fingertips of the gloves were dark green.

A dark green cowl covered his head, completing the look.

"Well ...how do I look?" Johnny asked.

Nassir and Brooks looked at each other and then looked back at Johnny.

"Perfect," they said simultaneously.

***

The next day, inside the gym, Johnny stood in full costume while Nassir explained the mechanics of the suit.

"First, Johnny," Nassir began, adjusting one of the earpieces, "the costume has a built-in transmitter. It works on a kind of experimental Bluetooth technology. It's very new so no one should be able to detect the frequency, but just to be safe, we'll only stay connected for short periods."

Johnny nodded, understanding the caution.

"The armored Teflon casing provides added protection," Nassir continued, "and the loosened sleeves give you extra maneuverability while you're in flight." He stopped tinkering and met Johnny's eyes. "Any questions?"

"Yeah," Johnny said, glancing down at his chest. "What does the 'V' stand for?"

"It's not a 'V,'" Doctor Brooks replied. "The light bands are positioned that way to distribute illumination evenly across your body."

"I thought it stood for *Vanguard*," Nassir added.

"That name's already taken," Johnny said dryly.

"They're just light bands," Brooks repeated.

"Okay," Johnny said. "You mentioned the suit would light my body up at night. How exactly does that work?"

"The gold sections are solar storage bands," Brooks explained. "Your body produces a tremendous amount of energy. The suit stores the excess and releases it when it gets dark. Interior cells reflect that light back onto your skin, causing the green sections of the suit to glow."

"So... I'll be glowing green?" Johnny asked.

"More or less," Brooks replied.

Johnny shook his head. "Whatever. Let's just get this started."

Nassir checked his watch. "It's eight o'clock. Time for your first night on patrol."

"You know I feel kind of whack going out there looking like this," Johnny said, glancing from Brooks to Nassir.

"Don't," Nassir said firmly. "You're doing this for a noble reason. Philly needs the kind of help you can provide. Relax. Once you get used to it, you'll be fine."

Johnny smiled at him. "Thanks, Doc."

"No, Johnny," Brooks said, catching his attention. "We're the ones who should be thanking you."

"You've given us something incredible to be a part of," Nassir added.

Johnny took a deep breath, looking between them. "I'm ready."

"Good," Nassir said. "As we discussed, your teleportation will be how you come and go—no one can trace your origin. Your first relocation point tonight will be the rear courtyard of William Penn High School, near the Girard Avenue side."

"Talk about de ja vu," replied Johnny in a low voice, reflecting on the last two encounters he had at that location. "Well, it is Friday night, there probably is a lot going on."

"Chosen because of the amount of activity seen near there in such short time," replied Brooks.

The sound of electricity started to crackle in the air around Johnny as the circle of yellow light swam around him, and he vanished.

***

A light, snapping sound accompanied Johnny as he reappeared—right on schedule—in the high school courtyard. The cool night air was almost completely devoid of light, and his costume responded instantly, beginning to glow.

The chill bit at his skin, but he still felt comfortable.

"I'm here, guys," Johnny said.

"Good," Brooks replied through the transmitter. "Now get out there and see if you can do some good tonight."

Johnny chuckled under his breath as he headed toward Girard Avenue, where a gap in the fence opened onto the street.

As he stepped through the gate, the glow of his illuminated costume drew immediate attention.

People stopped, stared, and openly mocked him as he walked past, listening in silence.

"What the hell is that brother wearing?" a woman asked from across the street.

"Yo, check the lights on that thing," a man beside her said.

"When I got shot, I was out here alone," started Johnny as he looked around. "I wear this thing and everyone's out!"

A drunk staggered toward Johnny, weaving into his path as he continued slowly up Girard Avenue.

Laughter followed in his wake.

"Hey, bro-thur," the drunk slurred, the sharp stench of vodka, beer, and something far worse rolling off his breath. "Can you fly?"

Johnny waved a hand in front of his face. "Hey, brother— would you like a Tic Tac?"

Through the transmitter, Brooks said calmly, "Go ahead, Johnny. Fly."

Johnny flashed the drunk a grin as his eyes started to glow and he rose smoothly into the air, lifting backward and upward as the laughter around them died instantly. Green and gold light engulfed his body from head to toe. A moment later, he shot off toward Center City, a streak of illumination cutting through the night sky.

"Whewee," the drunk muttered, craning his neck. "Look... at... that... brutter go!"

***

As Johnny flew above Broad Street in a southern direction, he elevated himself higher, catching the eyes of spectators who watched in awe as the greenish gold streak in the sky, darted past, just above the streets, and close enough to see the figure was humanoid.

Johnny beamed, taking in the scene as he went. As he approached Broad and Vine streets, he spotted a man with a small brown duffle bag and a gun running out of a mini - market two blocks ahead. He zoomed ahead as the running man happened to have turned around.

Upon seeing the glowing figure, the would-be thief screamed a high pitch scream and started shooting at Johnny.

As the bullets fell to the ground on their way to Johnny, he swooped down and picked up the screaming man.

The onlookers cheered.

"Hey, put me the hell down!" demanded the excited man.

"I will," started Johnny as the thief tried to look at his brightly lit face and correctly figured he was black. "Just as soon as I get you to the proper authorities."

"Proper authorities?" asked the man. "Are you sure you're black?"

Johnny raised up higher with the kicking, screaming man and noticed a parked police car with an officer inside on Cuthbert Street outside of the Department of Human Services building.

He descended towards the car as the cop, who was sitting inside eating a hotdog, watched as the glowing figure landed in front of him and Johnny's energy lights dimmed down. Johnny was still with the criminal in hand.

"Good evenin' officer," started Johnny as he walked around to the driver's side of the car with the frightened man, "this man was running out of a nearby mini market while firing this gun." Johnny handed the gun and small bag of money he had taken from the man and gave them to the police officer.

"Officer, I was just trying to make sure I could drop my night deposit off without being hustled by anyone," said the criminal.

"Really bruh?" asked Johnny.

"Word!" said the criminal. "I start runnin' and shootin' like I'm crazy and people automatically stay away!"

The police officer placed the gun and the money on the seat beside him and then got out of the car, tossed his half-eaten sandwich into the trash can near the front of his car on the sidewalk, and handcuffed the criminal while mirandizing him.

Johnny then took off into the air as his body converted to its glowing form with the bright green and gold streak following him as the cop and criminal both watched him fly away.

"Looks like you've had a pretty interesting night," said the cop as he opened the back door to the car and forced the criminal into the back seat.

"You saw him," said the criminal. "You tell me!"

***

"Very good Johnny," started Nassir over the transmitter. "We heard everything."

Johnny smiled at the approval. "I was the shit, wasn't I?" He then heard some laughter in the background.

"We didn't exactly say that," started Brooks. "But now that you've mentioned it, I suppose you are the greasy emulsification that comes out of one's anus."

"You had to go and make that weird," laughed Johnny as he shook his head in the negative. "Now that I let part of Center

116

City get a quick look at me," started Johnny. "I think I wanna go back and play down North side!"

"Be careful," said Nassir.

"Don't worry," said Johnny. "I'll be fine. By the way, I think I'm really enjoying this flying stuff."

Johnny turned around and flew back in the direction of North Philadelphia as the bright greenish gold streak followed him through the air. As he flew around the area, he decided to head towards Lehigh Avenue.

When he neared Eighth Street and Lehigh Avenue, he took notice the traffic was heavy, but the only thing occurring out of the ordinary was that everyone was standing around pointing at the glowing figure in the air.

Johnny then turned and headed westward, back in the direction of Broad Street. Upon reaching Thirteenth Street, he saw a man standing outside of the driver's side of a car with a gun in his hand.

"Lady I swear, if you don't get the fuck out of that ca..."

"Damn man...that' s no way to talk to a lady," interrupted Johnny as he levitated in the air behind the gunman who quickly turned around and looked up at him. "If you want her to get out of the car," said Johnny. "You really should say please."

"Man, who the hell are you?" asked the gunman as he looked up at Johnny. Maybe he was high, maybe he was tired, but the carjacker never seemed fazed a glowing man was floating in the air just above him.

"You just love cursing at people, don'tcha bro?" asked Johnny with a now angry look on his face.

"Why don't you just...MIND your business," suggested the gunman as he raised the gun and pointed it up at Johnny.

"I really don't like guns," said Johnny angrily as he descended to the ground in front of the carjacker and dimmed his light out.

The gunman fired three shots in Johnny's direction, and for a brief second, Johnny remembered the last time he had gotten shot, via a flashback. He remembered the searing pain the bullets caused when they entered his chest. He also remembered his slow agonizing drop to the ground. *Maybe this creep needs to feel some of that pain,* he thought.

Johnny held up his right hand, and the approaching bullets developed a yellow light around them as they quickly turned around and hit the gunman in his right lower leg.

"OH SHIT!" yelled the gunman in pain as he dropped the gun, hunched over and guarded his injured leg.

The surprised woman in the Lexus LS 400 looked over at Johnny with a happy yet shocked look on her face. "Whoever you are... thank you."

"You're welcome," said Johnny while smiling. "Now you better get out of here, I have to take Professor Yahoo here to the hospital, and don't know who else will try to do what he just tried to do."

The woman smiled at him and pulled off, taking his advice.

As a crowd of people watched in awe, Johnny walked over to the injured man, who was still cowering over his wound with tears in his eyes.

Johnny looked down at the man and smiled. "You should've thought about the pain of those bullets before you fired the gun," said Johnny. He then grabbed a hold of the guy as the sound of electricity crackled along with the bright spiral of yellow light which circled around them. "I hope this works for your sake."

They both then vanished.

***

A quick snapping sound announced Johnny's reappearance in front of Temple University Hospital's Emergency Room entrance, where there were a number of people scurrying about.

People looked on in curiosity and awe at the glowing figure with the injured man.

Johnny walked over towards a police officer with the now shaken man who had just uncomfortably experienced teleportation for the first time. "Good evening, sir," Johnny said to the officer whose mouth just hung open. "This man was attempting to car jack someone when he shot himself in the leg."

He handed the gunman and the gun over to the officer as the gunman just looked at him as if he were crazy.

"Get outta here man, I aint shoot myself in no leg," whined the gunman as Johnny just looked at him.

"You fired the gun those bullets came out of," started Johnny. "Therefore, you shot yourself."

He then looked back at the officer. "You may need a witness for the jacking but since you don't have one, I suspect this gun to be a little on the illegal side and the bullets in his leg are from said gun."

Johnny then smiled at the criminal as the cracking electric sound, along with the spiral of yellow light, which spiraled around him, allowed him to vanish.

***

With the sound of a light snap, Johnny reappeared falling high over Center City Philadelphia and his body then converted to his energy form as he started flying and as he started laughing.

"This is almost too easy Doc, these chumps can't hang with my game."

"Don't start getting cocky just yet Johnny," said Nassir via the transmitter. "This is your first night out. Do a sweep of Philadelphia and the surrounding areas, if everything seems calm, then come on back. Then we can consider this the first of a few successful trial runs."

"No problem," replied Johnny as he flew off in a northeast direction.

CHAPTER 18

EVERYONE SAT DOWN at the table as Miss Jenkins prepared to say grace. A very sweet woman with a soft brown complexioned skin tone. Her hair was in thick and long locks, black with some shades of gray in it. She had been left to her own devices when it came to raising her children.

April's father stopped coming around when she was a young girl, and Sorrie's father died within the last year.

Sorrie Cerhess was now fourteen years old and resembled her mother except she had her late father's slanted Haitian eyes. A freshman in high school, she was only certain about one thing; her love for her mother and sister couldn't be matched by any love she would ever have for any other human being.

Her mother and sister were all she had, and she loved them very much. Sorrie admired April, who worked in the fiscal department at Biotech Laboratories. Sorrie, herself, one day hoped to be a scientist working for Biotech.

On the table there was a spread which would make any man salivate as if he had been conditioned to do so by Pavlov himself.

The meal consisted of mashed potatoes with gravy, candied yams, baked macaroni and cheese, potato salad, stuffing, cabbage and a turkey, oven roasted and browned to perfection.

The aroma of the meal swam gently in the nostrils while playing in the taste buds of the four people who sat around the table ready to eat.

Johnny was sitting next to April as she looked over at her mother who closed her eyes.

Everyone else did the same.

As Miss Jenkins gave grace, Johnny reflected on how lucky he had been over the past few months. If it were not for his abilities developing at the time they had, he might not have been here now.

Johnny opened his eyes and looked over at Aprils' face. He loved her.

When Miss Jenkins finished saying grace, the family said in unison, "amen."

As the food was being passed around, Miss Jenkins looked over at Johnny. "So where's Pauline and Tanya?" she asked.

"They went down south to visit with my great aunts," replied Johnny. "Greenville, South Carolina. They'll be back next Sunday night."

Miss Jenkins shook her head in the affirmative as she started decorating her plate. She understood.

"So whatta yall think about this glowing man who's been flying around the city?" asked April as she dipped a large spoon into the mashed potatoes, pulled it back over her plate and plopped it down.

"I think it's an alien," Miss Jenkins said. "Things were just fine when the police were handling them. Now this no named thing is flying around dressed like a glowing Christmas tree, trying to take their jobs away from them. Nothing good can come from this."

"He aint tryin to take nobody's job away from them, he's just helpin' out," replied Sorrie. "Right Johnny?"

Johnny just looked at her curiously. "I guess," he shrugged.

"Besides," started April, "we need a little help these days, if you hadn't noticed. It's getting crazy out here. Banks and businesses being robbed every week!"

"I suppose you're right," replied Miss Jenkins as she reached for the stuffing.

"And he does have a name," started Sorrie as Johnny looked at her with a surprised look on his face. "Two of them actually. Some call him Light man and others call him Jade."

"What do you think the 'W' on his chest stands for?" asked April.

"Weirdo," replied Miss Jenkins.

"It's actually a 'V'," started Johnny.

"I thought Vanguard," started Sorrie, "but I think that name is taken."

That's what I said, Johnny thought to himself as he put a spoonful of mashed potatoes in his mouth.

"What you think Johnny?" asked Miss Jenkins, catching Johnny off guard.

"Johnny looked at everyone as he soon swallowed the potatoes. "I like the second name," he said.

"I was asking about my garlic mashed," chuckled Miss Jenkins.

Johnny looked around at everyone and swallowed another spoonful of potatoes as Sorrie chuckled. "Oh you talkin' 'bout the potatoes, they're tight Miss Jenkins!" he said as his spoon headed back to the plate.

"Jade's a girls' name," replied Sorrie smugly.

"Whuz up with your sister?" asked Johnny as he turned to April.

April shrugged as she ate.

Everyone just looked at each other and started laughing.

***

The next day, in the basement lab at Brooks' home, Nassir and Brooks looked with Johnny as they compared notes on the types of abilities he had developed since getting shot, notably his ability to review residual energy trails. So far, he has only viewed his own experiences, and he has not been sure how that exactly works.

They also noted his augmented strength, his ability to teleport or to travel through portals, his telekinesis, which for some reason only affects non-living objects, and his ability to fly.

The physicians believed his powers hadn't fully developed yet, but they also believed whatever mutation Johnny was going through, would soon be completed.

It had to be.

With the things Johnny was able to do he was almost comparable to a deity.

Johnny's alter ego was decided by the media news to be Jade.

Johnny, Nassir and Brooks all celebrated the success of the newly born superhero, as his name started to become a household one.

Imagine if there was someone out there who was evil with Johnny's abilities, thought Brooks. *There would be nothing on earth to save us. I am glad Johnny is, who he is.*

CHAPTER 19

TWILIGHT HAD PASSED just a few hours earlier, surrendering its post to full darkness as it settled over the quiet row of houses lining Cambridge Mall. The streetlights hummed softly outside, casting faint amber pools onto the pavement below. Inside the house, still and undisturbed in the absence of his aunt and cousin, Johnny lay awake. Tonight, sleep refused him. There was simply too much to think about—too much that no longer fit into the life he'd known only days ago.

WDAS 105.3 murmured softly from the radio on his nightstand, Tony Brown's *Quiet Storm* drifting through the room like a low, comforting tide.

Normally, the smooth rhythm would have pulled him under without a fight. Tonight, he barely heard it. His eyes remained fixed on the ceiling as his thoughts circled endlessly around the same subject.

His powers.

They weren't just abilities anymore—they were variables. Unknowns. Questions that demanded answers.

If you can think of a better way to change into your costume, then go for it, Brooks' voice echoed inside his mind, calm and analytical, as if they were still in the lab.

Johnny exhaled slowly and swung his legs over the side of the bed, standing as his eyes adjusted to the dark. Shadows stretched long across the room, familiar shapes taking on new weight now that he understood what he was capable of doing within them.

We know, for example, Nassir's voice added, *that even in low-light environments your body still generates massive amounts of energy. That energy can fluctuate without warning.*

"We'll see," Johnny muttered aloud, more to himself than to either of them.

He crossed the room and stopped in front of the dresser. The mirror above it reflected a lean silhouette—barefoot, wearing shorts and a T-shirt, looking like any other twenty-three-year-old young man trying to make sense of the world. Johnny stared at his own eyes, searching for something different in them.

Then the sound came.

A faint crackle of electricity whispered into his ears, prickling at the edges of his hearing. His vision shimmered as a spiral of yellow light bloomed into existence, wrapping itself around his body like a living thing. The air grew warmer, vibrating with unseen force.

Through the mirror, Johnny watched himself vanish.

***

The living room was silent, steeped in darkness, when a soft *snap* broke the stillness. Johnny reappeared directly in front of the hallway mirror, his feet landing without a sound. He blinked once, then smiled—wide and genuine.

"Okay," he whispered. "That was clean."

He tilted his head back as a sudden *zip* echoed overhead.

The ceiling split open as if unzipped by an invisible hand, revealing an oval of absolute blackness. It wasn't empty—it felt deep, endless, like space itself had punched through the plaster.

Johnny stared up at it, awe stealing his breath.

The portal hung there, silent and patient.

After a few seconds, curiosity overcame caution. Johnny bent his knees and rose slowly, floating upward. The darkness swallowed him whole, and the zipper sound snapped shut behind him.

***

A loud *zip* tore through the quiet as the portal reopened at the foot of Johnny's bed, ejecting him unceremoniously onto the mattress.

"Oof!" He bounced once before rolling onto his back.

The portal sealed itself with another sharp zip, leaving the room exactly as it had been.

"Okay... okay," Johnny said, laughing to himself. "So that's how *those* work."

He sat up, rubbing the back of his head as his mind raced. Each method of teleportation had rules—patterns he could feel more than consciously understand. The destination was his choice. The exit, too. But the force? The momentum? That stayed consistent.

Same velocity. Independent direction.

Just like when he'd raced the SEPTA train and then saved the young child.

"Guess physics still gets a vote," he muttered.

Johnny stood again and turned toward his closet, concealed only by a plain beige curtain. Without touching it, he reached out with his thoughts. The curtain slid aside obediently.

Inside hung a black-and-red sweatsuit.

He glanced down at the shorts and T-shirt he was wearing, then back at the sweatsuit.

"Let's try something else."

Electricity crackled through the air as the yellow spiral enveloped both him and the garment simultaneously. For a split second, the world seemed to fold in on itself.

The sweatsuit vanished from the hanger.

Johnny's T-shirt appeared in its place.

He looked down.

Black and red fabric hugged his body perfectly.

"Oh—shit," Johnny blurted, bursting into laughter. He spun toward the mirror, turning from side to side. "It worked! Powered by *adding light*, my ass. They've gotta be wrong."

His laughter faded into wonder as a new thought struck him.

"I wonder how far I can go," he said quietly.

Johnny's grin widened.

"Paris sounds nice. Haven't been there yet."

The loud crackling sound of electricity returned, louder now, energized by anticipation along with the spiral of yellow light which wrapped tightly around him as the room bear witness-
—and Johnny vanished.

CHAPTER 20

SNAKE HAD ALWAYS been the toughest member of the crew. There were sixteen of them in total, scattered across from North Philly through K&A and near Torresdale, like loose teeth in a broken jaw, but none carried the same quiet authority he did. Snake wasn't their leader—that role belonged to his longtime friend Toothpick—but when things went sideways, when fists flew or bullets came out, all eyes instinctively drifted toward Snake.

At six-foot-two and a solid two hundred pounds, he carried himself like a man who never doubted the outcome of a fight. His skin was a smooth, even chestnut brown, his build dense and powerful rather than bulky. Even beneath the oversized hoodies he favored, strangers could spot the hard lines of his chest and the thick cords of muscle running down his arms. He was handsome in a dangerous way, the kind of man people noticed even when they tried not to.

But it was his eyes that unsettled people most.

They were narrow and slanted, never fully still, always tracking—measuring distance, timing, weakness. They gave the impression that he was constantly coiled, waiting for the precise moment to strike. That was how he earned his name as a young teen, and his actions backing it up as an adult is how he kept it.

Yet as intimidating as his size and stare were, they weren't what truly frightened the people around him.

It was what Snake could *do*.

Over the past few years, the crew had watched him change. Subtly at first. Then undeniably. He would vanish without warning, leaving behind nothing but a faint pressure in the air, only to reappear minutes later—sometimes blocks away, sometimes across the city—like distance itself meant nothing to him. They'd seen him lift crates, cars, even himself into the air without laying a finger on them. They'd watched him tear through steel doors, bend crowbars like soft wire, and walk away from situations which should have left him broken—or dead.

Snake didn't bleed like other men. And when he did, it never seemed to matter.

At night, when the crew went out *borrowing* from other, more shady Philadelphians, Snake made sure they never got caught. Doors opened. Cameras failed. People froze in place, paralyzed by fear. The only thing which limited him from using his wondrous abilities more frequently was his headaches. If his powers were a lion ready to attack, his headaches were the chain keeping him at bay.

Otherwise, no one could touch him.

The flickering glow of the color television washed over Snake and four others as they sat crowded into the living room of a narrow row home near Huntingdon and Torresdale.

The air smelled faintly of sweat, weed smoke, and cheap takeout. The news anchor's voice cut cleanly through the haze.

"And just who is this glowing man who's been flying around the East Coast doing nothing but good deeds?" the woman from Channel Ten asked, her tone half-curious, half-amused. "While no one's been able to track him down for an interview, he's certainly getting his share of attention. This unknown hero has been spotted as far south as Baltimore and as far north as New York—but his very first sighting was right here in Philadelphia."

Snake leaned back, arms crossed, eyes narrowing slightly.

"And whoever he is," the anchor continued, smiling into the camera, "the media has already given him a nickname—*Jade*. So, Jade, from the people of the City of Brotherly Love... thank you!"

The room stayed quiet for a beat.

Then Snake laughed.

It was low and sharp, humorless.

Toothpick glanced over at him and grinned, shaking his head. They both understood something the rest of the city didn't yet.

Snake had gifts of his own.

And Jade would learn about him soon enough.

Snake displayed his grin slow and wicked. His eyes gleamed as the green glow from the television reflected back at him. "Matter of fact... I'd really like to meet him."

The screen flashed with another image of Jade soaring across the skyline.

Snake leaned forward, elbows on his knees. *How dare this guy have all my strengths and no evidence of my excruciating weakness.*

"Let's see what makes a hero bleed."

"I know I can take him," Snake said with a wicked grin.

CHAPTER 21

IN THE HEART of Center City Philadelphia, behind mirrored glass and guarded doors, a handful of city officials and members of the city's power elite convened as the Philadelphia Chapter of the Trilateral Commission.

To the outside world, the commission did not exist. No charters, no minutes, no paper trail—only whispers and conspiracy theories dismissed by pundits and academics alike.

In truth, it was a clandestine organization dedicated to a single, audacious goal: the quiet destabilization and eventual overthrow of governments across the world's major nations, clearing the way for a unified, totalitarian global authority ruled by collaboration rather than borders.

Membership was not granted lightly.

Wealth was a prerequisite, money bought influence, leverage, and silence, though a few of the commission's earliest founders clawed their way up from modest beginnings before amassing fortunes of their own.

Power, after all, tended to attract more power.

The board room where the Philadelphia board members met reflected their ambitions.

The room was grand in scale, its floor blanketed in deep red wall-to-wall carpet that lay perfectly still beneath a massive oval table crafted from polished cherry wood. Twelve matching chairs surrounded it—five aligned along each lengthwise side, facing one another like opposing armies, and one positioned at either end, elevated slightly in authority.

Three-quarters of the way up the walls, Hershey-bar-shaped wooden paneling rose in the same rich cherry hue as the table and chairs, reinforcing a sense of weight and permanence. Above it, the remaining quarter of wall space was upholstered in the same crimson carpeting as the floor, swallowing sound and secrets alike.

At one end of the table, opposite a wide window overlooking the city skyline, a white hanging sheet bore a single bold red-letter *T*. Whether it stood for *Trilateral* or *Tanner* was a question no one in the room dared ask.

Steven Tanner, founder and undisputed authority of the Philadelphia Chapter, had called the meeting to address what had dominated the media cycle over the past week.

Tanner was a well-dressed, attractive man in his early fifties, his brown hair neatly groomed and lightly dusted with gray at the temples. His tailored suit was impeccable, his posture confident, but it was his reputation that commanded the room. Among his peers, Tanner was feared—not merely respected—because of his volatile temper and his willingness to wield power violently when he felt challenged. He never let anyone forget who was in control.

A risk-taker by nature, Tanner had spent over twenty years as a successful attorney before turning his sights on politics. Yet even law and legislation had proven too small for his appetite. He wanted more, more money, more leverage, more reach.

While drafting legislation for the Pennsylvania House of Representatives, he noticed something invaluable: business owners understood how to manipulate politicians far better than politicians understood how to manipulate business owners. Tanner adapted quickly. Strategic investments followed. Shell companies. Insurance plays. Manufactured losses that produced enormous gains.

He made money while writing laws that ensured he could keep making money.

Now, he circled the boardroom table slowly, hands buried in the pockets of his tailored Giorgio Armani slacks. When he reached the spot where a folded newspaper rested, he withdrew his right hand and picked it up.

"Ladies and gentlemen," Tanner began, studying the front page, "it would appear we have a potential problem."

No one spoke.

He dropped the paper face-up onto the table. The image splashed across the page showed Jade frozen midair, glowing as he streaked through the city sky.

"We pay people to rob our banks, hit our businesses, and torch our properties," Tanner continued, his voice rising as he resumed his slow walk. "We tell them where to strike, how to strike, and when. They get a modest cut. We collect the real money from insurance payouts on businesses we already control." He stopped and turned sharply. "Can anyone explain to me why this," he gestured toward the image, "might now be a problem?"

His gaze swept the room. "I have a ton of money invested in these operations. So do many of you. And I am not about to let some neon-clad kid derail years of planning."

"But Tanner," a voice began.

Tanner turned toward Martin Cole.

Cole was baby-faced, with jet-black hair, blue eyes, and a sharply tailored suit which matched Tanner's in quality if not authority. Years younger, he served as Tanner's confidant, vice president, and designated question-asker—the man meant to voice concerns others were too afraid to raise.

Next to Cole sat Tanner's long-time friend—his on-again, off-again lover—Katherine O'Mally, an attractive, busty figured redhead who is well into middle age. Despite the years, she had preserved a surprisingly girlish silhouette through discipline, restraint, and a strict diet which owed nothing to childbirth. Her confidence was effortless, settled, the kind which came from knowing exactly who she was and how easily she could still turn heads.

"We don't know anything about him," Cole said carefully. "We've tried to have him followed, but he disappears before our people can—"

"We'll bait him," Tanner interrupted, fixing Cole with an icy stare.

Cole leaned back, watching closely.

"We create a crisis," Tanner continued. "A situation where innocent people are placed in immediate danger. Our glowing friend will come running." A thin smile crept across his face. "We can't hurt him directly, but we *can* limit his actions. Threaten the hostages. Force him to choose."

He paused. "My scientist, Mark Stern, will be finishing one of his projects soon. His creations should help balance the scales."

"Tanner, you're crazy," blurted Richard—a plump man seated two chairs down from Cole.

The room went still.

Tanner turned slowly and began walking toward him.

"What if this Jade character plays along?" Richard pressed, panic creeping into his voice. "Pretends to cooperate, then wipes us out the second the hostages are released?"

Tanner kept walking.

"We will *not* put ourselves directly in harm's way," Tanner shouted, his voice echoing. "If Jade refuses to cooperate, someone dies. One random death per day until he complies. And eventually," his lips curled, "we may reach someone he actually cares about."

"We don't even know if he can be killed!" Richard snapped.

That was when Tanner struck him.

One swift, brutal punch to the side of the head sent Richard sprawling from his chair. The room froze as Richard clutched his skull, staring up at Tanner with shocked, furious eyes.

"I know what I am," Tanner said quietly, looming over him. "But don't you ever fucking call me crazy again."

He turned to walk away, then stopped.

"And Richard—by definition of being alive," Tanner added coldly, "*anything* can be killed."

CHAPTER 22

LIKE A SPINNING twister, Johnny tore through five of Sam Brooks' best students, never allowing contact without consequence. Limbs blurred. Bodies hit the mat almost as soon as they engaged him. The white mask and sparring uniform he wore—clearly meant to hide his identity—matched perfectly, spotless despite the chaos.

"That's it, Johnny—keep it up!" Nassir shouted.

Johnny's hand-to-hand skills had become razor-sharp. In minutes, all five opponents were down, aided only slightly by his growing abilities.

"Excellent," Brooks said, stopping his stopwatch. "Take a break. We'll resume metaphysical training later."

"Cool," Johnny replied, already heading for the adjoining office. He dropped into a lounge chair and flicked on the TV.

As it played, Johnny closed his eyes—and his body lifted.

Brooks approached Nassir as Johnny levitated, motionless, serene.

"I can't overstate how pleased I am," Nassir said quietly. "Watching you use your gifts like this... it gives Robert and me purpose. We stepped outside the social norm for a reason."

The phrase *social norm* snagged Johnny's thoughts. He had wanted out of it—desperately. Now, without meaning to, he was.

The television cut to blue.

"We interrupt your program for a special report."

The image shifted to a reporter. "This is Trevor Covington. Late-breaking news: a bomb has detonated at a Center City bank. Channel Ten's Mike Messina is on the scene."

Smoke poured from the bank doors behind Messina. "Two dead. Five critically wounded. What began as a bombing is now a hostage situation. Heavily armed suspects. No demands yet."

"Gotta go," Johnny said.

Nassir nodded. "Be careful."

The sound of crackling electricity played as the yellow light spiraled around him.

Johnny's sparring gear vanished—his costume snapping into place in a blink.

Brooks and Nassir stared.

Jade's eyes lit, pupil-less.

The crackling sound of electricity along with the spiral of yellow light danced around Jade's body. He vanished.

***

Dusk crept over Fifth and Market as a flash of light split the sky. With a light sounding snap, Jade reappeared midair, slowing his descent as spectators pointed and shouted.

Snake, hidden among them, watched silently.

Jade landed near the police chief. "What do they want?"

The chief stared. "You. They want *you*."

Cameras flashed as Jade turned toward the smoking doors. Then— The crackling sound of electricity along with the spiral of yellow light danced around Jade's body.

He vanished.

***

With the sound of a light snap. Inside the bank.

Jade appeared behind four gunmen, standing between them and the hostages.

"Ah, Mista Jaide," Mikey sneered in a fake British accent. "Our honored guest."

Jade scanned fast—bodies by the windows, hostages split across the floor, gunmen tense.

"What do you want?" Jade asked.

Mikey laughed, set his gun down theatrically. "You think that ridiculous outfit makes you a negotiator?"

"You asked for me."

"You've got a point, very well. I will achieve my goals by *any means necessary*. Interfere again, someone dies. Maybe even someone you care about."

"So how do I know which operations are yours?"

Mikey laughed. "You don't, so you just need to stop, or..." He then raised his gun and fired at a woman.

The sound of crackling electricity along with the spiral of yellow light circled the bullet, causing it to change course—

—then Jade was hit hard as the bullet ricocheted off of his assailant.

A dark red blur.

Snake.

"You shot me!" Snake snarled. He felt no pain, just annoyance—increased use of his abilities equals more rage and psychosis.

"No..." started Mikey.

But before Mikey could beg, Snake lifted him one-handed and snapped his neck.

Mikey's lifeless body fell from Snake's hand.

His first kill.

The room froze.

Snake stood tall, eyes glowing red.

Tanner, posing as a hostage, smiled.

Snake turned toward Jade. "You're no match for me!"

Red energy consumed him—he launched forward, grabbed Jade by the legs and hurled him through the bank window.

***

On the television screen, Jade hit Market Street hard.

Cameras exploded in flashes.

Snake followed, stepping through the shattered glass like a god descending.

On live television, Brooks and Nassir watched in horror.

We never prepared him for this, Brooks thought.

Nassir activated the transmitter. "Johnny, can you hear me?"

***

Jade groaned. "Aunt Paula?"

"Use what you've learned."

"He just threw me out of a bank window."

"Think it through."

Jade rolled up, checking his surroundings—brick wall behind him, civilians cleared. "Who are you?" he asked.

"Snake," smiled. "The last face you'll ever see." He then flew hard and fast towards Jade.

A portal ripped open behind Jade—zip—and he fell backward through it. Snake slammed into the brick wall.

Jade reappeared exiting a portal high above. "Come get me!"

Snake stood quickly and took off into the air after him.

They flew.

"What about the weapons in the bank?" asked Nassir from over the transmitter.

"Hold that thought," replied Jade.

Mid-flight, Jade used the sound of crackling electricity along with the spiraling yellow light and conjured the weapons and grenades from the bank, sealed them in an energy bubble, and detonated them a safe distance away.

"They're disarmed," he said.

Snake pursued.

Jade flew fast over the Richard Allen projects and led him to the courtyard of the William Penn High School. "Why do I keep coming back here?" he muttered.

They landed.

Brooks' voice crackled. "If his powers mirror yours, darkness should weaken him."

"I don't feel weaker?" questioned Jade.

"You have the costume, just try!"

As he moved towards Jade, the sound of crackling electricity followed by red spiraling light circled him.

Snake vanished.

With a light snap he reappeared directly in front of Jade and punched him down to the ground.

The sound of crackling electricity followed by yellow spiraling light circled Jade as he fell.

He vanished.

With the sound of a light snap he reappeared on the ground directly behind Snake and dropped him with a brutal kick behind his legs.

Snake fell back as Johnny rose up.

Snake then got up, enraged.

Jade countered again—caught Snake's neck with a right arm swing.

Snake grabbed his neck as he looked up malevolently at Jade. The sound of crackling electricity along with spiraling red light circled him.

Snake vanished.

Jade nodded in the affirmative. "Yeah...powers definitely like mine."

"Johnny, what's happening?" Nassir demanded.

"I'm coming in." Jade flew upward.

A zipper sound opened a portal and he flew through.

The zipper sound closed the portal.

CHAPTER 23

FULL OF LIFE and unapologetically vibrant, Market Street pulsed with motion as if the city itself were determined to prove it could not be shaken. Shoppers flooded the sidewalks, arms heavy with bags, breath puffing in the cold December air as they rushed to complete their Christmas errands—barely a week after the bombing at the Center City bank.

Fear, it seemed, had a short shelf life in Philadelphia.

The bombing incident at the Center City bank had become little more than background noise, a grim headline already fading beneath holiday sales and glittering window displays. Life went on. Commerce demanded it.

At Eleventh Street, a dense crowd spilled into the crosswalk, boots crunching against slush as carolers stood just outside J.C. Penney's, their voices rising cheerfully above the traffic.

"♫ *Joy to the world, the Lord is come...* ♫"

Their harmony rang out with forced optimism, bells jingling at their feet as donation tins rattled. No one sang louder than the city itself, daring tragedy to interrupt again.

From several stories above the street, Steven Tanner stood silently behind the vertical blinds of his office window. He parted them just enough to watch the masses below surge and scatter like a living organism. The glow of traffic lights reflected faintly across his face as he studied the crowd with detached satisfaction.

Chaos below. Control above.

Inside his office, the silence was complete—thick, deliberate, and calming. The kind of quiet money bought.

Then—

"Mister Tanner?" came a soft female voice over the intercom.

The calm shattered.

Tanner exhaled slowly, irritation flickering behind his eyes. He crossed to his grandiose black desk and pressed the intercom button.

"Yes, Cherie?" he replied evenly, though the steel beneath his voice was unmistakable.

"Martin Cole is here to see you."

"Send him in."

He released the button and turned toward the door just as it opened.

Martin Cole entered briskly, closing the door behind him. Though his tailored suit masked the rough edges of his upbringing, traces of urban life still clung to him—in the loose roll of his shoulders, the confidence in his stride, the way he claimed space without asking permission. He walked like a man who had grown up needing to project toughness.

Yet beneath that posture was a sharp mind. Cole's intelligence—cold, adaptive, ambitious—was what had elevated him from the streets to this office, making him the right hand of one of the most powerful men in Philadelphia.

"Tanner," Cole said without preamble, "what the hell happened at the bank?"

The slap came fast.

So fast Cole barely registered the sound before his head snapped sideways. Tanner grabbed him by the back of the skull and yanked him close, their faces inches apart.

"I love you like a son, Martin," Tanner said quietly, venomously calm. "But don't ever forget—I'm the president of this club. You're the vice president. Watch your tone."

He released Cole and turned away as if the assault were nothing more than punctuation.

Tanner began circling the office, eyes locked on Cole like a vulture assessing a wounded animal.

"Besides," he continued, "do you even watch the news? The story's been replayed a thousand times in the last forty-eight hours."

Cole touched the side of his face, stunned, anger and disbelief wrestling across his expression. "You said none of us would get hurt."

"Sorry about your friend," Tanner cut in sharply. "He was a casualty of war. What exactly did you expect me to do about it?"

He stopped walking.

"And I was referring to the *board members*, Martin. Our safety. Not the hired help." His jaw tightened. "But I didn't anticipate this Snake character showing up."

Cole shook his head. "Mikey tried to tell me about him a month ago. I didn't think we'd need someone like that until Jade appeared."

Tanner turned back to his desk, a slow smile forming. "I also didn't expect Snake to beat the hell out of Jade," he said almost fondly.

The *Daily News* lay open before him. The front-page photo captured Snake stepping through the shattered bank window, eyes glowing, while Jade struggled to rise from the street.

Tanner stared at it with naked fascination.

The gleam in his eyes mirrored that of a child staring at a long-desired gift on Christmas morning.

"Well," Cole said carefully, "we know Snake didn't finish him. So what's our play?"

Tanner extended a finger and pressed it firmly onto Snake's image. "I want him working for me."

Cole blinked. "You want *me* to confront that psychopath and ask him to work for you?"

"No," Tanner replied calmly as he stepped around the desk. "I want you to confront that psychopath and *get* him to work for me."

He stopped inches from Cole again. "Give him whatever he wants. Money. Identity protection. Freedom. With him on our payroll, I'll earn it back tenfold."

Cole eased out of Tanner's space and reached for the door.

"Oh—and Martin."

Cole turned.

"If he says no," Tanner said coolly, "then you're failing me. And failure's not an option."

Fear eclipsed contempt in Cole's eyes. He nodded once, understanding exactly what had been implied.

"Get out of my office," Tanner snapped.

Cole didn't hesitate.

He left.

CHAPTER 24

"ARE YOU ABSOLUTELY sure?" Brooks asked over the speakerphone.

Johnny, dressed in a tailored black three-piece suit, studied his reflection as he adjusted his tie for the third time. The mirror caught a man trying very hard to look ordinary—hands steady, posture relaxed—even though nothing about his life had been for weeks.

"We've been over this for the past week, Doctor Brooks," Johnny said calmly. "I'm positive." He tugged once more at the knot, then smoothed the lapels of his jacket. "If I had a brother, I'd know by now. My aunt would've told me."

He picked up the phone base and stepped out of the bathroom.

"I only ask," Brooks replied carefully, "because you once mentioned you were adopted and..."

"By my aunt," Johnny interrupted gently but firmly. "Doc knows the whole story. He's known me my entire life. My mother died giving birth to me. I was an only child. She never told him...or anyone...about older siblings."

A pause.

"What about a twin?" Brooks asked.

Johnny snorted softly. "What...another suave brother like *moi*?" He grinned at his reflection as he passed the hallway mirror. "I don't think the world's that lucky."

Brooks didn't laugh.

"Johnny, I'm serious. I find it strange this Snake character would reveal himself now...*after* you've made yourself known. He's roughly your age. He has abilities disturbingly similar to yours. I can't shake the feeling there's a connection. Some common origin."

Johnny shrugged as he crossed the bedroom. "Maybe we were exposed to the same thing. Same time, same place. Power plant, lab accident, radiation leak...who knows? Genetic mutations aren't exactly new."

"Not like this," Brooks replied. "This isn't common. And you can't dismiss Snake as some coincidence. You got lucky the other day, Johnny. If you forget that, you're going to get hurt...or worse."

The doorbell rang.

Johnny glanced at the digital clock atop his dresser—its bright red numbers staring back insistently.

"That's April," he said. "I've gotta go."

"Just think about what I said," Brooks urged, his voice low and grave.

The doorbell rang again.

"I will, Doctor Brooks," Johnny replied. "Talk to you later."

He ended the call, set the phone down, and hurried to the front door. When he opened it, April stood smiling in the hallway, arms full—a picnic basket, a folded velvet blanket, a VHS tape, and a chilled bottle of Chardonnay tucked carefully under her elbow.

"I know we were supposed to go out tonight," she said, stepping inside, "but I thought it might be more romantic if we stayed in. Picnic on the living room floor. Movie night."

Johnny looked from the basket to the blanket, to the wine— and finally to her face.

The weight of the world slipped, just a little.

"I love you," he said, smiling.

CHAPTER 25

THE DARKNESS OF the city, paired with a bitter winter wind, greeted Martin Cole as he stepped out of the 7-Eleven on Huntingdon Street at Torresdale Avenue. The automatic doors hissed shut behind him, sealing away fluorescent light and warmth. He twisted the cap off a bottle of Snapple iced tea and took a long pull, then crossed the slick concrete toward his BMW at the gas pumps.

The station was nearly empty—just the hum of traffic in the distance and the rhythmic clunk of the pumps doing their work.

After disarming the alarm, Cole unscrewed the gas cap and rested it carefully on the trunk. He slid the nozzle into the tank and set it on automatic.

"Damn thing's slow," he muttered, watching the numbers creep upward on the pump's display.

He never heard them approach.

A hand landed casually on the trunk of his car.

"Nice Beamer you got, mister," a voice said from behind him. "Don'tcha think it's nice, Snake?"

Cole turned—

—and suddenly hands were everywhere.

Several youths swarmed him, yanking him backward, slamming him against his own car, forcing his hips hard into the cold metal. One pressed a forearm against his chest while another twisted his arm behind him just enough to hurt.

Then the crowd parted.

Snake stepped forward.

He moved slowly, deliberately, like a man who knew time itself bent in his favor. He stopped inches from Cole's face and stared into his eyes. His nostrils flared faintly, not with rage—but restraint.

"Let Mr. Cole go," Snake said.

The grip loosened but did not release.

Cole swallowed. He wasn't surprised Snake knew his name—but that didn't make it easier to hear. "How'd you know my—"

"Don't," Snake interrupted. He raised a hand, and the others backed off completely. "I ask the questions. You answer."

He leaned closer.

"My people...and the shop owners around here...tell me you've been asking about me. So I already know *that* part." His voice hardened. "Now tell me why."

Cole's heart pounded. He'd faced Tanner's anger before—knew how far his boss could go. But Tanner was a man. Snake was an unknown. And the media had shown him beating Jade.

That thought chilled him more than the air.

"I have an offer," Cole said carefully. "From a very powerful man."

Snake didn't blink.

"My boss...Steven Tanner...controls a majority stake in Biotech Laboratories. He can provide cover. Resources. Funding. We can make sure your identity stays buried while you do...what you do."

Snake's lips twitched. "I suppose you're talking about the glowing green light bulb," he said.

"The enemy of my enemy," Cole offered, "makes us good business partners?"

"And once that enemy is gone," Snake replied evenly, "so ends our partnership."

"That depends on what you want," Cole said. "We can make you legitimately rich. Separate you completely from your alter ego."

That caught Snake's attention. "Tanner," Snake said slowly, tasting the name. "He sent you to hire me... to kill Jade?"

A humorless laugh escaped him.

"Hell," Snake added, "I was gonna do that shit for free."

Cole allowed himself a cautious smile. "So what'll it be?"

Snake waved his hand. His posse melted into the darkness without a word.

He circled the BMW, trailing his fingers along the paint as if considering how easily it might be crushed.

"Tell Tanner the bidding starts at two-fifty," Snake said. "Up front. Plus an annual salary." He stopped directly in front of Cole. "If he agrees, I'll do whatever he needs to keep his interests... straight."

The sound of crackling electricity, followed by a spiral of red light encircled Snake, and he vanished.

With the sound of a light snap, Snake reappeared instantly, inches from Cole's face.

His eyes burned crimson, pupil-less. "But if he screws with me," Snake whispered, "I become *his* problem."

Cole exhaled slowly. For the first time, he smiled—not out of confidence, but satisfaction. "I'll make sure he gets that message."

He removed the nozzle, screwed the gas cap back on, and reached into his jacket. A business card passed from his hand to Snake's.

"Call me tomorrow night. I'll have spoken to Tanner by then."

Snake examined the card.

"Is there a way I can reach you?" Cole asked.

Snake looked up—and smiled.

The sound of electricity crackled around him along with a spiral of red light.

He vanished.

Cole stood alone beneath the buzzing station lights, staring at empty space. "Yeah," he muttered to himself. "Guess it's better if you just call me."

CHAPTER 26

AS APRIL AND Johnny lay side by side in the quiet of their bedroom, she studied his face in the soft half-light, memorizing the familiar angles she knew so well. She loved him—deeply, unquestionably. Six years together, and the comfort between them hadn't dulled, hadn't calcified into routine the way she'd watched happen to so many couples their age. They still laughed. Still touched. Still wanted each other.

That alone felt rare.

Yet something had changed.

Lately, Johnny had grown more elusive—more guarded. There were pauses where there hadn't been before, glances that seemed to drift somewhere she couldn't follow. It wasn't distance exactly, but a quiet separation, like he was standing on a threshold she couldn't see.

April stared at the ceiling, chewing on the thought.

I hope he's not getting bored with me, she worried, the idea tightening her chest more than she liked to admit.

Beside her, Johnny lay with his hands folded behind his head, smiling faintly at nothing at all. His thoughts were elsewhere—on rooftops and flashing lights, on the exhilaration of being known without being seen. The quiet thrill of being admired by a city that didn't know his name.

He didn't notice the concern in her eyes when she turned toward him.

Curiosity tugged at her.

"What's on your mind, handsome?" she asked softly.

"Huh?" Johnny turned, blinking, then smiled at her. "Straight happiness," he said easily, leaning in to kiss her cheek.

"The past few months have been amazing. I don't even know how to explain it...they just have."

She smiled back, though her expression lingered on his words longer than he noticed. As he turned his gaze back to the ceiling, she watched him carefully.

"You and I are moving forward," he continued, almost to himself. "My new job's great. It feels like my whole life just... leveled up."

April's smile faltered.

"Johnny," she said gently.

"Yeah, babe?"

She took his hand, lacing her fingers through his. "About your new job... we don't talk like we used to. And I mean...if I could at least call you sometimes, I'd feel better. Especially after the hospital incident. I didn't like being kept in the dark."

Johnny looked at her, surprised—then amused. "What, you don't think I'm really working? Or are you afraid I am WORK...ing?" he teased, smirking.

She swatted his arm lightly. "I'm serious."

He laughed softly. "Baby, I'm kidding. Of course you can have the number."

She relaxed, smiling again, and leaned into him. "I love you," she whispered.

Johnny met her gaze, earnest now. "I know you do. And I love you too." He kissed her hand, holding it between both of his. "And I think you want to spend the rest of your life with me."

Her smile widened. "I do."

"There's so much I want to do for you," he said quietly. "For us."

"Well then," she replied with playful warmth, rolling over him, "stop talking and start doing."

She kissed him, slow and familiar.

Johnny reached over and turned off the lamp. Darkness settled around them, gentle and complete, as they drew closer—finding comfort in each other, the way they always had.

For now, it was enough.

***

Later into the night, Johnny slipped back into sleep—and the dreams returned.

They always began the same way.

A vast emptiness. Endless and soundless. Then the light.

The being formed slowly, its body composed of brilliant yellow radiance, features indistinct yet unmistakably aware. It hovered above the void, turning as if searching for him. When it moved, it did so with purpose—flying, stopping, then unleashing concentrated beams of light from its hands that sliced through the darkness like judgment.

Johnny felt himself frozen, unable to speak, unable to move.

Then the dream shifted.

April appeared.

She was screaming.

Her voice echoed from inside a coffin—her fists pounding against the lid as it sank downward into a sea of thick, swallowing blackness. No water. No air. Just darkness closing in on her from all sides.

"Johnny!" she cried.

He tried to run, but his feet wouldn't move. He tried to scream, but no sound escaped him.

The glowing figure descended, landing only a few feet away. The light intensified, pulsing, alive. Slowly, deliberately, the being stepped toward him and extended a hand.

Johnny jolted awake, drenched in sweat. "April!" he gasped, turning sharply to his left.

She lay beside him, breathing softly, untouched by his nightmare.

Johnny sat upright, heart racing, staring into the darkness of the room. He didn't know whether the dreams were tied to his powers or merely the subconscious strain of everything he'd become. He didn't know if they were warnings, memories, or something else entirely.

Or if they meant anything at all.

He stayed awake the rest of the night, replaying the images over and over, waiting for dawn.

***

Across the city, Snake bolted upright in his bed, breath ragged, his heart pounding against his ribs.

The dreams again.

He ran a hand across his face, trying to shake the sensation that something—or someone—had been inside his head. The glowing figure haunted him, not yellow like Jade's light, but familiar in its movement, its intent. And yet Snake rejected the connection.

They're not about me, he told himself.

There was no yellow light in him. Only red. Only pain.

The thought crept in anyway.

Is Jade doing this to me?

The idea ignited his anger. No one had the right to enter his mind.

No one.

The memories surged unbidden.

The screech of the train.

Michael—still a boy then—had turned at the bottom of the subway steps just in time to see them. The fear registered instantly, blooming across his face before crashing into his chest. He spun and ran, but they were faster.

Two hands grabbed him, dragging him backward.

"Wuz up, Snake?" the oldest of them sneered. "Ain't hearin' you talk shit now."

"That's 'cause you ain't let me get a word in yet," A young Snake shot back, even as his voice shook.

They threw him onto the tracks seconds before the train roared in.

Snake shut his eyes.

Someone screamed.

Electricity cracked.

Red light spiraled.

He vanished a heartbeat before impact.

When Snake opened his eyes, he was standing in his grandmother's house in Pittsburgh. Relief hit him first—pure, dizzying relief.

Then came the first headache as he doubled over in pain.

Then the psychotic thoughts.

Kill her.
The idea horrified him.
"No," he whispered. "I gotta get outta here."
The sound of crackling electricity danced around him
accompanied by a spiral of red light.
He vanished from out the home, undetected.
He reappeared at the train station as police searched for a
body that wasn't there. Panic swelled. Fear. Confusion.
Then the thought returned—twisted, intrusive.
Push a cop onto the tracks.
Snake backed away just as a witness spotted him.
"That's him!" she screamed. "That's the boy who was
pushed!"
A cop reached for him.
The sound of crackling electricity danced around him
accompanied by a spiral of red light.
Gone.

Snake snapped back into the present, breathing hard.

That day had changed everything. Whether it was the third rail, the fear, or something far worse, he didn't know. All he knew was Jade had similar abilities—and it seemed, none of the pain.

No headaches.

No madness.

Or, at the very least, good control of them and that made Snake furious.

He then remembered—he'd had the dreams long before Jade ever appeared.

They had started years ago when his abilities surfaced.

Snake knew the cost of using his powers. The headaches grew worse every time, pushing him closer to the edge. Violence quieted the pain—for a while. Restraint brought clarity—but only if he stayed powerless long enough.

Which he never did.

The jealousy burned.

Jade had a secret identity. A support system. Control.

Snake had none of that.

And whoever Jade was, he wasn't helping him—so he had no right to exist inside Snake's head if it indeed was him.

Snake reached over to the nightstand and picked up Martin Cole's business card. He turned it over slowly, studying it like a contract written in blood.

A smile crept across his face.

"Jade," Snake whispered to the empty room, "your days are numbered."

***

Brooks couldn't sleep at all tonight. He thought over and over again about how Johnny seemed to just blow off Snake after one swift fight.

Doctor Robert Brooks had never married and never had any children. He almost felt as if Johnny were becoming like a son to him. And like any overprotective father, he wanted no harm to come to his young son.

He thought about canceling the Jade project, but both Nassir and Johnny had objected, being sure that they would definitely need the hero around now.

What can I do to keep Johnny one step ahead of Snake, he wondered.

Brooks then thought about increasing the amount of money he had put into the project by doing things like building a larger practice gym, increasing the technology Johnny may be able to utilize with his abilities, and maybe increasing the technology to be used in getting Johnny to focus more sharply on his abilities. After all, Johnny had what Snake seemingly didn't have; money and technology protecting his identity and backing him up.

God forbid if Snake got into an alliance with someone powerful enough to finance him and give him a little technology. We would really have a problem then, thought Brooks.

After spending most of the night worrying about Johnny, Brooks then gathered up his dirty dishes sitting before him and took them into the kitchen. After washing the single serving of dishes, Brooks then turned off all the lights and went up to bed.

CHAPTER 27

"SO THAT'S YOUR call, Snake?" Toothpick said, disbelief edging his voice. "You really gonna play us for that *mista high-sadiddy?*"

Toothpick stood with his arms folded, eyeing Snake hard. He and Snake were close in age, but Toothpick had always carried himself like the elder—calmer, steadier, the reluctant leader of their small crew.

It hadn't always been that way.

Years earlier, Toothpick's older brother, Warren, had found Snake wandering the streets as a teenager—angry, grieving, and running from a life that had already taken too much from him. Snake's father had just died. His mother had been gone for years. When Warren tried to convince him to go home, Snake told him he was living with his grandmother in Pittsburgh.

Warren didn't push. He took him in instead.

Warren had been a cop—one of the good ones. Too good, some said. He didn't look the other way, didn't take bribes, didn't play favorites. And for that, he'd been murdered by crooked officers within his own department.

Snake and Toothpick eventually pieced it together.

The chief of police knew. The mayor knew. But the incident was buried, sealed beneath reports and reassigned cases. No charges. No justice.

That was when Snake and Toothpick truly bonded.

They started their crew not for money or power—but as rebellion. A middle finger to a city that devoured its own and called it order.

Over the years, Toothpick learned everything about Snake—his family, his guilt about leaving his grandmother behind, his anger, his dreams of one day going back. He was there when Snake decided to return to Pittsburgh to check on her.

That was when the headaches started.

The blackouts. The flashes of rage.

Snake told Toothpick about the intrusive thoughts, the violent impulses that didn't feel like his own.

This all came after the night at Thirtieth Street Station.

Snake was fourteen. Cornered. Two members of a rival gang threw him onto the tracks. As the train roared toward him, whistle screaming, Snake shut his eyes.

Electricity cracked.

Red light spiraled.

He vanished a heartbeat before death.

At first, no one believed him. Then it started happening again.

Strength. Speed. Endurance.

The crew got stronger—but Snake never claimed leadership. He didn't need it. His people were enough.

The headaches though came with the power.

And the thoughts.

Only Toothpick knew.

They stole only what they needed.

Snake used his gifts only when absolutely necessary.

He stayed away from his grandmother, only observing from the sidelines—not because he didn't miss his grandmother, but because he was afraid of what he might become near her.

Now, years later, the choice sat heavy between them.

"Pick, I'm tryin' to tell you," Snake said, rubbing his temple. "This is my shot at getting better. All I gotta do is take out this Jade guy. Tanner makes me rich. Legit."

"To hell with that," Toothpick snapped. "You wanna be rich? Just take *his* money. You can teleport into vaults. Take whatever you want."

"Rich *legally*," Snake shot back. "You know this is not why we started this fam...Let me finish."

Toothpick lifted his soda can in surrender.

"I checked," Snake continued. "Biotech Labs does cutting-edge work. If anybody can fix what's wrong with me...kill these headaches...it's them."

Toothpick tossed his empty can and grabbed another. "I'll fix your headaches," he said flatly. "Stop using your powers. Every time you do, you spiral. You get those episodes. You stop using them, the pain stops."

"I wish it worked like that," Snake said quietly. "This ain't like flipping a switch. My powers are automatic...like breathing. Anything I do can trigger them."

He gestured helplessly.

"They ain't just something I *use*. They're something I *am*."

Snake's eyes dropped to the two-week-old newspaper spread across the table. The pages were creased, thumbed through so many times the ink had begun to smudge. His own face stared back at him from the grainy photo—caught mid-motion, eyes glowing faintly, frozen in a moment that had already slipped beyond his control.

"And peep this shit," Snake said quietly, tapping the paper with his knuckles. "I'm everywhere. Front pages. News feeds. I killed someone and the city now has a target on my back."

He shook his head, jaw tight.

"If I work for this Tanner dude, I know he can keep my name on the D-L. He got reach—money, connections. I still wanna be able to walk the streets, hit a corner store, ride the train, without feelin' like the next stop is *America's Most Wanted*."

Snake paused, his voice lowering.

"I'm gonna throw some ends to the fam so you can make sure you all are cool. And once I get these headaches handled..." He swallowed. "I wanna go back home, Warren wanted this for me, I want this for me. Not to be lurkin' across the street watchin' my grandmother through a window like I'm already dead. I wanna hug her. Let her see I'm still me. That I'm alive!"

Toothpick crushed his empty Pepsi can and tossed it into the trash. He crossed the room slowly and stopped beside Snake, studying him like he was trying to read past the words.

"So you got it all mapped out, huh?" Toothpick said. "This Jade kid—looks like he reps the way Warren did. Straight arrow. Tryin' to clean up a dirty city." He shook his head. "And your solution is to kill him instead of seeing if he can help you?"

Snake didn't answer right away.

"You really think this gonna make all the ghosts disappear?" Toothpick continued. "The pain? The rage? The shit in your head?"

Snake finally looked up.

"I ain't sayin' it fixes everything," he said. "But it fixes *enough*. It's how I wanna deal!"

Toothpick sighed, then nodded once.

"You do what you gotta do," he said quietly. "I ain't gonna stand in your way." He rested a hand on Snake's shoulder. "Just know...if you ever decide to come back...we still here."

A crooked smile tugged at Snake's mouth. "If I decide to come back," he said, "it ain't like y'all could stop me anyway."

Toothpick laughed despite himself. "You really had to go there?"

They bumped fists, then pulled into a brief, tight hug—the kind that said goodbye without admitting it was one.

When they separated, Toothpick's grin faded. "Be careful, man. I don't think this Jade dude is jokin' around."

Snake glanced once more at the newspaper, then folded it neatly and set it aside.

"Don't worry," he said, voice steady, almost calm. "When I'm done with him... he won't be nothin' but a memory people joke about."

The room went quiet after that—heavy with the kind of silence that settles right before something irreversible begins.

Chapter 28

MARTIN COLE SAT alone in a vinyl booth at the American Diner, the low hum of conversation and clatter of silverware washing over him like static. A half-finished cup of coffee cooled in front of him. He preferred to keep his hands free.

The diner smelled of grease and old coffee, comfort food and secrets. Neutral ground.

A few minutes later, a teenager slid into the booth across from him.

The kid was dressed plainly—blue jeans, a blue turtleneck under a mustard-colored sweater, an open goose-down coat, Timberland boots scuffed but clean. His chestnut-brown hair was parted neatly down the middle, his face smooth and earnest. He looked like the kind of kid teachers trusted and neighbors waved to.

Reliable, Cole thought.

Which immediately made him suspicious.

Not again, he told himself. He wasn't about to repeat the mistake he'd made hunting Snake.

"I'm Michael Warner," Cole said smoothly, extending his hand—one of Tanner's many borrowed identities.

"Brian," the kid replied, shaking it firmly.

Cole studied him as Brian shrugged out of his coat and draped it beside him.

"So," Cole said evenly, "what makes you think you've got the right person?"

Brian opened his mouth to answer—

"What can I do ya for, sonny?" a waitress interrupted, pad already in hand.

Brian glanced at Cole.

Cole nodded once.

"I'll have a burger," Brian said, "fries with salt, pepper, and ketchup, and a Sprite."

"How you want that burger?"

"Well done. No pink."

"Alright, hon. Be right back."

As the waitress walked away, Brian leaned forward slightly.

"As I started to say... my taekwondo instructor asked a few of us if we wanted to make some extra cash. Sparring sessions. He said the guy would be real challenging."

Cole remained silent.

"We agreed," Brian continued. "But we had no idea how good this guy was. I mean—none of us could even touch him."

Cole shook his head slowly, unimpressed. "That ain't what I asked. What makes you think you've got the *right* guy?"

Brian hesitated, nerves flickering across his face.

"Well... every time we sparred, he wore a mask."

Cole's jaw tightened. "So do a lot of people. Vigilantes aren't new."

"You didn't let me finish," Brian said calmly.

Cole leaned back, eyes narrowing. "Go on."

"One day after practice," Brian said, lowering his voice, "I overheard one of the two men who were always with him thanking him—for being a superhero."

Cole's interest sharpened.

"And when I turned around," Brian added, "the guy was floating. Legs crossed. Just... hovering."

Cole's eyes lit up. "Did he do anything else?"

Brian shook his head. "No. But they kept calling him *Johnny.*"

The waitress returned rather quickly, setting the plate down. "Enjoy."

She vanished as quickly as she'd come.

Brian picked up his burger, took a bite, then looked back at Cole with quiet confidence.

"So, Mr. Warner," he said after chewing, "when do I get my fifty grand?"

"As soon as I get an address," Cole replied, smiling thinly.

Brian set the burger down and reached into his pocket, unfolding a small piece of paper and sliding it across the table.

"That's where we trained," he said. "Don't think he lives there. I wrote directions, too."

Cole scanned the note carefully, committing it to memory. Satisfied, he reached into his jacket and produced a tightly wrapped stack of cash, sliding it across the table.

Brian pocketed it without hesitation.

Cole folded the paper and tucked it away.

"If you're lying to me, kid," Cole said quietly, "my boss won't be happy."

Brian smiled as he picked up his burger again. "Then," he said confidently, "I think your boss is gonna be very happy."

Cole watched him eat, already planning the next move.

The diner buzzed on—unaware that another piece of the puzzle had just slid into place.

CHAPTER 29

AS APRIL AND JOHNNY sat curled together on the couch, the living room glowed softly in the low light. Christmas lights twinkled along the walls and around the windows, casting gentle reflections across the ornaments and framed photos scattered throughout the apartment.

From the entertainment center, Boyz II Men's *"Let It Snow"* played quietly, filling the room with warmth and nostalgia.

Johnny shifted slightly and reached behind the sofa, pulling out a small, neatly wrapped box. He held it out to her with a faint, mischievous smile.

"Another one?" April asked, genuinely surprised.

"It's just a little one," he said.

She laughed and carefully opened it. Her eyes widened.

"A personalized license plate!" she exclaimed.

"I know how long you've wanted one, so..." Johnny shrugged.

April didn't let him finish. She leaned over and wrapped her arms tightly around him.

"Damn," Johnny said with a grin, "I didn't know you liked license plates that much. Next time I'll just get you a whole box of 'em."

She pulled back and smacked his chest playfully. "I like it because of the thought you put into it." Her fingers traced the lettering—ME 4 U—before she hugged him again, lingering a moment longer this time.

The song drifted on in the background.

"Can you see it?" April asked softly.

Johnny glanced around the room, then raised his arm and peered at his shirt-covered armpit. "See what?" he asked innocently.

She laughed and swatted his arm. "Us, silly. You and me—sitting here years from now, listening to this song when it's a golden classic and we're old and gray."

"Old and gray," Johnny repeated, smiling as he imagined it. "Ten grandkids running around while their parents—our kids—are out partying."

April sighed contentedly. "Yeah. You see it too."

Johnny cupped her cheek gently and drew her closer. Their lips met briefly, a soft, teasing kiss.

"Don't tease," she warned with a smile. "Please."

Johnny answered by pulling her closer, kissing her deeply as the music swelled around them.

Then the song ended.

She leaned back slightly. "I'm gonna hit replay. That's my favorite Christmas song."

As she started to rise, Johnny caught her arm gently.

The song began again.

She smiled and sank back down until they were eye to eye.

"I know," Johnny said. "That's why I put it on continuous play."

"Merry Christmas," April whispered.

Johnny kissed her again. "Merry Christmas."

***

The next morning, the office in Brooks' home buzzed with activity. Brooks, Nassir, and Johnny maneuvered furniture through the spare room, clearing space for incoming computer equipment.

Cables lay coiled on the floor, blueprints and notes spread across a nearby table.

"Where do you want this?" Johnny asked, holding a massive desk several feet off the ground with telekinesis.

"Right there," Brooks said, pointing to an open corner. "Plenty of space."

Nassir peered into the room, nodding approvingly. "This'll be our main analysis hub. We'll monitor every fluctuation in your abilities from here."

"My powers," Johnny repeated, lowering the desk into place before lifting himself off the ground instead. He drifted lazily in a slow circle, hands clasped behind his head. "Man... the last four months have been almost perfect."

Brooks and Nassir exchanged amused looks as Johnny floated, smiling at nothing in particular.

"Johnny," Nassir asked, "you okay?"

Brooks chuckled. "What's the matter, Ben? Don't remember what being in love feels like?"

Nassir glanced from Brooks back to Johnny. "Alright, Casanova," he said. "Back to work."

Johnny descended to the floor, still grinning. "Sorry, Doc. I just—these powers, April, everything—it all feels right."

"Well," Brooks said carefully, "we can celebrate your happiness later. Right now, we need to make sure you stay one step ahead of Snake."

Johnny waved a hand dismissively. "I haven't run into him again. And if I do, I'll stall him till dark and—"

"—beat the hell outta him?" Nassir finished.

"Exactly."

"That won't work if you're surrounded by lights," Nassir said matter-of-factly.

Johnny and Brooks stared at him.

"What?" Nassir asked defensively.

Johnny laughed. "Relax, Doc. I know I gotta be ready for anything."

The tension broke. All three shared a laugh as they went back to work, the hum of preparation filling the room—joy, hope, and danger quietly coexisting, just beneath the surface.

CHAPTER 30

TANNER LIVED IN a sprawling, single-level ranch house set deep within acres of carefully maintained land. The isolation wasn't accidental.

Distance bought privacy, and privacy bought power.

The beige brick exterior blended neatly into the muted landscape, understated but expensive, while the wooden shutters—permanently fixed in place—had been freshly painted a crisp, confident blue. It was a home designed to look unassuming to passersby who would never pass by.

Cole pulled into the long driveway and cut the engine. The quiet was immediate. Before he could close the door, a massive Alaskan malamute bounded toward him, tail wagging with unrestrained enthusiasm.

"Hey, Zeus," Cole laughed as the dog jumped up, paws landing briefly on his chest before dropping back to the ground.

As Cole straightened up, the front door opened. Tanner stepped out carrying a full trash bag, dressed casually—slacks, a sweater, nothing that suggested the reach of his influence.

"Put this in the first can for me, Martin," Tanner said evenly, nodding toward the line of trash bins neatly arranged near the garage.

Cole took the bag without comment and deposited it as instructed. When he turned back, Tanner was already heading inside, Zeus trotting ahead of them like a silent escort.

The living room they entered was large and meticulously arranged—plush green-and-beige pillow-back sofas, framed artwork placed with intention, every surface clean without feeling sterile. It was the kind of room meant to impress without appearing to try.

"Where's Marguerite?" Cole asked, glancing around.

"Not here," Tanner replied flatly. He didn't elaborate. "What do you have for me?"

They sat. Zeus padded off toward the kitchen, nails clicking softly against the floor.

"We may have a possible I.D. on Jade," Cole said carefully.

Tanner's smile vanished.

"Don't shit me, Martin."

"I'm serious," Cole continued. "I've got Ace and Mack staking out a location past Horsham. Looks like a possible hideout."

Tanner leaned forward slightly. "Are they taking pictures?"

"Everyone who comes and goes, the place belongs to one of our consulting scientists, a Doctor Robert Brooks, should we reach out?"

"No, we don't need any attention, just make Stern aware." Cole replied. "If this plays out right, we'll know who Jade is under that mask—where he lives, and everyone connected to him."

Tanner held Cole's gaze for a moment, then stood. A smile slowly crept back across his face as he began to pace the room, hands clasped behind his back.

"Snake is working for me," Tanner said almost to himself. "Jade's secret identity will be mine." He stopped and turned. "Everything is moving exactly as it should."

He exhaled, satisfied.

"Have Katherine arrange a board meeting," Tanner added. "It's time we formally introduce Snake."

"Right away," Cole replied.

Tanner nodded once, already moving on in his mind— another piece placed, another trap tightening—while the house settled back into its quiet, as if nothing dangerous had just been set into motion.

CHAPTER 31

IT WAS A BRIGHT, unseasonably mild winter afternoon, the kind Philadelphia sometimes surprised itself with.

The sun hung pale and steady in the sky, and the wind barely stirred.

If not for the leftover holiday decorations—wreaths clinging stubbornly to lampposts and strings of lights still draped across storefronts—no one would have guessed it was the middle of winter.

This wasn't Minnesota. Philadelphia winters didn't always arrive buried in snow.

The streets were busy. People moved freely, laughing, talking, alive.

Which was why April never once sensed danger.

She slid into her car, shut the door, and flipped down the vanity mirror.

For a moment, the world narrowed to her reflection. She examined her face with practiced honesty—then smiled faintly.

She was beautiful.

Johnny had always believed appearances mattered. He thought the way someone carried themselves on the outside reflected how they felt within. April knew that about him. But it wasn't her looks that had kept them together.

It was her strength.

From the beginning, April had been the steadier one, a natural born leader—the one who stayed grounded when Johnny drifted, who spoke plainly when things grew complicated. That strength had only deepened his love for her over the years.

She was intelligent, too—quick-witted, articulate, blessed with a gift for conversation that allowed her to outtalk anyone foolish enough to underestimate her. Lively. Funny. Confident.

April Jenkins was all brains and beauty—the kind of woman who didn't need saving.

Satisfied, she snapped the mirror back into place.

That was when something felt... wrong.

She looked up—and froze.

A tall man stood directly in front of her car, close enough that she hadn't noticed him approach. Her pulse jumped, startled more than afraid—yet.

She rolled down the window and leaned out slightly.

"Excuse me," she said, irritation edging her voice. "Do you mind?"

Snake smiled. "No," he said calmly. "I don't."

Before she could react, he raised both hands.

The sound of crackling electricity along with the spiral of red light burst into existence, wrapping around her car like something alive. The vehicle shuddered—and then lifted.

The ground dropped away.

April screamed.

The car hovered five feet in the air, suspended in a glowing crimson haze.

People on the sidewalk shrieked and scattered. Some stood frozen, mouths open. Traffic screeched to a halt.

"PLEASE!" April cried, gripping the steering wheel. "PUT ME DOWN!"

Her mind scrambled, grasping for anything familiar—and then memory surfaced.

The news.

The tall dark figure.

The man who fought the city's masked hero.

"Oh my God..." she whispered, horror flooding her voice.

Snake leaned closer, his face eerily calm.

"I'll put you down," he said evenly.

Relief surged—only to die instantly.

"But you're coming with me," he continued. "And if you scream again, fight me, or try anything stupid—"

His eyes glowed, empty and merciless.

"—I'll kill you."

The red light pulsed.

April's breath hitched as the reality settled in—not panic, but cold, focused terror. This wasn't random. This wasn't a robbery.

She didn't know *why* he wanted her.

Only that whatever he wanted, it was dangerous.

And somewhere across the city, completely unaware, Johnny's trajectory was about to be thrown off.

CHAPTER 32

AS JOHNNY CONTINUED practicing his basic martial arts moves in Brooks' home gym, the phone rang.

Watching from the corner near the phone Brooks reached for it. "Hello?"

A pause.

His brow furrowed. He glanced at Johnny and extended the receiver. "It's for you."

Johnny wiped sweat from his brow, surprised. *April wouldn't be calling until after work*, he thought. He took the phone. "Hello?"

Silence.

His jaw tightened. "Who is this?"

Another pause.

Without thinking, Johnny's eyes flicked to the television. A surge of yellow light snapped it on—Fox 29—then the channel changed to Channel 10.

Nassir and Brooks exchanged looks as Johnny stood frozen, still holding the phone.

On the screen, an elderly man spoke breathlessly into a microphone. "...then the man lowered the car, grabbed the woman's arm, and they both just disappeared."

"They vanished?" the reporter asked.

The old man squinted. "Isn't that what I just said? You might wanna clean your ears out."

Johnny leaned closer.

The camera panned to a 1996 Ford Escort with the driver's door hanging open.

Johnny's heart stopped.

The license plate read: **ME 4 U**.

"Shit—that's April's car!" Johnny shouted.

Brooks hit the speakerphone button.

Laughter crackled through the line. "That's right, Johnny," the voice purred. "Or should I call you *Jade*?"

Johnny's breath caught.

"I have your girl. Fairmount Park. Near the Dell East. Twenty minutes."

A pause.

"Any later... she dies."

The line went dead.

The room fell silent as the television cut away.

Nassir turned, already knowing. Brooks couldn't meet Johnny's eyes.

A tear slid down Johnny's cheek.

"This is my fault," Johnny whispered. "April doesn't deserve this."

Before either man could speak, the sound of electricity cracked. Yellow light engulfed him. His clothes transformed into his costume. His eyes ignited—brilliant gold, pupil-less.

And Jade vanished.

***

With a light snap, Jade materialized high above Horsham, already falling. He caught himself midair and accelerated forward, checking the built-in chronometer on his wrist.

Too slow.

A zipper sound opened a portal ahead of him.

He flew through.

The zipper sound closed the portal.

***

The zipper sounding portal reopened near the Dell East, and Jade burst out into the cold afternoon air.

The zipper sound sealed the portal behind him.

He checked the chronometer again.

Ten minutes early.

He descended quickly as a black van curved into the drive. The sound of electricity crackled along with the yellow light which spiraled around him.

Jade vanished.

***

With the sound of a light snap, Jade reappeared behind the rear wall of the Dell and peered around the corner, watching the van roll to a stop.

The front doors opened. Cole stepped out on the driver's side. Steven Tanner emerged from the passenger's seat.

Jade studied them carefully and realized he didn't recognize either man. He watched Tanner bark orders at Cole, but he couldn't hear the words. For the first time, Jade wished for super-hearing. Invisibility wouldn't hurt, either.

Cole walked around to the cargo doors and flung them open.

Four-armed men hopped out, followed by a fifth who kept April close, a gun pressed at her side.

Jade's chest tightened.

He moved without thinking—stepping from behind the wall.

Everyone's attention snapped to him at once.

April's eyes widened as she saw the glowing figure in person for the first time. She'd heard reports, seen footage, watched the city argue about whether he was real—but here he was, bright and impossible, standing in front of her. Unreal in the way Santa Claus felt unreal to a rebellious seven-year-old.

Tanner grinned at Jade's impulsiveness, satisfied. "A little anxious to save our beloved, aren't we?"

"Let her go!" Jade snapped, anger and strain roughening his voice. "It's obvious you want me. I'll do whatever you want."

Tanner shook his head. "I've tried to get your attention before," he said lightly. "It didn't work out as planned. But I did make a new friend."

As if on cue, Snake flew in and descended beside Tanner, as the business mogul smiled a devilish smile.

Jade didn't care about the evil alliance before him. He repeated himself—harder. "Let the girl go!"

"If I do that," Tanner said, "then I don't have a hold on you. Now do I, Johnny boy?"

Upon hearing Tanner's comment, April stared at Jade, confused and frightened. *It couldn't be.* Johnny might look tough, but he wasn't the hero type. "Johnny?" she whispered. "Is that you?"

Jade looked at her and the sound of electricity crackled along with the yellow light which spiraled around him.

He vanished.

A heartbeat later, with the sound of a light snap, he reappeared behind April and set his hands on her shoulders.

The sound of electricity crackled along with the yellow light spiraled around both of them.

They both vanished.

Tanner looked around, furious. "Shit. I don't believe this asshole." He turned to Snake, who was grasping his head with both hands as if in pain. "Please bring them back."

The sound of electricity crackled along with the red light which spiraled around him.

Snake then vanished.

***

All was quiet—until, with the sound of a light snap, April and Jade reappeared in the Philadelphia Zoo near the children's section.

Apparently unfazed by teleportation—Snake had already forced her through it—April shoved Johnny away.

"Johnny, what the hell is going on?" she demanded. "Why would you keep something like this from me?"

Every lie he'd ever told her slammed into Jade at once. He knew he couldn't explain everything—not now—but he had to say something.

"April... I was going to tell you, I was waiting until I thought it would be safe."

"I guess I'd have to be dead to qualify for..."

"Do you love me?" Johnny interrupted.

She stared into his eyes and then grabbed his face and kissed him harder than she ever had—then pushed him back again. "I love you," she said, voice shaking. "Very, very much. But you're making me lose trust in you."

"I know," he said. "I'm sorry. And I'm going to fix this starting right now."

He held out his right hand. Electricity danced in his palm as a small ring case formed in a spiral of light. He lowered to one knee.

A knot tightened in April's stomach. She already knew what was coming.

Johnny opened the case, revealing a diamond ring. He looked up at her. "This is not how I wanted to do this... April, will you marry me?"

Tears gathered in her eyes. Anger still simmered—but love rose higher. "Yes," she breathed. "Yes!"

Johnny stood to slide the ring onto her finger, then paused, just to look at her. Six years of love condensed into one shaking moment.

"Do it," she said, half-laughing through tears.

He slipped the ring into place. They laughed—giddy and stunned by the sudden shift of their lives—then kissed.

Jade eased back, levitating slightly, smiling down at April as she stared up at him—at the ring, at the impossible glow.

How did he get the ability to do all of this? she wondered.

"Find security," Jade said gently. "Stay with them. I've got to go take out the trash. When this is over... we will talk about all of this, and we've got a wedding to plan!"

He rose and streaked away in a bright yellow-green trail, leaving her staring at her hand.

***

Jade returned to the Dell and landed several yards in front of Tanner and his men.

Tanner spotted him first. "Shoot him!"

The gunmen fired. The bullets flared with yellow light and dropped harmlessly before they could reach him.

Jade walked forward, steady and furious.

The gunmen panicked and threw their weapons. The guns hit the ground as if dragged down by invisible weight.

"Really?" Jade said, voice low.

A thick beam of light surged outward from his fists, knocking the armed men off their feet. Jade kept walking toward Tanner and Cole.

"Give me one reason," he said, "I shouldn't kill you both right now."

"I'll give you a good one," Snake's voice growled.

Jade turned his head—just in time to see Snake gripping April's neck tightly, from the back.

"Don't move," Snake warned, "or she dies."

"Let her go," Jade said, barely containing himself.

Snake sneered. "You teleport her out, take her somewhere safe, then fly right out of the zoo with your bright trail following like you ain't got sense? Not very *bright*, Johnny boy."

Tanner's smile returned. "I would listen to him if I were you," he said. "He will kill her!"

Snake leaned in. "C'mon, Jade. I dare you."

Jade didn't blink. "Let her go."

"Make me."

"I'll kill you."

April struggled. "Kick the living shit out—"

A loud crack interrupted her words as Snake held her up by her neck.

As she stared at Johnny her view grew dark as her eyes stayed fixed in his direction with tears coming from them.

"APRIL!" Jade screamed a heavy sounding, dark and loud scream.

Tanner and Cole looked at Snake in shock. Killing the girl was not part of the plan. Tanner was enjoying the leverage he currently had on Jade and was hoping it would be his permanent card with which he would always hold the winning hand, but with Snake's malicious move, he lost his perceived winning hand.

Jade fell to his knees and started glowing brighter and brighter until he looked as if he were made entirely of yellow light. His pupils were still non-existent, though it was apparent there was anger in his eyes. Jades' costume was also now well hidden by the bright light.

Tanner and Cole immediately started running.

The underpaid henchmen were already gone, having disappeared because of the involuntary and painful laser beam which hit them.

"A little heart Broken?" asked Snake. He then withdrew her heart out of her chest. "Here take this one, she won't be needing it anymore." He threw the heart at Jade as he let go of her and as April's lifeless body fell from his hands.

Jade stood up angrily and aimed both fists at Snake who was now laughing uncontrollably.

The sound of cracking electricity formed around his fist and a thick light beam shot from his hands and contacted Snake just as he threw up a force field, but the beam forced him to fly back some one thousand feet across the park and into a tree. Jade then quickly grabbed April's lifeless body and flew off with her.

The sound of the giant zipper opened up a portal, and he flew through with April's body.

The zipper sound closed the portal.

Thirty seconds later, a zipper sound opened up another portal and Jade flew out just as Snake jumped up with his eyes glowing crimson red.

"What's wrong?" Snake asked. "Feeling a little outside of yourself? Wait, that would be the girlfriend? She's outside herself."

Jade power flew hard towards Snake at the speed of light but caught a fist with his face which sent him back about sixty feet, where he connected with a tree which had at least a hundred annual rings.

Jade, who was dazed from Snake's blow and not from the tree, then looked up as Snake appeared in front of him with a light snap and grabbed a hold of his brightly lit body.

Snake then hurled the grief-stricken Jade over his head and approximately eighty feet behind him, where this time, Jade had gotten personal with the black van Tanner and his allies had arrived in, giving it a huge dent and knocking it over onto its side.

Snake's eyes, which were still glowing, then emitted red lasers from them, hitting Jade as he was attempting to get up. Jade was knocked back down.

***

Tanner and Cole, still running through the park, both headed towards thirty-third Street when Cole looked over at Tanner.

"Was killing the girl part of your plan too?" asked Cole.

Tanner looked over at Cole as they kept running. "Don't fuck with me Martin. We both knew there may be casualties, but this was definitely not how I planned for things to go."

Upon reaching the end of the parkway, they crossed the street.

While still running Tanner said, "I had in fact, no intentions of killing her. I only wanted to get Jade's attention so I would be able to control his actions, not so he'd want to kill me."

"Well, if Snake doesn't kill him now, then that plan's shot to shit."

After crossing the street, Tanner flagged down an approaching cab, and as soon as they got in, it sped away.

***

Back in the park, a very deranged Snake was stomping a very angry and very brightly lit Jade. It was soon apparent there were spectators, and even though they had kept their distance, Jade thought to himself it might be better for him to move the fight somewhere else.

Jade then looked up and flew off in a northeast direction, leaving behind him a trail of green and yellow light and missing the last stomp of Snake's foot.

Snake took off behind him like a rocket, and grabbed one of Jade's legs, but Jade kicked him in the face with his free leg. The impact of the kick sent Snake hurling back, giving Jade some distance.

Before hitting the ground, Snake caught his bearings and took off again like a rocket behind Jade. Then, realizing he was not going to be able to catch up with him, Snake started shooting lasers from his eyes in Jade's direction.

As the lasers whizzed past him, Jade thought hard about diverting Snake's attention and upon doing so, light poured out from either side of him and on each side a being of pure light, each looking exactly like himself appeared. Slightly shocked, Jade and his decoys started rotating and changing places with each other in a way similar to the way the colors of a kaleidoscope did.

The constantly changing positions of Jade and his decoys confused Snake, causing him to stop firing.

Snake then started gripping his head, trying to deal with the unbearable pain he had now somewhat grown accustomed to. Then Snake, in blind anger, again started firing lasers at Jade and his decoys, missing them all.

Jade soon located his chosen destination, Frankford High Schools' football stadium which, because of the cold weather, was devoid of any human life. He descended to the ground but was quickly tackled by a speeding Snake. Jade went flying backwards because of the hit, crashing into a fence and then falling to the ground.

Snake, with the sound of cracking electricity and the spiraling red light, soon disappeared and then quickly reappeared with a light sounding snap right in front of Jade.

Snake grabbed Jade by his neck and started lifting him up until his feet were a foot off the ground.

"Do you even know what you've done?" gasped Jade.

"You think you can beat me," started Snake as he ignored the question, "that you're better than me, but I will kill you just as easily as I killed her." He laughed. "I have the upper hand."

Jade grew even angrier than he already was. "Wrong answer!"

Jade looked down at Snake, his eyes a mixture of red and yellow light, flushed with anger and rage. Anger because this ass hole came into his life in the first place, rage because he not only killed his girlfriend in a cruel and malicious way, but because he was also dragging her name into the pit from which he came. Jade then yelled as with great effort, the sound of cracking electricity along with the spiraling light, helped him to vanish from Snake's grip.

Snake turned around and his face caught Jades fists, both of which were moving at a blinding speed, and hitting him in various places over his mandible and left and right parietals. Snake then kicked Jade in the midsection with his right foot, sending him back about twenty feet.

Snake quickly followed with long strides and quickly recovered the fallen Jade. He then spun him around and hurled him across the football field.

Jade produced the sound of the cracking electricity and his spiraling yellow light, causing him to disappear mid drift.

Snake looked around and as his head was turned, a quick and loud zipper sound opened up a portal right in front of him as he turned around to face the sound.

Light blasts then shot out, shoving him back about ten feet before he fell to the ground.

Before Jade flew out.

Jade then landed a few feet in front of Snake as the bright light had hidden his own costume had faded away. As Jade walked closer towards Snake, the anger rested on his face put an obvious look of fear on the evil giant's face.

Jade felt the malevolence was now running through his blood stream, the contempt he felt for this bastard now rested in his stomach as he thought about the joy, he would experience from finishing him. Jade then eyed Snake over the length of his brawny frame and noticed the energy beam he had shot out through the portal had done more damage than he thought would have been possible.

The injured Snake slowly looked down at the hole in the side of his abdomen and then looked up at Jade.

Snake's flesh was singed and intestines revealed. A rib could be seen on the right side as well, even in the darkness. But somehow, he felt relief from the headaches and the episodes of psychosis.

Red light then started to emanate around the edges of the damaged organs and flesh within Snake's body as well as his skin.

Jade looked up and saw the lights from the football field were gleaming down upon them. "Fuck that," he said in a low voice.

Snake, still lost in the imbalance of his episode, looked up at Jade. As his headache pain was gone, he felt it might be because of his fast-approaching death. He would now welcome it as it seemed to be the only way he could get rid of the pain which has tormented him over the last nine years. Snake said, "I guess this is it light bulb...you're finished."

"Not quite," said Jade as he grabbed him and flew upwards until he was about three hundred feet in the air. Jade then flipped in a downward position and started flying straight down towards the ground.

Snake developed one of his rare looks of fear on his face as he struggled to free himself from Jade's grip.

"Jade felt a glitch in his powers for a brief moment."

Right before they hit the ground, the loud zipper sound opened a portal and Jade dropped Snake in and right before he himself could go through the portal, the cracking sound of electricity along with the spiral of light quickly circled Jades' body and he vanished.

As the zipper sound assisted with the portal closure, Jade reappeared falling from high above and then slowed to a hover.

He then stopped until he was standing next to the spot where the portal just closed up. The spot where he had dropped Snake into the ground. He looked at the ground with contentment and anger still on his face as a tear came out of his eye. Jade then flew up towards the sky and the loud zipper sound opened a portal.

Jade then flew through.

The zipper sound closed the portal.

***

Back at the park, where the dented van was being gawked at by the curious and the news cameras which had arrived only moments ago, the loud zipper sound opened a portal up and Jade flew out and landed as the people looked at him in wonder. Jade looked around in the crowd for the strange men he saw earlier but knew deep down they were not there.

Jade then walked over to the spot where he was kneeling when Snake had thrown Aprils' heart at him and stooped down slowly, picking up the organ which was so viciously ripped from her fragile, lifeless body. As he started to cry, Jade stood up and a woman who was standing nearby covered her mouth and pointed to the bloody organ in his hand.

Tears streamed down his cheek as the sound of cracking electricity along with the bright spiraling light wrapped around him.

The reporters started running towards him.

Jade then vanished.

***

With a light snap, Jade soon reappeared back at Brooks' home, where he had so swiftly taken Aprils' damaged and lifeless body.

The two physicians looked at Jade with empathic eyes as he walked over to April and pulled the sheet halfway off of her body.

As the tears continued to run down his cheeks, his hand turned into pure yellow light and he placed the torn heart back into her chest, in the same manner Snake had removed it. After removing his hand from her chest, light emanated from off of her skin and sealed the aperture.

182

"Me for you," he said with a scratchy voice. Jade then picked up her body, wrapped the both of them in the sound of cracking electricity and spiraling yellow light.

Jade, with April in his arms, soon vanished.

CHAPTER 33

THE RADIO PLAYED in Johnny's apartment. This time he was not listening to music as he normally did, today he was listening to the news.

"And just what is the connection between this Jade and April Jenkins is the question being asked tonight as the city remains to be shocked at the tragic death of this young college student who was also employed at Biotech Laboratories. Now even though sources say there seems to be no apparent connection between the two, everyone remains baffled at this tragic incident."

The night was painfully cold and silent for Johnny. Just a short time ago, he felt as if he had everything, yet now he felt as if he had nothing. There was nothing in the world he wanted more than April, and now he felt his brief time as the hero Jade, ended the world as he cherished it.

As the news broadcast was continuing to play on the radio, Johnny sat on the couch with the lights off as tears poured out of his eyes.

He started having flashbacks of the last six years of his life.

Johnny relived the big thanksgiving dinner he attended when he was seventeen years old. *He had just met April for the first time. They were at the residence of a mutual family friend, and as the dinner took place, they constantly exchanged glances and smiles with each other. The practice of shy eye glance exchanges kept up throughout the whole night.*

After the dinner, while the other guests were mingling with each other, Johnny and April had escaped to the front porch for their own conversation.

"I'm Johnny," he said as he extended his right hand towards her.

"I know," she replied smiling.

The vision ended as a tear came to his eye, as he heard her voice say, "I'm April."

Johnny then looked into the mirror and started crying as he then saw a vision of April with her arms around his neck.

"We make a beautiful couple," she said smiling.

Johnny laughed and said, "We're gorgeous!"

Johnny then looked around the darkened bedroom and saw his botany text. *He then saw a vision of the two of them in their botany class, passing notes to each other. The vision ended with them laughing.*

Johnny smiled briefly and then started crying as he remembered the snowball fight, they had a few years ago in which *she had gotten him dead in the face with a snowball.*

"Now punk, paybacks are a motherf ..., AI-E-E!" April screamed as she started running from Johnny.

He then saw the more recent memories. All of the events which had taken place prior to April's death, all the way up until that actual apocalyptic moment where Snake killed her. Johnny cried all through the night. His lost was one which could never be found.

***

April looked down and saw what she thought was a bright red light in her chest. Her eyes lost sight of Johnny and she saw nothing but darkness.

She felt a strange yanking sensation pulling her backwards slowly, and then suddenly, she felt as if she were being pushed forward very quickly through the vast darkness and she looked on as she saw a bright light in circular form which grew bigger and bigger until it filled what she perceived as her field of vision.

The next thing she knew, she suddenly felt as if her eyes were closed and she slowly started to open them and she immediately squealed in fear as she observed what appeared to be giant pigs around her. She then attempted to look at her hands and quickly realized as she saw the snout on her face she didn't have any hands.

Suddenly, everything again went dark.

In the darkness, she could sense emotions, fear and anxiety. She then saw a bright blue light fluttering around before her.

"That was a close one," started a soft female voice.

"Where am I?" asked April.

"You're sort of in an in-between realm," replied the voice.

"Why can't I see you?" asked April.

"You're comprehension of this realm is delayed due to your manner of death," replied the voice.

"I'm dead?" asked April.

"Sort of," started the voice, "but someone with great power cares a great deal for you and you were imbued with a protection spell. The combination of such mixed with infant Nelarian D-N-A, has put your body in sort of a suspended animation while your body heals itself."

"Who are you?"

"You can call me Crystal."

"Crystal?" started April, "are you my fairy godmother?"

"Think bigger dear."

"Bigger?" asked April. "You're an angel? My guardian angel?"

"I am!"

"So there is a Heaven?"

"There is a Heaven, but it's not what you think, and only a select few ever make it there."

"So there is a hell too?"

"Hell is a real concept, not a place, difficult to explain."

"Why did I see giant pigs a few moments ago?"

"They weren't giant pigs," laughed Crystal. "Your soul quickly reincarnated into the body of a male piglet."

"A male piglet? Reincarnated?"

"Yes," started Crystal. "The majority of souls from your world reincarnate, sometimes into the same species, sometimes into other species, because the fight for bodies is a tough one and sometimes there aren't enough human bodies to go around, so some souls are pushed into animal bodies. The same is true for when animals reincarnate."

"So humans can be eating animals who were once human?"

"The body you eat is merely a shell but this is the way of your world. Animals and humans are more connected than many of you know."

"When can I go back?"

"When your physical body finishes the healing process you will go back, but it will take external Nelarian energy to help you recall your memories. So relax while you can, this can take a bit of time."

CHAPTER 34

EVEN THOUGH IT was daytime, you couldn't see the sun today. One would think the sun must've been hurt by the loss of April Jenkins for he refused to show his face.

His cousin, the wind, blew his cool air heavily by, but the breeze wasn't really welcomed.

The sky also frowned down upon them with a dull, dreary expression as the mourners stood around the casket, listening to the minister's eulogy.

Johnny stared blankly at the casket with teary eyes, this has been the longest two weeks of his life.

His Aunt Pauline grabbed a hold of his hand as he looked over at Ms. Jenkins and Sorrie, both of whom were dressed in black and sobbing.

"I know our grief has struck us this early into the new year and we...we need to praise him still. Let us bow our heads in prayer," started the minister as all of the saddened and grief-stricken friends and family members bowed their heads.

The minister was tall and lanky with brown hair, which was balding in the middle, yet his voice was soothing and graceful, and made many of the mourners strong during this time of grief. "The Lord is my shepherd; I shall not want. He maketh me to lie down in green pastures. He leadeth me beside still waters. He restoreth my soul and leadeth me in the path of righteousness for his namesake.

Yay, though I walk through the valley of the shadow of death, I will fear no evil, for thou art with me, thy rod and thy staff they comfort me. Thou hadst preparest a table before me in the presence of my enemies. Thou hadst anointed my head with thy precious oil and my cup runneth over. Surely goodness and mercy shall follow me all the days of my life - and I will dwell in the house of the Lord forever. Amen."

"Amen," repeated the small crowd in unison.

The crowd all raised their heads in unison as the mahogany casket was slowly lowered into the ground.

April's family then cautiously walked past the six-foot hole as they each dropped a single red rose into the ground where the casket was descending.

Miss Jenkins started crying heavily as Sorrie grabbed a hold of her arm and led her away from the large hole, making sure her mother didn't fall in.

As the mourners started to disperse, Johnny and Pauline walked over towards Sorrie and Miss Jenkins. He looked into her teary eyes trying to reach somewhere inside of her, just to say I'm sorry. Johnny gave the grieving woman a hug of compassion and slowly pulled back.

"Miss Jenkins," started Johnny, "If there is anything I can do for you, please let me know."

"Unless you can get rid of this Jade person," started Ms. Jenkins with an obviously upset expression on her face, "there isn't much you can do."

Johnny looked at her with a look of surprise on his face.

"He's the one who got my daughter killed," replied Ms. Jenkins.

"Jade didn't...," started Sorrie as she pointed in the direction of the hole in the ground. "It was all over the news there were others implicated in..."

"Yeah, well who then?" Miss Jenkins asked, with intent on interruption. "As far as I'm concerned, all of this strange shit started happening when this Jade person showed up. He was probably an experiment from that crazy place she worked at, if I could..."

Johnny continued staring at Miss Jenkins with a blank expression on his teary face and realized she was partially right.

189

If he had not taken on the responsibility of being a hero to Philadelphia, April, without question, would be alive right now.

Miss Jenkins said, "It's all his fault." She then touched Johnny's face and kissed him on the cheek as tears streamed down hers. "I gotta get goin' baby, don't hesitate to come see me, you here?" Miss Jenkins then turned and touched Pauline gently on the arm as Pauline sent her an empathic smile.

Sorrie turned and faced Johnny and mouthed the words, "It's up to you to bring her back!"

Johnny developed a look of confusion on his face.

"It's up to you!" Sorrie exclaimed. She then turned around and walked away with her mother as a tear rolled down Johnny's cheek.

He cried feeling as if her sister didn't fully understand April was gone. "I'm sorry," he said softly.

***

The next day, inside of the majestic Horsham house, Johnny, Nassir and Brooks all sat around trying to make sense of everything that transpired over the past week.

There was no way anyone could've gotten information about Johnny, they were sure they had taken great steps to ensure his identity remained private, yet somehow, someone found out who he was and all the other aspects of his life which were separate from Johnny's alter ego.

"How did they know where to find me, how to find April?" Johnny asked in frustration.

"Who are they?" Nassir asked while looking back and forth between the two.

Brooks looked grimly at his two friends. "You two are asking the wrong questions," started Brooks. "What we need to know is, where are they now?"

Johnny looked over at Brooks and then over at Nassir. He then looked back over at Brooks. "How are we supposed to find out where they are if we don't even know who they are?" Johnny asked.

They all just looked at each other in a stupefied manner as the ringing of the phone intruded in on their silence.

Brooks walked over to the telephone and picked up the receiver. "Hello?" Brooks asked.

He paused as he listened to the response of the person on the other end of the phone.

"Okay we're all here, I guess we'll see you then." Brooks then hung up the phone and looked at his two friends. "Sam is on the way over. He has some information for us."

CHAPTER 35

BACK AT TANNER'S house, Tanner and Cole were sitting in the living room when a small Philippina woman brought out two beers on a tray.

Tanner and Cole each took a beer and the woman started heading out of the room.

"Salamat Marguerite!" said Tanner.

"Walang Anuman," responded Marguerite as she walked away from the two.

"Well at least he doesn't know our names," started Cole as Tanner opened up the can and took a gulp.

Tanner then sat the can on a coaster on the table in front of him. "He doesn't need to know our names," started Tanner. "He knows our faces. A man who has suffered the type of loss he just suffered will spend the rest of his life hunting us down if he has to. And I frankly, don't have time to spend running."

"Then what do you think we should do next?" asked Cole.

Tanner pondered for a moment as to how he could best handle the situation. He was sure Snake was dead by now since he hadn't heard from him. He had to think of something and fast, for he wasn't sure what information Snake had coughed up in his last few moments of life. Maybe in desperation for his life to be spared, he had given Tanner up to Jade. Tanner then quickly picked up the receiver of the cordless phone and dialed.

The phone rang a few times and then someone answered.

Tanner said, "Jim, I want you to fuel up one of the jets and prepare a flight plan to Paris."

Cole looked at his boss with a curious look on his face as Tanner waited for the response of the person on the other end of the phone.

Tanner caught the look Cole had on his face while he was put on hold. Tanner said, "I have a version of Stern over there who's also a terrific plastic surgeon."

Cole placed his right hand on his face. He disapproved.

***

The doorbell rung and Johnny, with the sound of cracking electricity and the spiraling light, quickly changed into his sparring outfit with the mask in place.

Brooks headed over to the door as both Nassir and Johnny followed. When he opened the door, his brother Sam walked in followed by one of his students, Brian Baker.

Brooks looked at his brother, at Brian and then at Nassir, with a look of understanding of what might have happened. Brooks then hoped this youth could give them a name or anything which would lead to the two men Johnny spoke of.

Sam nudged at Brian. "Well?" He then pointed towards the trio. "Tell them!" he demanded angrily.

Brian looked at Johnny, who had an obvious look of anger on his face and of whom he felt intimidated by as he got a better look at him. Brian then looked from Johnny and over at his two friends who also displayed faces of disappointment. "Someone was posting flyers throughout some areas of the hood," said Brian. "Mostly 'round the off beaten paths, offering fifty thousand dollars to anyone who could give up info leading to him," he said as he pointed to Jade.

Johnny looked at the two physicians, Sam and then back at Brian.

"Was there any type of phone number on the flyer?" Johnny asked.

"Yeah ...well it was a pager number. I paged him from a pay phone, and he called me back almost immediately."

"Do you have the number?" asked Nassir.

"No," said Brian as Johnny, Nassir and Brooks all sighed in frustration. "But he did tell me his name."

"What is it?" asked Brooks.

Brian looked over at Brooks. Brian said, "Michael Warner."

Johnny turned around and started to walk away.

"What did this Warner guy look like?" asked Brooks.

"Tall, about six feet even, a baby face with jet black hair and blue eyes."

"That sounds like one of the guys," added Johnny, while still facing the other way.

Brooks looked at his brother and said, "Thanks Sam, now get him out of our sight!"

"No problem," replied Sam as he reopened the door and pulled Brian by his jacket and shoved him out.

As Sam started to leave out the door, Nassir tapped him on the shoulder.

"What? He just came to you and started confessing?" asked Nassir.

Sam said, "He came to practice driving a brand-new car and bragging about how he paid cash for it. When I found out about it, I had to start asking questions. The kid's always broke, never has money for anything, yet out of the clear blue, can afford to buy a new car?"

Nassir shook his head in the negative. "Thank's again Sam."

"His sheer stupidity was definitely a disappointment to me as his teacher." Sam then said in a low voice, "please give my condolences to the kid."

"I will, thanks Sam," replied Nassir as he closed the door behind Sam.

Johnny produced the sound of cracking electricity along with the spiral of yellow light and changed back into his regular clothes with nothing more than a mere thought and he then turned around to face the two physicians. "I lost the love of my life 'cause I chose to play hero and 'cause some kid wanted some money?" asked Johnny angrily. "I'm gonna get these mother fuckers! Doctor Brooks, can you try to find information on this

Michael Warner person and see if you can find anything out on the black van they found at the park?"

Brooks shook his head yes. "Already on the van."

Johnny said, "I'll be back, I've got something I need to take care of." Johnny then produced the sound of cracking electricity along with the spiraling light and vanished from out of the house.

CHAPTER 36

LOOKING DOWN FROM the heavens, the sun wore a warm, almost knowing smile, its golden light spilling gently across the earth below. It filtered through the branches of tall oaks and maples, setting their leaves trembling as though they wished to wave hello to every creature that passed beneath them. A soft breeze whispered through the cemetery, and the grass responded in kind—thin green blades bowing forward, then rising again, as if offering quiet respect to the dead.

At the center of Chelten Hills Cemetery, surrounded by orderly rows of stone and shadow, Johnny stood beside April's freshly turned grave.

The soil was still dark and raw, its edges sharp where the shovel had bitten into the ground only days earlier. A faint scent of earth lingered in the air, damp and heavy, mingling with the sweetness of fallen leaves. Johnny stared at the headstone, his eyes tracing each carved letter as if committing them to memory for the rest of his life.

April Jenkins
Sunrise 06/29/75 · Sunset 12/27/96
Beloved Daughter
And Friend to All

The words felt too small. Too final.

Johnny swallowed hard and slowly lowered himself onto one knee. He placed his hand against the cool gray granite, the stone unyielding beneath his fingers, real in a way he still struggled to accept. His lips curved into a faint, broken smile.

"Hey, babe," he murmured, his voice barely louder than the breeze. For a brief, foolish moment, part of him expected to hear her laugh, to feel her hand brush his shoulder. "You know you lied to me. You were supposed to marry me."

Silence answered him.

Johnny tilted his head back and looked toward the sky, squinting against the brightness. He reached down and pulled a single blade of grass from the ground, rolling it between his fingers, twisting it absentmindedly as he searched for the words he had rehearsed a thousand times in his head.

"April... I'm—" His voice cracked, forcing him to pause. He took a breath and tried again. "I'm so sorry. If I thought telling you about my abilities would've kept you alive, I would have told you everything. Every secret. Every fear." His grip tightened around the blade of grass. "If I'd known this was even possible, I swear to you... I would have never done any of it."

The cemetery remained still, the world holding its breath.

Johnny's gaze drifted across the empty paths and silent stones. A tear escaped the corner of his eye, cutting a slow line down his cheek. His eyes burned, but he didn't wipe it away.

"This battle isn't over," he said, his voice steadier now, edged with something colder. "And I will make every single person responsible for your death pay. I won't rest—" his jaw tightened, "—not until I know you can."

The blade of grass slipped from his fingers and fluttered uselessly to the ground.

Johnny rose to his feet and stood over the grave, shoulders squared, grief hardening into resolve. He wiped his face with the back of his hand, then bent down once more. Pressing his lips to the top of the stone, he closed his eyes.

"I love you," he whispered.

Straightening, Johnny turned and walked away, his footsteps fading along the gravel path. The trees rustled softly behind him. Birds perched above fell silent, and even the squirrels seemed to pause, as though the weight of his words had reached them too.

But they were not the only witnesses.

From a distance, unseen by human eyes, a being composed entirely of light observed the moment in silence. Its form shimmered faintly against the air, radiant and untouchable, bound by laws that prevented interference. It could not speak. It could not reach out.

It could only watch—as grief transformed into purpose, and love into something far more dangerous.

And the light pulsed softly, as if acknowledging that what had just been set in motion would not end quietly.

CHAPTER 37

WITH THE EXCEPTION of the halogen lamps mounted high atop their metal poles, the world lay swallowed in darkness. Their cold white light washed over the grassy expanse of Frankford High School's football field, carving out pale islands of visibility amid the surrounding void. Beyond that glow, the night was absolute.

The arctic air had emptied the streets. No cars passed. No voices carried. Even the animals seemed to have retreated from the bitter cold, leaving the city eerily hollow—as if life itself had briefly stepped aside.

The silence was broken by a sudden *thump* beneath the turf.

The ground ruptured in a small explosion of dirt and sod, and Snake burst upward from below the surface, propelled just far enough to rise a foot above the earth before gravity reclaimed him. He slammed back down hard, the impact driving the air from his lungs.

He lay there, staring up at the glare of the lights, breath ragged, chest rising and falling unevenly. For a moment, the world spun.

Then the pain arrived.

A deep, searing agony flared along the right side of his abdomen, forcing a low groan from his throat. Snake twisted slightly and looked down at the spot where Jade's laser had torn through him. His shirt was shredded, burned clean through, the fabric stiff with dried blood and caked dirt. The wound *should* have been fatal.

But it wasn't.

His skin had closed.

The flesh beneath the torn shirt was intact—unbroken, smooth except for faint discoloration, as if the injury had never fully existed. Snake touched the area cautiously, half-expecting his fingers to sink into a hole that wasn't there.

Nothing.

His body had healed itself.

A stunned laugh escaped him at first—quiet, uncertain. Then another followed. Louder. Sharper. Soon the laughter grew unchecked, echoing across the empty field, rising into something jagged and unhinged.

"A miracle..." he muttered, shaking his head.

Snake had always known he was different. He had always known he possessed extraordinary abilities. But *this*—this went beyond anything he had imagined. His body hadn't just survived. It had adapted.

No hospital. No recovery. No weakness.

He pushed himself up onto his elbows, eyes burning with a fevered light.

"I'm not just strong," he said aloud, as though confessing a sacred truth. "I'm not just gifted."

He rose slowly to his feet, ignoring the lingering ache in his side.

"I'm immortal."

The word felt right as it left his mouth.

No—*better* than right.

"I'm a demigod."

The realization sent a surge of exhilaration through him, electrifying his nerves. With this new understanding of his power came clarity—and with clarity, obsession. The madness he had fought so hard to suppress returned, curling through his thoughts like smoke.

Jade had hurt him. Jade had challenged him.

But now?

Now Snake knew he could destroy him. Still, raw power alone wouldn't sustain the life he intended to live. Money, resources, influence—those still mattered.

That meant Tanner.

Tanner was a necessary evil, a means to an end.

Snake threw his head back and laughed again, the sound wild and unrestrained, carried away by the wind into the empty night.

"Jade," he rasped, his voice dry and venomous. "Your ass is mine."

The field bore silent witness to his vow.

***

Across the city, beneath warm lights and polished surfaces, Cole paced the living room of Tanner's house like a teenager waiting for his first date. He ran his fingers through his hair, then stopped, then started pacing again.

Every thought circled back to the same fear.

The plastic surgeon's knife.

Cole's reflection stared back at him from a decorative mirror—smooth, youthful, untouched. He had a baby-soft face, jet-black hair that fell naturally into place, and ice-blue eyes that stood out sharply against his pale complexion.

At six feet tall and one hundred eighty pounds, he was well-proportioned, effortlessly attractive.

And tonight, he was supposed to lose it all.

"What if they mess up my face?" he asked, his voice tight with anxiety.

Tanner, lounging comfortably nearby, looked at him with amused contempt. "Which would you rather have?" he replied dryly. "A messed-up face or a dead ass?"

"You know what I mean," Cole said, stopping his pacing. "I've had this face all my life. And now I just... get rid of it?"

"Relax," Tanner said calmly. "You'll probably get a better one."

Before Cole could respond, Tanner's pager began to vibrate insistently. Tanner glanced down at it—and froze.

"Six, six, six," he muttered, staring at the number.

Cole frowned. "I told you," He said nervously. "We're gonna get it."

But Tanner smiled.

Recognition dawned on his face.

Snake.

So Jade hadn't finished him after all.

Tanner reached for the phone and dialed immediately, his movements sudden and purposeful. Cole watched him, curiosity replacing fear.

"Hello?" Tanner said when the line connected.

"Tanner, it's—"

"I know who it is," Tanner cut in. "Don't say anything unless I ask you. Where are you?"

"Oxford Avenue and Pratt Street, in Philly," came Snake's strained reply.

"How do you feel?"

"Like someone burned half my insides away," Snake answered, his voice betraying the pain he refused to acknowledge.

Tanner smiled. "I'll be there in thirty minutes. Hang tight— I've got a plan."

The call ended.

Tanner turned to Cole, eyes gleaming. "My adopted son is still alive," he said. "Plans have changed. I'm taking Snake to France with me."

Cole blinked. "And me?"

"You're staying here."

Almost on cue, a car horn beeped outside.

Cole smiled.

For the first time that night, he felt relieved.

Whatever fate awaited Snake and Jade, Cole would keep his beautiful face—untouched by scalpels, shadows, or madness.

CHAPTER 38

"THE REPORT ON the van came back," Brooks said quietly as he crossed the room.

Johnny didn't look up.

He sat motionless behind Brooks's desk, shoulders slumped, a small collection of photographs spread out before him like pieces of a life no longer fitting together. They showed him and April laughing, arguing, kissing—moments frozen in time, untouched by the violence which had ended her story.

From the way Johnny stared at them, it was clear his heart wasn't in this hunt—not because he lacked the will, but because the task felt impossibly large. Finding the men responsible for April's death felt like chasing shadows. Still, there was nothing else he wanted—or *could*—do.

Brooks stopped a few feet away. "The license plate was a false tag. Nothing came back from Philadelphia, New Jersey, or Delaware. Completely clean."

Johnny didn't respond.

His eyes lingered on a photo of April squinting into the sun, her hair blown wild by the wind. He traced her smile with his thumb; barely aware Brooks was still speaking.

"I was also thinking," Brooks continued, adjusting his glasses, "if this Warner character handed fifty thousand dollars to a teenager like it was pocket change, then he's far wealthier than we think. Which raises a question." He paused. "Why would someone like him risk telling a kid his real name?"

That did it.

Johnny slowly lifted his head, the movement heavy and unsteady, as if he were waking from a brutal hangover—except there was no alcohol to blame. Only grief. He glanced briefly at Nassir, then back at Brooks, who was already watching him closely.

"I was thinking the same thing," Johnny said hoarsely as he pushed himself to his feet.

He looked down at the desk once more, then turned away from the photos.

"Why would Warner give up his real name," Johnny continued, "especially to someone who was so quick to sell me out?"

The fog in his eyes began to clear, replaced by a sharp, dangerous focus. The hunt was back on.

Johnny turned toward Nassir. "Doc—my suit. Is it ready?"

Nassir nodded and pointed toward the metal footlocker against the wall. "Patched up. Reinforced. Good as new."

A faint hum filled the room.

The sound of electricity cracked through the air, bright and alive, as a spiral of yellow light wrapped itself around Johnny's body. In a blink, Johnny's clothing changed into his suit, and he stood before them as Jade.

The room fell silent.

Jade's eyes ignited with a glowing intensity that made Brooks instinctively take a step back.

"I've been meaning to ask you something," Brooks said cautiously. "How do you do that? And...where do your clothes go when you change?"

Jade glanced down at himself, then back at Brooks. "I don't know how I do it. I just know that I can." He shrugged slightly. "And you told me—if I ever figured out a better way to change, I should go for it."

He nodded toward the footlocker.

Brooks hesitated, then walked over and opened it. Inside, neatly hanging on a metal hook, was the outfit Johnny had been wearing moments earlier—untouched, intact.

Brooks stared at it, stunned.

Jade offered a tired, humorless smile. "I'm going to see if I can find anything. Anything at all. Something that leads me to the two men who were working with Snake."

Before Brooks or Nassir could respond, the sound of electricity surged again. Yellow light spiraled outward—and Jade vanished.

***

A sharp snap of displaced air echoed in the night.

Jade reappeared at the highest point of the Ben Franklin Bridge, suspended high above the Delaware River—and immediately began to fall.

"Damn it," he muttered as the wind tore past him.

He righted himself just in time, stabilizing his descent and shifting into flight. The city rushed up to meet him, lights streaking beneath his feet.

"I really need to start paying attention to where I teleport," he said to no one but the night.

Jade flew through the city aimlessly at first, scanning streets, rooftops, alleys—faces blurred together as desperation drove him forward. Every passing figure sparked a brief, irrational hope. Every shadow felt like it might hide an answer. He returned to the park where everything had gone wrong.

The park was quiet now. Too quiet.

Jade hovered low and scanned the ground, searching for anything—a wallet, a dropped weapon, a forgotten clue. There was nothing. Just footprints half-erased by time and weather.

Frustration boiled over.

Jade's body shifted, dissolving into pure energy as he shot straight into the sky, faster and faster, until the city vanished beneath him. He circled the planet in a blur of light, fury driving him beyond reason.

If I go fast enough...

He clenched his fists.

I saw it in a movie once.

He pushed harder, hoping—praying—that time itself would bend.

It didn't.

Jade screamed into the void and tore open a series of abysmal portals, diving through one after another, each leap fueled by blind hope.

None of them took him back.

Each attempt failed.

Eventually, exhausted and defeated, Jade slowed and landed on a nearby rooftop. He dropped to one knee, breathing hard— not from exertion, but from the weight of reality crashing down on him.

April was gone.

No amount of speed, power, or rage could change that. Maybe Sorrie's last words to him made him believe otherwise.

He closed his eyes, realizing how badly his anger had clouded his judgment. This wasn't helping. This wasn't what she would have wanted.

"I'm sorry," he whispered into the empty night.

For the last time that evening, the sound of electricity crackled around him. Yellow light spiraled outward around him.

And Jade vanished—returning home, carrying grief heavier than any enemy he had yet faced.

CHAPTER 39

AFTER SECURING HIS ally a fresh change of clothes, Tanner wasted no time.

Within hours, he and Snake were airborne, crossing the Atlantic in a private jet bound for Paris, France, where a very specific kind of doctor awaited them. The kind who asked no questions, accepted untraceable payments, and understood that discretion was more valuable than credentials.

Doctor Girard Shremmer was not merely a physician by profession. He was an anomaly—renowned, feared, and quietly purchased. His expertise spanned molecular biology, histology, nuclear physics, and biochemistry, a résumé so dense it bordered on absurd. He was also, according to Tanner's dry internal assessment, fully capable of tying his own shoes—an achievement Tanner privately considered optional in most academics.

Shremmer flicked off his penlight and stepped back from Snake, his brow furrowed.

He had been peering into Snake's eyes for several long seconds, searching for signs of trauma, disease, *anything* that would justify the urgency of this visit. He found none.

"How do you feel, monsieur?" the doctor asked at last, his French accent clipped but polite.

The office itself was immaculate—too immaculate. Bright white walls, antiseptic to the point of sterility, and a wide window overlooking the Paris skyline. The examination table Snake sat on gleamed unnaturally clean, its paper covering untouched. Still, Snake found it preferable to the alternative, his shallow grave he climbed out of.

"Never felt better," Snake replied, flashing a grin that held no warmth. "The pain in my side's gone. The headaches aren't as bad either. Still come though." His eyes darkened slightly. "And when they do... they make me crazy."

The doctor took a cautious step backward.

He turned toward Tanner, lowering his voice as if Snake weren't sitting ten feet away. "Why is zis man here?" Shremmer asked bluntly. "I do not see anyzing wrong wiz him."

Tanner glanced at Snake, amused. "You hear that? The good doctor says you're perfectly fine." He folded his arms. "Care to tell him otherwise?"

Snake slowly turned his head and fixed Shremmer with an unblinking stare.

"Every time I use my powers," he began calmly, "I get those headaches I told you about. If I push too long, I start losing myself." His smile crept back, thin and unsettling. "I border on insanity."

Shremmer swallowed.

"During the day," Snake continued, "I'm stronger. Faster. I can do just about anything that glowing freak Jade can do. But at night..." His jaw tightened. "I get weaker. Slower. I can't fight him as well as I should be able to."

Tanner stepped in smoothly. "So you see, Doctor, we have a dilemma. And I know you can—*and will*—help us."

Shremmer hesitated, then moved toward a metal tray. He snapped on a pair of latex gloves and prepared a syringe with practiced efficiency. Drawing blood was routine. Comforting, even.

He approached Snake, tied a tourniquet around his upper arm, palpated a vein, swabbed the area with alcohol—

—and the needle bent the moment it touched Snake's skin.

Metal curled uselessly.

Shremmer froze.

"Ze needle—" he stammered. "It will not go in!"

Snake chuckled.

Tanner sighed and pinched the bridge of his nose. "Snake," he said patiently, "is there any way you could *allow* the doctor to do his job?"

Snake glanced between them, enjoying the moment. Then he nodded. "Go ahead."

The doctor prepared a second needle, hands trembling now, and tried again.

This time, the needle slid in effortlessly.

Blood flowed immediately.

Shremmer worked quickly, changing vials one by one, his earlier confidence replaced by awe and fear. When he untied the tourniquet and withdrew the needle, he reached for a bandage—only to pause.

The puncture wound had already sealed.

A faint red glow shimmered where the skin had been breached, then vanished entirely.

Shremmer stared up at Snake, face pale.

Snake smiled.

The doctor crumpled the bandage in his fist and turned slowly to Tanner. "I am... finished," he said carefully. "Where may I contact you with ze rezults?"

Tanner stepped closer, his smile gone. "Do I look like someone with time to waste?" he said flatly. "Have your technicians analyze the samples now. We'll wait."

Shremmer blinked. "But zis could take hours—"

"That's fine," Tanner replied, glancing at Snake.

Snake met his gaze, anxiety flickering behind his eyes for just a moment.

They both turned back to the doctor.

"We will wait," Tanner said, his tone leaving no room for negotiation.

Shremmer nodded stiffly and hurried from the room, the door closing behind him with a soft, ominous click.

Snake flexed his fingers.

Somewhere beneath the skin, power stirred.

CHAPTER 40

IT WASN'T SUNNY, but it wasn't dreary either. The weather rested comfortably in between—clear blue skies stretched overhead while a gentle breeze drifted through the air. In the distance, people played, walked, and talked, absorbed in their own routines, unaware of the trio's sudden arrival.

Nassir parked across the street from the football field where Jade had buried Snake. The plan was simple: exhume the body so Brooks and Nassir could examine the structure of Snake's DNA.

The three of them exited the car and entered the small stadium. As soon as they passed through the open gate, Johnny's eyes locked onto a mound of disturbed dirt.

"There it is," Johnny said, already moving faster. "Oh—shit!" His voice jumped with urgency. "He was right here. I shoved him into a portal *right here.*"

Brooks leaned over the hole. A person could have fit inside—barely. It would've been a tight squeeze.

Johnny glanced around, then raised his hands. Crackling electricity formed, wrapped in spirals of yellow light. He fired downward, blasting a larger hole into the ground.

"What the hell?" Brooks snapped, scanning the area nervously. "The last thing we need is attention."

When Johnny stopped, the three of them peered inside. Nothing.

"He's not in there," Johnny said flatly.

"Well," Brooks replied, "it's possible he crawled out."

"I blew a hole through the right side of his abdomen," Johnny shot back. "He shouldn't have been able to do *shit!*"

"Calm down," Brooks said firmly. "Up until now, we assumed Snake's abilities worked exactly like yours. That may not be the case. He's out there—probably learning more about what he can do. Which means you're going to have to find him and stop him."

Johnny clenched his jaw. "I blew a *hole* in him. That's contraindicated with life. And it obviously didn't work."

Nassir crouched and scooped up a handful of dirt. "There's something I don't understand," he said thoughtfully. "If Snake's abilities are similar to Johnny's, then why didn't putting him in a dark environment stop the healing process?"

Brooks nodded slowly. "I think it's time we go back to basics, like I said, that may not be the case."

***

Rachel Madison had always been Doctor Robert Brooks's most trusted employee—which was why she served as his personal assistant. She loved her job. Beyond her administrative duties, Brooks had encouraged her to learn, to observe, to understand the science around her.

Rachel was twenty-eight years old and the mother of an eight-year-old daughter, Michelle, whom she loved more than anything in the world. Because of Michelle, Rachel valued stability above all else. She would never jeopardize her position—especially not when she doubted, she would ever find another employer as kind, sincere, and generous as Doctor Brooks.

Today, Rachel was conducting inventory on Brooks's cultures—a routine but critical process designed to prevent cross-contamination.

After donning the appropriate protective suit, she moved through the clean room, checking refrigeration units against her clipboard. One by one, she examined each culture.

When she opened the third unit, the internal light flicked on. Rachel froze.

Three culture dishes glowed brightly—tiny pools of light resting calmly within their containers.

She lowered herself until her eyes were level with the dishes, staring in disbelief. The light didn't flicker. It didn't spread. It simply *burned*.

Curious, Rachel pressed a small button along the door frame, turning off the refrigerator's internal light.

The cultures continued glowing.

Her breath caught. What are these...*bioluminescent bacteria*, she thought.

What could they mean? I need to tell Doctor Brooks immediately.

When she released the button, the refrigerator light came back on.

Moments later, the glowing dishes dimmed—one by one—until the unit was dark and ordinary once more.

Rachel stood silently, heart racing.

She had just seen something which wasn't supposed to exist.

CHAPTER 41

"YOU'RE TELLING ME," Tanner said slowly as he circled Snake, "that his body gets energy from the sun?"

"The sun, the moon, or any type of light source," the physician replied. "Unless he is somehow capable of producing it himself."

Tanner stopped pacing. "And how is any of this even remotely possible?"

The doctor folded his hands. "It appears your friend has an organelle in the outer cells of his body that functions much like the chloroplasts in plant cells. It absorbs light and converts it into energy." He paused. "The only difference is he is not green."

Tanner resumed walking, absorbing every word as the doctor continued.

"That has been the only reason Jade has been able to defeat you," the doctor added, turning toward Snake.

Snake's expression shifted to curiosity just as Tanner stepped away from the window and joined them.

"What do you mean *has been*?" Tanner asked. "If Jade knows adding light keeps him charged, then he may know things we don't."

"I do not believe so," the doctor replied calmly.

A glint of ambition flashed in Shremmer's blue eyes. Knowledge meant leverage.

Leverage meant money.

"Before I tell you anything further," he said carefully, "I would like you to consider hiring me as his personal physician."

Tanner smiled—thin, dangerous. "How about before you decide not to tell me anything, you consider the possibility I might kill you for trying to haggle with me?"

Snake chortled.

The doctor frowned but pressed on.

"It is obvious," Shremmer said, "that whoever has been helping Jade has not allowed his body to reach its full potential. While exposure to light initially strengthened him, his body would have eventually adapted to darkness—just as Snake's has."

"What are you saying?" Snake asked.

"Yes," Tanner added. "What exactly are you saying?"

"I am saying that when Snake was blasted, the trauma accelerated the mutation already occurring in his body. Light may enhance strength, but once maturation is complete, neither of them will ever run out of power. That is why Snake's body healed itself."

He gestured toward Snake.

"And as long as Jade continues wearing that bright costume, his body's full development may be further delayed."

Tanner smiled and looked at Snake, who returned the expression.

Then Tanner turned back to the doctor. "Shremmer, you've just earned yourself a bonus."

"What about the headaches?" Snake asked.

"I cannot fully explain them," Shremmer replied, "but your body appears to be producing compounds similar to morphine and ketamine."

Snake blinked. "Morphine and ketamine?"

Tanner echoed, "Morphine and ketamine?"

"Powerful painkillers," Shremmer explained. "Though they are not behaving in a typical manner within your system and they seem to be locked within your system as a genetic component."

Tanner pulled out his phone and dialed home. "Thanks Shremmer!"

A pause.

"Marguerite, est-ce que Martin est là?"

He paused, listening.

"Martin—good news. We don't need to do anything drastic. I do need a favor. Contact Mark Stern. Tell him I want the EMFRA suit prototype ready by Monday."

I'll discuss additional modifications when I'm back in the States."

Snake would soon be back in action. He would need something to protect his identity.

Tanner had already decided to install him as a board member of the Philadelphia Chapter of the Trilateral Commission. With Snake at his side, there would be little he couldn't accomplish.

And with what Shremmer had just revealed, Tanner was confident of one thing above all else:

Snake would defeat Jade—once and for all.

CHAPTER 42

A TALL, MEDIUM-BUILT man with dark brown hair streaked with gray strode into the morgue of Chestnut Hill Hospital. His arrival cut sharply through the stillness, interrupting the young coroner who stood over a body, dictating notes into a microcassette recorder as he worked through an autopsy report.

The coroner glanced up, startled, and immediately switched off the recorder.

"Doctor Feinstein," he said, forcing a polite smile. "To what do I owe this unexpected visit?"

Doctor Feinstein crossed the room without answering. He stopped in front of the stainless-steel table and placed a thick folder into the coroner's hands.

"What the hell is this?" Feinstein demanded.

The coroner opened the folder and scanned the first few lines. His expression tightened. Slowly, he looked back up. "That's my report."

"I know that," Feinstein snapped. "What I want to know is why it says you were *unable* to cut into the body to perform a thorough autopsy. What is that supposed to mean? You don't know how to make an incision?"

Without a word, the coroner—Jerry—reached for a small circular bone saw. He leaned over the corpse on the table beside him and powered the blade on, making a clean lateral cut down the leg. When he finished, he switched the saw off and set it back onto the metal surface.

"Yeah," Jerry said calmly, "I know how to make a slice."

He gestured toward the folder.

"But the woman in that file wasn't like this guy—or anyone else I've ever cut. Saying I *couldn't* cut sounded better than explaining that every time I did, the wound healed itself almost immediately. It made the process nearly impossible."

Feinstein stared at him.

"And there's more," Jerry continued. "The authorities said her heart had been removed and replaced. I saw faint scarring over the chest cavity, but nothing that would support an organ extraction. No trauma. No surgical markers. Nothing."

Feinstein looked at him as if he wanted to believe every word—but couldn't allow himself to.

"What about the broken neck?" Feinstein pressed. "You don't need to open a body to determine that. You can tell if the neck was snapped—even if, for some ridiculous reason, you couldn't cut into her."

Jerry shook his head. "There was no evidence her neck had ever been broken. No fractures. No bruising. Nothing." He hesitated. "I couldn't even determine a cause of death."

Feinstein slammed the folder down onto the table. "Dammit, Jerry. What did she die of? Natural causes?" His voice dropped.

"You couldn't take more time? Get a second opinion? *Something*?"

"What was I supposed to do?" Jerry shot back. "The family demanded the body back. They wanted to bury her."

Feinstein exhaled sharply, pacing now. "If the media gets hold of this report, they're going to tear us apart. You have to make your findings match the police report—or we're going to look like a pack of incompetents."

Jerry reached for the microcassette recorder but hesitated before turning it on.

He was young, confident, and far from naïve. Despite his age, Jerry possessed the intelligence and precision of a seasoned physician. His blue eyes, soft blond hair, and athletic build made him an unlikely coroner—one whose profession frightened off most potential admirers. He understood exactly what Feinstein was asking.

And why.

Feinstein turned toward the door, leaving the folder behind. "You're going to have to revise the report," he said over his shoulder. "I'll attach an addendum explaining the delay. Do it that way—or you're going to lose your job."

The door closed behind him.

Jerry stood alone for a moment, staring at the folder.

Then he switched the recorder back on and turned toward the body on the table, his voice steady as he resumed the autopsy—though nothing about that previous case felt steady at all.

CHAPTER 43

THE DOOR TO Brooks's home laboratory slid open, and Johnny stepped inside, immediately spotting Brooks hunched over his computer, fingers flying across the keyboard.

"Where's Doc?" Johnny asked, glancing around the room.

The steady clatter of keys answered him. Johnny's gaze dropped to Brooks's hands as they continued their relentless rhythm.

Without stopping, Brooks glanced up briefly. "He's picking up his wife and kids from the airport."

Johnny nodded. "That's right—they stayed in Florida until just after New Year's." He walked over to an empty chair beside Brooks's desk and dropped into it as if his legs had simply given out. "Must've been hard on him, being away from them that long."

"It's always difficult," Brooks said evenly, "making sacrifices *with* the family for the benefit *of* the family."

Johnny tilted his head. "Is that why you never married?"

Brooks smiled faintly, finally pausing his typing. "That ship sailed for many reasons, Johnny." He met Johnny's eyes for a moment—then turned back to the screen and resumed working.

Johnny leaned back, rubbing his face. "What am I gonna do about Snake?" His voice was tired now, stripped of bravado. "If he crawled out of that hole like nothing ever happened to him, what chance do I have? How do I even start finding him?"

Brooks stopped typing and rotated his chair just enough to face him.

"I know how discouraged you feel," Brooks said gently. "But you *can* beat Snake. He has a weakness—just like you do. We simply haven't found it yet."

"Found it?" Johnny scoffed bitterly. "That's the thing. I thought we *had* found it. And yet—"

"We were wrong," Brooks cut in. "If he survived your blast and escaped total darkness without issue, then we can't assume his powers resemble yours at all. Until we have proper DNA analysis, we can't even assume he's anything like you."

Johnny exhaled sharply, frustration etched across his face.

"I've been reviewing everything you told me about Snake," Brooks continued. "As things stand, you probably won't be able to defeat him head-on. But if you think strategically—if you stay ahead of him—you can survive."

Johnny laughed, humorless. "So what—you're saying I fight him for the rest of my life until one of us finally kills the other?" He shook his head. "There's got to be another way. Something that neutralizes him."

"I agree," Brooks said quickly. "The fact that you were able to damage him at all means something. There may be a common link—something that affects both of you." He hesitated. "I know it's a long shot without comparative data."

Johnny stood and began pacing.

"What if you're right?" he said suddenly. "What if Snake and I are connected somehow?" His voice gained momentum. "The dreams I've been having. The similarities in how our abilities manifest. Maybe Uncle Eric had a kid he never knew about. Hell—Snake even *looks* like him."

He let out a sharp breath. "This is all messed up. If I could take these powers and give them away, I would. In a heartbeat."

"But you can't," Brooks said quietly. "You were chosen to have them. You can choose to walk away—but that isn't who you are. You won't."

Johnny stopped pacing.

His eyes began to glow—bright, volatile yellow.

Brooks watched silently as Johnny turned toward the metal footlocker containing his costume. Electricity crackled along Johnny's arm, yellow light dancing around his hand. A focused beam erupted, welding the locker shut along every seam.

Johnny lowered his arm and faced Brooks again.

"There are too many variables," he said, his voice tight. "I've got a family to think about. I need time. I need to figure some things out."

The sound of crackling electricity along with the spiraling yellow light began to dance around him.

"Johnny, wait—" Brooks started.

Johnny vanished before Brooks could finish the sentence. The room fell silent.

Brooks stared at the sealed locker, then sighed heavily.

"You didn't have to seal the locker," he muttered to himself.

Chapter 44

AT BIOTECH LABS Tanner and Cole stood on the spotless white tiles of Conference Room Three, the sterility of the place at odds with the criminal ambitions that had brought them there. Fluorescent lights hummed faintly overhead as they waited for Mark Stern to arrive.

Their conversation drifted back to France.

Tanner filled Cole in on everything Shremmer had revealed—every unsettling detail about Snake's evolving abilities, the implications of his power, and the possible ways that knowledge could be exploited. The more Tanner talked, the more focused Cole became. France had changed the game, and both men knew it.

The door slid open.

Biotech's top scientist entered the room holding an Erlenmeyer flask low at his side, as if it were an afterthought rather than something volatile. Doctor Mark Stern was a small, unimposing man—maybe five foot nine on a good day. His blond hair hung in stringy curtains parted neatly down the middle, brushing the sides of his narrow face. Thin, gold-framed glasses perched on his nose, magnifying sharp, restless eyes. Beneath his white lab coat, his clothes were baggy and ill-fitting, lending him a perpetually disheveled look.

Stern cleared his throat.

"Ahem. Excuse me, gentlemen," he said politely, already smiling. "But I would like to introduce you to the new and improved—Snake."

He gestured back toward the door he'd just come through.

Snake stepped into the room looking exactly as Tanner remembered him: blue jeans, a plain sweater, and a pair of scuffed Lugz boots. Nothing about him suggested improvement—at least not yet.

Tanner frowned. "What the hell is this?"

Stern glanced at Snake, confidence etched into his grin. "It's his new costume."

Tanner bristled. "Stern, don't—"

"Show him," Stern interrupted calmly.

At the cue, a red glow flared around Snake's body. The light pulsed once, then twice, and his clothes began to liquefy, melting into a silvery, mercury-like substance that flowed over his skin. The liquid surged upward, coating his hands, crawling across his chest, and sealing over his face like living metal.

As the substance settled, it hardened and reshaped itself.

When the morphing was complete, the six-foot-two, two-hundred-pound man standing before them wore a full black bodysuit. A crimson-red snake ascended the right side of his leg, coiling upward around his torso in a tight, predatory wrap. Its head rested over his left shoulder, mouth open in a frozen strike. His left arm was short-sleeved, revealing chestnut-brown skin, while both hands were encased in sleek red leather gloves. The mask concealed his entire face, its eyes marked by glowing red, diamond-shaped patterns.

Crimson boots completed the ensemble, their polished finish perfectly complementing the suit.

"Whatta ya think?" Snake asked.

Tanner stared, then slowly smiled. "Dangerous," he said, clearly impressed.

He turned to Stern, curiosity replacing his earlier irritation. "How'd he do... *that*... with the liquid?" Tanner asked, gesturing toward Snake.

Stern lifted the flask he'd been holding. "This is the prototype of an experimental synthetic fluid," he explained. "It's based on the same compound we used for the bank robbery masks and related applications." He extended the flask toward Tanner. "Go on. Touch it."

Tanner hesitated, then dipped his hand inside. "Feels like some kind of gel," he said.

"Wait a few seconds." Stern suggested.

The substance clinging to Tanner's fingers stiffened, unraveling into thousands of tiny fibers until it became a patch of flexible cloth.

"This is similar to the masks I designed for your crew," Stern said. "Minus the solar deconstruction components of course."

"This alone is incredible," Tanner admitted, showing it to Cole. "But how did you get it to respond like that to *him*?" He stepped closer to Snake, inspecting the suit.

"Embedded in the fluid are programmable nanites. I designed the fluid to be programmable in its conglomerate state," Stern replied. "After extensive testing of Snake's abilities, I modified the formula so it would respond specifically to his energy signature—and his telepathy. As long as he remains within fifty feet of the fluid, he maintains full control. His body also charges the fluid as well as the nanites."

Stern turned toward Snake. "Show them how the suit comes off."

The costume shimmered, then reverted to liquid, peeling away from Snake's body in smooth streams until it pooled onto the floor in a gleaming silver puddle.

Cole couldn't help but stare. Snake now stood wearing nothing but a pair of boxers, his muscular, brawny frame fully exposed. Cole himself aspired to be so brawny.

Tanner shook his head in disbelief. "Son, what possessed you to come up with something like this?"

Stern smiled, clearly pleased. "When you asked my team to develop flame-resistant bodysuits, I thought perhaps I could offer you something far more... useful."

As if on cue, the liquid surged upward again, crawling back onto Snake's body and reshaping itself into his street clothes.

Tanner placed a heavy hand on Stern's shoulder. "Good answer," he said. Then, with a grin, added, "So what else have I been paying you to do off the books?"

Stern's smile widened.

"I'm very glad you're ready to see my other projects."

CHAPTER 45

JOHNNY WALKED INTO his Aunt Paula's house just as she was beginning to prepare dinner.

When she heard the front door close, Pauline stepped out of the kitchen and spotted him hanging up his jacket. "Hey, baby," she said, greeting him with a kiss on the cheek. She immediately noticed the sadness on his face and placed a hand on his forehead.

"Johnny, are you okay?"

"I don't know, Aunt Paula," he replied, sinking onto the sofa and looking up at her.

His mind felt like Swiss cheese—full of holes punched through by the events which have been changing his life over the past few months. As he looked at his aunt, questions spiraled through his head.

What secrets does she have? Can she do some of the things I can, but chooses not to use her gifts? Is she really my mother? Was the story of my mother's death fabricated along with the pictures on the wall?

No. Uncle Eric and Tanya are real. But will Tanya develop the same abilities I have?

Johnny hoped she wouldn't. He didn't want her to ever go through the ordeal he was facing now.

"Does Uncle Eric have any kids?" Johnny asked.

"If he does," Pauline chuckled, "he'd have a lot of 'splainin' to do, seeing as how I missed out on any more nieces or nephews!"

Johnny shifted, then redirected the conversation. "Did my mother really die in the hospital while giving birth to me?"

Pauline turned away as a tear slipped from her eye.

"Well, Aunt Paula," Johnny pressed, anger creeping into his voice, "were you tellin' me the truth or not?"

Pauline spun around sharply and raised a finger in his face. "Don't you dare take that tone with me, young man. I'm still your aunt, and I will put you over my knee just as fast now as I did when you were five."

Johnny lowered his gaze. "Sorry."

"I told you the truth," Pauline said firmly. "Your mother died in the hospital while giving birth to you."

Johnny looked up, guilt twisting in his stomach. He started to speak, but Pauline raised her hand, signaling him to stop.

"There are things I didn't tell you," she continued softly. "Things you deserve to know."

She sat beside him on the sofa. "Your mother—Lee Anne— and my father had a terrible argument about two years before you were born. She ran away from home. Since she was only seventeen, my dad had to call the police. Lee Anne stayed gone for fourteen months. We never heard from her—no postcards, no phone calls. Nothing. We assumed the worst."

Pauline stared down at the floor. "Then one day, she came home. We were all so ecstatic. She was sweet, kind—especially to Dad. It was like nothing had ever happened."

"The fight between her and Pop Pop?" Johnny asked.

"We never brought it up again," Pauline replied. "I can't even remember what it was about."

Another tear slipped down her cheek.

"About three weeks after she came home, Lee Anne started talking about being abducted by aliens—beings made of light. She said she'd fallen in love with one of them." Pauline shook her head. "Every time she tried to tell the story, people would cut her off out of disbelief. Me included."

Johnny wiped a tear from his eye as he listened.

"Dad thought she needed psychiatric help," Pauline continued. "He had her committed to Norristown State Hospital. After an evaluation, they transferred her to Byberry State Hospital. Dad fought like hell to get her out, but once she was court-committed, there was nothing he could do."

She paused, swallowing hard.

"Then he found out she was pregnant. Dad tried everything to get her to tell him who the father was, but she kept saying a name none of us could understand. When she insisted the father was from another planet, both the psychiatrist and her OB-GYN demanded she stay committed. The only thing the hospital did right was keep her off psych meds."

"Then what happened?" Johnny asked quietly.

"The day you were born, we were notified your mother had died during childbirth. Dad was too grief-stricken to go, so Mom and I went to identify her and bring you home." Pauline looked at him through tears. "I should've told you all of this a long time ago."

"And I was the only child?" Johnny asked.

"Lee Anne believed she was having twins," Pauline said. "But as far as we were told, you were the only child."

Johnny stood slowly. "Aunt Paula, there's something I think you should see."

"What?" she asked, wiping her eyes.

"You'll see," Johnny said, glancing toward the kitchen. "Where's Tanya?"

"With her father, I don't expect her back for another hour. Why?"

With the sound of the crackle of electricity and a spiraling burst of yellow light which circled him, Johnny's clothes transformed into his costume right before her eyes.

His eyes began to glow.

Pauline screamed and recoiled into the sofa, staring at Jade in disbelief.

"Wait—Aunt Paula, sh—" Jade whispered urgently, peeking toward the window to make sure no one had heard her scream.

Pauline covered her mouth. "I'm sorry," she said shakily.

"It's okay," Johnny said gently. "It's still me. Just... try not to scream when I show you this."

Jade then shifted into his energy form, bright yellow.

"Oh my God," Pauline whispered.

Johnny now matched the description Lee Anne had given years ago—his body blazing as if made entirely of light.

Pauline slowly reached out and touched his arm, her fingers moving through the glowing energy like legs kicking in water.

She smiled. "Feels like tingly Jell-O."

Jade dimmed and reverted back to Johnny via the sound of electricity crackling as yellow light spiraled around him.

Johnny sat beside her.

"How long have you been able to do... that?" Pauline asked nervously.

"Since around my last birthday," Johnny said. He took her hand. "I've been pretending to be someone's superhero while walking around scared outta my mind. I lost April because someone discovered my identity. And this Snake guy—he's giving me hell."

Pauline's eyes widened. "Johnny...that Snake—could he be your brother?"

Johnny shook his head. "I don't care about that. He killed April."

Pauline placed her hand over his and nodded her understanding. "Johnny, you can't blame yourself for everything that goes wrong. Bad people existed long before you—and they'll be here long after you're gone. No matter what planet your family tree comes from, you're human first. And humans make mistakes. That's how we learn."

She squeezed his hand.

"April would tell you to stop focusing on what's going wrong and look at what's going right. If you've got a job to do, then do it. Things will get better."

Johnny smiled and hugged her.

"I think you're a pretty good superhero," Pauline said warmly. "And knowing it's my nephew out there doing all that good? That makes me very proud."

Johnny kissed her cheek. "My secret's safe with you?"

She laughed. "Like I'm gonna tell people my nephew's Jade—you done bumped your head."

Johnny laughed as he grabbed his jacket. "And as the hero of this city, I promise I'll clean up its garbage problem!"

Pauline smiled. "You've got my vote!"

With the sound of crackling electricity along with a spiral of yellow light dancing around him, Johnny vanished.

Chapter 46

RICHARD DALTON WAS usually a man of few words—especially since the day Tanner had clipped him upside the head—but today, he had found his voice.

The pleasantly plump man, his chestnut-brown hair retreating steadily from a once-proud hairline, stood red-faced and indignant as he spoke. Years of silence had finally boiled over, and for the first time in a long while, Richard Dalton had plenty to say.

He would soon learn the true cost of free speech.

Inside the boardroom, members of the Philadelphia chapter of the Trilateral Commission sat around the long mahogany table as tempers flared.

"We can no longer have Steven Tanner representing us," Richard barked. "Working with us. Tied to us in any way. It was bad enough when he suggested blowing up a bank just to get Jade's attention—but now things are completely out of control!"

"If you had a problem with his methods," Katherine O'Mally said coolly, "you should have said something before everything started."

Richard turned on her. "Don't tell me you don't think innocent people getting hurt is wrong."

Katherine folded her arms. "As long as Tanner was keeping us rich, you never complained."

"Well, now there are too many people getting hurt!"

"That's bullshit, Richard," she snapped. "Far more people were getting hurt when this chapter first began. Tanner built this operation, and I'm not voting him out."

The boardroom doors opened.

Tanner entered first, calm and unhurried. At his side walked Snake, dressed in an immaculate black Brooks Brothers three-piece suit, followed by Martin Cole, whose confident smile never wavered.

They had heard enough.

"Who wants to vote me out?" Tanner asked.

Katherine didn't hesitate. She nodded toward Richard. "He does."

Tanner approached Richard slowly, every step measured.

"After everything I've done for you," Tanner said quietly, "you want me gone? From the chapter I built?"

Richard swallowed hard. The bravado he'd displayed moments earlier drained from his face. His eyes darted nervously, his voice faltering.

"Tanner, I—"

"—am finished!" Tanner interrupted. "You think you've made enough money, so now it's time to cut me loose? Dump me somewhere in the middle of the ocean with a bunch of hungry sharks and pretend I never existed?"

Richard stared at him, confused and terrified.

"Perfect timing," Tanner said pleasantly. "Snake."

Every eye in the room shifted to the only Black man present.

Snake stepped forward, commanding attention without trying.

He was keenly aware of the stares, the whispers, the unspoken rules of the room—but he didn't acknowledge any of it. To him, they were irrelevant.

Tanner tilted his head toward Richard. "Take this garbage out."

"My pleasure," Snake replied.

As he reached Richard, his business suit liquefied into shimmering silver, then reshaped itself into his black-and-red costume.

The room erupted in gasps.

Richard screamed as Snake seized him.

The sound of crackling electricity filled the air. A spiral of red light enveloped them both—and then they were gone.

Tanner turned back to the table. "Is there anyone else who'd like me removed?"

Silence answered him.

"Good." Tanner pressed the intercom. "Linda, call Richard Dalton's home and ask if he's still coming to the meeting. If there's no answer, leave a message on the answering machine."

"Yes, Mr. Tanner."

Tanner released the button.

"Before we continue," he said, "the gentleman who just departed with Richard is now one of our investments. His name is Michael Jones, and he is an equal member of this chapter. He'll be receiving Richard's current and future earnings."

Murmurs rippled through the room.

"No one loses except Richard," Tanner added. "If anyone objects, you may take it up with Mister Jones—but I wouldn't recommend it. He's efficient. And he has a bit of a temper."

He smiled. "But he's worth every penny."

*Michael Jones...*The name nagged at Katherine's thoughts. *Why does that sound familiar?*

***

High above the Pacific Ocean, Snake and Richard reappeared with a sharp sounding snap.

They were falling.

Snake intended to dispose of Richard where no one would ever find him.

In the open ocean, death came quickly—or painfully. Sharks, whales, things far worse in the depths. If Richard was lucky, he'd drown before anything noticed him.

"PLEASE!" Richard screamed over the rushing wind. "I'LL PAY YOU WHATEVER TANNER'S PAYING YOU!"

Snake looked down at him, unmoved. "IT AINT ABOUT THE MONEY!"

The water rushed up fast.

Snake released him.

Richard hit the ocean hard and vanished beneath the waves.

Snake slowed his descent, grabbed his forehead as the headaches started to show up. He took a deep breath, then turned back towards the United States, specifically, Philadelphia—already moving on.

CHAPTER 47

"WHAT DO YOU mean he quit?" Nassir asked, his voice tight with frustration.

"He just did," Brooks replied, pushing himself up from his chair and pacing. "He sealed the locker shut, disappeared before I could talk him out of it, and I haven't seen him since. It's only been a day—I'm sure he'll come around."

Before Nassir could respond, a soft *snap* echoed through the room and Johnny materialized between the two physicians.

"Johnny!" Nassir exclaimed. "I'm glad you're back."

Johnny smiled at him, then turned to Brooks. Brooks returned the smile—subtle, but relieved.

"I'm sorry I acted the way I did," Johnny said. "When you asked me to help fight crime in Philly, I wanted to. I felt like that's what I was made for. I can't really explain it, but after April died... I wanted to quit. I just couldn't."

He placed a hand on Brooks' shoulder, glanced at Nassir, then back again.

"Truth is, over the past few months, you two stopped feeling like my doctor and my employer. You became family. These abilities would've come whether I was ready or not, and I don't know how I would've made it this far without either of you."

"Oh, Johnny," Nassir said, stepping forward and pulling them into a tight, emotional group hug.

Johnny laughed softly, eyes wet, as they pulled apart.

"I've been talking with my aunt," Johnny continued. "I learned some things about my mother's past—things that might explain my powers and my connection to Snake."

"Relative?" Nassir asked.

"Brother," Johnny said.

"I *knew* it!" Brooks blurted.

"Not definite but quite possibly!" Johnny shook his head in the negative. "It changes nothing. Family or not, I've got a score to settle. I plan on avenging April's death—with or without your help. So what'll it be?"

Both men nodded without hesitation.

"Good," Johnny said. "Let's catch ourselves a Snake."

"Johnny," Brooks said, "you sealed the locker with your suits in it."

Johnny smiled.

Crackling electricity filled the air as spiraling yellow light enveloped him, transforming him into Jade right before Brooks' eyes. His eyes ignited with a familiar glow.

"Since when did that matter?" Jade asked.

Nassir chuckled.

Brooks huffed. "Oh yeah."

"Johnny," Nassir said, "I'm turning on the transmitter. Keep us updated. We'll monitor media coverage, but we want your firsthand account. We might be able to guide you."

"You got it, Doc," Jade replied. With the sound of crackling electricity along with the spiraling yellow light which danced around him, he vanished.

***

Jade reappeared high above Roosevelt Boulevard near Friends Hospital—falling fast.

He slowed, then hovered, scanning the city below. Car horns blared as drivers spotted him waving and calling out.

Jade turned southwest toward Center City.

"Doc?"

"I hear you, Johnny," Nassir replied.

"I've got a feeling I should head downtown."

"Alright. Keep us posted."

Jade accelerated toward Center City Philadelphia.

CHAPTER 48

SNAKE RETURNED TO the city and touched down on the dock at Penn's Landing, his boots striking wood with a hollow thud which echoed across the waterfront.

People noticed immediately.

Whispers spread, then shouts. Cameras came out. A small crowd rushed toward him, excitement rippling through the air as some mistook him for a new kind of hero.

Snake didn't wait to correct them.

The sound of crackling electricity burst around his body as a spiral of red light engulfed him. He vanished—leaving behind only stunned faces and unanswered questions.

***

Snake reappeared inside the boardroom of the Trilateral Commission.

The room was quieter now. Most of the members were gone. Only Tanner, Cole, and a red-haired woman Snake had never seen before remained.

The woman stepped forward and extended her hand—but startled slightly as Snake's costume liquefied into shimmering silver and flowed away, reforming him into his civilian appearance, still wearing the suit he entered the board room with earlier.

"How you doin', stranger?" she asked, recovering quickly.

Snake shook her hand. "Mike Jones," he said. "Most folks call me Snake."

"No," Tanner corrected without looking up, "around here we'll call you Michael."

The woman smiled. "Katherine O'Mally. Everyone calls me Kat." Her eyes narrowed slightly. "Michael... your name sounds familiar. Have we met before?"

Michael chuckled. "Doubt it. I'm from Pittsburgh. If we crossed paths there, I was probably under fourteen."

"Pittsburgh?" Kat asked. "Your parents still there?"

"They're dead," he replied evenly. "Just my grandmother."

He turned toward Tanner, who stood near the window overlooking the city. "Trash discarded."

Kat watched him closely. *That name...* she thought again. *Why does it sound so familiar?*

"Michael," Tanner began, "to bring you up to speed—besides your new role with us—the board agreed to funnel additional funding to Mark Stern at Biotech Labs. We want to accelerate some of his more interesting pro—"

The silver liquid surged back over Michael's body, cutting Tanner off mid-sentence as Snake reclaimed his costume.

"What's wrong?" Tanner asked.

Snake didn't answer him. His glowing eyes apparent through the diamond patches were fixed on the city beyond the glass.

"I've gotta go play with an old friend," he said, his voice low and venomous.

Tanner and Cole turned just in time to see Jade streaking through the sky in the distance.

With the sound of crackling electricity along with the spiraling red light, Snake vanished.

CHAPTER 49

With the sun hidden behind fast-moving clouds and a steady wind cutting through the air, Jade descended toward Penn's Landing. Though he knew he was drawing attention, he ignored the onlookers and focused instead on the tightening sensation in his chest.

He *felt* Snake.

Jade scanned left, then right—

And there he was.

Snake walked toward him calmly, wearing the same torn outfit he'd had on at the football field—the shirt still ripped where Jade had shoved him through a portal. He pressed a hand over the hole as he approached.

"Lookin' for me, bubby?" Snake asked.

Jade glanced at the torn fabric splattered with dry blood. The wound beneath it had healed, though Snake still guarded the spot.

"You might as well give up," Jade said. "Even if you crawled out of that hole, you don't seem like you were able to fully heal. You won't last long."

Snake looked down at his shirt, then back up and smiled. "You're right."

His clothes liquefied into silver and reformed into his costume right before Jade's eyes.

"How's this?"

Jade's surprise lasted a heartbeat too long.

Snake rocketed upward and slammed into him, launching Jade nearly a thousand feet over the water. Screams erupted from the dock below.

Jade recovered quickly and charged back—but just before they collided, he tore open a portal with the familiar zipper-like sound and vanished through it.

Snake slowed, turned—

—and caught Jade's boot square in the face.

The impact sent Snake spinning end over end through the air. Jade hovered, waiting.

Snake regained control and locked eyes with him.

Jade turned and flew toward Center City.

Snake followed.

"I found him—or he found me," Jade said into the transmitter. "I'm pulling him away from people."

"Be careful, Johnny," Nassir warned. "We don't know what else he's capable of."

"Don't worry, Doc. I got this."

As Jade zipped past Twelfth and Market, he glanced back—and cursed.

Snake had stopped.

He stood casually on the street below, arms folded, as a crowd gathered around him, mistaking him for a new hero.

"Aw, shit," Jade muttered, slowing.

"What's wrong?" Nassir asked.

"He stopped. He's drawing attention."

"Maybe he'll follow if you keep moving."

"No," Jade said grimly. "He wants me to come back."

And he did.

Jade descended.

"Look at 'em," Snake laughed as the crowd cheered. "They adore me."

"Don't do this," Jade warned.

"Don't do what?" Snake mocked—then suddenly clutched his head, staggering as pain surged through him.

Jade hesitated.

Snake grinned through it. "You mean don't attract attention? Too late. Or don't do *this*—"

He grabbed a bystander.

Jade rushed forward—but Snake's uppercut as he let go of the bystander caught him midair, sending him skidding across the street as the crowd scattered screaming.

Snake shot straight up two hundred feet.

"Damn it," Jade snapped, climbing to his feet. "He almost killed someone again," Jade said into the transmitter. "I'm ending this."

A zipper sounding portal ripped open.

Jade launched through it.

Snake, still laughing, flew upward—until Jade burst out of a zipper sounding portal and collided with him head-on.

They plummeted together and slammed into Market Street, leaving a crater.

Jade grabbed Snake.

The sound of electricity crackled.

The yellow light spiraled around them both.

They vanished.

***

They reappeared a thousand feet above Lincoln Drive, near a police station—mostly unnoticed.

Jade's costume dimmed suddenly.

They began to fall.

Snake's mask quickly liquified and melted away to his neck, panic flashing across his face. "Let me go!"

"No," Jade said.

Snake elbowed Jade hard and then kicked away from him.

Jade lost his grip.

Snake flew upward as Jade crashed to the street below.

A car screamed toward him.

At the last second, the sound of crackling electricity along with the spiral of yellow light circled Jade and he vanished.

The car missed him by inches.

***

With a light snapping sound, Jade reappeared on the side of the road as painless bullets of rain struck him from above.

"Great," Jade muttered as he started walking, his costume lighting back up. "Another addition to an already perfect day."

"What's happening now?" Nassir asked through the transmitter.

"We ended up at Lincoln Drive. It's cold, it's raining. Why didn't you make this thing with a heater or something?"

"I'll keep it in mind next time," Brooks replied.

"Well, there might not be a next time. Check this out—I think I discovered Snake's Achilles' heel."

"Johnny, that's great, now you c—"

"Unfortunately, it's mine too," Jade interrupted.

"What do you mean?" Nassir asked.

"If we hold onto each other for too long, our powers get dampened."

"Then there's a common thread between the two of you," Nassir added.

"I'm not even gettin' into all that," Jade said as he lifted off, flying along the drive. His illuminated costume left a streak of green and gold light behind him. "I just want to put an end to—"

Jade's words were cut short by a sneak attack from Snake. The missile-like blow hurled him into a nearby wooded trail.

Jade crashed into a tree and dropped hard onto the muddy ground. A deer bolted away. He pushed himself up, scanning the area, but Snake was nowhere to be seen.

"Doc, I'm takin' off my costume," Jade said as crackling electricity and small spirals of light stripped the mud from him.

"Why?" Nassir asked.

With the sound of crackling electricity followed by the bright spiraling yellow light, Jade's costume changed back into his clothing.

Johnny continued moving through the woods. "Because he can see me when my costume's lit," he said. "I can hide better in the dark without it. It's only fair—"

He stopped short.

The realization hit him—the transmitter was in the costume.

"Damn. Now I can't talk to—"

"Johnny..." Snake's voice came from behind him.

Johnny turned slowly, contempt burning in his eyes. Snake grabbed his hand.

"What's wrong, Johnny?" Snake asked. "Feeling a little weak?"

Johnny yanked his hand free.

"I'll tell you what," Snake said. "I'll take my costume off—level the odds."

The suit liquefied into silver metal and changed into blue jeans and a white T-shirt stretched tightly over his chiseled torso. The rain immediately began soaking the fabric.

"You like that, dontcha?"

Johnny's expression darkened as he saw the face of the man who had viciously murdered April. He felt a fleeting sense of familiarity in Snake's slanted eyes—but his rage smothered it instantly. He ignored the obvious pain behind Snake's gaze.

"I like the rain," Snake said. "It can bring life or bring death—depends on its mood."

"I'm not a big fan," Johnny replied, looking him up and down. "So what are you waitin' for? We doin' this?"

Snake laughed malevolently. "Hell yeah. I mean—we could. But I've been thinkin' about our little clashes. Don't you see? You and me—we're more than everyone else on this planet. Together, we could rule the world if we wanted to."

"Nigga, you done bumped your head," Johnny snapped. "You murdered my girlfriend."

"You gonna hold that against me forever?" Snake shrugged. "So I made one itty-bitty mistake. You can always get another one."

Snake smiled.

Johnny's eyes burned. "You're so fucked up in the head, I'm startin' to think you're not worth my time."

Snake raised his middle finger. "Fuck you."

"Oh—how original," Johnny said coldly. "You know, you're the one that's fucked. Because I *am* going to kill you. Believe it or not."

Snake's eyes filled with rage. "Your call."

The sound of crackling electricity followed by the spiraling red light quickly engulfed him—and he vanished.

Johnny scanned the rain-soaked darkness. Then he saw it: a fast-approaching red glow cutting through the downpour.

Snake slammed into him from nowhere, launching Jade into another tree. Johnny's head struck the trunk and snapped forward. His eyes closed.

Snake stood over the unconscious body, sneering.

"You fuckin' idiot," he muttered. "Can't use your powers against me if you're asleep, baby boy."

Snake's clothing morphed back into the silver liquid and then his costume.

He grabbed Johnny and quickly produced the sound of crackling electricity along with the spiral of red light.

They both vanished.

***

With the sound a light snap, Snake and Johnny reappeared atop the Empire State Building. The rain was gone, replaced by bitter, cutting wind.

Johnny began to regain consciousness as Snake blasted a hole through the fence overlooking 34th Street—Johnny still clutched in his arms.

The sound of crackling electricity flared. A spiral of yellow light restored Johnny's costume.

Snake, distracted by a pounding headache and his task at hand, didn't notice.

Snake stepped onto the ledge and looked down.

"Doc, are you there?" Jade asked.

"Oh—you're awake, light show?" Snake sneered. "Who you talkin' to?"

"Yes, Johnny, I'm here," Nassir replied. "Are you okay?"

"No. Not really," Johnny said. "Is that Dyneema rope still in the lab?"

***

"Yes—it's here," Nassir said, glancing toward the corner.

The sound of crackling electricity along with the spiral of yellow light danced around the rope.

The rope vanished.

***

With the sound of a light snap, the rope appeared in Jade's hand as Snake watched with cruel curiosity.

Snake's mask changed into the silver liquid and melted away. "You got an invisible friend handin' you rope, light show?"

Jade moved fast. The sound of crackling electricity along with the spiraling yellow light influenced the rope to wrap tightly around both of them. It knotted.

243

"Bet you haven't practiced your telepathy like I have," Jade said. "Judging from the looks of things, you also figured out what weakens us, and maybe your plan was to kill me, but now, we can die...together!"

The grin slid off Snake's face.

As Jade's costume dimmed with the two of them bound together on the ledge, he propelled them outward—twenty feet away from the ledge and downward.

They started their descent.

Powerless. Defenseless.

Time stretched. Fear filled Snake's eyes as Johnny closed his own—and smiled.

"Like I said, Doc," Jade said calmly. "Both of our Achilles' heels."

***

Back in the lab, Nassir shook his head as tears streamed down his face.

Brooks stood silently beside him. *There has to be another way*, Nassir thought. But he knew Johnny couldn't hear him. And even if he could—Johnny would already have a thousand reasons why this was the only choice.

***

They felt every second of the twelve-hundred-foot descent. Air forced its way violently into their lungs, but both remained conscious.

A split second before impact, Jade was snatched away in a burst of blinding light.

Snake—still powerless—hit the street below.

A woman screamed.

A crowd rushed forward as a patrol car screeched to a stop, sirens wailing.

Snake lay motionless, bloodied, maskless.

He did not move.

CHAPTER 50

SILENCE FILLED THE lab at Brooks' home.

The hum of equipment—normally comforting—now felt intrusive, almost disrespectful. Brooks stood motionless near the workstation, his shoulders slumped, his hands clenched into tight fists at his sides. His eyes, glassy with uncertainty, drifted toward Nassir.

Nassir swallowed hard and reached for the television remote. His expression was hollow as he clicked the set on, hoping—desperately—for answers. Or perhaps hoping for proof that this was all a mistake.

A commercial.

Nothing yet.

The room felt smaller, tighter, as if the walls themselves were closing in.

Both men were grieving in silence over the loss of Johnny Thompkins—*Jade*. They had heard everything through the transmitter. Every word. Every warning. Every terrible second.

And still, neither of them could accept it.

This can't be how it ends, Nassir thought. *Not for him.*

Clinging to that fragile hope, Nassir reached for the desktop transmitter, his fingers trembling as he pressed the activation switch.

"Johnny," he said quietly at first. Then louder. "Johnny—Johnny, please answer me."

Only static replied.

Brooks turned toward him, his face crumpling as a single tear slipped down his cheek. He didn't wipe it away. He didn't have the strength. At that moment, the television cut away from the commercial.

A red banner flashed across the screen.

BREAKING NEWS.

The anchor's voice was grave.

"This just in—authorities report that a man believed to be a dangerous outlaw from Philadelphia fell from the top of the Empire State Building in New York just moments ago."

Brooks' breath caught.

"The description of the man matches that of an individual who had been wreaking havoc in Center City Philadelphia earlier today."

Nassir slowly lowered the transmitter, his knuckles white.

"The man also fits the description of the mysterious figure seen throughout the Philadelphia region engaging in multiple confrontations with Jade—the emerging hero who has been credited with stopping violent crimes across the Eastern States."

Brooks' knees felt weak. He reached for the edge of the desk to steady himself.

"At this time, authorities do not know why the man fell from the skyscraper, nor do they have information regarding the second individual witnesses claim was present with him at the top of the building."

The anchor continued speaking, but the words blurred together, losing meaning.

The room went quiet again—except for the muted sound of the broadcast and Nassir's shallow breathing.

Slowly, Brooks turned to Nassir.

Nassir met his gaze.

No words were needed.

In perfect unison, they moved.

They grabbed their coats from the rack by the door, hands moving on instinct alone. Whatever doubt still lingered, whatever hope remained, it no longer mattered.

Johnny was out there.

And if there was even the slightest chance, he was still alive—

They weren't staying behind.

The lab door swung open, spilling cold night air inside, and the two men disappeared into it without looking back.

CHAPTER 51

JOHNNY WAS LYING in bed as he woke up to the ringing of the telephone. As soon as he jumped up to answer the telephone, the ringing stopped. Johnny rubbed his eyes as he then heard a loud pounding at the door.

Damn, that was a messed-up nightmare, he thought.

Johnny then got up and headed for the door as he looked at the time on his clock. It was eight thirty-four A.M. "What?" he asked out loud and to himself.

The loud pounding at the door started again.

"WHO IS IT?" Johnny asked angrily.

"It's Robert and Ben," said Nassir through the door.

The view through the peephole confirmed what the voice had said so Johnny opened the door and Nassir rushed in, giving Johnny a tight, fatherly hug as Brooks strolled in behind him smiling.

"What are you two doing here?" asked Johnny in a gasping breath as Nassir let go of him. "Doc, I thought you were at the hospital today?"

"You mean, you don't remember what happened last night?" asked Brooks.

Johnny looked at him with a puzzled facial expression.

Nassir put his right hand on Johnny's shoulder and looked him in his eyes. "Johnny, you did it," said Nassir. "You finally defeated Snake. He fell to his death in the heart of New York."

"They've been trying to remove the costume from off of the body for the past few hours," added Brooks, "but they're not having any luck with it so his body is being sent back to Philly to a molecular specialist at Biotech Labs."

"New York?" asked Johnny. "I thought I dreamt all of that."
He walked away from the two physicians and then placed his
hands on the sides of his face, in disbelief, he had extorted
revenge on his girlfriend's murderer. *That's it? I did it?*

"Johnny," started Nassir, "there's one thing I don't quite
understand about last night. We heard on the news eyewitnesses
swear they saw two people falling, Snake's body was the only
one that was accounted for with the rope around him still. If
your powers were dampened, how did you manage to teleport?"

"I remember closing my eyes on the way down," started
Johnny. "But that's all I remember."

"So you're saying," said Brooks. "That you don't..."

"Remember teleporting?" interrupted Johnny. "I don't think
I can teleport myself while I'm powerless."

"You think someone did it for you?" asked Nassir. "Who?"

"I don't know Doc. Maybe I have someone more powerful
than me, looking out for me. I really don't have a clue." They all
looked around at each other then Brooks walked over to Johnny
and gave him a hug.

"We're glad you're okay Johnny," said Brooks.

"Thank you Doctor Brooks," replied Johnny as he returned
the hug. "Thank you!"

***

The dreary sky started to darken the colors of the clouds,
announcing the rain was going to fall soon.

The wind, which was usually ahead of the sun and the rain in
the race toward the earth, had once again proved to be first as it
blew forcefully on Johnny's open leather trench coat.

Johnny stood over top of April's grave as a tear started to
roll down his cheek. "We did it April." Johnny then looked up
towards the sky. "I knew killing Snake wasn't gonna' bring you
back, but I had to stop him before he killed any more. You know,
I don't think he knew this, but the fucked-up part about my
whole ordeal with him is that he is my brother."

The wind again blew slightly, and his leather trench again
volunteered to go in the direction it went in earlier.

Johnny stooped down and laid the neatly wrapped one dozen roses next to the base of the stone and he then stood back up with teary eyes. "I will always love you," he said tearfully. Johnny hesitated for a moment or two and then turned and walked away.

***

Tanner sat in his office, tapping a pen on his desk, as he waited for the telephone to ring.

The phone soon rung.

Tanner then depressed the speaker button. "Hello?" he asked forcefully.

"Everything is just as we expected it to be," said Stern's voice from the other end of the phone.

"Thanks Stern," replied Tanner. "Keep me updated on his status." A smile now grew across his pleased face as he hung up the phone. "Perfect!"

CHAPTER 52

IT WAS A cool yet sunny day, and traffic was normal for a Tuesday morning.

Johnny came down the steps of the post office at Thirtieth and Market Streets and quickly crossed Market Street. Johnny then started walking in the direction of Center City. While walking down Market Street, he glanced two blocks ahead in the direction of the Peco Energy building and saw Snake wearing a jacket zipped up and a pair of blue jeans. Upon the moment of recognition, Johnny started running towards him.

Snake smiled upon seeing Johnny coming in his direction. He then made his clothing morph into the silver liquid and then again into his costume as people continued to walk blindly past him as if nothing happened. Snake then flew straight over Johnny going in the direction Johnny was coming from.

In anger, Johnny ran through a portal.

The portal immediately reopened ten feet in the air above where it had closed up, and Jade flew out.

Jade didn't care who saw him do what he had just done. No longer seeing Snake, he immediately descended to the ground and started looking around as people continued to walk blindly past him, as if he were not there. Jade then looked over the stone railing of the bridge and into the water as he was tapped on the shoulder from behind.

Upon turning around in order to respond to the tap on the shoulder, Jade caught a fist from Snake which sent him backwards in a somersault motion over the railing and into the water.

Snake then jumped up onto the railing and looked down into the water. "Pay backs are a mother fuck," said Snake. He then dove off of the railing into the direction of the water, but before he could hit the water, Snake turned sharply upward and flew under the bridge way between two large stone pillars and kept going as Jade reached the surface of the water and then flew fully up and out of the water.

Jade remained hovered above the water and a look of anger displayed across his face. He huffed. "I killed you once, and I'll do it again," said Jade as he took off and flew under the roadway.

***

The dimly lit lights and the smell of pasta sauce and other delicacies distracted Johnny for a second until he remembered he was after Snake just a moment ago. However, when Johnny looked around, he saw he was in a crowded restaurant. "What the f..."

"Johnny!" interrupted a voice from off to the side. He turned and looked to the side as April soon joined him at the table. "Sorry I'm late babe," started April. "Traffic was a bitch!"

"April?"

"Yeah silly," replied April as she laughed lightly. "Are you okay?"

"I was just..." Johnny cut himself short because he wasn't sure what was going on. He had never heard April curse casually like that. If they were making love, yes, but not out in public like she had just done. Then he remembered April was murdered just a short while ago, or at least he thought she was yet she was here sitting opposite him in a crowded restaurant.

He then again remembered chasing Snake just a few short moments ago, even though he had just had a hand in killing him. Johnny looked around at the other people in the restaurant as they just ate.

No one was having any type of conversation they were all just eating. They all appeared to be lifeless or more appropriate, automated, as if robots. As he looked back at April's face, a tear just started to roll down his cheek.

"What's wrong baby?" asked April.

"You died."

"Died?" laughed April, "I was murdered is more like it! Do you know I reincarnated in the body of a pig?" She laughed again. "I'm never eating bacon again!"

***

Again, it was a bright and sunny day, and traffic seemed to be normal.

Johnny looked out the window of the trolley he was on and saw he was going down Baltimore Avenue. The thirty-four trolley, he thought.

"What's going on?" he asked out loud as he noticed other passengers just sitting there on the trolley staring blankly towards the front.

Just then, Johnny witnessed from the window as a parade of police cars swarmed around the trolley as it stopped at a traffic light.

As the officers got out of their cars and boarded the trolley, the other passengers continued to stare ahead.

Johnny continued to watch out of curiosity.

The cops then scrutinized the faces of the zombie like passengers as they made their way to the back of the trolley where Johnny was sitting.

One of the cops pointed in Johnny's direction, Johnny looked behind himself in order to see who it was they were pointing at, thinking maybe Snake was now behind him.

"Sarge, we've located a suspect who matches the exact description of the perp!" yelled one of the cops.

Then another cop, apparently a sergeant, boarded the trolley and slowly walked down the aisle towards the back where Johnny was sitting. His cap skewed the view of his face as his head was tilted as he moved towards the back.

The first cop grabbed a hold of Johnny's arm. "Come with me!" he demanded angrily.

253

"What?" asked Johnny as the sergeant grew closer and raised his head up.

The sergeant was Snake dressed in a cop's uniform. "Your final lesson in life son will be, not to fuck with me," said Snake as he raised a gun and aimed it at Johnny's chest.

"No-O-O!" yelled Johnny.

The gun went off and three shots were fired.

***

The night air was fresh and warm, apparently a result from the summer day.

Jade's body was fully lit as he flew through the dark skies of Philadelphia in his energy form. He looked around, feeling slightly dazed about the sequence of events he had just experienced. Jade soon flew over the park where he last saw April alive and he descended to the ground.

He then dimmed his body out.

Jade then walked around in the dark park as his costume glowed the greenish gold color which gave him his name. He walked over to the spot where April had been murdered and got down on one knee. As a tear rolled down his cheek, he looked down at the ground. When he looked back up, the gray granite which had April's name engraved on it, stood before him.

He was now in the cemetery.

"I'm sorry April," he said as he touched the stone with his right hand.

Just then, the ground exploded from underneath him and Zombie April, with torn clothes and missing flesh, jumped out of the ground and wrapped her hands around his neck.

"You bastard," she started. "You lied to me. Now I'm condemned to this hell hole down here, because of you!" April continued to yell as she choked him.

Everything suddenly went dark.

***

Drenched in sweat, Johnny quickly sat up in bed holding his neck and he started breathing heavily as if he had been unable to so for some time.

He looked down at his palms, both of which were clammy. Johnny then looked around his bedroom until his eyes located the clock whose bright red numbers displayed; four thirty-three a.m. Johnny then realized he had not merely been reliving experiences in which he had previously gone through, nor did he just get home from a weird turn of events in which he fell victim to.

As Johnny looked in the mirror, the horrible and vividly real experiences in which he had just experiences were simply fabricated from his mind.

**

Johnny shared the dreams with both Brooks and Nassir. He explained the vivid realness and lucidity of each segment and how he felt it to be strange there were only two people who were interactive with him in the dream, but who were dead in the real world.

No one else had existed in his dreams except for the cop who grabbed him on the trolley, but that part was a blur compared to when Snake fired the gun at him.

"Every time I think I've come to a solution about something, I find myself with more questions than answers," said Johnny as he walked around the small lab with his hands tucked in the pockets of his denims.

Nassir looked at him with empathic eyes.

"Is there anything you need from us?" asked Brooks in an attempt to be supportive.

Johnny shook his head no. "I'll be fine," he said. "If there is an emergency the police can't handle, then call me."

"Well, if you need anything at all," started Nassir, "don't hesitate to call us."

Brooks shook his head in agreement. "What about the two men who were involved with April's death? We still don't have any leads?"

"We will get them," replied Johnny.

***

The bright sun beamed down on Cheltenham as the night wind sent crisp air sweeping through the barren trees, their skeletal branches swaying and clattering softly at its touch.

At Chelten Hills Cemetery, two preteens darted between the headstones, laughing breathlessly as they cut across the graveyard. The sound of a faint *snap* cracked the air behind them.

April Jenkins materialized atop her own gravesite.

Her sudden appearance—solid, silent, and impossibly wrong—froze the children mid-stride. For half a heartbeat they stared, eyes wide, mouths open. Then terror took hold. They screamed and bolted, scattering in the opposite direction from where they had been running, their footsteps fading into the distance.

April remained where she stood.

Her dress was dirty and soiled, clinging to her frame as if it had been pulled from the earth itself. She looked around slowly, her expression vacant, unfocused—like someone waking from a long, disorienting sleep.

She glanced down.

Her name stared back at her from the cold stone beneath her feet.

April's brow furrowed. She took a tentative step away from the grave, then another, her movements stiff and uncertain. The wind tugged at her dress as she turned and began walking toward the cemetery's exit on Washington Avenue.

Behind her, the headstones stood silent. The earth remained undisturbed.

The grave was empty.

And somewhere beyond the iron gates, the living world waited—unaware someone meant to stay buried had just begun to walk among them again.

CHAPTER 53

DRIVING DOCTOR BROOKS jeep, Johnny pulled into the parking lot of the abandoned hospital and parked the jeep in a nonconforming manner. As he got out of the jeep, the wind blew hard on his unzipped, down jacket, blowing it back and revealing the well-defined torso in the white sweater which was pulled neatly over his denim blue jeans.

He looked at the building with its boarded-up windows, walls scarred by time, and as he slowly surveyed the property, vivid images began to flood his mind.

Johnny saw his mother in various counseling sessions, telling the psychiatrist what she had been through when she was abducted by aliens. He felt a pang of guilt; without his own strange abilities, he would've dismissed her claims as crazy talk.

The vision shifted.

He saw his mother being pushed down the long dark hospital hallway as she was crying, sweating and holding her pregnant belly. Then came the red headed nurse who injecting two syringes with clear fluid into his mother's arm.

Another image followed.

A being composed entirely of light, the same being from his dreams, *my father*, he realized.

The being touched his mother's face and professed his love.

A passing car horn blared, snapping Johnny briefly back to reality. He turned away, then looked at the hospital again.

Two physicians cutting open the stomach of his mother's lifeless body and removing the two infants, only one of them was alive. Johnny kept watching and witnessed the nurse storming out of the operating room with the dead infant in her arms.

He shook his head no. He didn't need to see any more.

Johnny turned around and walked back over to the jeep and got in. After backing up and turning the jeep into a position where he could pull out of the parking lot and into the street, he pulled out onto Southampton Road and stopped at the red traffic light. When the light turned green, he turned right on the inner drive of the Roosevelt Boulevard and sped away.

***

April walked aimlessly through the streets of Philadelphia. As she walked down Washington Lane, she passed a fruit stand outside of a small grocery store and picked up two apples and two oranges without stopping.

"Hey you!" shouted a stout older black man with salt and pepper colored hair.

April turned around as she took a bite out of one of the apples.

"Where do you think you're goin'?" he asked angrily as he then took notice to her attire. "You have ta pay for those!"

"But I don't have any money," April replied innocently.

"Don't I know you?" the man asked. "What's your name?"

April smiled and then, with the help of the sound of cracking electricity along with a spiral of purple light, she vanished.

***

With the sound of a light snap, April reappeared in the middle of a park, giggling as she continued eating her apple. She wandered over to a bench, sat down, and once again the parade of visions flooded her mind.

The man in the dark body suit with the design of a red snake ascending up his side.

The green and gold clad figure who was fighting against him.

The being who looked as if he were composed entirely of a yellow light.

What do they mean? She wondered.

Taking another bite of her apple, she watched two squirrels playing off in the distance.

She laid the other pieces of fruit next to her on the bench, never taking notice a short distance away of the man who was staring at her with a shocked facial expression.

Mark Stern was sitting at the park eating his lunch when he witnessed April Jenkins materialize before his eyes.

***

Michael lay in bed sleeping in a tastefully decorated condominium provided by the Trilateral Commission. With his regeneration nearly complete, Tanner had arranged for him to recover somewhere comfortable.

Michael flinched suddenly.

The visions were active again.

He saw the glowing figure reaching his hand towards him. He saw the face of the woman he had so viciously killed when he was experiencing his episodes. Then he saw himself carrying a fallen Jade.

Michael woke with a gasp, drenched in sweat, hands running over his chest as if to confirm he was real. He looked around and noticed a black and gold designer beer keg which sat tastefully against the wall far opposite his bed. Next to the bed, a large fruit basket filled with flowers, a card sticking out from the arrangement. Next to the basket, a new rolled up pair of boxer briefs, *Fruit of the Loom*.

He pulled the card out of the basket and read aloud. "Welcome home, Tanner."

Michael smirked as he grabbed the underwear.

He rose from the bed and entered the bathroom to pay his water bill while sitting the roll on the sink. The bathroom was tastefully decorated with gold and black accents against the beige walls.

He absently flushed the toilet and then moved to the sink to wash his hands.

For several minutes Michael stared blankly at his reflection. *Something's different*, he thought.

The phone rang.

He then exited the bathroom and looked around to see where the phone was located until he saw it and moved towards it.

The answering machine clicked on.

"Mike, it's Katherine, I'm guessing you may be awake by now. Welcome home, I hope you like the condo. Your...uh suit, is in the keg in your bedroom. Tanner asked if you could meet us over at Biotech Labs today by around two...two thirty. Bye."

The line went dead.

Michael stared at the phone. He wasn't sure why, but he always felt uneasy when he heard her voice. He glanced the clock and headed into the shower.

With a thought he switched the radio on.

'Say Amen' by Howard Hewett filled the room.

♪ *I wanna thank you God* ♪,
♪ *For giving me one more chance,* ♪
♪ *To raise my voice and to sing your praise* ♪

Michael chuckled as the hot water pelted his muscular frame. "Mom's favorite," he muttered. "I hear you. Loud and clear!"

After showering, drying himself off and putting on a pair of boxers, he donned his deodorant. Michael then went back into the bedroom and looked in the direction of the old designer beer keg which was positioned against a wall in his room.

The lid to the keg had a hole which was two inches in diameter, and the silver liquid contained inside, flew out and onto Michael's body, becoming an outfit.

He eyed himself in the mirror. Michael was wearing a gray dress shirt, black Armani dress slacks, and a pair of black Georgio Brutini Loafers.

Michael then went into the bathroom and looked at himself through the mirror. "Perfect," he said. He then produced the sound of crackling electricity along with the spiral of red light and vanished from out of the condominium.

Johnny went back to Brooks' house and explained everything he saw in the visions.

Brooks listened intently as Johnny revealed to him that he could visualize recordings through the residual energy signatures.

He told him of the woman whom he believed to be his mother, the fact there were two babies and not just one, about the duplicitous nurse who had stolen one of the babies after killing his mother.

"You could just watch this?" asked Nassir. "As if things were happening in front of you?"

"Yeah, again I don't know how I'm able to do it, just that I can," started Johnny. "A short time after I was shot, I went back to the area where it happened and I watched everything as it went down, so it must be one of the ways my people communicate."

"You think your father is trying to reach out now?"

"Maybe he has been all this time," started Johnny, "those weird dreams...I haven't connected all the dots yet."

"Okay," started Nassir, "So you are still having dreams about Snake. Maybe we need to see his body. Last we heard, his body was being sent to Biotech Labs, we can start there."

"April's still a part of my dreams, or nightmares," Johnny shook his head in the negative. "I'm not ready to exhume her body, besides, I don't see the connection there yet."

"Don't worry Johnny," started Brooks, "we'll take this one piece at a time."

Johnny nodded in agreement. "But we still need to get to Biotech and see Snake's body!"

"We have to make sure he's really out of commission," agreed Nassir, "see if we can learn anything from his autopsy, then once we are sure we're done with him, we can revisit the April situation. Rob are you still consulting for that lead scientist over at Biotech, what's his name?"

"Mark Stern," replied Brooks, but we haven't touched base in some time, I'll try to reach out to him and see if he can get us in to see Snake's body."

CHAPTER 54

BAFFLED, TANNER, COLE, Katherine, and Michael all stared at the glass enclosure staring at the creature as it seemed to have been in a catatonic state. The creature appeared to be a black panther but was obviously something more. It stood at about seven feet eight inches tall and weighed a good four hundred and seventy-five pounds. Its form was humanoid, but it didn't look as if it should have a name. His eyes were closed.

"What is it?" asked Katherine.

Michael looked at Katherine and said, "Any idiot can see it's half man and half feline."

"Actually," started Stern as he pointed in Michael's direction, "you're wrong."

"I am?" asked Michael with a confused look on his face.

"Yup, but good guess," replied Stern.

"Enough with the guessing games," started Tanner in his normal malevolent tone. "What is it?"

"It's just a black panther," said Stern as he held his hand up to the cage.

"Just a black panther?" asked Katherine. "It's got arms and legs just like we do."

Stern smiled and replied, "well its' not, JUST a black panther. He was a cub from Africa. From the time he was a few months old, I've been altering his genetic code, so he would somewhat match that of a human."

"Wouldn't making him more human make him genetically inferior to other cats?" asked Michael.

Everyone just looked at him. Since his latest return from the grave, the man who had the alter ego they called Snake seemed different of late. He was actually engaged in conversation with an intellect such as Stern.

Tanner kept his concerns about Snake to himself, for now.

"What?" asked Snake, knowing they were looking at him differently.

"Technically, he's right," interjected Stern. "I had to mix the initial injections of H-g-h with the equivalent feline hormones somatotropin, thereby keeping his strength and speed at a constant rate of growth."

"What is H-g-h?" asked Cole.

"Human growth hormone," replied Stern. "It's what gives us our developing characteristics as we sprout from childhood into adulthood."

"You can do this to an animal just by injecting it with some H-g-h?" asked Tanner.

Stern nodded in the affirmative. "With many modifications to the hormone of course."

"How long has that thing been in there?" asked Tanner.

"Since he was a month old," replied Stern.

"What?" asked the small group in unison.

"Well, that's only three years," added Stern.

"Three-years-old?" asked Kat as she examined the anatomically correct creature. "But he looks like a full-grown man."

"Well," started Stern, "you've got to remember, cats age differently than we do."

The group all stared at the catlike creature in amazement.

"That's a wild animal," said Tanner. "How do I know it won't attack me?"

"Come with me," said Stern as he led the small group over towards a metal cabinet.

They all walked across the white tiled floors of Biotech labs until they reached the other side of the room.

Stern then opened the cabinet, revealing a number of bands which resembled wristwatches. The only difference between the bands Stern had and wristwatches were Stern's bands didn't have clock faces on them. Instead of a clock face, the band had a funny looking letter 'T' on it.

Stern pulled one of the bands from out of the cabinet and held it up in front of the small group. "Anyone who wears one of these bands will be protected from the cat."

"The cat?" inquired Michael. "Doesn't it have a name?"

Katherine said, "I like it just fine."

"His name could be Mud for all I care, long as he does what I want him to do," replied Tanner.

"What if I forget to put the band on one day and I come face to face with the creature?" asked Katherine.

Stern looked at her with a blank expression on his face. "You love life?" asked Stern.

Katherine shook her head yes.

"Then don't forget to wear the band," he replied.

"I like it," started an anxious Tanner, "when do we get to play with it?"

"As soon as I finish fine tuning the frequency bands and after I take his muscles out of atrophy," replied Stern. "And boss, with the adjustments I made on your band, he will be under your complete control whenever in your vicinity."

"What possible application would he be useful for?" Michael asked Tanner.

"We'll always need ways to get rid of enemies," replied Tanner.

"What about the other prototype you wanted to show us?" asked Michael.

"Model BT two thousand and one?" asked Stern. "Right this way." He held his hand out and led the small oasis through a set of double doors to another section of the laboratory. As they walked inside the darkened room, Stern turned on a light switch.

The large square shaped glass cage in the room immediately caught everyone's attention. Contained within the glass cage stood an imposing android type figure—silver robotic hands and torso, a red T emblazoned across its chest, silver boots, and long titanium jet-styled wings spanning six feet. Its limbs and head were humanoid, entirely encased in red Kevlar.

Tanner's eyes lit up brighter than a child's eyes in a toy store at Christmas time. "Wow!" started Tanner as he pointed to the figure in the glass cage. "Martin?"

Cole stared, transfixed. "I see it!"

Katherine rolled her eyes. "It's just a robot."

"Unit BT-two thousand and one is *not* just a robot," Stern snapped defensively. "He is a cybernetic entity composed of reconstructable synthetic skin, titanium alloyed steel, and a molecular self-reconstruction device housed in the skull."

He pointed to the eyes. "Optic sensors see up to thirty miles and emit lasers capable of disintegrating organic matter on contact. Audio sensors detect a pin drop in a crowded ballroom."

He gestured to the wings. "Retractable titanium wings capable of cutting through brick. Automatic guidance sensors ensure flight stability—even during combat."

"What are those two round things under his belt?" Cole asked.

Michael chuckled as everyone just looked at him. "Sorry—that question caught me off guard."

No one else laughed.

Getting the joke, Stern smiled. "Those are thirty-second damper discs."

"What?" asked Katherine.

"Thirty second damper discs," replied Stern. "Upon contact, they will cause any powered unit to lose power for about thirty seconds or so."

"Any powered unit?" asked Tanner.

"Any - powered unit," replied the convincing young scientist.

"Thirty seconds doesn't seem like a whole lot of time," replied Cole.

"Think outside the box," started Stern with confidence rising from his voice. "If a vehicle loses power for thirty seconds, that's enough to cause a three-mile long wreck on a major interstate." He then looked at Tanner. "What better way to distract our law and rescue workers? Planes can be brought down...Martin, what do you think would happen to you if both your brain and your heart stopped working at the same time for about thirty seconds?"

Tanner smiled. "Stern, you've done well," said Tanner as he stared at the cyborg admirably. "When will he be operational?"

"I'm just waiting for a willing donor."

"A donor for what?" Katherine asked sharply.

"What do you need a donor for?" asked Tanner.

"You tell me this boss," started Stern, as he quickly glanced at Katherine with a look of irritation on his face. He then slyly put his arm around Tanner's shoulder. "What is the fastest computer in the world?"

Tanner nodded his approval.

He then looked at his three companions and signaled them to follow him out.

As they started to leave the lab, a look of disappointment fell across Stern's face. "Wait," started Stern as Tanner and company all stopped and turned around with curious looks on their faces.

Tanner, Cole, Michael, and Katherine all stood around for about fifteen seconds waiting for Stern to say something.

"Well what is it?" asked Tanner impatiently.

"There's' one more I have to show you," said Stern nervously.

"I thought you said you only finished two prototypes," said Katherine.

"This one isn't exactly a prototype, she's the real thing," replied Stern as he directed them to follow him to another section of the laboratory.

"She?" queried Cole.

"What's the matter Martin?" asked Katherine. "You don't think a woman could be a cold-blooded killer?"

"I happen to think women make the best cold-blooded killers," replied Cole grinning.

"Don't make me prove you right," said Katherine as they all followed Stern into a well-lit room where a woman dressed in a pair of jeans and a purple sweater stood abruptly.

"Don't be afraid," started Stern, "these are friends."

When the woman smiled, Michael started having flashbacks of the time when he had killed April Jenkins. His eyes then widened with remembrance.

He looked at the woman and realized he had just killed her not too long ago. He couldn't have been mistaken about killing her because he not only broke her neck, but he removed her heart from her lifeless body. It can't be, he thought.

April was a little thinner now and had longer hair than when he last saw her, but it was definitely her. It was April Jenkins!

"I've got to talk to you," whispered Michael as he pulled Tanner back out of the room by his arm.

They all watched as Michael and Tanner both left the room. April looked at both Cole and Katherine nervously.

Outside of the room, Tanner looked at Michael as if he were crazy. "What's this about?" Tanner asked angrily.

"That's April Jenkins!" exclaimed Snake.

"Who?" whispered Tanner.

"April Jenkins, Jade's girlfriend. The one I killed a short while ago!"

"How is that possible?"

"I don't know, Stern's behind this one."

"I'll find out what the hells' going on," started Tanner as he and Michael rejoined the small group in the room. "Stern – Where'd this young lady come from?" he asked as soon as they had gotten into the room.

"I discovered her while on my lunch break, she materialized out of thin air at Bums' Park and I recognized her immediately," replied Stern. "Poor thing doesn't remember who she is."

"She doesn't remember?" asked Tanner.

April stood up. "I can speak for myself Mark!"

She walked over towards Tanner with confidence and seduction in her stride. She had lost her memory. She did not remember any part of her life before her death. If she remembered she used to work for him and he was the one who ordered her kidnapping, she might have attempted to take him out, but instead, she embraced the thought of working for him in a different manner. "I woke up in a coffin and suddenly found myself on top of my grave site. That's when I learned my name, but I don't remember much else. As I was trying to figure out my way, Mark here found me and told me you would be able to help me get my life back in exchange for use of my skills."

She then started floating upwards. "I am willing to do whatever it takes to reclaim my life."

"How do I know that I can trust you?" asked Tanner.

"Because you're still alive," she said. "I could kill you right now in less than five seconds, if, I wanted to." While still afloat in the air, she made herself appear to be made of a bright purple light. A second later, she dimmed her body out and said, "I heard you could use someone with talents such as mine, and frankly, along with reclaiming some lost memories, I could use some money without having my face plastered in the papers."

"That's similar to what I said," Michael said under his breath.

Everyone in the room, except for Michael, smiled as she extended her hand to Tanner while still floating in the air.

Michael felt uneasy about this new addition to the Trilateral family and was not quite sure of how he would handle it.

Tanner took April's hand and kissed it. "You're hired, Stern get her a costume and ensure she's up to snuff, wake your Cat and get him out on a test run. We need to start flexing our muscle."

CHAPTER 55

BROOKS AND RACHEL hurriedly donned the containment suits in order to enter the clean room where Rachel had witnessed the skin samples burning brightly like little pieces of light. Brooks called Rachel in order to check in and discovered she had some quite surprising news for him.

Hearing the news, Brooks couldn't help but to rush over to the lab in order to see what it was she had gotten excited about.

Now they were both there, it would seem he would get his chance to witness the miracle himself.

Brooks turned his back to Rachel because he had a difficult time with fastening the suit. "Do you mind?" he asked.

Rachel zipped him up and then turned her back to him, hoping the good doctor would reciprocate, which he did.

"Are you sure it wasn't some sort of a reflection?" asked Brooks.

Rachel followed Brooks into the airlock and then closed the door behind her as she gave Brooks a smug look. "I know what a reflected light off of a culture dish looks like. There were three dishes in there that had their own light source."

"Bioluminescent bacteria?" he suggested.

"I initially thought that," she said, "but there's nothing in the supply or manifest saying we should have any."

A green light came on above the entrance door to the lab and they walked in.

Rachel led Brooks over to the third refrigeration unit and opened the door. She pointed out the dishes, but all Brooks saw were petri dishes labeled skin cells, but seeing the barcodes given him by Nassir, he immediately recognized those dishes as the culture dishes Johnny's cells were in.

"So where are the lights?" Brooks asked in as much of a disbelieving voice as he possibly could.

Rachel looked at him sarcastically and pressed the little button which laid discreetly in-between the edge of the refrigeration unit door and the edge of the box. With her action, the light to the refrigeration unit went out and the three samples in the box once again provided light to the interior of the box.

Brooks thought this discovery was amazing, because the cells didn't have a main collective or brain to tell it what to do, so it responded to the environment to atone for the absence of light. This latest discovery made him more confused about Johnny and his abilities.

"Well Doctor Brooks," started Rachel, "is there something you want to tell me?"

Brooks looked at her and smiled, but he knew this was one of those times he had to remind her she was his employee. "No," he said without further explanation.

CHAPTER 56

THEY WERE ALL good kids.

Not little kids—no scraped knees or bedtime stories—but teenagers standing at that fragile age where freedom still felt new and invincible. There were four of them: Michelle Howard, Thomas Kershaw, Elena Abrams, and Richard George.

They had gathered behind the Philadelphia Museum of Art, their usual spot—far enough from the road to feel hidden, close enough to the city to feel alive. The trees were thick here, their branches intertwining overhead, swallowing what little light the city offered. They stood atop the palisade, the stone edge overlooking the dark, slow-moving stretch of the Schuylkill River below.

The air was crisp, cool enough to sting their lungs when they laughed too hard. This was what life was supposed to be—school during the day, part-time jobs when they could get them, and nights like this as the reward. A few blunts. Maybe a beer or two. Nothing stupid. Nothing dangerous.

They were good kids.

"Pass it this way," Elena said, her voice bright with anticipation as she reached toward Richard. He had just taken an obnoxiously long pull, smoke spilling lazily from his lips.

Michelle laughed. "He's fuckin' up the system. We're supposed to go counterclockwise."

Thomas smirked. "You'll say anything to get your way."

Michelle licked her lips slowly, deliberately, like she was savoring a lollipop. "Do anything too."

Thomas groaned and pointed at Richard. "Pass it this way, dude!"

They all laughed as Richard handed the joint to Elena, shaking his head.

"Punk," Thomas said.

"I do what I gotta do for me," Richard replied, grinning. "You do what you gotta do for you."

More laughter followed—carefree, loud, careless.

They never noticed the eyes watching them from the darkness.

The low growl came first.

It wasn't loud. It wasn't sudden. It was deep, resonant felt more than heard. It slithered through the trees and curled around their spines.

Hidden within the shadows was a massive, catlike creature. Its black fur absorbed the darkness, rendering it nearly invisible. Only its eyes betrayed it—two predatory embers burning with intent.

It had been watching.

And now, it wanted to play.

Thomas stopped laughing.

The color drained from his face in an instant, leaving him pale and rigid. His body locked up unnaturally, as though his instincts had seized control before his mind could catch up.

"What's wrong?" Elena asked, her smile faltering.

Thomas whimpered. His voice barely worked. "It's... it's gonna kill us."

Warmth spread down his legs as his bladder gave out.

Richard snorted. "Did you just pee your pants? Man, I think you took one puff too—"

The sentence never finished.

A massive, black-furred claw flashed through the air.

Richard's head separated from his body in a single, horrifying motion. His corpse crumpled to the ground as his head rolled away, eyes still open, mouth frozen mid-word.

Michelle screamed.

Elena screamed louder when she finally saw it.

The creature lunged with impossible speed, knocking Elena to the ground. Its jaws tore into her as if she were nothing more than prey, ripping and chewing until her screams dissolved into wet gurgles—and then silence.

"Oh shit!" Michelle cried, terror stripping her of all reason.

She dove over the wall.

The cat grinned.

It sprinted to the edge and snatched Michelle by the legs mid-fall. Her scream echoed as the creature yanked her back and swiped viciously across her torso. Her legs tore free from her body, and the rest of her disappeared over the edge, tumbling into the darkness below.

Thomas watched, frozen in place, as the creature lifted Michelle's severed legs and began to eat.

His stomach revolted. Vomit spilled onto the ground.

I gotta get outta here.

The thought jolted him into motion.

Thomas turned and ran.

Behind him, the cat dropped its meal and grinned wider. This was its favorite part. Cat and mouse. Especially when the mouse was big enough to be satisfying.

Thomas sprinted blindly through the trees, lungs burning, heart slamming against his ribs—

—and without warning, the creature landed in front of him.

It struck the ground like a living missile, stone cracking beneath its weight. For one fleeting, absurd second, Thomas thought of Superman landing—only this thing bore no red S, no suit, no mercy.

The cat roared.

Thomas tried to scream, but no sound came.

The creature swung.

He missed me! Thomas thought as he collapsed backward. *I gotta get help—*

Then he looked down.

The cat hadn't missed.

His body had been sliced clean in half.

As the last pint of blood rushed through his fading vision, Thomas understood the final thing he would ever see: the creature hunched over him, already devouring the lower half of his body.

Darkness then took him.

CHAPTER 57

WEARING NOTHING BUT a pair of shorts and a tee shirt, Johnny had just finished making himself a cheese steak and homemade French fries when the ringing of the phone interrupted him.

"Happens every time," he said as he sat the plate down. He then picked up the phone. "Hello?" he inquired.

He paused as he listened to the response of the person who was on the other end of the telephone.

"Its' on right now?" he asked.

Johnny then looked in the direction of the television and the tape which was playing in the video cassette recorder stopped without warning and channel three displayed on the television screen. Johnny had caught the news in the middle of a broadcast.

On the screen was a barrage of police cars with blaring lights, ambulances and a vehicle belonging to the animal control unit.

A camera pans to the reporter.

"...One witness to this horrifying act," continued the reporter. "Once again, the police have advised everyone to stay out of the area of The Philadelphia Museum of Art, as it is dangerous. To reiterate, a large, catlike creature was seen around the art museum area, where it viciously mauled four people to death. An eyewitness to the situation stated, "the creature looked like a black panther but stood on two legs...it also had two arms, just like a person."

Johnny tuned out the reporter as he continued and just shook his head in the negative. "This city is getting stranger by the day," interrupted Johnny as he spoke into the telephone. "I'll be there in a few," he said as he, with the assistance of the sound of cracking electricity and the spiraling bright light, changed into his suit.

The television then cut off as he used his cracking electric sound along with the spiral of yellow light to vanish from out of the apartment.

***

Jade reappeared at the lab, where Brooks was watching the news report. "Have they found it yet," he asked as Brooks turned around from the television set and faced him.

"No - not yet," he replied.

"What was the last known location of this cat?" asked Jade.

"As far as we know," started Brooks, "it hadn't left the art museum area - as a matter of fact, the authorities are looking for the beast now."

"Well just stand by, just in case I need anything."

"You got it," said Brooks as Jade used the cracking sound of electricity along with the spiraling yellow light to vanish again.

***

With a light snap, Jade reappeared in the area of the art museum. When he saw the media news had spotted him, he just flew straight up and over them, in order to keep attention away from him at the moment.

The media watched as the greenish gold lit figure just flew down the parkway and away from them.

"Dangerous creature walking around, and they want to take pictures," said Jade as he landed, thinking he was far enough away from the circus of the media. He then started looking around for clues as to where the creature might be.

As he looked through the area, he saw sporadic outlines of small creatures, but nothing synonymous to the appearance of a large black panther. He spent ten minutes around the location but couldn't find any clues. "You there Doctor Brooks?"

"I'm here and I hear you loud and clear," said Brooks.

276

"I don't see anything out of the ordinary, but I'm sure it's around here somewhere, it couldn't have gotten too far."

"Okay Johnny, just...."

A loud screeching noise interrupted the transmission, startling Jade.

"Doctor Brooks?" asked Jade as he slapped himself on the side of the head in an attempt to get the transmitter to work properly.

A low growl from behind caused him to turn around slowly.

From out of the brush, a large black panther emerged on all fours.

"Nice kitty," he suggested nervously.

The cat slowly rose himself to where he was just standing on two legs. He then licked his lips, roared, and then pounced on Jade.

As he fell back, Jade felt the wind leave his body quickly.

Jade was still shocked from seeing the creature stand up to where it was more than a foot taller than he was.

The cat immediately started tearing away at Jade's costume, until Jade finally produced the sound of cracking electricity along with the spiraling yellow light and vanished, right before getting his face swiped by the mighty talon-like claws.

With the sound of a light snap, Jade then reappeared standing directly behind the cat.

The cat turned around slowly and then prepared to pounce on Jade, but before he had a chance to, Jade gave him a swift kick in the groin.

The large cat fell over like a maple tree just cut down by a lumberjack. The cat laid there for a moment, wincing in pain while covering the delicate area.

The swift kick was an unfair fight tactic his Aunt Paula had taught him when he was in the third grade.

"When nothing else will seem to do, just line your sight and kick the two...Pauline Thompkins, nineteen eighty-one," said Jade as he looked down at himself and his ripped costume.

"Robert's not gonna like this," Jade said. "Sorry but now I'mma haveta shock ya!" He then reached down for the fallen cat and as he grabbed a hold of it, Snake materialized with the sound of a light snap, standing in front of Jade.

In full costume.

"Snake?" asked Jade in disbelief.

Snake gave Jade a backhand fist which sent the surprised hero across Kelly Drive and into another wooded area.

Snake then grabbed a hold of the cat by its underarms. With the sound of cracking electricity and the red spiraling light, Snake and the cat both vanished.

***

Cole pulled into a Sunoco A Plus on Broad Street across from William Penn High School and just down the street from The Philadelphia Freedom Theater.

He was on his way to Center City to meet with Tanner and Katherine but decided to stop for gas and to get a snack on his way. After he left the store, he took a bite of his hot-dog as he disarmed the alarm on his BMW. He opened the car door and prepared to get in, but a gun was aimed at the left side of his head.

"All right mother fucker," started the voice that came from his left, "give up da wallet and da keys."

"Okay, but please don't shoot, I just have to reach for my wallet."

He raised his hands, then spun suddenly, knocking the gun from the man's grip. Cole then drove his fists into the attacker's face with brutal precision.

"I'm sick of you punks trying to rob me," he growled. "You want a Beamer? Get a job and buy one."

Inside the store, the attendant glanced out the window, saw Cole pummeling the man, and reached for the phone.

Cole grabbed the assailant by the shirt, his fist cocked inches from the man's face—

Click.

Cole turned slowly.

Four shots slammed into his back.

278

Cole collapsed, releasing his grip as his body hit the pavement.

The shooter kicked Cole onto his side as the first attacker and two more youths burst from the shadows. They jumped into the BMW, backed out of the lot, and sped onto Broad Street toward Center City.

Two minutes later, a patrol car screamed into the lot. One officer leapt out while the other grabbed the transmitter.

"Officer Tyson. Male victim, late twenties, multiple gunshot wounds—corner of Broad and Master..."

**

"He didn't say a word," started Johnny as Brooks scrutinized the various rips in his Kevlar costume. "He just hit me hard enough to get me away, so he and the cat could vanish."

"The cat creature *and* Snake?" Brooks muttered, shaking his head. "Where are all these freaks coming from?"

"At first," Johnny said, "that thing scared the hell out of me. Then I realized—he's built like a man. You bring him down like one."

Brooks laughed. "The proverbial swift kick?"

"You got it."

Brooks looked up from the costume. "The transmitter's intact—but you won't be wearing this suit for a while."

"That's what spares are for."

Nassir, silent until now, stepped toward the window.

"Now we're dealing with the cat *and* we know Snake's still alive," he said. "So what the hell *is* he?"

"The same thing I am," Johnny replied. "But something was different. He didn't taunt me. No threats. No theatrics."

"Maybe he had bigger priorities," Nassir said.

"Or bigger plans," Brooks added. "And Jade isn't part of them."

**

"Tanner I'm telling you," Started Katherine, I feel like something isn't right with him."

Tanner nodded in agreement as he stared out of a nearby window. "Ever since he took that spill off the Empire State Building, he hasn't been the same. I haven't even heard him complain about those headaches he used to complain about all the time."

Katherine moved closer to him.

"Stern told me his D-N-A was different after the fall. He had some sort of chemical locked within his D-N-A which is similar in structure to Morphine Sulfate, and Shremmer as well as Stern, both surmised those chemicals somehow had a negative effect on Snake, causing issues with the use of his abilities."

Tanner then turned and faced Katherine.

"With that component somehow wiped from his genetic code, no restraints," he said.

"You think he will flip on us?" asked Katherine.

"I don't know," replied Tanner. "But you can never be too sure anyway so, I asked Stern to create something which will somehow transform energy into a form of inert matter. Rendering Jade, Snake, or even April, killable."

"He can do that?" she asked.

"He is certainly going to try," Tanner said dryly. "Stern's a genius and I'm hoping he can even surpass his own smarts."

Just then, Tanner and Katherine were interrupted by a brief knocking on the door followed by a young man, Stewart Warthog, barging in uninvited.

Tanner snapped, "What is it?"

"Sorry Mr. Tanner," Stewart said, "but Mrs. Hunter just got a call from Hahnemann Hospital, Martin Cole was gunned down during a carjacking in North Philadelphia. He doesn't have a next of kin in his chart, so they are trying to contact you."

"What?" asked Tanner.

"Oh my God," added Katherine as they both grabbed their coats and ran.

***

The cat paced back and forth inside of the electronic cage as he eyed the masked Snake, who stood there staring back at him.

"I thought he was supposed to destroy some property; he mauled those kids!"

Stern was sitting at his desk writing an entry into a log about the cat's activities. He then looked back up at Snake and continued their conversation. "I'm not happy about that either, I thought I satiated him enough to hold any hunger down while he carried out our tasks."

Snake turned from the cat. "I don't think he did what he did out of hunger, I think he was enjoying it!"

"And you didn't stop him?"

Snake lowered his head for a moment pondering that thought. He then looked back up at Stern. "No...no I didn't."

"Well the important thing is he got Jade's attention, which is exactly what Tanner wanted!"

Snake turned and looked back at the cat who was still staring at him. "Can he talk?" he asked.

"No, not yet anyway. I haven't been able to shape his vocal cords genetically, so I've been taking a more cosmetic approach."

Stern watched as Snake used the silver liquid and morphed back into his alter ego. "You know, the nanites in your suit have bonded with you in a crazy way."

"What do you mean?"

Stern looked up from his computer. "When you died, they didn't want to leave you. It's like they not only responded to your energy signature, they bonded with it."

"That's possible?" asked Michael.

Stern went back to his tasks. "Artificial intelligence is still very new; I guess anything is possible."

"I'm going home," said Michael as he headed towards the door.

Stern grabbed another folder and started writing in it. "Monday, I'm going to test a viewer displacement formula for your suit, hopefully you'll be able to cloak your body."

"Cool," replied Michael as he walked slowly out of Stern's lab. *If I'm here*, he thought.

The cat growled as he watched Michael leave out of the lab.

***

Tanner stood next to Cole's bed as he lay still and as Katherine walked in beside him and gently rubbed Cole's arm as a tear came out of her eye. Not only was he heavily sedated but he was connected to a ventilator which was helping him to breathe.

The low hum of the machine along with the constant alarms going off as his vital signs fluctuated between stable and un-stable values intruded on their auditory canals more often than they would like them to.

"His vertebrae was shattered from C one to C eight. He's never gonna walk again," started Katherine as Tanner stood there and stared at him. "He may always need external support to breathe. What kind of life is he going to have?"

Tanner just continued to stare blankly

"Martin I, I'm sorry this happened to you, but we are here and we love you!" said Katherine as she looked at Tanner and signaled him to say something.

Tanner just kept staring angrily at Cole. He then touched Cole's arm lightly turned and then walked out of the ICU.

Katherine ran out after him. "Steven!"

He kept walking.

"STEVEN!" yelled Katherine as she got in front of him and started walking in a backward motion until he stopped. "You gonna do the same thing to me when something happens to me? Ignore me? Small family my ass you lying son of a ..."

Tanner throwing up his hand as if he were going to give her a backhand slap interrupted her. He knew he wasn't going to hit her, but he threw his arm up in frustration.

"Well go ahead, I'm not afraid of you!"

He just pointed at her. "Just come on," he said impatiently.

***

"This costume," started Brooks as he was holding the sleeve of a costume which was hanging on a hook in the second locker, "is made the same way as your original costume, from the Teflon

282

coating all the way to the transmitter." He then walked over to a third locker and opened it, revealing another costume. "But this one," he started as he touched the armored torso, "is the shadow."

The costume was very similar to the original except the color was darker, and the gloves and boots had translucent strips around the edges where they met the costume.

Brooks said, "When you need to keep your cover down in those dark situations, just change into this costume. It doesn't light up like the other costume, but if you feel as if you're running low on power," he paused as he pushed a button on the side of the torso, lighting up the translucent strips. "You should be able to use your telepathy to turn these on. The earpieces also have transmitters for communication. I don't want what happened at Lincoln Drive to ever happen again."

Johnny ran a hand over the armor.

"It works," he said. "Feels right."

CHAPTER 58

*JOHNNY LOOKED AROUND and knew he had no idea where
he was. Upon first glance, all he could see was darkness, but
when he looked again, he saw two beings looked as if they were
made entirely of light. The beings looked similar to each other
except one of them was a bright yellow and had more
definition to his form than the other one who was red.*

*Johnny then looked down at himself and noticed he
appeared to look the same as the other two beings who were
there, and just like the other two beings, he was floating. He
attempted to speak but the sounds coming out of his mouth
sounded like the playing of a flute.*

*"You will not be able to speak here because you are still in
the learning and development process with your true natures,"
started the glowing figure, which had the more defined form. "I
am Shakkar, an operative for the high council of Nelaria. I
have tried to communicate with both of you through your
dreams but have had little success in the past because of the
immature development of your Nelarian D-N-A.*

*The more you switch back and forth between your human
selves and being full Nelarian, communication with you gets
much simpler for me. I have much to tell you but little time to
tell you everything, so I will tell you what I can. Before you two
were born, your mother was abducted by some of my people. I
was part of a regime which helped her and a few others escape.
In order for her to survive on my world, we had to do what
was called a synergistic merge. It allowed your mother and I to
become one. During her time on my home world, while
planning to get her and the other captives back to your planet,*

we befriended each other. We then soon fell in love. Shortly after, a few of my comrades discovered the Nelarians who had abducted some of Earths' inhabitants were about to engage in some unethical experiments on the people they had gathered from your home world, so my team took all of the Earthians back home while the council dealt with my rebellious clan.

Sometime after returning your mother home, I soon started missing your mother terribly but was constantly denied permission from the council to visit Earth because of the actions of the rebellious ones. I used what your people call astral projection to visit your mother while she was asleep much of the same way I visited with the two of you. During one of my many visits, I learned she was locked away at one of your state hospitals. To ease her mind, I increased my visits to daily ones. On one of my visits, she told me she was carrying the two of you, a phenomenon which was thought impossible with my people, but I surmised our bonding time is what created you two. I again attempted to get permission from the high council so I would be able to help her, but again they denied me."

Shakkar glided around the dark void the same way a professional figure skater glides across ice while Jade and Snake stayed motionless with the exception of following his movements with their heads. "On my final visit with her, I was surprised to find she wasn't asleep yet, but able to see me in a waking state. This is when I knew she was dying. She felt it too. I stayed with her past death and before her ascension as we watched as the two of you were removed from her womb. She cried upon the belief one of you had died as well, but as she ascended to her new home, I assured her you both would be fine because of your then dormant, Nelarian DNA. Because of your genetic coding, Michael and Johnny, whatever the substance was which took your mother at her young age, couldn't kill the two of you. The substance did, however, encode into your D-N-A and blocked certain neuropathways in each of you, causing your sparks to be mostly delayed. Michael, you *were affected the most by the substance which took your mother and when your Nelarian D-N-A started to develop, your second nature abilities would give you those headaches and cause your human brain to be - imbalanced which in turn caused you to experience those moments of insanity. I knew falling like you did along with the death of your human body would allow for your enhanced D-N-A to correct your human D-N-A.*

The two of you already have learned when in opposition, your abilities will dampen an inherent biological feature which prevents any one of us from harming another, but together there is a synergistic effect which is greater than any of you individually. Right now I await my fate from the high council for breaking the rules to save you Johnny, but I hope the three of us will unite one day. And Johnny, April…"

Everything then went pitch black, interrupting Shakkar.
Johnny then suddenly sat up in bed.

***

Michael sat up in bed and started holding his head. He wanted to believe what he had just experienced was nothing more than a mere dream, but deep down inside he knew the revelations were true. As he sat there, he thought about his childhood. He thought about how he had lived his life believing he was actually Michael Jones junior. He thought about how he had grieved when his mother died from cancer, and when four years later his father had been murdered. He then thought about the year after his father's death when he turned thirteen. He had become rebellious with his grandmother and ultimately ran away from home, leaving her all alone.

Almost from that point in his life, up until last year, he had spent his life in a gang, running territories and opposing the law. He hadn't started killing people until the person who shot at him at the Corestates Bank in Center City, during his first confrontation with Jade, who he now knows to be his brother. He always knew the episodes were what caused him to kill, but giving up using his abilities were never easy for him, as they were ingrained in him. He believed Tanner, via Shremmer and Stern, were the ones who helped him with his headaches. He was deceived. Michael then wondered what Johnny's life was like. Did their grandparents, aunts, and uncles or perhaps older siblings raise Johnny? Or was he brought up in a way similar to his own up bringing. For the first time since the time of his father's death, a tear came out of his eye.

***

The next morning, the aroma of coffee took center stage in Brooks' home lab.

Nassir walked into the lab as Brooks was sitting behind his desk drinking a cup of coffee. "Look at this," started Nassir as he sat the Sunday edition of the Philadelphia Inquirer on the table in front of Brooks.

On the cover of the paper, in bold print it said, 'Man and Woman, Both Struck by Lightning, Live'. "You remember Doctor Harding, don't you?" asked Nassir.

"Doctor Jennifer Harding?" asked Brooks as Nassir shook his head in the affirmative.

"Very young and very intelligent," started Brooks, "Yes, I remember her, she gave a brilliant dissertation a couple of years ago on magnetic fields and gravitational forces."

"It says here in the paper she created an anti-gravitational magnetic disrupter cannon which blew the power in her building while she was testing it during a huge funding demonstration. And, to add insult to injury, she caught a flat on the way home in the middle of a thunderstorm. A good Samaritan was trying to help her, and they were both struck by lightning. She's alive, but I imagine she's quite hurt."

Brooks examined the front of the newspaper and shook his head in the negative.

Johnny then soon walked into the lab and found a seat. "You two won't believe what happened to me last night," said Johnny as he shook his head in disbelief of the information he learned.

"What happened?" asked Nassir.

"Last night," started Johnny, "I had an out of body experience, and I learned everything I needed to know in regard to my relationship with Snake and why he acts the way he does." He paused as he looked between the two physicians. "I also met my father."

"What?" asked Brooks.

Nassir said, "Your aunt doesn't even know who your father..."

Johnny quickly held up his hand signaling them to stop talking.

"My father," started Johnny, "is an alien from another world."

Nassir and Brooks just looked at him.

They found it hard not to believe him; after all, he did have a lot of strange abilities.

"Snake is my twin brother, and his real name is Michael. I learned a lot about our connection, why he is the way he is..." He sighed.

The two physicians looked at him with expressions of curiosity on their faces.

"That does explain a lot about you," replied Brooks.

"Did he say anything else?" asked Nassir.

"He started to say something about April, but we were cut off."

"April?" asked Nassir.

"Cut off like a phone call being cut off?" asked Brooks.

He looked at Nassir. "Yes," and then at Brooks, "yes, I think."

"What could April have to do with this?" Nassir asked.

"I don't know other than she was a victim." Johnny grunted. "There is way too much information to process!"

"Well I think I know where we should start," suggested Brooks. "I reached out to Mark Stern and he's been pretty much blowing me off and we now know Snake is alive."

"So Biotech?" asked Nassir.

"Biotech," said Brooks.

Johnny nodded in agreement. "Biotech!" He then looked at the pair. "Where is Biotech?"

"Their offices are in Center City of course," started Brooks, "but their research Facility is in Willow Grove, thirty-nine hundred Welsh Road."

Johnny's eyes hardened. "Then that's where we go."

CHAPTER 59

TANNER, MICHAEL, AND KATHERINE all walked into the
testing atrium at Biotech Labs, where Stern was observing April
through the tinted glass window in a booth which sat up two
stories, high enough for them to look down at April and the floor
of the atrium.

The atrium looked like the typical American high school
gymnasium, but was devoid of the basketball courts and
bleachers, and with the addition of an observation room.
Initially designed to be an area to test highly volatile substances.
Some of the walls were padded with blue cushioned mats while
others appeared to be slightly off white. At one side of the room
there sat a backless bench as a prop for April to use in order to
practice with. April was wearing purple boots, a purple spandex
set which had blue legs, and dark blue baggy sleeves in the arms.
Her torso was purple also and her medium breast were covered
well. She also wore a purple mask, and her eyes were lit with a
purple light, appearing to be pupil-less.

"Nice outfit," started Tanner as he observed April through
the glass window. "Though I would've covered her face since her
boyfriend is still out there and all!"

"She designed it herself," replied Stern as he looked over at
Tanner. "I gave her the same synthetic fluid given to Mister
Jones with the exception of one modification."

Tanner huffed. "What's that?"

"You'll see soon enough," replied Stern.

As they watched April flying through the small gym, they
observed her opening up a number of portals and flying

through. They then watched her shooting various targets with lasers, which she emitted from her hands.

"Snake, get in there and give her a challenge," Tanner said calmly.

Michael just looked at Tanner.

"I want to see if she can hold her own on an equal footing fight."

With the sound of cracking electricity accompanied with the spiraling red light, Michael vanished.

With a light snap and in full costume, Snake then reappeared inside of the gym. He stood around and watched April as she smiled at him.

Again, with the sound of cracking electricity along with the spiraling red light, he vanished.

With a light snap, this time he reappeared falling over top of her, but she disappeared, leaving him to fall to the ground.

April started laughing as she reappeared standing over top of him with her legs positioned at the sides of his waist. She looked down at him. "Why are you hiding that face?" she asked.

As Snake looked up at her, his mask turned into the silver liquid and morphed down off of his face.

April smiled with approval of his compliance as a bench circled with red light hit her from behind and sent her flying involuntarily to the other side of the gym.

Snake's mask morphed back into the silver liquid and then moved up onto his face as he stood up and faced her.

She stood up and faced him as she slowly faded out of sight.

As he looked around for her, expecting her to reappear somewhere different from where she was standing, lasers shot from in front of him as he saw her image for a brief second. *What the fuck?* He thought as point zero one seconds later, the blast sent him back against the wall of the gym, under the booth.

"How'd she do that?" asked Tanner.

"Oh you caught it that time?" asked Stern. "I added cloaking technology to her costume, she essentially works the cloaking the same way she changes the only flaw is she can't use any of her laser fire abilities while she is cloaked, which is why we saw her for a brief second when she fired at Snake. The cloaking will make her an excellent spy."

Down in the atrium, April reappeared standing over Snake, picked him up and slung him to the other side of the gym.

Back up in the booth, Tanner looked over at Stern.

"Where are we with Martin?" he asked.

"I had to make a few adjustments figuring he'd want some of his own extremities, but I made them. I've uploaded a bunch of additional skills into his mainframe such as his fighting ability and ability to fly, but there has been no negative feedback reported."

"Mainframe?" asked Katherine. "You mean his brain?"

Stern looked at her with a sarcastic expression on his face. "Yeah Kat, his brain which is connected to his mainframe."

"What's the status of the cat?" Tanner asked.

Stern laughed. "Oh he's nice and pissed."

He then looked back into the gym as he heard Snake crashing into another wall. "He is definitely holding back," added Stern as he pointed at Snake.

Katherine gave Tanner an '*I told you so*' look.

CHAPTER 60

JOHNNY STOOPED OVER and laid the flowers next to the tombstone.

He then looked around the cemetery and over at the crowd of people in the distance who were all standing around a casket which was sitting above ground, waiting to be lowered. "This seems to be a very popular place these days," Johnny said as he looked back at April's tombstone. "I just recently found out a lot about myself." Johnny held up his right hand and started to count down his fingers. "For one, I am part of an alien race whose language I can't even speak. Number two, my mother was murdered in a state hospital right before she gave birth to me. And three, you're really gonna love this one, Snake is my twin brother."

He dropped his hands and briefly started laughing the demented laugh of a raving lunatic. "Who the hell am I kidding?" he asked in frustration. "I have been dancing around here for the last five, six months, pretending to be somebody's superhero, and I couldn't even save your life." He teared up and then started, "I don't have a clue as to the name of the woman who murdered my mother, and my own twin brother is my arch enemy." He paused again as he wiped the tears from his eyes. "By the way, I forgot to mention, Snake is still alive, the one fault of our D-N-A that in any other circumstance would be an ideal trait."

Johnny looked up to the sky as he again wiped a tear from his right eye. "April, I need you back."

***

"Phase one of our plan is complete," said Tanner as he walked cautiously around the boardroom. "Of course, you all know any money we vest into this project will not reap in any profits until our small Trilateral Commission army does everything we ask them to do and the first thing, we're going to have them do is destroy that little glow worm Jade."

Tanner continued to walk around the table. "The Cat, however, is a wild card and he will need to be dissuaded from harming commission members. After all, I wouldn't want any of you accidentally mauled or killed or anything like that."

The small business attired crowd all looked around at each other as Stern got up on Tanner's cue. Stern said, "These wrist bands will keep you safe from the cat." He grabbed the wristbands from out of the box and started passing them out around the room. "The band works by emitting an invisible ultrasonic frequency around your body and if you happen to be in the path of the cat, he'll simply just avoid you."

Tom Herman, one of the older members of the board, older by age and not length in the commission, stood up and said, "what happens if the battery dies?" Tom Herman was one of the more conservative members of the board. He was in incredibly good shape, and his white hair was the only way anyone could tell he was around seventy years old.

While a kind man in the public eye and a wonderful grandfather to his seven grandchildren, he was just as corrupt as the other members in the room. The cause for his drive was financial greed. His money was a large part of the backbone which funded the Trilateral Commission, right under Tanner.

"Then you're already dead," replied Tanner sarcastically.

Herman looked over at Tanner as if he were crazy and Tanner just smiled.

"Your body is the battery," interjected Stern as he lowered the box from off of the table and on to the floor. "The band will be feeding from your bodies' heat which is released from the brown fat which constitutes part of your weight. While the frequency is being maintained around you, you'll be slightly losing weight on a continuous basis."

The crowd of board members all put their wristbands on.

Tanner, watching Herman, said, "Tom your light isn't on, chances are you have a defective wrist band."

Tom looked around at the other board members' bands and saw theirs also didn't have any type of light. He then looked at Tanner who smiled sarcastically. *Damn I hate him*, he thought.

"What about those of us who have kids," asked one of the board members.

"The band works conglomeratelike," started Stern. If you hold onto your loved ones, it will expand your protection."

If you're not happy with your wife Mark," started Tanner, "just let go of her. The cat will handle the rest."

Stern shook his head.

"Cheap divorce," added Herman.

"Nothing gets past you Herm," chortled Tanner. Thank you, Mister Stern," started Tanner, "and I will contact the rest of you if anything further develops. Meeting adjourned."

***

As the sun started to descend for the night, Jade flew through the city of brotherly love when his costume started to illuminate. As he flew over East River Drive, he looked down and over all of the ground area and observed everything was quiet.

"I haven't seen any sign of that cat thing. Do you think my swift kick scared it away for good?" asked Jade.

"That sounds like a good theory," said Nassir through the earpiece. "Just continue to circle the parks and..." Nassirs' words were cut short by a loud ear piercing, screeching sound which caught Jade off guard, causing him to scream out and fall to the ground. "What the hell was that?" Jade asked as he stood all the way up.

There was no response.

"Doc? Doctor Brooks?" He tapped hard on the earpiece transmitter. "Where is every..." Interrupted by the black cat, who lunged at him and knocked him into a nearby tree, Jade looked up as his eyes ascended up the furry black form. The cat stood over him, roaring majestically. "I'm more than ready for you this time," said Jade as he kicked up towards the creature's groin area.

The cat quickly blocked the kick with his arm but winced in pain from the force of the kick.

Jade looked up as the cat raised its right arm, ready to strike. He then, with the cracking sound of electricity along with the bright spiraling light, vanished as the mighty claw took up some of the ground.

With a light snap, Jade then reappeared standing just a few feet behind the cat.

Irritated, the cat turned around and roared some more.

Jade stared at the cat who then just returned the stare without making a move. Come on you big dummy come to daddy.

The cat just continued to stare.

What are you wait...? His thoughts interrupted, Jade was soon knocked over hard by something which made him hurt a little. *Snake*, he thought. When he turned around in order to see his attacker, he saw a being who was dressed in red and silver armor, a robotic-looking type of person.

"What the fuck?" he said. "Where these fuckers coming from all of a sud..." Interrupted again, by mini missiles which came at him quickly, and exploded upon contacting his costume.

Jade quickly flew up into the air, in order to give himself some distance.

The Biotech android creation then released two little round discs from just around his belt and into the air after Jade.

The two discs whizzed through the air sounding like a small posse of bees planning to hit their target.

One of the discs hit Jade.

Jade's costume dimmed out quickly as he started falling towards the ground. What the hell?

Five.

I can't fly!
Four.
C'mon, up up!
Three.
Aw shit!
 Two - one.
Right before Jade hit the ground, a loud zipper sound opened a portal and he fell through.

***

The portal then reopened with the zipper sound, one thousand feet above where it had closed, and even though Jade was still not glowing, it was because of the shadow outfit he was now wearing. His powers were restored. Jade quickly descended into the wooded area.

"Unit B T Two Thousand and One?" said Sterns' voice coming from the left wrist of the robotic looking figure. "What's your status?"

"I said, call me TURBINE!" said the unit angrily as he looked around the wooded area. He soon noticed Jade with the help of the infrared sensors in his optics. Through his field of vision, Jade was outlined in a red light. He fired a laser from his left arm in the direction of where he saw Jade.

"You can't fire a laser beam at an energy based being," said Stern from over the transmitter.

Turbine watched as Jade flew fast out of the brush and as the light bands around his wrist and ankles became illuminated. "You can harm him in his humanoid form," started Turbine as he looked on at Jade, "or you can scare him from his hiding spot."

The Cat growled as Jade ascended upward.

Turbine laughed as he watched Jade swoop around.

Snake rammed hard into Jade, causing him to fall to the ground again.

The trio of villains than swarmed quickly around Jade like vultures who had just discovered a cuisine of rabbits, squirrels and possum stretched out in front of them.

As Jade looked up, the cracking sound of electricity along with the spiraling light, changed his costume from the shadow version, to his brightly lit green and gold outfit, thinking he may need more power.

Turbine then released two damper discs as Jade produced the cracking sound of electricity along with the spiraling light and vanished.

Both discs hit the ground.

***

With the sound of a light snap, Jade then reappeared wearing the shadow again, some one hundred yards from where his attackers were currently standing.

This time the light bands were off and soon illuminated.

"Nassir, Brooks, anybody?" he called nervously.

"We're here Johnny," replied Brooks. "We kept getting cut off from..."

"They've ganged up on me," interrupted Jade. "If one isn't kicking my ass, then another one is. They got this robotic looking thing with long metal wings working with them now. The robot has these things that somehow drain my powers."

"How about using your..."

Loud screeching and static cut Brook off.

The same loud screeching sound Jade had heard when he had first encountered the cat, and the same loud screeching sound he had just heard a few short moments ago, when he was attacked. Jade then turned around as he heard the clicking sound, but he never saw the two discs which landed on his back. The light bands on his costume quickly flickered off.

The cat smacked him and the claw marks tore through the costume leaving paths of blood on the left side of Jade's torso as he quickly put his left hand over the delicate area.

Jade then looked down at his bloodied left hands.

Snake gave Jade an uppercut, but it wasn't much of a hit so Jade's head flew up and back and he fell to the ground.

Jade then looked upward at Snake as he recovered from the punch. *No*, he thought to himself.

The thought went unheard, even though Snake was thinking the same thing.

But he hated Jade.

At least he thought he hated Jade.

Well, he hated the fact Jade could use his abilities without appearing to be suffering. But then again, now he could too. *This Jade boy sounds like he stands for the same things Warren stood for*, he heard Toothpicks' voice repeat from inside his head.

Turbine gave Jade a hard elbow on the small of his back.

Jade fell down with the blow.

He thought he felt his spinal cord snap as he cried out and because he couldn't move, he decided not to argue the thought. He also felt the pain radiate all over his body as the titanium steel fist assisted him with falling down.

The cat took another swipe.

Blood splattered.

The pain suddenly went away.

Snake stepped back as the pair took turns beating the shit out of him and as Turbine constantly released damper discs onto Jade every time a minute had elapsed, just in case his powers would reactivate.

Jade's last few moments felt like an eternity.

After they were finished pounding on him, a small circular saw extended from out of Turbine's right forearm, and he began to guide it over various sections of Jade's body, cutting the costume from off of him.

After removing the costume from off of Jade's body he kicked his body over to the side. Turbine extended his majestic looking, silver titanium wings. He then grabbed a hold of the cat, who slightly resisted, and took off with the beast and costume in hand.

The costume was a present for Tanner, proof of the destruction of the young hero.

Snake agreed to and was left to destroy and discard the body. He picked up Jade's half naked and bloodied body and looked down at him as he carried him off. With the cracking sound of electricity assisted by the spiral of red light, they vanished.

CHAPTER 61

"JOHNNY COME IN!" yelled Brooks but he received no answer from over the transmitter. "SHIT!" he yelled as he grabbed his coat and headed to the door. "Ben, keep trying him! I'm gonna head over to Biotech!"

Nassir ran over and grabbed Brooks arm. "Whoa, whoa Robert, what do you think you can do?"

"I can get a hold of Stern, I still have consultant level clearance," started Brooks angrily, "make him give me some answers!"

"You can get yourself killed!"

Brooks slammed the coat rack down to the floor. "Ben I just can't sit here and do nothing!"

"I know how you feel Robert," started Nassir. "I've known Johnny his whole life. One thing I know is that he is strong willed, resilient, intelligent, and above all he is a good person with a good heart, and he will prevail." He led Brooks to a nearby chair and slowly sat him down. "What you will do, is patiently wait for him! Neither of us will be any good to him or anyone else if we get ourselves killed. If he takes too long, we'll go to his apartment like we did before. Plus, we're gonna need you to keep your credentials at Biotech."

Brooks stared up at him, knowing Nassir was right.

In the short time he has known Johnny, he has proven to them that he is the true definition of a hero. Not only because of his remarkable abilities, but because of who he is as a person.

Johnny Thompkins, even with all of his losses, will still come out of this on top.

***

With the sound of a light snap, Snake materialized in his condo with Johnny in his arms. He carried the lifeless hero into his room and laid him on the bed. He then morphed his costume into the silver liquid and then into an outfit; a black sweater, some blue denims, and a pair of white Nikes.

He looked at his brother with less and less disdain and increasing admiration. He then heard his father's voice in his head from their brief conversation with him. *You already know when working against each other and touching, your abilities cancel each other out, but when you merge and become synergistic, you can become so much more.*

Michael sighed. "Yeah...we need to end this now!" He converted his body to his energy form and merged his form with Johnny's still body.

Johnny's body lit up a bright orange as it elevated off of the bed and burned brightly as if on fire.

While merged, Michael became privy to many of Johnny's recent memories regarding his energy walks, seeing the moment Johnny was shot, witnessing their altercations through Johnny's eyes, and seeing the events which transpired at Byberry State Hospital almost twenty-three years ago.

Johnny's body then dimmed down and lowered back to the bed as Michael's red energy form emerged and he dimmed his body out and looked down at Johnny.

The bruises, cuts and blood from Johnny's badly beaten body were all gone and Johnny laid there asleep as if he had not been hurt at all.

Michael smiled. "Damn, that worked! You rest; I'll be back. We have a lot to discuss when you wake up." Michael produced the sound of crackling electricity along with the red light which surrounded him, and he vanished from out of the condo.

CHAPTER 62

STEVEN TANNER WALKED into the lab, interrupting Mark Stern who was completing documentation in a notebook.

Stern then closed up the book and looked up at Tanner with a wicked smile. "You think you're ready for this?" asked Stern.

"Please just get on with it," replied Tanner.

Stern got up from behind his desk and grabbed a set of keys from off the hook sitting on the wall to the right of his desk. "Just come with me," Stern said.

He led Tanner through the room where they had first saw Turbine when he was patiently waiting for a donor and where he was currently in a large cylindrical charging station with a glass enclosure, to the other end of the room where a door was locked.

Stern quickly dug through the stack of keys as Tanner sighed with the breath of annoyance. Stern then located the key and unlocked the door.

They then went in.

Tanner smiled with amusement.

Steven Tanner was amused because of the fact he was looking at himself through the window of an incubation tube. Not actually himself, but his clone, a replica of him, and if he could be fooled by the identity, then he was sure everyone else would be fooled also.

The plan was for the Tanner clone to take over everything; with the belief he was actually Tanner, while the real Tanner controlled everything from the background.

Stern's task was to wake Tanner the clone, educate him, and convince him he was just in a coma suffering from a loss of amnesia. Then, when the Tanner clone would figure out where they were at strategically, he would be anxious to get back to work.

"Stern this is absolutely amazing," started Tanner. "What does he know?"

"He knows everything about you, including your aspirations and goals and everything that transpired up until last week, only what you wanted him to know as per your instructions."

"I just want him to believe he is actually me; I don't need him to know everything I know about my money. He may actually try to do what I'm going to do."

"Whatever you want boss," replied Stern.

"Does anyone else know about this?" asked Tanner.

"No - nobody knows about this except for you and I."

"Make sure no one finds out about this and when the smoke clears, I'll be back for you. You are definitely an employee I do not want to lose."

***

With an uneasy feeling in his stomach, Nassir unlocked the door to Johnny's apartment and walked in followed by Brooks. They looked around in all of the rooms and saw everything appeared to be neat and in order. If anyone had been staying there, neither one of them could tell.

"I just don't get it," said Brooks. "It's been over four hours since we've heard from him. There's been nothing on the news about finding him anywhere and this place is so spotless, if he had been here, we would never know."

Nassir continued to look around the apartment. His concern grew. The last time they couldn't find Johnny he was asleep in bed. This time, Johnny was nowhere to be found.

"Johnny wherever you are," started Brooks, "I pray you're okay."

***

Michael couldn't believe the images he had seen since his brief merge with Johnny. It was as if his own mind were feeding off of the thoughts Johnny had in his mind. He decided he would have to confirm what it was he saw for himself. Dressed in a pair of blue jeans and a sweater, he started walking slowly around the interior of the darkened and abandoned hospital, wondering if he was indeed at the right place or not.

He held up his hand and produced a soft red light to try and brighten the halls a bit. He soon made his way to the second floor and immediately recognized the vision he had of the sign which said surgery over the double doors.

Then he saw the images.

Michael saw everything from his biological mother in the counseling sessions, to the nurse who injected the lethal needle into his mother's arm. *The nurse*, he thought, *looks somewhat familiar*. He continued watching as the nurse with the short red hair turned fully around.

The soft yet wicked smile caught his attention as he immediately recognized it. *Katherine O'Mally!* He then became enraged as he saw the young nurse carrying him out of the hospital. He saw the events which altered his life, keeping him from a life and family he now would never know.

As his anger grew, his headache started to surface. This was just a simple tension/stress headache from what he learned. Thank God it wouldn't produce the same kind of results it had in the past. He reached into a pocket in his pants and pulled out a bottle of pills Stern had made for him. He remembered Stern saying the ones Doctor Shremmer had given him wouldn't help, but he was no longer under the belief his current supply would work as well. He stood there and looked at the pills.

"Tanner - Katherine, you're both gonna pay!"

***

Laying down in bed with the blanket half exposing his bare chest, Tanner looked over at Katherine as she slept, and he smiled his devilish yet boyish grin. He liked her. More than a feeling of simply liking her, he admired her.

Katherine was the only person whom he has ever known, who has ever stood up to him. Whenever he would talk shit, if she didn't agree with him, she wouldn't just disagree with him, she would logically challenge him. If at any time he were being truthful yet manipulating, she would stand up to him.

Katherine O'Mally had more balls than any man he has ever known and he liked that the most about her.

The fact she was pleasing to look at helped out also.

Her spicy red hair hung over her face as she slept, partially covering her eyes. To him she looked just as good now as she did when he first met her in college over twenty-eight years ago. Her lips were naturally pink and unnaturally full. Her skin was slightly pale but creamy in appearance.

The telephone then started ringing and Tanner turned away and picked up the receiver. "Hello?" he said dryly as he looked away from Katherine and listened.

"So Cole and the cat were the last ones to see him?"

Again he listened.

Hearing his voice, Katherine slowly opened her eyes and looked at Tanner as she listened to him on the phone.

"They returned with his torn costume and Snake volunteered to get rid of the body?"

Tanner pulled the receiver away from his face and slapped his hand with it several times. "You didn't know this when I was there?"

Tanner paused as Katherine sat all the way up.

"Did they at least bring his head too?" he asked and then paused.

"Send them back out to him tonight, and just in case Jade is still alive, I think we need to try plan b, use the girl as back up if you need to."

Tanner then hung up the phone.

"Who are you sending the children after?" asked Katherine as she yawned out her words, stretching her bare arms in the process.

"Stern just called," replied Tanner as he ran his fingers through his hair. "Cole and that cat creature returned with Jade's costume as proof of defeat, but Snake took off with the body."

Katherine sat up quickly. "I told you he needs to go!"

"I know, I'm working on it, and he is a mistake I'm willing and ready to correct."

***

With the sound of a light snap, Michael materialized inside of a house in Pittsburgh. The house was a traditional three bedroom with contemporary styled furniture; a sofa and loveseat, which were both hunter green with a cream splash pattern design. There was also a chestnut brown coffee table with a matching end table on which there sat a hunter green touch lamp with a beige colored lampshade.

The window, which was covered with cream mini-blinds and hunter green curtains were closed tightly. The blinds were slanted downwards, and the curtains were fully drawn.

No one would have been able to witness Michael's arrival into the house because of the non-existent visibility into the residence.

Michael's grandmother had her brother secure the place after her son died so they didn't lose it. She intended for Michael to have it after he had gotten old enough, now the place just sat there. The same yardman who cared for his grandmother's house was taking care of this house, not for the money, and definitely not because of his generosity, but because someday he aspired to obtain the property himself, after the old lady had passed away.

Michael looked around the living room first and recalled all of the family pictures, all of his baby pictures, all of the trophies he had won running track when he was in elementary and the beginning of junior high school, most of which were first place.

As Michael studied the pictures and other artifacts of his past, he realized he really had no complaints. His childhood was one most children were never blessed with seeing.

His parents showed him nothing but love and respect, the only problem though was they lied to him about who he was. Had Michael never found out about his abilities, he would have lived his whole life believing he was someone he wasn't.

Michael then headed over and up the stairs, past a bathroom and his old bedroom until he reached his parent's bedroom. He put his hand on the doorknob and hesitated for a minute before going inside.

Inside the room was a large oak canopy bed, obviously his mother's taste. There were a matching mirrored dresser and tall chest, as well as two nightstands which matched the set.

Michael went across the room and opened a closet door which sat adjacent to the left side of the bed. On the top shelf of the closet was a fireproof Sentry Safe, which he remembered well from his days as a snooping child. He didn't have a key but knew where it was and had no desire to get them at the moment.

Michael's eyes started glowing a crimson red and lasers shot out of them and at the lock, blasting the safe open in order to see the contents inside. Michael rustled through the safe, hoping to find a birth certificate, but deep down inside, knowing he wouldn't find any such piece of information. He searched again, hoping to find something, anything which would tell him his visions were nothing but mere lies.

Again, fate did not work in his favor.

What Michael did find, however, was interesting enough. He found his parents will, naming his grandmother executor of their estate and which stated all of their personal belongings were to go to him upon his eighteenth birthday. He found saving bonds, certificates of deposits, stacks of them which had maturity dates of nineteen eighty-five, over eleven years ago. Bank account statements with generous sums of money his parents had opened up for him, and a notarized letter stating everything would be solely his, after his eighteenth birthday.

Michael had left Pittsburgh way before that time and his grandmother had no way of knowing whether or not he was dead or still alive. Just the same, she held onto everything in the hopes he was alive.

He was now twenty-three.

"What am I doing?" Michael asked in frustration as he put the box back up on the shelf. He realized, even though he was obtained illegally, the two people who raised him, did so unconditionally. And he couldn't love them more. He knew the truth now, whether or not he liked it. Now he had to deal with it.

Assisted with the sound of cracking electricity and a spiraling red light, Michael vanished from out of the house.

***

As if waking from a bad dream, Johnny suddenly sat up in bed. "What?" he asked out loud.

He got no answer.

Wearing nothing more than a pair of boxers, he got out of bed and began to investigate his current environment.

The bedroom he was in didn't belong to him.

The room was lavishly furnished with black lacquer furniture and an old beer keg which was positioned against the wall added a nice touch. The black vertical blinds were metal and the cream accessories complimented the color scheme of the room nicely.

Then Johnny happened upon a small family picture.

In the picture, there was a man, woman and child and all three of them wore Kool-aide smiles. As he scrutinized the picture, he decided the child was around eight or so, and then he thought the child looked similar to himself at that age. *Snake,* he thought, *it has to be.*

Suddenly scenes from his brief encounter with The Cat, Snake, and Turbine started to play in his head. *Did I die? I should be dead,* he thought as he touched himself wondering how he could still be alive and in one piece.

Why am I at Snake's place? Johnny then produced the sound of cracking electricity along with the spiral of bright yellow light and teleported an outfit from his home onto himself.

He was now wearing a gray sweatsuit with a hoodie. He again produced the sound of crackling electricity along with the spiral of yellow light and vanished from out of the room.

***

309

With a slight creak and a light slam, the front door to Johnny's apartment had just closed.

A second later, with the sound of a light snap, Johnny reappeared in his living room and walked over to the telephone.

After depressing the speaker button, he heard a dial tone and acknowledged it by dialing.

The phone on the other end rung three times.

"Hello?" said Brooks over the speaker phone.

"Doctor Brooks, I ..."

"I'm not home right now," interrupted the voice, "but if you leave your name, number, a brief message and the time you called, I will definitely get back to you."

The machine beeped.

"It's Johnny, I'll be there as soon as I shower, so if you get this message before I get there, please call Doc and let him know." He then pressed the button again, hanging up the phone. "I wish everyone could have carry around phones."

Johnny quickly headed into the bathroom.

***

With the sound of a light snap, Michael arrived back to his condominium and went to his bedroom. When he looked in, he immediately saw Johnny was gone.

"Damn," he said out loud and to himself. A surge of disappointment ran through his veins.

Michael then turned around quickly in response to a loud explosion.

He was immediately confronted by Turbine who tore down the door frame to his condo, followed by the cat.

"What's up, Snake?" asked Turbine as a faint humming sound started to play.

Michael looked at the two intruders with angry eyes. "Get outta my way Cole."

The cat growled.

"We know what you did, Tanner would like a word with you," started Turbine.

Michael's eyes started to glow a crimson red. "That's not gonna work out well for either of you then!"

"After all he's done for you." Turbine shot two damper discs out towards Michael, but he quickly threw up an energy shield which shorted the discs out as they hit it.

He then produced the sound of cracking electricity along with the spiral of red light and vanished from out of the condo.

The cat roared in anger.

"No worries," Turbine said calmly. "We've got another stop to make."

CHAPTER 63

BROOKS WALKED BACK into the room as Johnny continued to explain to Nassir all of the strange details of what happened. The constant dimming out of his body, the way he felt when he believed he had experienced death, and all of the oddities he felt when fighting against Snake, Turbine, and the cat.

"... and every time I tried to listen to what yall were saying, I would hear this loud screeching noise."

"This android character must have a radio frequency close to ours," replied Brooks. "We can probably use that to our advantage."

Johnny looked puzzled. "Meaning?"

Nassir walked over to the transmitter and switched it on. A slight static sound with some squeaking could be heard. "What I think he means Johnny is - we can use the wavelength of interference in order to track them down."

"If we do that, aren't we going to have a problem keeping in contact with each other?"

Nassir walked back over to Johnny. "Well we're going to have to communicate in order for you to be able to pick up their signal, but beyond that, if you find them, we're going to have to wait in order for you to be able to communicate with us."

"What about the shadow?" he asked. "I woke up in my underwear..." he shrugged.

"Don't worry," started Brooks. "Because Ben couldn't make up his mind about which one looked better, we made two versions of the shadow."

Nassir went into one of the two functional metal lockers and pulled out the suit.

The other version of the shadow was black with dark green sleeves and legs. The light bands contoured perfectly with the shape of the boots and gloves. Other than those few differences, the suits were exact matches.

"You'll just have to use this one instead," said Nassir.

"Where do you two find the time to make these suits?" Johnny reached for the suit and touched the torso. He smiled signaling his approval. "I like it."

***

"Alright Tanya, time for bed," said Pauline as she walked out of the kitchen and into the living room where her daughter Tanya was sitting and watching television.

Tanya huffed. "There's only ten minutes left in *E.R.*!"

A loud explosion blew in the front door.

The red and silver, android stood in the doorway.

Then the large black panther looking creature jumped in and started roaring.

Pauline and Tanya grabbed each other in fear, screaming and crying.

"You can either come with me," started Turbine as the cat licked his lips, "or you can stay with him."

***

"What's wrong?" asked Nassir as he and Brooks ran over to Johnny, who had fallen to his knees.

Ever since his reawakening, Johnny's empathic abilities seemed to have been heightened. He now could sense when there was a problem with any human whom he cared about.

"No! Aunt Paula," was all Johnny said right before he and his costume, with the cracking sound of electricity and the spiraling yellow light wrapped around each of them, and they vanished.

***

With the sound of a light snap, Jade, in his shadow suit, reappeared at his aunt's house or what was left of it.

The police were there already when he arrived.

As Jade walked through the living room, he took notice to the blasted hinges which seemed to have still been smoking.

"What happened?" he asked of the approaching police officer.

"Neighbors said that giant cat was here with some sort of robot. They took a woman and a little girl away."

"Thanks," replied Jade as a portal opened up with the sound of a large zipper in the ceiling above him.

The cop watched in wonder as Jade flew into the black abyss.

The zipper sound then closed up the portal.

***

The zipper-sounding portal reopened over Center City Philadelphia and Jade flew out.

"I swear to GOD if they hurt them," started Jade.

"Where are you now?" asked Nassir through the transmitter.

"Center City," started Jade. "Where is this Biotech place again?"

"No, go to Willow Grove," started Brooks. "That's where the lab facilities are!"

"Willow Grove it is," said Johnny as he started flying in that direction.

As Jade flew through the city, the greenish gold light from his costume caught the attention of everyone along the way.

Like a shooting star within the Earth's atmosphere, Jade flew fast across the city until he reached the corner of Welsh Road and Computer Avenue where he landed in the parking lot of Biotech Industries, as the alarms started blaring at his presence inside the fenced perimeter.

Jade didn't care about anyone watching. He lost April and was not about to lose anyone else he loved.

"WHOEVER YOU ARE!" he yelled. "WHEREVER YOU ARE, I WILL FIND YOU!"

Nassir started, "Johnny..."

314

A loud screeching sound through the earpiece transmitter cut Nassir off as something streaked across the sky from behind him.

They're here!

The silver and red clad android landed in plain view in front of Jade.

The retractable wings retracted with the sound of metal clanging together.

Turbine immediately noticed Jade was devoid of the bruises, cuts, and blood which plagued him earlier. "Nice suit...by the way, my life is ruined because of you!"

Jade looked angrily at Turbine. "Am I supposed to know you?"

Turbine looked down at his own metallic body. "No, not yet!"

The cat then roared loudly from behind Jade, alerting the hero to his presence without him having to turn around.

"The woman and child!" Jade demanded angrily.

"You'll never see them again," said Turbine as the cat lunged towards Jade as he converted his body into his pure energy form and flew straight up.

Turbine expanded his wings with the clanging sounds of metal as he took off after Jade.

***

With the sound of a light snap, Snake, in his full costume, appeared inside of Tanner's house. As he started walking, he bumped his foot into the couch.

Zeus, the Alaskan Malamute, could be heard barking outside.

The light thump along with Zeus's announcement got Katherine's attention and caused her to run into the living room.

Her red hair was hanging just past her shoulders, and she was wearing only a tee-shirt which came down just past her waist and a pair of slippers, so the fact Snake was standing there and not Tanner, startled her.

"Snake?" she said trying to sound pleased he was there, but the tone in her voice was a dead giveaway she was indeed nervous.

Snake looked her up and down as he slowly started walking towards her. He was actually there to see Tanner, but she was a bonus.

"Why don't you call me by my real name?"

The liquid morphed down Snake's face and stopped at his neck merging with the rest of his costume.

Katherine slowly walked backwards matching Snakes steps as he moved towards her.

"Okay," she said as she shrugged her shoulders. "Michael." She fake smiled as she continued backing away from him.

"No!" he said angrily. "My full name!"

"Your full name?" she shrugged her shoulders.

Snake nodded in the affirmative as they both kept moving.

Katherine bumped into the love seat and turned around briefly as they both stopped. "Mike - Michael Jones," she replied, tripping over her words.

"Why am I not surprised my name has never rang a bell in your head?" he asked as he towered over her.

"Should it?" she asked nervously.

"Think back to nineteen seventy-three, and maybe you'll jog your own memory."

"Nineteen...seventy-three...nineteen...seventy-three," she repeated to herself in a low whisper. "Michael Jones, Michael Jones..."

"Byberry," he said angrily.

She looked up at him slowly as her eyes widened with remembrance. "You can't be," she started as he grabbed a hold of her.

Snake smiled as he produced the sound of cracking electricity along with the spiraling red light which wrapped around both of them.

They both vanished.

***

316

With the sound of a light snap, Snake and Katherine reappeared somewhere in the arctic, in the middle of a large iceberg and he let go of her.

"What are you crazy?" she asked. "I'll freeze to death out here."

Snake smiled at her revelation and flew upward. He then looked down at her.

"Damn you," said Katherine.

"It's okay to let life go," he said as a zipper sound opened a portal a few feet above him.

"Michael wait!"

Snake waved goodbye to her and then produced the zipper sound, opening a portal.

He then flew through.

Katherine watched as the portal close.

She cried as she wrapped her arms around herself in a futile attempt to warm herself.

"He'll come back for me, he won't just leave me!"

She heard a growl coming up behind her and turned around nervously to investigate.

The last thing Katherine saw was the white teeth of a polar bear as it lunged at her.

***

Pauline stared hard at Tanner as he paced back and forth in front of her and Tanya. She struggled to pull her hands through the rope which bound her arms behind her back.

Her legs were tied to the legs of the chair she sat in, in the same fashion.

Tanya cried silently as she looked at her mother.

"How dare you send those - those things to my house!"

Tanner looked at her and huffed. "Blind fold them and gag their mouths!"

Stern walked over to Tanner as the two henchmen followed his orders. "Do you really think it's necessary to blind fold them?"

Tanner slapped him. "Don't question me!"

317

Stern held the side of his face. He then smiled. *Perfect*, he thought.

***

Just outside of Biotech, Turbine was firing missiles and lasers at Jade, who was flying in and out of portals at random as the cat stood by and waited for his chance to pounce on the hero.

As Jade came out of one of his portals, a damper disc hit him.

He soon fell to the ground.

As he hit the ground, two more discs hit him. In pain from his impact into the ground, he slowly stood up as his lighted suit bands dimmed and eventually went out.

Jade then wiped the trickle of blood, which was coming from the right corner of his mouth, off.

The cat, who was standing a few feet from where Jade was, licked his furry lips and then lunged at Jade, but found he couldn't quite reach him. When the cat looked back, he saw Snake holding his tail.

"Bad - bad kitty," said Snake.

The cat growled and started to reach his talon-like claws back at Snake.

Snake flew straight up into the air with the cat's tail in his hands, pulling the ferocious feline with him.

The cat couldn't touch him.

Turbine aimed his right fist towards Jade and a mini-scope came out, and locked onto Jade, making him the target. He then quickly retracted the scope as he changed his mind and extended his wings with the clanging sound of metal, quickly flying straight towards Jade.

The light bands on Jade's costume quickly lit back up right before Turbine reached him.

Jade then slid down on the ground directly under the android as Turbine was starting to pass over him, and Jade quickly made his feet connect with Turbine's midsection. He

318

pushed up hard with his legs, sending the android somersaulting through the air.

Simultaneously, Snake finally let go of the cat, who was now dizzy from being spun around.

The cat's body crashed into Turbine's, sending them both to the ground.

The cat's head hit the asphalt, and he fell unconscious as his body remained partially on Turbine.

Jade jumped to his feet. "Dumb and Dumber!" said Jade as he watched Snake descending to the ground next to him. "Thank you!"

Snake nodded, not knowing if he was saying thank you for taking his body to safety, or for taking care of the cat, but nonetheless acknowledging the words of gratitude.

As the cat lay still, Turbine pushed him off, stood up, and faced the duo standing before him.

"They have my aunt and my little cousin," said Jade.

Snake said, "I got a good idea where they are. I'll get them, 'cause Tanner's got more surprises than a little bit!"

"Tanner," repeated Jade aloud to himself.

"You keep the space ranger here busy," started Snake as the sound of crackling electricity along with the spiral of red light started to encircle him. "When he releases the little round disc towards you, throw up your shields, they'll be taken away, but at least you'll be able to throw them back..."

A blast from Turbine's optic lasers interrupted Snake's words as he vanished.

Jade then took off straight up and into the air.

Turbine then followed Jade up into the air.

As Jade elevated higher and higher, Turbine started slowing down.

Jade looked down and laughed. "C'mon heavy metal...What you waitin' on?"

While still looking at Jade rocket boosters came out of the soles of his metallic boots, increasing his speed.

"Oh shit," said Jade as he increased his speed with Turbine following right behind him.

***

With the sound of a light snap, Snake reappeared in the dimly lit Atrium training gym, where he saw who he assumed to be Jade's aunt and little cousin, tied up, gagged and blind folded.

As he walked over towards them, the lights to the gym came on, causing him to stop in his tracks. He looked up at the darkened glass booth where he knew Tanner was.

"SNAKE!" started Tanner's voice over a loudspeaker. "THIS TRAP WASN'T INTENDED FOR YOU, BUT SINCE YOU'VE MADE IT CLEAR YOU HAVE INTENTIONS WHICH DIFFER FROM MY OWN..."

A purple light blast struck Snake from behind, causing him to hit the wall hard and then fall to the ground.

As Snake got up, he turned around and saw April in costume with a purple glow in her eyes.

April laughed. "Shit, this is going to be fun!"

CHAPTER 64

CUTTING THROUGH THE wind like an aerodynamic knife, Jade flew through the city at a remarkable speed with a trail of green and gold light following him.

Turbine was also right behind him.

Turbine, with both of his arms extended out in front of him, armed himself with the mini missile launchers which came out of both forearms.

They too were now armed.

Jade sensed what was about to happen behind him.

He briefly thought about when he had awakened inside of Snake's bedroom, he discovered he had a new ability which was tied to his telepathic nature. His awareness of events seemed to have been more prevalent than before his deep sleep.

Continuing his flight, Jade allowed his decoys to emerge from either side of him.

Turbine started firing as he saw the decoys appear beside Jade.

Jade and his decoys started rotating and changing positions constantly, just as they had done with Snake during their earlier encounters.

Turbine fired numerous shots of missiles and lasers at Jade constantly missing him. Through his optic sensors, the visual field had darkened, and the real Jade was outlined in a red light by Turbine's thermal detection sensors. Turbine then fired two damper discs.

One of the damper disc hit the decoy on the right side of Jade and it vanished.

The other damper disc hit the decoy on the left side of Jade and it vanished.

Turbine then fired a third disc and it whizzed through the air looking like a mini flying saucer buzzing as if a bee.

Jade shielded himself right before the disc reached him, and the shield vanished when the disc contacted it.

Jade then opened up a portal with the sound of a loud zipper, and he flew through.

The zipper sounding portal opened five miles ahead of where Jade previously was and as he exited the portal, Turbine saw him and so proceeded to dart forward.

"Doc - can you hear me?"

"Loud and clear," replied Nassir.

"I wanna use the shadow."

"Why are you telling me? Go for it."

As Jade continued flying, with the cracking sound of electricity along with the bright spiraling light which circled him, his costume changed from the illuminated version, into the second shadow version Brooks designed.

The light bands which were positioned around the gloves and boots came on.

Jade led Turbine to an empty field in Horsham.

Turbine landed and retracted his wings. He then fired two damper discs in Jade's direction as they ran towards each other.

***

From up in the booth, Tanner and Stern witnessed as Snake crashed involuntarily into the wall of the atrium back first.

Tanner smiled.

In the atrium, Snake wasn't sure how to handle his present situation. He knew he could easily let loose and beat the shit out of her, but he didn't want to do that. He was just starting to deal with the guilt of killing her in the first place.

As Snake got up, recovering from the crash into the wall, the bench he had used a couple of weeks ago to hit April with went flying into him.

He fell back down.

Snake produced the cracking sound of electricity along with the spiraling red light which wrapped around him.

Snake vanished.

With a light snap, he reappeared standing behind April and grabbed a hold of her.

April quickly produced the crackling sound of electricity along with the spiraling of a purple light and vanished.

With a light snap, April quickly reappeared on all fours right behind him, swooping her leg around so it made contact with the back of his leg, causing Snake to fall backwards. She then stood up quickly and grabbed his arms and flung him into the wall on the other side of the atrium, where he fell and hit the floor.

"I've just about had it wit these freakin' walls," said an angry Snake.

Tanner, still watching from the booth, laughed. *His holding back is gonna cost him this fight,* he thought.

***

As Jade rushed towards Turbine, Turbine raised his right leg while keeping his arms crunched inward.

The foot caught Jade in the abdomen, and Turbine then lowered his leg and punched him in the face.

The impact of the punch sent Jade flying back twenty feet.

Jade landed on his back and Turbine jumped up into the air and started to come down over Jade feet first.

Jade rolled over before the robotic feet had landed on him, and he witnessed the impression Turbines' feet made into the ground.

Just after Turbine hit the ground, Jade then swung his right leg around until it met the back of Turbine's legs, knocking the cyborg onto his back.

As Turbine started to sit up, Jade, on his hands and knees, brought his foot back around and kicked Turbine hard in the face, knocking him back down.

***

"LOOK!" yelled Snake as he picked April up by her neck, "I'm tryin' to be nice but you aren't makin' it easy for me."

April struggled to get free but couldn't. She felt as if she were losing her abilities and couldn't figure out why. April then felt as if the grip on her neck was starting to get tighter, starting to hurt, and she now wanted Snake to let go.

Snake said, "Jade taught me a little trick, if I just hold on to you for a little bit, our abilities disappear and all that is left is pure - human - strength."

April's costume morphed into the silver liquid and covered her body. She then appeared to have disappeared, and Snake lost his grip, thinking somehow, she managed to use her abilities in order to teleport.

She then reappeared in front him, holding her neck and looking at him with contempt in her eyes while breathing heavily.

"Tanner told me you didn't agree to my being here from the start," she said while gasping for breath.

"What?" asked Snake.

"He told me I woke up in the cemetery because I was buried there after you murdered me. He also told me I should take you out first before you attempt to do it again."

Snake looked up in the direction of the glass booth and, with the sound of cracking electricity along with the spiral of red light, he vanished.

April stood up straight as she continued to cough. Her eyes then started to glow a bright purple. She then smiled as she looked up in the direction of the booth.

With the sound of a light snap, Snake reappeared standing in the booth, in between Tanner and Stern.

His sudden appearance startled them both.

"You!" said Snake with a bit of malevolence in his voice as he grabbed Tanner.

Snake knew the perfect way to exact his revenge on Steven Tanner.

Tanner, after all, used him more than he helped him. Sugar coated his problem and tried to keep him under his command.

Snake and Tanner then, assisted by the cracking sound of electricity and the spiral of red light, both vanished.

**

With the sound of a light snap, Snake and Tanner reappeared in the parking lot of Biotech Industries.

"What the hell'd you bring me out here for?" asked Tanner.

The sirens of the police cars could be heard in the distance.

Snake smiled at him as Tanner felt him rip his watch off of his wrist. He then produced the cracking sound of electricity along with the spiraling red light, and vanished.

"What an idiot, doesn't he realize I OWN THE COPS!" yelled Tanner angrily. "And my watch, well I can always buy another watch."

As he turned around and started to walk back towards the Building, Tanner noticed the cat out of his peripheral waking up.

Tanner then stopped suddenly and looked down at his wrist with a horrible feeling in his gut. He then noticed he still had his watch on and what Snake had removed was the frequency band provided by Stern.

The band was to deter the cat from killing any board members.

The cat growled and licked his lips.

"Awe shit!!" yelled Tanner as he turned to run but the cat roared and lunged at him with the force of a four-hundred and seventy-five-pound lion.

The cat landed on Tanner's back crushing him as he started clawing at him, ripping him into shreds.

Tanner screamed in agony right before the cat raised his mighty claw and swung down hard, knocking Tanner's head off of his neck. The cat then finished eating off of Tanner's body as the tycoon's lifeless eyes just looked at him.

**

Back at the field, Turbine spun Jade around by his arms and then let go of him sending him upwards.

Jade caught his bearings and released numerous pulses of light energy, which circled around Turbine.

Turbine, looking like he had been tied up with a rope made of light, extended his wings, cutting the energy rope in the process, and then flew straight up towards Jade. Turbine then made a sharp turn, allowing his sharp wings to slice the hero in half.

When he landed, he saw Jade, the decoy, was standing there as if nothing happened. Then he felt a tap on the shoulder and turned around.

Jade flashed his body as if he were a camera taking a picture and the bright light temporarily blinded the android's optics. Jade then kicked him dead in the chest, sending him back about fifty feet.

Jade then produced the zipper sound and flew straight into a portal.

As he got up, recovering from the kick, Turbine looked around for the hero but saw nothing. As his head was turned, a portal opened up in front of him and a thick light blast shot out at Turbine, followed by a fully lit Jade.

The blast separated all of Turbine's extremities from his body and singed his torso and midsection.

Jade then landed and looked over the dismantled Turbine.

Then Jade saw something he had not expected to see.

There was exposed flesh and blood through the torn parts of the Kevlar exterior.

Jade's fully lit body went out, exposing him to be still wearing the shadow. He walked over to the android and pulled off the Kevlar face mask, with the same curiosity which was well known by the kids in the cartoon 'Scooby-Doo'.

The face was unmistakably one of the men he saw the night April was murdered. The only thing different about his face was where his blue eyes used to be, there were now round silver things which looked like a pair of binoculars which were somehow lodged into his head. He also had all types of wiring on his head and not only was he bald, but the top of his dome was completely metallic. Turbine's eyes then started to flicker.

"I have no intention of making the same mistake twice," said Jade. He disintegrated the disconnected extremities of Turbine with an energy blast from his right hand and blasted a hole in Turbine's chest with his left.

The flickering lights of Turbine's eyes soon went out.

"Program deleted," said Jade as he opened a portal up under the damaged cyborg, who then fell through.

A zipper sound then closed up the portal.

"I really need to work on my tag lines." Okay Snake, where'd you go?" Jade then opened a zipper-sounding portal and flew directly into it.

The zipper sound then closed the portal.

***

Snake reappeared inside of the atrium but didn't see April.

After looking through the room, he saw Johnny's aunt and little cousin were still safe. He covered his face back up with the silver liquid, which then turned into his mask.

Snake walked over to Pauline and Tanya and untied them.

When Pauline removed the blindfold, she jumped back upon seeing the masked face.

"Don't worry," started Snake as he continued to untie Tanya. "I'm here for Jade."

A silver silhouette of a woman started forming from the bottom up behind where Snake was standing and after it fully formed it decloaked.

April's eyes and hands glowing as Jade flew out of a portal which opened a few feet behind her.

Snake turned around as Pauline and Tanya ran aside.

Jade's hands then started to glow as he prepared to fire a laser at the strange woman who was about to fire upon Snake.

"Wait!" yelled Snake as he, with the sound of cracking electricity along with the spiral of red light, vanished just before April's lasers could hit him.

327

With the sound of a light snap, Snake then reappeared just behind April but in front of Jade just as he fired a thick laser beam at her.

The beam hit Snake.

Jade, in anger he had hit Snake instead of his intended victim, prepared to fire another laser as April turned around.

"NO!" yelled Snake, "that's April!"

Jade looked confused. "What?"

Snake stood up! "She came back to life somehow, but without her memory."

Damn, he thought as Jade scrutinized April hard as the purple light started to develop again in her eyes. He then looked at Snake.

"I need to go get the cat!"

Snake then produced the sound of cracking electricity along with the spiral of red light which wrapped around him.

Snake then vanished.

A purple blast fired in Jade's direction as he also produced the cracking sound of electricity along with the spiral of yellow light which wrapped around him.

Jade then vanished.

The laser blasted a hole the size of a standing bathtub into the wall of the atrium, leading into other areas of the building.

With the sound of a light snap, Jade then reappeared standing behind April and he quickly grabbed a hold of her.

"Let me go," she said angrily as she started to struggle.

"C'mon baby," started Jade, "Just remember me!"

Jade then converted his body into his pure energy form and merged himself with her.

April then stiffened up as her body appeared to change into a black void with a yellow rim outlining her body. She then relaxed and floated upwards as her mind began to flood itself with memories.

Meeting Johnny.

Spending time with Johnny's family.

Taking classes with Johnny.

Spending holidays with Johnny.

Being proposed to by Johnny as he was in the guise of Jade.

Jade then separated from her as April fell to the floor.

As he dimmed his glowing body out, Jade stared at her as she faced the other way appearing to be confused as to where she was and what she was doing there.

A tear came out of his eye as he watched her looking around in shock, her mind somewhat Swiss cheesed from the recent events she had been through.

April then turned around and looked in his direction.

"JOHNNY!" she exclaimed as she threw her arms around him.

"Johnny?" asked Tanya, who was standing nearby.

"You didn't hear that," suggested Pauline.

A parade of sirens could be heard darting by outside.

* * *

April, in full costume, kept talking as she stood inside of the lab in Brooks home with Johnny, Brooks and Nassir.

They all examined her with curious expressions on their faces though Johnny's was more of a look of joy and less a look of curiosity.

"...And then Stern gave me this really neat suit," she said as she made the costume morph into the silver liquid and then morph again into a pair of jeans and a long sleeve shirt, right before the trios' eyes.

"Wow, they can both do that." said Johnny with amazement. "Why can't I do that?"

April shrugged and smiled as she walked over to Johnny and rested her buttocks into his non-existent lap. She then elbowed him on the right side of his abdomen.

"What was that for?" he asked.

"Don't you dare keep anything from me again," she replied.

Nassir and Brooks both smiled as he turned her around, so they were face to face and he kissed her on the cheek. "I won't" he said softly as he kissed her on the cheek for a second time. "That's a promise."

"So where did Snake go?" asked Brooks.

"I don't know," Johnny said. "I went back to his condo, but the door was blasted off, the police had tape around his building. I learned I could use my abilities to connect with him, but I think he needs some time to figure himself out, I can only imagine what he is going through right now."

"So April," started Nassir, "are you sure we can't convince you to join our little team?

April smiled. "it's really tempting, but with everything that's come to light with the company I work for, my quote unquote, death, etcetera, I have too many things on my plate to handle, but I will say if you all really need me in a pinch, I'll be glad to help!"

Brooks nodded in the affirmative. "That's fair enough. If there is anything we can do to help, please don't hesitate."

April smiled.

"But should we need you," started Nassir, what do we call you? We can't very well be calling you April when you're helping us!"

Johnny, Brooks, and April all chuckled.

April touched her finger to her chin as she thought about it.

"I know," said Johnny. "We can call her flower girl."

She again elbowed him in the side.

Nassir and Brooks laughed.

"What about Star Girl?" asked Brooks

"What's' up with all this girl stuff?" asked April as she let go of Johnny and morphed her clothing into the silver liquid and then into her costume. Her eyes started to glow.

"Just call me Gemini."

Nassir and Brooks both looked at Johnny.

Johnny smiled. "It's her birth sign."

"Two sides," started Brooks as he shook his head in the affirmative. "It fits."

They all laughed lightly as Johnny stood all the way up. Johnny looked at April and said, "now there's one more thing we need to do."

The sun shined brightly as Michael walked slowly northward along route 476. For him, it wasn't enough to take down Tanner, dispose of the android, not even to exact revenge on the woman who killed his mother and forever altered his life.

He took the money he earned working for Tanner and gave a large majority of it to his friend Toothpick with the hope to affect positive change in the community which embraced him. He shared all that he had been through with his old friend and also shared his future plans with him. Including going home without using his powers and then sitting down and having a long conversation with his grandmother.

A black Chevrolet Lumina, with a United States Government license plate on the back of it pulled up in front of him.

The man driving the car rolled down the window and stuck his head out. "HEY BUDDY, WHERE YOU HEADED?" he asked.

"PITTSBURGH!" Michael yelled.

The man smiled. "WELL IT'S A LONG WALK TO PITTSBURGH, BUT I'M GOIN' THAT WAY!" he yelled. "C'MON, GET IN!"

Michael ran up to the passenger side of the car and got in.

"Alex Callahan," said the man as he pulled back into the traffic flow. Once he was sure he was moving correctly with the flow of traffic, he then offered his hand to Michael.

Michael smiled as he took the man's hand and shook it. "Michael Jones," he said.

"You have family in Pittsburgh?" asked Alex as he continued looking at the road.

"My grandmother lives in Green Tree. I just thought I'd go stay with her for awhile."

"That's real nice - family's' important," said Alex as he reached for the radio and turned it on. "I hope you like country music."

In the middle of playing a country western song, the radio station then, without warning, turned to Power Ninety-Nine F.

M. *'Up Jumps Da Boogie'* by Timberland and McGoo was playing.

♪I'm up on this tracks ♪
♪Like Pam Grier in movies...♪

Alex quickly tried to change the station back but kept getting the same results. "Damn," he said as he banged on the radio. "What the hell's wrong with this thing?" He then attempted to cut the radio off, but it kept turning back on. "Gotta get this thing fixed!"

Michael smiled. He liked Dolly Parton, Willie Nelson, and Garth Brooks but none of them were on so he telepathically changed the radio station.

♪Up jumps da boogie♪
♪ da boogie jumps for me...♪

"What the hell is that?" asked Alex in frustration. "A song talking about boogies that jump? The radio waits for a road trip to not act right."

Michael laughed. "That's always the way ain't it?"

***

In Hatboro, Pennsylvania, just down the street from the Naval Air Station in Willow Grove, a group of teens walked past the Horsham Fire Company station fifteen B and then across an adjacent field in order to get to Hatboro-Horsham High School.

The sun shone brightly and seemed to have lit up the bright green grass.

Fifty feet under the footsteps of the children, Turbine's dismantled body lay still as his optic sensors lit up. Through his eyes, the words *'battery backup'* came on followed by the words *'initiating self-reconstruction sequence'*.

A red light formed around the damaged ends of the android as dirt, stones, and grass seemed to move towards the androids body and turn into materials he needed as his face and mask reconstructed itself over Turbine's head.

"Thank you Stern," said Cole's voice as the rest of his body continued to reconstruct within the dark confines of the environment.

***

Back at Biotech Labs, the cat paced back and forth inside of the electronic cage as he stared intently at the mayor, who stood there with two Biotech scientist, a handful of police officers, and a couple of Horsham Township officials.

"As soon as the new super max prison is ready, you'll be the first to be a guest," promised the mayor.

The cat stopped pacing, looked the mayor dead in the eyes and licked his lips.

He then started pacing again.

Somewhat startled, the mayor looked at the rest of the small crowd who was with him and said, "ladies and gentlemen, shall we?" He extended his hand towards the door which led the way out of the room. They left out of the room and passed the two policemen who were standing guard outside of the room.

Back inside of the room, the cat stopped pacing again and walked up to the electrified cage, so he was standing no more than an inch away from the electrified bars. "Ladies and gentlemen, shall we?" he repeated in a raspy voice.

CHAPTER 65

"SO WHEN'D YOU get the jeep?" asked April as her and Johnny got into the Grand Cherokee which was parked in Brooks' driveway.

Johnny closed his door and started the jeep up.

Like the sound of a kitten purring while getting his back stroked, the jeep hummed quietly.

Johnny said, "it belongs to Doctor Brooks, but he rarely uses it so he lets me use it."   Johnny then looked at her curiously as he started driving. "You literally found out I was Jade, died, came back to life, and the first thing you ask me when we're finally alone together - when did you get this jeep?"

April laughed. "Well it's all strange, I don't know what to say or how to feel, everything seems so unreal."

"I know you didn't have your memory when you first came back, but now that you do, do you remember anything from the time you, you know, up until your memories came back?"

April nodded in the affirmative. "I actually kind of remember everything. I remember how it felt to die, I was moving towards this bright light and when I got there, I was reborn as a piglet. I remember meeting some sort of light, she told me she was my guardian angel."

"What?" asked Johnny in disbelief.

April nodded again in the affirmative. "I'm not kidding Johnny, even about the part when I was reincarnated as a piglet!"

"No," started Johnny, "it's not that. I had a nightmare a while ago of you telling me you were a baby pig and you said you were going vegetarian."

"I would probably actually become a vegan," replied April. "and the guardian angel hinted at knowing my sister."

"Sorrie?"

"Yes, Sorrie! and the angel said it wasn't my time."

"Ever since I became Jade, life has been increasingly weird and everything I thought I knew before then..." Johnny huffed. "It was Sorrie who told me at your funeral to make sure to bring you back." He shook his head in the negative. "I am starting to believe that as a species we have death and dying and space time all wrong."

Driving down Easton Road, they stopped at a red light near the Horsham Air Force Base.

"Only thing I'm certain about right now is that I've missed you and I'm just glad to have you back!" he said as he took his right hand off the steering wheel and grabbed her left hand.

"Oh shit!" she replied looking past him.

"What?" he asked as he turned around and looked out of his window. Turbine was flying straight into the air with his wings fully extended. The light turned green and the traffic started moving. Then a car two places ahead of them slammed on their brakes. Johnny, still looking up at Turbine, stepped on the gas.

"John - KNEE!" yelled April as the jeep proceeded to slam into the back of the Mercedes Benz in front of them.

Upon hearing April screaming Johnny's name, Turbine looked down and smiled. He didn't think Jade would be so close.

A loud zipper sound allowed a portal to open right before they hit the Mercedes, and the jeep slid through.

The zipper sound then closed the portal up.

***

The zipper-sounding portal opened up in the field behind the Horsham Fire Station and the jeep slid out as people far off in the distance watched.

Johnny quickly produced the sound of cracking electricity along with the spiral of yellow light around his body and turned into Jade.

He then looked over at April who was holding onto the left side of her seat and the handle of the door panel with her eyes closed.

She opened her eyes.

Jade said, "Take the jeep and see if you can get Stern to tell you how to terminate or deactivate missile man here, and I'll try to hold him off."

With the sound of crackling electricity along with the spiral of yellow light, Jade then vanished from out of the jeep.

April quickly moved over into the drivers' side of the jeep and started driving. She opened a zipper sounding portal and then drove through.

**

Prior to exiting the portal on Welsh Road in Willow Grove, April could see the traffic she was getting into and immediately cut in precisely while getting honked at by some surprised drivers. "Sorry yall, didn't see you back there," she said out loud and to herself.

**

Turbine swooped down towards Jade as he was hovering in the air looking at the large, crater like hole in the ground from where he correctly assumed the once dismantled Turbine had come from.

"Like I said, wrong about death, wrong about space, wrong about time." said Jade out loud and to himself as he turned around in time enough to see the large knife-like wing coming at him.

He quickly converted his body turn into its energy form, and Turbine's wing passed right through him. Jade laughed. "I'm so glad that worked!"

Turbine then swooped around and landed while keeping his wings extended.

He quickly fired damper discs in Jade's direction.

The damper discs hummed as they quickly headed in Jades' direction but then they both developed a yellow light around them, turning them around quickly and contacting Turbine.

Turbine buzzed with electricity, froze and then fell backwards to the ground.

Jade landed and walked over toward Turbine. "For a robot or android or whatever you are, it's pretty dumb of you to be deploying weapons that can be used against you."

    ***

A loud zipper-sounding portal opened up inside of Stern's cell at Biotech as he sat on his bed and watched to see who would come out.

Gemini flew out and landed. "Solitary confinement huh?"

"My temporary housing 'til they figure where they want to extradite me to," he replied, "but I'll take it. The township officials thought it would be in my best interest to have my own suite...for now anyway."

"Well - I need your help."

"My help?"

"Cole has somehow reconstructed himself and he's going to put a lot of innocent people in dan..."

"It worked!" interrupted Stern as he jumped up in excitement.

Gemini looked at him and felt the desire to slap him in his scrawny head. "Yes whatever you did to him worked, and if he kills anybody, the blame is going to be placed on you. Again."

Stern slowly sat back down on the bed and removed his thin, wire framed glasses from off of his face. "When I found you at the park and convinced you to come with me for observation, I hypothesized that your coming back to life and subsequent abilities had to do with your manner of death. Before then, I collected Snakes D-N-A after his death in New York but I was unable to reproduce what I thought would be the obvious answer which was inoculating others. So I then started experimenting with his D-N-A and my nanite fluid and found that the energy from his body could heal or reproduce as long as there was a central computer to tell it to repair the tech."

"So your robot will keep rebuilding himself?"

Stern shrugged. "What do you expect me to do from here?"

"I know you," she started.

"You never do anything without a back-up plan. Tell - me - how - to - DESTROY HIM!" she demanded angrily as she grabbed him by the collar and lifted him up off of the bed.

Gasping for breath, Stern said, "you, you can slow him down but you can't destroy him."

"What do you mean I can't destroy him?"

"I created the artificially intelligent reconstruction chip so small that - he could be blown into a million bits and as long as there are an abundant supply of the proper elements around, the chip can reconstruct him out of any matter bit by bit, each time making him more powerful than the last, thanks to Snake's D-N-A."

Gemini lowered Stern back down and displayed a look of disappointment on her face. "How were you able to produce something so powerful?"

"I used the law of thermodynamics in my creation of the prototype."

"What?" she asked.

"Matter and energy cannot be destroyed but are merely transformed from one form to the other, therefore when the unit is destroyed, it draws up the energy provided by Snake which sits dormant until the chip tells it about the damage.

Then the reconstruction chip uses that energy to help it gather the necessary elements allowing Cole to reconstruct himself."

Gemini turned around. "What are the necessary elements?"

"Carbon, hydrogen, oxygen, potassium, sulfur - a whole list of them, and there isn't anywhere on Earth where you could put the chip and it wouldn't be able to reconstruct the unit."

Gemini smiled and turned back around. "And you said damage activates the chip?"

"The chip is activated when it receives a message from the brain that there is bodily damage."

"So if the brain is destroyed..."

"It'll start by reconstructing another brain with the same thought pattern as the original one."

Gemini grabbed a hold of Stern. "So you created a chip which is a mate to Cole's chip which provides a loop feedback telling the reconstruction chip everything is fine."

Stern looked up at Gemini like a small child who just got caught with his hands in a cookie jar.

Gemini smiled. "Like I said, you're the type who thinks of everything. She then grabbed a hold of Stern and, with the sound of cracking electricity along with a spiral of purple light, they both vanished.

***

With the sound of a light snap, Gemini and Stern reappeared inside of Stern's darkened lab.

Stern had just experienced teleportation for the first time. "Ooh that was fun," Stern said. "Can we do that again?"

Gemini, looking around said, "sure, when I take you back to your cell. Now, where's the chip?"

"Relax, don't be so on edge," he said.

"When there are lives at stake, I tend to get a little on edge," she said angrily.

Stern walked over to his desk and pulled out a small plastic, translucent case which he had taped under the desktop.

"Here it is," he said.

"What do we do with this?" she asked as she walked over towards him.

Stern pointed to the copper end of the chip. "Take this end of the chip and melt it to the identical end of the matching chip."

"How do we get the matching chip?"

"Oh yeah - I forgot. You have to get him up into space, most of his reflexes will be slower up there, blow him up just as you would if you were still on Earth. If all of the parts are disconnected, remove the metal dome from off of his head and remove the chip from off of the left parietal side of his brain. Once you have welded the two chips together, he'll have no way of reconstructing."

"That's it," started Gemini. "You're giving up all this information for nothing?"

"Well I hope one day you will consider talking at my parole board in the future."

"You're getting ahead of yourself, aren't you?" replied Gemini as she grabbed his arm and produced the sound of cracking electricity along with the spiral of purple light around the two of them.

"I want to continue my research in the future"

They both vanished.

***

As Turbine flew downwards and backwards into the ground, Jade looked up and saw a helicopter hovering high above the field where they were fighting. "Oh just great, anything for a news story," said Jade.

Turbine looked up and fired missiles from his right hand at the helicopter.

Jade then fired energy lasers in the direction of the missiles.

The energy lasers exploded the missiles before they could hit the whirly bird.

Turbine then shot his lasers in the direction of the helicopter and Jade flew straight up and in front of the whirly bird.

Jade threw up his shields and the lasers stopped and dispersed in front of him. He then turned around and looked at the pilot of the helicopter.

"DON'T YOU THINK ITS TIME YALL GOT OUT OF HERE?" he yelled, attempting to compete with the loud sound of the helicopter blades.

The pilot quickly shook his head yes.

Turbine then shot two damper discs out, one hit Jade's shield and the other hit the helicopter.

The engine from the helicopter could be heard sputtering as it started to tip to the side.

Jade threw an energy pulse under the helicopter, holding it steady in the air.

A damper disc smacked him in the back and the energy pulse vanished.

Both Jade and the helicopter started to fall as the onlookers from the school and fire house watched in horror.

Suddenly, a purple pulse light circled under both Jade and the helicopter keeping them in the air long enough for Jade to get his powers back.

Jade's eyes lit up and he produced another energy pulse under the helicopter.

Gemini then darted into Turbine as Jade lowered himself and the helicopter down to the ground.

Turbine picked himself up and looked at Gemini.

"What's wrong?" asked Gemini. "Didn't expect to see me here?"

"You turn on Tanner," started Turbine, "Then know you'll be looking over your shoulder for the rest of your life."

"That's right - you don't know," started Gemini. "Your furry homeboy made a meal out of Tanner."

"What?" said Turbine as he shot two damper discs onto Gemini, causing her lit eyes to dim out. "I'll skin that puss with my bare hands."

He then kicked Gemini in the midsection, causing her to fly backwards and onto the ground.

Jade quickly ran over to where Gemini was on the ground as Turbine took off. "Are you okay?" he asked.

She grunted from the pain. "I'll be fine, you've got to stop him!"

"What did Stern say?"

"You've got to get him into space where his movements will be slower." She pulled out a microchip the size of a quarter. "There should be a piece under the dome of his head lying right on top of the left parietal of his brain and it matches this one." She handed him the microchip.

He took the microchip in his hand and examined it. "What the hell am I supposed to do with this?"

"Take the two matching ends and weld them together, it'll shut him down for good," she started, "he's on his way to Biotech now to off the cat."

He helped her up. "Doesn't matter, he'll probably just come back to life anyway."

"Huh?" asked Gemini.

"Never mind," replied Jade. He then, produced the sound of cracking electricity along with spiral of bright yellow light which danced around him.

Jade then vanished.

Gemini's eyes then started to light up, and she then took off into the air and opened a zipper sounding portal.

She then flew through the portal which closed up with a zipper sound.

CHAPTER 66

ALL WAS QUIET at Biotech labs as the two policemen sat outside of the small room where the cat was being detained.

Without warning, a loud explosion at the end of the hall broke the silence of the almost empty building and filled the halls with smoke.

When the smoke cleared, Turbine stood there looking powerful, a metallic tower with the Trilateral 'T' majestically displayed across his chest. He walked slowly towards the two officers who, in fear, drew their guns and started firing.

The bullets deflected off of Turbine like rubber balls repelling a brick wall, but with the sound of metal clanging against metal. They didn't even chip his paint.

When Turbine got closer to the two officers, he simply swung his right arm in their direction and knocked them hard against the wall.

They fell unconscious.

Turbine then blasted in the door to the room where the cat was being detained.

The cat looked up in wonder and saw Turbine standing there.

Turbine said, "You killed Tanner."

The cat just stared at him.

"Don't just sit there and stare I know you can talk!"

The cat, in a raspy voice, said, "My feast was unpure, I killed an imposter!"

Angered by the sarcastic comment, Turbine shot the control panel on the wall, shutting off the electricity to the bars.

The cat bent the bars open with his mighty hands and stepped out of the cage.

"You should be glad I freed you from false proclivities."

Turbine fired a missile and it grazed the cat's arm, forcing an angry growl.

The cat roared and lunged at Turbine with the force of a five-hundred-pound lion.

***

Jade, in his pure energy form, emerged through the walls of the hallway and saw the unconscious bodies of the two police officers. He dimmed his body out and walked over to the first cop and felt under his chin for a pulse. He then went over to the other cop and did the same thing.

"Whew!" he said. He then heard a loud crash accompanied by what sounded like a very large cat getting his tail stepped on, so he moved over to the smoky doorframe and looked in.

The cat lunged back towards Turbine, but then an energy rope surrounded his body and Turbines, keeping them still. The cat was suspended in air.

"THIS ENDS NOW!" demanded an angry Jade.

The yellow light which surrounded Turbine dissipated as his damper disc hit the energy rope.

Turbine freed himself and slammed the huge metallic fist of his right hand into Jade's face, causing him to lose his grip on the cat.

The momentum trapped inside of the energy rope with the cat, forced him to continue flying in the direction of Turbine.

Turbine raised his left arm and smacked the cat as if he were just a nuisance ball coming his way.

Jade swung at Turbine, who ducked and then extended his metallic knife-like wings, right before the cat recovered and jumped back towards him.

Jade then quickly grabbed the androids' arm and tossed Turbine over to the left, in order to keep him from flying anywhere.

The cat let out a high-pitched roar as his body was sliced in half at the waist by Turbine's wings as they collided.

Jade heaved. "I'm gonna be sick," he said as he watched the two halves of the cat hit the floor, jittering uncontrollably.

Turbine's rocket boosters ignited and he started to fly through the roof, but a zipper-sounding portal quickly opened up in the ceiling above him and he flew through, followed by a fully lit Jade.

Chapter 67

DARKNESS WAS ALL he saw as Turbine flew out of the portal and looked around in confusion. Although it was involuntary, it had been his first time traveling through one. He looked around and saw darkness which occasionally revealed a small planet, or a star. *I'm in space?* He wondered.

"I'm apparently from out here somewhere," started Jade sarcastically as Turbine turned around and saw the fully lit being, "So I'm guessing I'll be able to move around a little bit better than you."

Angered by the sight of the energy-based being, he fired a couple of missiles.

The missiles moved at the speed of an overweight cop running after a rebellious teen.

Jade fired his energy beams at the missiles causing them to explode on contact.

"I guess Stern didn't plan on having you fightin' up here when he designed you."

Turbine released rocket boosters out of his back and retracted his wings in order to minimize drag as he flew straight towards Jade.

The dense air around Jade started to crackle like a bowl of *Rice Krispies* splashed with milk and a spiral of yellow light swam around him.

Jade vanished.

Turbine slowly turned to his left as he looked for the brightly lit Jade, but when he turned back around, he caught a fist in his face.

The punch sent Turbine backwards in a slow flipping motion.

Jade said, "Michael Warner, Martin Cole, Buzz Lightyear - whoever you are, you really messed up by interfering in my life. I don't know how else to put this but, you got to go!"

Turbine fired his damper disc, a wasted effort for he knew they weren't going to reach Jade.

Jade threw energy laser lights around the discs and forced them back onto Turbine's torso.

Electricity seemed to have buzzed around Turbine as the lights in his eyes blinked on and off.

Jade fired a thick energy beam towards Turbine causing him to explode.

The debris from his blasted caucus hurdled through space as Jade quickly flew over and caught up to his head.

"Sickening," said Jade as he turned the head, which was looking in his direction, so it faced the other way. He then emitted focused lasers from his eyes and separated the metal dome from the synthetic flesh.

He stopped the lasers.

He then opened up the dome and pulled out the chip which sat on the left parietal side of his brain.

"Technology is a mother fuck," he said as he pulled the matching chip from out of the area where his belt would've been. He then placed the matching copper ends together, so the tips met enough to touch.

Focused energy lasers again shot from out of his eyes bonding the two connecting ends of the chips together.

Jade then looked at the back of Turbine's head as it slowly started to drift away. He then fired an energy beam from his right hand, blasting the head to bits. "That's just in case," he said.

He then darted in the direction of Earth as a zipper-sounding portal opened up in front of him.

The zipper-sounding portal closed after he flew fully through.

***

"Hey captain look at this," said a sailor as the ship he was on cruised slowly past a small iceberg. The captain walked over and looked at the small berg which was drifting in the water.

"What the hell is she doing out there?" he asked.

Lying on the iceberg was a lifeless, partially eaten, frozen and half naked Katherine O'Mally.

"We'd better report this," said the captain.

"Yes sir," replied the sailor as he walked off.

***

"I can't believe we missed all of that," said Brooks.

"Where's Johnny now?" asked Nassir.

April raised her arms up, "I don't know. He went to take care of the android created by Stern, I thought he'd be back by now."

Just then, a zipper-sounding portal opened against the wall of the lab and a dimmed Jade flew out and landed.

"I've got to get a bigger place," said Brooks.

April ran over to Jade and hugged him. "I'm so glad you're okay."

He returned the hug and asked, "was there ever any doubt I would be?" She looked up into his pupil less eyes. "I mean - thanks." He then pulled slightly off of April and gave the chip to Brooks, who pulled back slightly because of the heat radiating off of the chip. "Be careful it's hot. Those two halves can never be separated."

"Okay," replied Brooks as Jade produced the sound of cracking electricity and the spiral of yellow light, changing his costume into his clothing, consequently, changing into Johnny.

***

All over the Delaware Valley, people were watching the news, teens, young adults, adults and senior citizens. Everyone who's anyone has been watching, because of the numerous events which have transpired over the past six months.

In the Johnson household, all were quiet as the twenty seven-inch color television situated in the living room took center stage.

"...and Steven Tanner, majority share owner of Biotech Laboratories was viciously mauled by the strange black cat who - sources say - was created by Tanner's own Biotech Labs. Mark Stern, the top scientist at Biotech, has been charged with the unethical experimentation of people and animals. His other experiments included a murderous android and Snake, the anti-hero who was Jade's most powerful archenemy in the short time he has been a hero.

Our sources state Snake wasn't actually created by Stern, but is an alien just like Jade, and they say he was under a powerful mind control device as part of Tanner's plot to overthrow the U - S - government. His shares of Biotech will be held in trust by Philadelphia City Trust pending a decision of how to dispose of his interest in the company. A Doctor Robert Brooks was asked to step into the role of Lead Scientist over at Biotech as the company is dismantled and or possibly relocated, he has yet to accept the offer...In related news, The Federal Bureau of Investigations attempted to freeze the late Steven Tanner's bank accounts which were all estimated to be worth over fifty three million dollars, but the funds were found to have been moved to parts unknown.

Talk about strange. In other news, an unidentified woman was found mauled to death by what authorities believe to have been a polar bear attack. She was found on a floating iceberg. Authorities have released this composite sketch of the woman and asks if anyone knows of her to please contact area code..."

As the broadcast continued, a composite sketch of Katherine O'Mally was displayed on the television screen.

CHAPTER 68

THE ROOM WAS dark and the slow music was playing softly.

The candles which sat on top of the dining room table started to sweat with beads of wax as the flame sat majestically on its throne, flickering.

The shadows which arose from the flames danced across the adjacent wall.

Johnny, sitting across the table from April, watched as she twirled the spaghetti around her fork and placed it in her mouth.

Catching the fixed gaze, which was resting upon her body, April looked over at Johnny as she swallowed her food.

"What?" she asked.

"I was wondering if you would like to dance," he said.

"Right now?"

He smiled.

She rested her fork in her plate as they both stood up simultaneously.

They moved close to each other only leaving an inch of space between the two of them.

Her hands found his as his hands found hers, meeting at a level which laid in-between the height of their individual shoulders.

They started dancing slowly, staring into each other's eyes, as the flickering shadows from the candlelight seemed to move with them.

"Have you decided what we're going to tell my mother?" she asked.

"Yes."

"Well - are you planning to tell me or do I have to beat it out of you?" she asked while laughing softly.

Smiling, Johnny said, "the truth."

"Johnny - do you know what telling the truth could do to her?"

"I know what it did to you when I didn't tell you the truth."

She pulled back slightly and stared into his eyes, ready to initiate a debate, but decided not to. She knew he was right. What else would they tell her. If her mother was going to hear a reason why her daughter is alive, it would have to be the truth. She kissed him on the side of his face. Never mind the fact that Sorrie may already know.

He returned the kiss. "I love you," he said softly.

She said, "I love you too." She then started hugging him and started crying.

He was waiting for it.

She had never had the opportunity to feel upset about everything that happened to her over the last three months.

They each had felt their own lives end in different ways.

As he held onto her, tears came out of his eyes also. Not just because she was brutally murdered and they were apart for over three months, but because prior to her death, he had shut her out of his life. Before he was blessed or cursed with his gift, he shared everything with April. Everything. There was nothing she didn't know about him, likewise there was nothing he didn't know about her.

Now she would have doubts.

They looked into each other's eyes and started kissing with a passion which had been contained with time.

Approximately three long months.

***

The White Jeep Grand Cherokee pulled up in front of the Mount Airy home and parked behind the red Ford Escort which was parked on the street.

April and Johnny both got out of the jeep wearing dark sunglasses and they walked up to the front door.

Johnny rung the bell as April stroked the sides of her hair down while looking around.

Miss Jenkins answered the door and saw Johnny first. "Come on in baby," she said as she gave him a hug. She looked at April strangely as April came in and started to close the door.

Sorrie came running down the steps as April closed the door and when April turned around, Sorrie threw her hands over her mouth, "Johnny you did it!"

"Johnny how could you bring someone over here who looks like..."

"It's me mama," interrupted April as she removed the sunglasses from off of her face.

Miss Jenkins threw her hand over her chest as she looked as if she lost her balance for a moment.

"Lord, how is this possible?" asked Miss Jenkins as she started to cry. "I identified you at the morgue!"

Sorrie screamed, ran down the steps and hugged her sister tightly.

"Neither one of you can ever tell anyone what we're about to show you," said Johnny. "It's for your own safety but we feel you need to know to at least understand."

"What?" asked Ms. Jenkins.

Johnny looked at April and nodded his head, and they simultaneously stepped back as not to startle them.

Johnny produced the sound of crackling electricity along with the spiral of yellow light which swam around his body.

Simultaneously April changed her clothing into the silver liquid and then into her costume.

Standing before Miss Jenkins and Sorrie were now their alter egos, Jade and Gemini respectively.

Miss Jenkins plopped down on the sofa. "I gotta sit down!"

The two then changed back into their alter egos and started to tell her mother and sister the whole story.

***

"Okay Miseur Tanner," started Doctor Shremmer, "when I put this over your face, I want you to start counting backwards

352

from ninety-nine. Is there anything you think I should know before I start working on your face?"

Steven Tanner smiled because his plan with the clone Stern created worked. Everyone had believed he was dead because his clone was mauled by the cat. Now he had plenty of time and money to devise a new strategy to expunge of Jade. Once his surgery was complete and once his identity established.

"From here on out, just call me Michael Warner," he said.

"Okay Miseur Warner," started the French physician as he placed the anesthetic mask over his patient's face. "Whatever you want."

***

Back at home, Brooks turned on the television in the middle of a news broadcast as he sat down in his lounge chair.

"In a related incident, a young woman who was reported murdered over three months ago, had not been murdered at all. It seems the young woman, had discovered her boss, Steven Tanner, tried to have her killed when she discovered he was using the investor money to fund an assortment of strange experiments at Biotech Laboratories. The young woman, with the help of Jade, faked her own death and remained well hidden for over three months. The young woman, who shall remain nameless for privacy, is now back with her family safe and sound."

As the news broadcast continued, Brooks laughed out loud and to himself.

About the Author

Derrick J. Truesdale is a healthcare professional who spent over thirty years wanting to tell the stories he believed would both entertain and inspire. Today, those long-held ideas have become interconnected science fiction and fantasy novels that stand alone while forming a larger, evolving universe.

His worlds can be dark at times—but they are never without purpose. He writes with the hope of encouraging others to explore their imagination, embrace transformation, and discover strength in unexpected places.

Welcome to the world of Semaj, where seemingly separate stories share deeper connections waiting to be discovered
www.SemajBooks.com.

www.ingramcontent.com/pod-product-compliance
Lightning Source LLC
Chambersburg PA
CBHW030347120726
47901CB00007B/1939